Driven b_____ to
a newbor_____

DESTER GRANVILLE—tall, magnetic, aggressive
—had a soaring dream—to create the richest plantation in Louisiana and found the proudest dynasty.

His adored young wife ZELMA was a blue-eyed,
auburn-haired Savannah beauty. Only unending love
for her bold, handsome husband brought her—reluctantly—to the new frontier to face the bitter hatred
of envious neighbors, the violence of secret lust, the
cruel hurt of betrayal and death.

Parisian-born owner of a New Orleans brothel, MA-
DAME CELINE developed a sheltering friendship
with the naïve Zelma—and then shattered her in-
nocence forever.

The beautiful, bronze-skinned mulatto slave PIER-
ROT was Madame Celine's sensuous pet. He was a
mute, but she knew enough endearing words for
both of them.

MATILDA, a dark, sassy, passionate young slave,
lusted helplessly for her white master—until one
night when she went to him, naked, in the woods.

DARK DESIRES
is an original POCKET BOOK edition.

Dark
Desires

by Parley J. Cooper

PUBLISHED BY POCKET BOOKS NEW YORK

DARK DESIRES

POCKET BOOK edition published April, 1976

3rd printing.........................April, 1976

This original POCKET BOOK edition is printed from brand-new
plates made from newly set, clear, easy-to-read type.
POCKET BOOK editions are published by
POCKET BOOKS,
a division of Simon & Schuster, Inc.,
A GULF+WESTERN COMPANY
630 Fifth Avenue,
New York, N.Y. 10020.
Trademarks registered in the United States
and other countries.

To the memory of
my grandfather, Granville Clayborn Cooper,
my grandmother, Vianna Smith Cooper,
and my father, Howard Cooper

What we have, we prize, not to the worth
while we enjoy it; but being lacked and
lost, why then we reck the value; then
we find the virtue that possession would
not show us while it was ours.

—Shakespeare

PART ONE

CHAPTER ONE

ZELMA GRANVILLE ARRIVED late at the party of an old Savannah friend, and unexpectedly, she arrived alone. Judging from the increased whispering behind the ladies' fans, she had already precipitated a scandal. Ladies of Zelma's station did not attend parties without their husbands, even when the husband was almost beneath her, socially.

Why had the daughter of a wealthy senator consented to marry a farmer such as Dester Granville? Granted, he was handsome and could be charming if it suited his mood, but he was not "well-off" and could not lay claim to the title of "gentleman." His manners were often coarse, and he was blatantly critical of the social standards by which his wife's friends guided—or pretended to guide—their lives.

"The cheek of her," a woman remarked loudly to her husband.

"As beautiful as a spring day," he murmured. Then, catching his wife's scowl, he saved himself from argument by adding agreeably, "Yes, cheek, my dear."

Zelma was aware of the commotion her lone arrival had created among her friend's guests. It pleased her. She had deliberately started the tongues wagging. Silly, perhaps. Childish. Maybe a little scandal would strike back at Dester for making another trip so soon after his last, leaving her behind while he rode to Washington on business. She had pleaded with him to take her. She could have visited her family while he went about his business, but he had refused, telling her the trip must be made in all haste. A carriage would have slowed him down. That

morning, he had swung into the saddle at daybreak and
ridden away with a wave—and no apology. Anger and
frustration had welled up in her chest, and it was then
she had decided to attend the party alone. She knew the
gossip would reach him on his return.

Now, determined to enjoy herself, she straightened her
shoulders and swept into the midst of the crowded drawing room. She knew from the approving glances of the men
and the envy of the women that she looked her best. She
had spent a full three hours preparing herself. Her new
gown, a pale blue silk, had a full seventeen yards of material in the skirt and flattered her eyes. Her auburn hair
had been brushed to a healthy sheen. Her waist was
cinched tighter than usual, so tightly that sudden or quick
movements were impossible. The blue sapphire pendant
about her neck nestled in the pale valley of her cleavage
above a neckline that was shockingly low. The rumors that
reached her husband would have it even lower, perhaps
expose her completely in some contrived accident. Well,
it served him right for abandoning her during the most
important party of the spring season.

Nodding and smiling, she made her way to the punch
bowl. She had anticipated the commotion her arrival
would create, but she had expected it to be momentary.
But it had not stopped. Some of the older women, her
mother's friends, continued to whisper and avoid her gaze.

Dorothea Farris, the hostess and her friend, appeared
at Zelma's elbow. "All right, darling," she murmured beneath her breath, "if you wanted to create a sensation, you
succeeded. Crossing the drawing room, I heard that you
and Dester were divorcing, that you've taken leave of
your senses, and that your coarse, farmer-husband—their
expression, not mine—had finally dragged you down to his
level."

Zelma continued to smile, but the humor was gone from
her face. "I'm merely showing that in the year of our Lord
1803 a woman does not have to cling to her husband's
arm," she said lightly.

"What you have succeeded in proving, I'm afraid, is that
the old mores are as strong as ever," Dorothea told her.

"It's up to you, of course, but if you left suddenly and quietly, I'm sure they'd dismiss the incident."

"Are you asking me to leave?"

"You know better than that," Dorothea said. She lay her hand on her friend's arm. "I'm merely saying there's no disgrace in retreating when the strategy of the attack is misconceived." The pressure of her hand increased, meant to convey her understanding. "We know one another pretty well, Zelma. What did Dester do to make you angry enough to attend my party without him?"

"Is it that transparent?"

"Only to a close friend."

"He went to Washington," Zelma explained. "He said a carriage would slow him down. Men are so inconsiderate," she said bitterly. "He knows I haven't seen my parents since Congress convened. I'm tired of being left alone, tired of being the devoted wife, and . . ." She broke off speaking when two women passed behind them.

"But it's not Dester you're hurting today," Dorothea said after the women had passed out of earshot. "He doesn't give a damn about these people and their mores. He laughs at them openly. Forgive me, my dear, but it'll be you who'll be hurt by not receiving invitations to future parties, not Dester." The hostess sighed and withdrew her hand from Zelma's arm. She glanced fleetingly over her powdered shoulder at the crowded drawing room. "Frankly, I admire your husband's views on most of these people," she said. "Of course, if you quote me, I'll deny it. You and I, we're part of them. What would we do without Savannah society?"

Zelma couldn't imagine it. She left her punch cup on the edge of the table. She smiled at Dorothea. "I'm good at dramatic entrances," she said, "but I'll need your assistance for an unnoticed retreat."

Dorothea took Zelma's arm, and chatting, they made their way out of the drawing room without attracting too much attention. In the library, Dorothea closed the doors, and they were alone. "I'll have your carriage brought around to the side of the house," she said. "I doubt that anyone will see you leave."

Zelma moved to the chesterfield and sat down. "In the year of our Lord 1803," she repeated bitterly, "women are still victims of the archaic." She rose again to accept Dorothea's parting peck on the cheek, and then paced about the library until she heard her carriage pull up outside the french doors.

Bessie Lou, her personal slave since childhood, sat pressed into the far corner of the carriage. She had a smug expression on her wrinkled, black face. "I told you it wasn't right attendin' a party without the master," she said.

Zelma's temper flared. "I don't need a slave reminding me of what's right and what's wrong," she snapped.

"Seems to me you do," Bessie Lou mumbled. "I heard how them people reacted when you came in alone. And in that Jezebel cut dress. What's the master goin' to say when he hears about this?"

"The *master* may say what he pleases," Zelma shouted.

She stamped her foot on the floor of the carriage to signal the coachman to drive away.

Dester Granville was not a handsome man, but there was an aura about him that compensated for his too big frame, unruly blond hair, and jutting chin. He had a sexuality that was obvious to both women and men, and a drive for power and success that impressed all who encountered him. Had he not been a farmer by choice and birthright, there were those in the Washington of 1803 who would have feared him and felt challenged by his sheer dedication. But he was an outsider, the stranger who had married the daughter of the senator from Georgia, and because his visit to the capitol was to be a short one, he was readily accepted into the tightly woven social circle of the senator's friends. The women flirted with him from behind their fans, and the men chatted with him amicably about everything from the war in Europe to the admission of Ohio as the seventeenth state of the union.

The senator's parties and friends bored Dester Granville, but he concealed this. He disliked his mother-in-law and hoped his wife would not be like her, shrill and complaining and given to incessant gossiping; if he was forced to listen politely to one more tale about James Madison's wife, he swore to himself he would find an excuse to take lodging at a nearby inn. He always felt like a released animal when he managed to escape his mother-in-law's presence.

On this crisp, clear day in late March, the fifth day of his visit, he left his wife's mother and sister immediately following the noon meal and walked the short distance to the White House. The senator had agreed to meet him later, but he was too impatient to wait. He wanted to have his business done with and return to Georgia. He disliked cities, Washington in particular. He preferred the country life to which he had been raised and seldom left the farm outside Savannah. His last trip had been three years earlier, when he had gone to Philadelphia prior to the moving of the capital. That was when he had married Zelma and brought her home. He had planned a trip of one week, and it had taken him five days to convince the senator that he would make a better husband for his favorite daughter than any of the other suitors.

But affairs of the heart were easier to deal with than politics. This time, the senator was being cagy. The Republicans and the Federalists were creating one helluva row. Bonaparte had, to Dester's knowledge, delayed responding to President Jefferson's threat to make common cause with England, and there might be war over Louisiana instead of negotiations to purchase it.

If there was war, his plans were lost.

The plantation, his dream, would never see fruition. The money he had invested would be wasted; he would be penniless, with only the farm and not enough to sustain that until the next harvest.

Dester wandered down the corridors of the White House in search of the Senate chambers. The building was a hive of frantic activity and confusion. The politicans and visitors to the capitol who wandered to and fro had to raise their voices to compete with the din of hammering and sawing created by the carpenters. Dester, glancing up at the workmen on scaffolding, who had months yet ahead of them before the completion of the building, wondered how any man, even President Jefferson, could retain his sanity amidst such pandemonium.

He thought of his father-in-law, and smiled. It was no wonder the senator could not bear the slightest disturbance at home and locked himself in his study after dinner, for-bidding the servants—or his wife—to converse above a whisper in the entryway. After a day at the White House, the man deserved the solitude of his locked room, and on the evenings when he was not entertaining, the quiet.

Dester liked the senator, but he felt now that the man was putting him off.

As he strode down the White House corridors, Dester thought of Zelma and their son, Vance, and for the first time in months wondered if his planning had been sound or if he had allowed his plantation dream to cloud his reasoning. Zelma knew of his dream, but not that he had taken steps to make it a reality. When he returned home, he would either be telling her they were plantation owners in Louisiana or that they had been ruined.

"Dester, my boy!"

The senator came hurrying toward his son-in-law. It had been impossible not to pick Dester out of a crowd, even a crowd such as that gathering in the White House corridors to hear President Jefferson's speech. His son-in-law was a tall man, six-foot seven-inches, with blond hair and mus-tache that literally glistened under the naked lights.

Dester took the smallish man's hand in his own. "I couldn't wait until the meeting," he said apologetically.

The older man's eyes gave off a mischievous twinkle. "Not to mention the fact that you were driven away from my house by those two chattering females I call family," he said. "You know, of course, that my wife will never forgive you for not bringing Zelma with you? She's having her retribution by attempting to talk you to death." He laughed. Then, turning away from Dester, he nodded to two passing men. "President . . . retired President Adams and his son John Quincy," he told Dester.

Dester's gaze followed the man he had heard so much of but had never seen.

"The White House is full of notables today," the senator told him. "I've just been chatting with Secretary Madison and his charmng wife, Dolly."

The younger man flashed a smile, revealing even white teeth beneath his thick mustache. "Your wife would dispute her charm," he said.

"Jealousy, my boy," the senator laughed. "There's not a woman in Washington who wouldn't change places with her." He winked. "And not a man who wouldn't like being James Madison."

But Dester had ceased to listen. His face had taken on a serious expression. "Any news?" he asked. "About . . . ?"

"Let's go for an ale," the senator interrupted, "and escape this infernal noise. That is, unless you want to stay for President Jefferson's speech."

"An ale would be fine," Dester said.

They did not speak again until they had reached the tavern and seated themselves at a corner table. Dester sat back and stretched out his long legs beneath the table. He tried not to display his impatience, but it was in his eyes. The future of his family depended on the news from France.

The older man ordered two ales, sat back, and stared at Dester. He was fond of his son-in-law. He had known his parents in Savannah before their deaths in a carriage accident, and had watched Dester, then twenty years of age, take control of his father's farm and succeed in doubling the cotton crop in less than three seasons. Although Zelma occasionally complained of her husband in letters to her mother, the senator considered Dester an ideal husband. The thoughts of the complaints caused him to smile. *Too much of a man,* his daughter had written, *which makes my one duty as a wife most painful.* As a daughter, Zelma had been spoiled; the senator wondered if Dester had taken that out of her. He was not a man to waste time on foolishness. As for being "too much of a man," well, Zelma would have to handle that on her own. The senator only wished that he, himself, had been "too much of a man" to make women complain.

After their ales arrived, the senator said, "If you weren't my son-in-law, I wouldn't discuss these affairs with you until they were made public, even if you pressured and cajoled me for five days more."

Dester leaned forward, his elbows resting on the table-top. "If you can't give me facts, then give me specula-tions," he said. "Rumor has it that Bonaparte has opened negotiations. Why can't President Jefferson confirm this?"

"And have the Republicans and Federalists at each others' throats? As it is, they're arguing on every street corner."

"There's nothing different in that," Dester said. "If there was nothing more important to argue, they'd debate the architectural design of the White House to delay its completion."

The senator laughed. "That's already happened," he said, amused. He studied his son-in-law as he sipped his ale. "You know, my boy, I think you've gone further into this Louisiana deal than you've told me."

"I have," Dester confessed.

"How far?"

"As far as I could go without selling the farm and borrowing." Dester met his father-in-law's eyes to judge his reaction, but the older man was a practiced statesman and had long ago learned to keep his opinions veiled.

"I see," the senator said thoughtfully. "Why not stay in Georgia? And expand?"

"It wouldn't be the same," Dester told him, "even if I could afford the price of land there. Besides, Senator, I want to raise more than cotton."

"More than *cotton?* What, then?"

"Sugarcane."

Surprise crept into the senator's voice. "But it's not na-tive to Louisiana soil."

Dester nodded. "But it can be grown there," he said with assurance. "The topsoil is as deep as a man can dig and rich enough not to need fertilizing. The growing season is long because of the climate. You should see the land, Senator; then you'd surely understand my enthusiasm. It's there, it's mine, and it's waiting for me." He stopped talking for a moment and ran a long, calloused finger thoughtfully around the rim of his ale cup. His enthusiasm was dimmed by concern as he went on, "But I don't dare proceed unless I can determine what will happen between us and France. If war is imminent, then I'll be forced to accept my losses. There's a French plantation owner named Faviere who's after the same land. He was holding out for a lower price when I bought out from under him. If there's a war, my claim won't be honored, and the bastard will get the land." He drank and then brushed the froth from his mustache. "Damnit! Maybe I shouldn't have taken the gamble. If I lose the Louisiana land, chances are I'll also lose the farm. But, God Almighty, there's no limit to what I can do if everything goes as I hope!"

"I understand better now why you came hounding me," the senator told him. "What about slaves?"

"I have twenty-eight on the farm. I bought twenty more, and I've hired them out to various farmers until I'm ready for the move."

"And the farm?"

"I've a buyer for top value," Dester said. "It's James Worth. His acreage joins my farm, and he's been after it since before my father died. Either way, it looks like he's going to get it."

"You're ambitious, aggressive, and adventuresome," the senator said. "In short, my boy, you're made of the stuff that will make our country great. It's the Jeffersons and Madisons and Washingtons who created the foundation, but the country will be built by men such as yourself who are willing to make such gambles as you have made. Providing. . . ."

"Are you telling me there will be a Louisiana Purchase?"

"Providing," the senator went on, "that other men such as yourself are as fortunate in their speculations."

Dester's eyes sparked to life, questions forming behind them so rapidly they could not be voiced coherently.

"I'll give you the facts as I know them, my boy," the senator said quietly. "I think you'll agree with my interpretation of them. First, let's consider the French position regarding Louisiana. Bonaparte kept the Treaty of Ildefonso, which restored the territory to France, a secret since 1800. Only he understands his reasons there, but it is obvious he became indifferent to the acquisition. When he did announce the retrocession, President Jefferson instructed Robert Livingston, our minister in Paris, to inform Bonaparte that the occupation of New Orleans by France endangered the relationship between our nations and that we might even be forced to make common cause with England. If the French controlled the Mississippi, American commerce would most assuredly suffer. The conflicts of interest between America and France would undoubtedly lead to war."

"I realize all of this," Dester said.

"But let's carry it through," the senator told him. "Our Emperor Bonaparte is no fool. By putting the territory of New Orleans into our possession, he not only creates a counterbalance to the maritime power of England but gains an ally as well. There's also the probable chance that if he retains New Orleans the English will take it from him anyway. It's a well-known fact that they have twenty warships in the Gulf of Mexico."

"Then you feel the sale to us is inevitable?" Dester pressed.

The senator leaned back with a sigh. "Bonaparte has asked for an excess of fifty million francs," he said, lowering his voice. "James Monroe has already departed for France to assist in the negotiations. So, you see, my boy, your fears can be put to rest—as far as the land itself is concerned. As for planting sugarcane in foreign soil, ah, well, I would have more trepidations about that. It would be my advice to. . . ."

Dester ceased to listen to his father-in-law. He was lost to his own thoughts, feeling as if a great uncertainty had been lifted from him. The only obstacle in the way of his plantation dream had been removed.

The senator touched his arm to reclaim his attention. "And Zelma?" he asked. "What does she think of being carted off to Louisiana?"

"I haven't told her."

The senator scowled. Then he became amused. "She'll object," he said knowingly. "She likes her comforts and her Savannah friends. She'll not be easy to convince. There's much of her mother in Zelma. . . ."

Dester winced, unnoticed.

". . . and, the value disputed, much of me as well. I'd admire another man for doing what you will do, but I wouldn't undertake it myself."

"I'll manage with Zelma," Dester said confidently. "She'll soon have comforts far greater than she's known on the farm. I intend to build a plantation home our children and grandchildren will be proud to be born in, to live in and to marry in, and, yes, even to die in. In fact," he added with a laugh, "I've already had an architect in New Orleans draw up plans."

"That, too, without Zelma," the senator mused. "I can anticipate the next series of letters to her mother. My boy, you are going to make a hell of my life. You'll be accused of dragging Zelma into the wilderness, a land of barbarians who will surely rape her and cut her throat. I can already see my wife's tears and smell the burned leg of mutton. But rest assured, I shall play the game and say nothing. I approve of you. I approve of what you are going to do."

"Thank you, Senator." Dester rose and shook the man's hand. "Now, I must leave you. I want to start for home immediately."

"Yes, I understand. Good-bye, my boy. I'll keep you informed of any news from France." He noticed his son-in-law pull absently at the constricting crotch of his trousers, saw the bulge, and was reminded again of his daughter's complaint. *Too much of a man.* As Dester walked away from him, he called, "Stop along the way, and buy Zelma some pretty trinket. You had best soften her up before delivering your news."

Outside, his heels clicking over the cobblestones as he hurried to the stables, Dester concluded that the senator did not know Zelma as well as he. He anticipated only minor resistance, if any, against the fulfillment of his plantation dream. It was, after all, as much for her, their children and grandchildren, as it was for him.

He stopped for a passing carriage and was oblivious to the inviting stare of the lady passenger.

At a small shop near the stables, he stopped and bought Zelma a ridiculous hat that he knew she would adore.

CHAPTER TWO

"NEVER! NEVER! NEVER!" Zelma, her blue eyes flashing, flung the hat Dester had brought her onto the hearth. "How could you even suggest it?"

Dester was taken aback by her vehemence. He stared at his wife in disbelief, finally finding his voice to say, "But I told you often about my plantation dream. You always approved."

"That was a dream!" she cried. "This is a reality!" She turned away from him, her long, auburn hair slipping from its pins with her quick movements. "How could you have done this? How?" she sobbed.

Dester started to go to her but found he could not. He hung back, pale and confused. In three years of marriage, he had never seen Zelma react so violently. He did not know how to cope with her outburst.

Young Vance, playing on the floor before the chesterfield, was startled by his mother's cries. He looked from one to the other of his parents, trying to determine in his two-year-old mind the dangers that were confronting them. His father was obviously the villain; he had caused the upset. Crawling across the floor, the child clutched at the hem of his mother's gown and began to cry.

Dester, for one brief instant, thought Zelma was going to kick the boy. Instead, she vented her anger by kicking the hat from the hearth. Blue ribbons flying, it sailed across the room and disappeared beneath a chair. Bessie Lou, the slave who was both cook and child-watcher, stuck her head through the door to investigate the commotion.

"Take the boy away," Dester commanded her.

Bessie Lou obediently undid the child's grasp of his

15

mother's skirt and carried him, still wailing, from the
room. A distant door closed, and a hushed quiet settled
about the house. Even the slaves, coming in from the fields
for their noonday meal, must have sensed the distress between their master and mistress, because they had ceased
their usual songs and clamor.

Dester sank into a chair and stared at his wife's heaving back. Her words, *That was a dream! This is a reality!*
kept echoing through his head. True, it *had been* a dream,
but he was not of the nature to ever have considered a
dream beyond his achievement. Always, since his parents
had died, in the back of his mind after each harvest or the
purchase of a new slave, he had told himself they were
that much closer to the realization of the dream. How
often he had confided the scope of his dream to Zelma in
the privacy of their bedroom, and she had pretended to
understand. She had encouraged, fed the dream with her
own fantasies of wealth and plantation ownership. Once
upon waking, she had told him she had dreamed herself
a plantation mistress beyond compare, and that had
pleased him. He had made love to her and promised he
would make it come true.

Now as he looked at her, rejection of the reality of it
stunned him, sickened him in the very pit of his bowels.
And it angered him also that he had believed her excitement
over the dream. He stared at her. She was beautiful, this
woman, with her auburn hair and pinched-in waist and
pale skin. The breasts, which were heaving now with her
anger, were ample and inviting. Beneath the yards of
muslin material of her skirt was a fine body. Dester shook
himself. "Zelma," he said, but could say no more. He
now understood the senator's anticipation of his daughter's reaction. How foolish he, the husband, had been to
think he had known her better.

Zelma spun around to face him, the anger blazing in her
eyes. "Aren't you going to tell me I should be a dutiful
wife?" she cried. "That I should sacrifice everything and
let myself be carried away to some godforsaken backwoods?"

"It's no backwoods," he answered calmly. "The land

is no further from New Orleans than this farm is from Savannah."

"New Orleans!" she scoffed. "Nothing but French and Spanish, and half the darkies freemen who call themselves Creoles." She turned away again and stood with her back to him.

"Who've you been listening to, Zelma?" His anger with her was growing, but he attempted to keep the evidence of it from his voice. With as much patience as he could muster, he said, "A Creole's any person born of pure European parentage regardless of rank or wealth. A Creole Negro is a Negro who's been reared in a Creole section. It doesn't make him any less a slave."

"I won't go!" Zelma cried. To give the statement more finality, she stamped her foot. "You can't force me! You won't force me!"

"No," he said. "I won't force you."

"You are a fool!" she groaned. "Did you talk to my father about this?"

"I did."

She walked to the chesterfield, sat down, and then, because she could not bear to sit when she was upset, rose and began to pace about the room. "Of course, he tried to talk some sense into your head, but you wouldn't listen," she said.

"Yes, we talked sense, your father and I," he said quietly. "He advised me to plant cotton as well as sugarcane in the event the sugarcane fails in foreign soil."

Zelma's pacing came to an abrupt halt. She met his gaze, disbelief mirrored in her eyes. Her father would not have sanctioned their leaving the security of the Georgia farm for the uncertainty of Louisiana.

"He also told me what reaction to expect from you," Dester went on. "I didn't believe him. I thought I knew you better."

"Well, you were wrong, Dester Granville!" she cried with renewed anger. "About me! About this plantation dream! It's madness! Nothing but madness!"

Dester sprang to his feet, his anger now demanding to be vented. "Perhaps I was wrong about you," he shouted, "but not about the plantation. My only madness was believing that you shared my dream and hoped for an opportunity to build something fine for ourselves and Vance and the children we are yet to have." He brushed the hair back from his eyes with a quick gesture. "If there's madness here, that was it—my belief in you!"

If Dester had been surprised at the anger in Zelma, she was doubly surprised at his anger vented against her. She had witnessed him lash out at a disobedient slave, at a buyer who had attempted to cheat him, at a farmer who had forgotten himself in her presence, but never had Dester so much as raised his voice at her. She felt her own anger quickly giving way to injury and fear. In one last feeble attempt, she cried, "I grew up in Savannah. My father's plantation is less than ten miles from this farm. My friends are here. Everything I love is here."

Dester glared at her for a long, frightening moment, his face flushed. Then he said flatly, *"I* won't be here! Neither will *our son!"*

He did not wait for her reaction. He stormed from the room, slamming the door so violently that one of Zelma's prized figurines toppled from the table and broke into pieces on the floor.

Zelma fell onto the chesterfield and began to cry her heart out.

In the kitchen, Bessie Lou had quieted young Vance with a piece of toffee and crept back to the door to listen to the argument. She had known her mistress since girlhood, having come from possession of the senator to Dester Granville as a wedding present, and she had not known her mistress to create a tantrum of screaming and tears as she had often done before her marriage. The sudden explosion of the old ways could only mean serious trouble, and Bessie Lou thought it her place to listen and know so she would be prepared for whatever would be expected of her.

When she heard the master shout and saw him hurry from the drawing room, she eased the kitchen door closed and went back to the kitchen table, where she had been

preparing rhubarb for a cobbler. She stared down at young
Vance, who was playing on the floor at her feet and pondered what she had overheard.

Bessie Lou had heard many stories about Louisiana
from travelers who had stopped off at the farm for water
or food. It was a place of swamps and giant, poisonous
snakes and summers that crowded winter into a single
month of God's fury, of floods from the Mississippi, naked
savages who lived in the swamps and stole children away,
and civilized white men who spoke in mixed tongues.

The child interrupted Bessie Lou's thoughts by holding
toffee-covered hands up to her and making a sound that
was half-talk, half-gurgle. She got a washcloth and cleaned
his hands and then sat with him balanced on her broad
lap.

Bessie Lou had grown extremely fond of the Granville
farm during her three years as Dester Granville's slave.
She was happy with the routine of her life. The oldest
slave on the place, she had the respect of the younger
ones, even those who worked the fields and did not come
under her directing eye. As much as her mistress, she disliked the prospects of leaving Georgia. It was a well-
known fact that slaves were worked to death below the
stateline.

Still, Bessie Lou knew in her heart that they would both
follow the master wherever he took them, the mistress out
of love and herself because the Good Lord and a band of
slavers had seen fit for her to be born black and made a
slave.

Rocking the child, she began to sing to him in hushed,
troubled tones.

When the mistress rang for her, she sent one of the
younger girls. Bessie Lou was in no mood for pampering
her mistress when she herself needed consolation.

Jingo was the only slave on the farm who knew about
his master's purchasing land in Louisiana. They had made
the trip to Louisiana together. Jingo had told no one, had
waited, knowing the mistress's reaction. When he saw the
master come storming out of the house, he understood and

sympathized, although he knew sympathy from a slave was as dangerous as rebellion.

But in the end, the master would have his way with the mistress. He was not the sort of man who lost battles.

And then, too, hadn't he, Jingo, seen the future in a dream? Wasn't he known among the other slaves as the one who was gifted with seeing into the future? Of predicting things to come?

In his dream, he had seen the Louisiana land as vividly as the day he had stood on a knoll beside his master and stared out over it. Except in the dream he had seen a great, white house and fields of rich crops and more slaves than he had ever seen in a single place. He had seen the mistress in a gown of emerald green silk with jewels about her throat and on her fingers.

There had been more to the dream, but he had only told the master about the land and the mistress and that the house did not stand on the knoll where the master had planned but at the bottom, closer to the creek.

He did not tell what was on the knoll. He couldn't because on the knoll was a cemetery and a large, granite tombstone with the name *Dester Granville* chiseled across it.

Jingo watched his master walk away toward the stables. Then, gathering up the wood for Bessie Lou, he walked around the side of the house and in through the kitchen door.

CHAPTER THREE

DESTER ORDERED HIS horse saddled, and he rode away from the farm.

The slaves knew by the manner in which he sat his mount and drove his riding crop into the flesh of the animal's flanks that their master was riding out in a fury. Already rumor had spread to them from the house slaves that trouble was brewing between their master and their mistress. They watched their master ride across the fields and disappear among the trees bordering the creek. Then, their songs forgotten, they went quickly back to their work. Their personal fates being decided by their master's moods and decisions, they wondered at what lay ahead for them.

Dester, reaching the creek bank, dismounted and walked his horse. He pondered the quarrel with Zelma, their first of any serious nature since they had been children, and wished he had had the foresight to handle her differently. He should have left her until her anger and upset had subsided and then let her come to him. He should never have threatened her with the loss of their son should she refuse to accompany him to Louisiana; although if it came to that, he would most certainly take the boy without her. If he were without a family, the entire plantation dream was without purpose.

He walked until he was tired, and then, tying the horse's reins to a branch, sat down on the creek bank. He watched the trout in their never-ending quest for food beneath the clear water's surface and listened to the gentle breeze stir the treetops. He pushed Zelma from his mind, and his anger waned. Then, because the sun was still high

21

and there was much to be done, he remounted his horse and rode to the Moore farm to give notice on his hired-out slaves.

Elaine Moore came onto the porch as he rode up. She was a shriveled-up little woman with enormous dead eyes and features that always reminded Dester of a hawk. He had never liked her, but she had been kind to his mother, and he forced himself to be always politely attentive toward her.

"James is out behind the slave sheds," she told him, a measure of excitement in her usually lifeless voice. "He's about to lash a renegade nigger. Go on, hurry!" she urged, "or you'll miss seeing the devil's due." Her intonation told him that she wished herself to be present, but her husband had forbidden her to witness punishments, having told Dester he feared she would intervene on the slave's behalf. But the farmer would have had no cause to worry.

Dester tipped his hat and walked on down the pathway, around the house, and past the slave sheds.

There were twelve men present: James Moore, holding the whip, his white overseer, Henry, and ten darkies who had been required to watch the punishment because Moore thought it would teach them a lesson. The slave to be put to the whip was a giant of a fellow, well over six feet, with as black a skin as Dester had ever seen. Stripped naked, he was bound between two lashing posts, his arms and legs both secured by leather straps so that he was forced into a standing spread-eagle position. The afternoon sun glistened off the solid, muscular contours of his taut back and arms. As he waited to feel the bite of the whip, he could have been lifeless for all his lack of movement, a statue modeled by some sculptor to perfection from black marble.

Moore, who was about to deliver the first lash, stopped with hand poised in midair when he saw Dester come around the side of the sheds. He was a tall, gangling man with a face scarred from a fight. The scar, running along the side of his cheek, cut along the corner of his right eye and gave it the appearance of being useless, bulging, and constantly filled with mucous. He looked younger than his fifty-odd years, despite the scar, and although he had over twenty years on Dester, his hair had no more gray. He had the same hawklike profile as his wife, and because of this it was rumored that he had married a first cousin. When a witless boy had been born to them, the rumor had been intensified.

Moore was known for his cruelty to his slaves. Dester had only agreed to hire five of his new slaves to him under the condition that if they deserved punishment it was to be dealt out by Dester himself, not Moore.

"Afternoon, Granville," Moore called. He handed the whip to his overseer and stepped forward. "What brings you callin'?"

Dester returned his greeting and told him he had come to give notice on the hired slaves. "Three weeks," he told his neighbor. "We leave for Louisiana no later than four."

A light sparked in Moore's left eye. "That meanin' you're aiming to sell to me?" he asked. He was mentally calculating the harvest he could reap from the two farms combined.

"It does if you can meet my price," Dester told him, "in cash."

Moore stroked the stubble on his chin and tried to hide his excitement. "Don't give me much time," he mumbled, "but I suppose I can raise it."

Dester knew the cash could be raised. He had already checked with Moore's banker. He had the feeling Moore was going to attempt to bargain with him, and to prevent this, he turned his attention to the bound slave. "What's he done?" he asked with casual interest.

"The black bastard!" Moore said. "Third time I've caught him drinkin' in the fields." He kicked at the ground with the toe of his boot and sent dirt and gravel against the slave's naked backside. "If I could find the sonofabitch who's given them liquor, I'd do more than just beat him."

"He looks like a good strong slave," Dester observed. "Too bad you can't tame him."

"I'll tame him, or kill him," Moore said strongly. "I'd have killed him before this if it wasn't that he's such a

good worker when he ain't drinking. The bastard cost me
a pretty penny."

Dester walked up to the slave and examined the old lash
scars across his back. There were too many to count.

Moore said, "He's a strong nigger. It takes more than
most to make him feel the pain." He knew his reputation
with his slaves and had no wish to have it spread.

Dester said nothing. He walked slowly around the slave
and stared into his face. The eyes that stared back at him
from the black face were filled with hatred. When he continued to meet the slave's gaze without the slightest aver-
sion of his eyes, however, the slave dropped his lids.
"What's your name?" Dester asked him.

"Africa."

"Africa, sir!" Moore shouted. "I'll teach you to show
respect for white folks!" He stepped forward and slammed
his palm against the side of the slave's face.

The slave did not flinch at the blow. "Africa, sir," he
said.

"That's what I named him," Moore said, "because he's
as black and savage as the continent they brought him
from."

Still staring at the bound black man, Dester asked
Moore, "Will you sell him?"

Moore looked confused. "Why do you want to go and
buy trouble?"

"I'll need strong slaves like him in Louisiana," Dester
answered. "Is he for sale?"

Moore looked thoughtfully at his overseer. A glance
passed between them; then he said hesitantly, "Well, if I
could get my money back out of the bastard, I might just
consider. . . ."

"Be sure that's all you ask," Dester interrupted. "He
knows how much he went for, and I'll get it out of him.
If it's more than I pay, the price of the farm will go up
double that amount."

Africa met Dester's eyes again and an unspoken agreement passed between them.

"Hell's fire, I wouldn't go and cheat you," Moore blus-
tered. The knowledge that he would at long last become

the owner of the Granville farm had put him in good
spirits. "Let me think," he mumbled, "if my recollection's
right, he cost me six hundred dollars."

Africa's eyes said, too high!

"Too much," Dester said flatly.

"But that's what I paid for the bastard!" Moore protested. "I've got to get my investment out of him."

"How long you had him?"

"Six months, maybe seven," Moore answered uncertain-
ly.

"At two dollars a day you've had more than half your
return already," Dester reminded him. "Besides, judging
from your marks on him, he's going to soon be a maroon
anyway."

"What makes you think he won't be a maroon after you
own him?" Moore asked with controlled anger.

"I'm willing to risk it."

Moore stared at the slave. He had bought the goddamn
nigger from a farmer who had been forced to sell out and
return to Rhode Island, paying only four hundred dollars.
And Granville was probably right, the bastard would soon
be a maroon.

"Well?" Dester pressed. "How much?"

Forcing a laugh, Moore said, "Since we're neighbors
and friends, Granville, I'll sell you the renegade for less
than I paid for him. Give me five hundred, and he's yours."

Africa's eyes still said, too high.

"Four hundred," Dester counteroffered.

"But he's worth at least double that on the block."

"This isn't the block, and he's a renegade," Dester said.
"You said as much, and your marks on him show it to be
true."

"All right, all right!" Moore cried. "As long as I can
make use of him without charge until I return your five
hired slaves in three weeks."

"Agreed."

"Shall we include him in the deed for the farm?" Moore
asked.

"No, I think a separate bill of sale," Dester answered.

Moore nodded. Grumbling, he motioned his overseer to

him, walked away with him to the edge of the shed, and stood talking.

Dester took the opportunity to speak softly to Africa. "You belong to me now," he told him. "You'll find I treat my slaves fairly. But if I catch you drinking, I won't put you to the lash. I'll hang you. Is that understood?"

Africa nodded.

Moore came strolling back toward them. "What about the farm? When can we sign the documents and make it legal?"

Dester told him to meet him at the justice of the peace the following morning. "And cut down this slave," he said. "My rule regarding the hired slaves also stands with him. The only lashing he'll get will be given by me."

Moore frowned and cast his shifty good eye on the Negro. "He'll think he's gotten away with something and be twice as hard to tame, but it's no longer any concern of mine." He took his knife from his belt and cut the straps, unable to resist giving the Negro a shove in the ass with the toe of his boot.

Africa went for his clothes and began pulling them on over his nakedness.

Moore yelled at the overseer, "Get these niggers back to the fields!" The group of them, Africa included, were led off at a fast pace.

"Until tomorrow," Dester told Moore. As he walked away, he noticed Africa turn and glance back at him. He wasn't certain, but he thought the look of pure hate had gone from the slave's eyes.

Elaine Moore came onto the porch again as Dester rounded the side of the house. "Did you see that devil get his due?" she asked.

"Yes," he answered. "That I did." He touched the brim of his hat with his fingers as a greeting of farewell and swung onto his horse.

"My best to the Missus," the woman on the porch called.

He nodded and rode away, his thoughts returning to Zelma and how he should handle her. He urged his horse into a fast gallop, intent on giving notice to the other farmers who had his hired slaves.

CHAPTER FOUR

BESSIE LOU LET the curtain fall across her mistress's window and turned into the room. "The master's riding across the field," she said. "It ain't right for a man to come home and not see his wife."

Zelma, her eyes red from crying, clinched the handkerchief tightly in her fist and glared at the slave. "It's not right for a man to drag his wife off to some godforsaken wilderness," she cried. She slammed her fist into the soft down of the mattress. "All for a dream! A dream!"

"A man without a dream ain't no man at all," Bessie Lou said quietly. "And a woman who don't encourage that dream ain't no wife."

Zelma sprang from the bed. "Are you calling me a bad wife?"

Bessie Lou began picking up her mistress's scattered articles, returning them to their proper places. "I'm not calling you no names," she said. "It just seems like foolishness to act the way you are when you're going to give in later. We're going to Louisiana and that's that."

"Is it now?" Zelma snapped. "I suppose you're some kind of fortune-teller like Jingo now. You looked into that black crystal ball of yours, and you saw it all right there in front of you." She walked quickly to her dressing table and sat down, deliberately avoiding her reflection in the glass.

"Jingo's had his visions," Bessie Lou said, ignoring her mistress's mocking tone. "He says. . . ."

"Don't tell me what that fool nigger said!" Zelma cried. "I've had my visions too, and they don't include Louisi-

27

ana. Someday Dester's going to inherit Papa's plantation. We'll have to settle for that."

"You expecting your Papa to die soon?" Bessie Lou asked. "Last time I saw him he looked mighty healthy."

"Don't take that attitude with me, Bessie Lou!" Zelma cried. She spun about on the bench and faced the slave. The fury she had felt over Dester's news had not yet left her; otherwise, she would have hesitated venting anger at Bessie Lou. She knew from girlhood experience that the old slave would stand for none of her nonsense.

The formidable Bessie Lou paid little attention to the anger in her mistress's eyes. "A man like the master would never be satisfied inheriting your Papa's plantation," she said, "not just so his wife'd be around her *friends.*" Her emphasis on the word *friends* clearly expressed her opinion of them, those women who gathered weekly for "social evenings." "Master Granville has got to build for himself. He can't take what some other man's built."

"I should have known you'd take his part in the matter," Zelma said hotly. "Even Papa's taken his part!" Tears formed anew in her eyes.

She's still part-girl, part-woman, Bessie Lou thought. "Listen, child," she said, "we've all got our duty in this life. Yours is being a proper wife to the man you married. Up until now, you've been a good wife, but then there ain't been no reason you shouldn't have been. When you married, all you did was change houses, that grand plantation house of your Papa's for this one. Now it looks like you've been thinking that change was temporary, that you've been waitin' around for your Papa to die so you could get back into the big house. But that ain't what your husband wants, and it's not what going to be. Now, why make it harder on him and yourself by acting like you could change things?"

"Don't preach to me! I don't need some darkie telling me what I ought to do!"

"Well, then, you'd best turn around and face that mirror there and tell yourself," Bessie Lou said flatly. "Someone's got to do some telling."

The door slammed below, and Zelma, about to lash out

at Bessie Lou, fell silent. She heard Dester call her name. "Go down and tell him I have a headache," she said. She added firmly, "Go on, damn you!"

Shaking her head hopelessly, Bessie Lou left her mistress's room and went down the stairs. She found the master in the living room and delivered her mistress's message.

"When did she get this headache?" Dester demanded.

Bessie Lou knew there was no possibility of lying and being believed. "It came on her suddenly," she said quietly.

"Tell your mistress I shall expect her down for dinner," Dester told the slave. "If she doesn't come down, I'll come and fetch her!"

They sat quietly picking at their food. Zelma made no effort at conversation, and Dester did not feel obliged to force her.

Zelma had not changed her gown, as was her custom for dinner, but wore the same muslin frock. A wisp of hair had slipped free of its combs and dangled about her slender neck. Her face was extremely pale and her eyes red from weeping. The hand that held her fork trembled ever so slightly. When she thought him unaware she would glance at him but would turn quickly away if she felt he was about to engage her gaze.

Finally, after his coffee had been served and he had lighted his pipe, she looked at him directly. "When," she asked, "is this upheaval to begin? Or is that also to be kept from me until it pleases you?"

He chose to ignore the bitterness of her tone. He sipped his coffee for a moment, watching her quietly. Then, he said, "I apologize for not telling you about purchasing the Louisiana land, but I didn't want news of it spread around. One word to one of your friends and. . . ."

"It seems unanimous that my *friends* are not highly regarded in this house," she said.

"Women talk," Dester said. "A word to any possible buyer of the farm and they might have forced my price down." He stared at her over the brim of his cup. "As for our departure, I estimate four weeks, no longer."

"Then the farm has already been sold?" she asked, feeling her final hope dwindling.

"It has. To James Moore."

"That low-bred bastard!" she cried incredulously. "How could you?"

The angry flush of her face suddenly amused him. She had never spoken of her dislike for Moore, although he had understood it. "Your own language, my dear, fails to speak highly of your own breeding," he said and laughed.

Her flush deepened. "Don't amuse yourself with me," she said. "There are times when even a lady should be allowed to forget herself. How, Dester? How could you have sold to Moore? You know what he is. You know he will deplete this land, your father's land, him with his greed and cruelty. I don't understand you. You've become a stranger to me."

"Moore was the only potential buyer who could give me cash," Dester told her. "He wants the farm so badly he's paying a price well above its value."

"And that is all you thought of?" she asked pointedly. "Cash?"

"I'll need cash if I'm to build the sort of house I promised you, Zelma," he said. He almost forgot himself and told her about the architectural plans he had had drawn up in New Orleans. If he had, she would have only felt more slighted. There would have been another scene comparable to the one of that afternoon. He did say, "I'm planning a house that'll put the grandeur of Georgia's richest plantation home to shame, just the house I always promised you."

"The dream again," she said distantly.

"Yes, the dream. *Our* dream. It's going to come true, you'll see." He felt she was weakening. He thought he saw that old look in her eyes that came when they talked about the dream. Hesitantly, he asked, "You have come to your senses? There'll be no more talk about not going with me?"

"Have I a choice?" she cried with a sudden renewed anger. "I'm no more than another of your slaves!"

Matilda, the mulatto serving girl, who was about to leave the room, hesitated upon hearing her mistress's statement. She rolled her eyes expressively and pushed through the door, a muffled laughter reaching them from the adjoining room. Dester knew word of the quarrel and his plans would soon spread from the kitchen to the field slaves. He told himself he must tell them of his intentions that very night . . . as soon as he had settled things with Zelma. It would be necessary to assure them that none of them would be sold or treated any differently because of the move.

He let Zelma weep and did not speak. When she calmed down, he said very quietly, "You are my wife, Zelma, the mother of my son. I love you. If you feel I've treated you like a slave, I'm sorry. However, I do not feel it unjust to ask my wife to support me in whatever I might undertake. As I've said, this realization of my dream is not for me alone, but for you and our children as well."

She averted her gaze and said nothing.

"Both our parents were among the first settlers to brave the wilderness that was Georgia. Louisiana is my wilderness —and yours. Surely we haven't become so soft that we cannot do what our parents did."

"Why not content ourselves with what our parents did achieve?" she demanded. "They did this for us. Just as you want to build in Louisiana for our children. But, no, you want more."

"Yes, more," he agreed. "Is it wrong to set a higher goal?"

Zelma pushed her chair back and rose. Clutching the chair, she stared across the table at her husband. "I'll go with you, Dester," she said flatly. "But don't delude yourself into thinking it's because I wish to do so. Our parents were accustomed to hardships. I'm not. They began with next to nothing. I didn't. I'd be perfectly content here, where my friends are. The goal you have set is *your* goal, a man's goal. I'll follow you because I am helpless to do otherwise. I'll not lose my son, and if my father decided in your favor, he will not take me back." She saw the hurt from behind his eyes and added, almost as an afterthought, "You are my husband, and I love you." Turning, she moved to the door, stopped with her hand on the knob, and said, "But I do not know if I shall ever forgive you for doing this to me."

Before he could speak she was gone.

Dester sat for a long while, his pipe unsmoked, the coffee growing cold in his cup. Then, sighing wearily, he pulled himself out of his chair, went through the house, and out the door. He summoned the slaves from their sheds and spoke to them at length about his plans and hopes for Louisiana, telling them the things he had been unable to share with Zelma. They listened quietly, but when he went inside, he heard their excited chattering and wailing. He sent for Jingo and instructed him to keep close watch on the slave sheds for the following nights. He did not want to be troubled with a maroon slave. He had trouble enough with Zelma and the preparations for the move.

When he climbed the stairs for bed, he found the bedroom door bolted to him. At first, he entertained the idea of breaking down the door. Then, shaking his head, he retreated down the stairs and ordered a bed made up for him in the parlor.

He found it difficult to sleep in his own house away from his own bed, without the warmth of Zelma close to him. It was a moonlit night, and the draperies had not been drawn. The painting of Zelma above the mantel, which the senator had commissioned the year before her marriage, was well illuminated. Dester lay staring up at the painting of the woman he loved, with her soft, smooth complexion, long auburn hair, and laughing blue eyes, and the thought occurred to him that the real Zelma might prove as unyielding as the image of her that stared down at him.

Matilda had made up the master's bed in the parlor and had deliberately left the draperies undrawn. After being dismissed, she slipped from the back door and crept around the house to the parlor window. Stationing herself behind a tree where she had a clear view of the interior of the parlor, she watched quietly, longingly, as Dester began to shed his clothes.

Since Matilda had been fifteen, she had had a secret love for her master. The feeling had come on her suddenly, like the fever of a summer cold. She had experienced nothing like it. It had devastated her with its hopelessness. She had lost considerable weight, been listless, and given to frequent tears. Bessie Lou had put her to bed for two days, treated her with mustard packs and herbal teas, and had made her return to work, when the symptoms did not improve or worsen. Serving dinners, Matilda had been forced to drive her desire for her master into the recesses of her mind so that neither he nor the mistress would suspect her devotion.

Matilda hated her mistress, out of deep jealousy which grew in the secret part of her along with the love for her master. Never had she been happier than when the couple had argued at dinner. As she had made up the master's bed in the parlor, she had thought, *Now that she's turned him away, maybe he'll look at me.* Her hands had trembled so that she had almost been incapable of tucking the quilts about the foot of the bed. But he had not looked at her; it could have been Bessie Lou or any of the household slaves tending to his wants.

Outside, clinging to the shadows of the tree, silent tears of frustration streaked her cheeks as she watched the man inside systematically remove his boots, shirt, and then riding breeches. She thought he would stop there, but he did not. He hooked his fingers under the waistband of his underdrawers and pushed them down over his thighs. He sat to pull them over his feet, and then stood again, turning, almost as if he suspected her presence, to the window. Matilda's breath caught in her throat; her heart pounded against her rib cage as if it would break through. She stepped back farther into the shadows, her eyes riveted on the golden patch of hair at her master's loins from which his enormous cock swayed. His hand moved, he absently cupped himself, scratched, then reached for the lantern.

The parlor became dark, and Matilda, alone with her

frustration and a burning fever, ran around the house and
to the slave sheds, where, if she could arouse Job from his
exhausted sleep, she could find temporary satisfaction.

The following days did not seem to have enough hours
for all that must be done. The sale of the farm to Moore
was legalized. Moore had tried to bargain at the last
moment, but when Dester threatened to walk out of the
office of the justice of the peace and put the farm in the
hands of an auctioneer, he quickly produced cash in the
full amount. The blacksmith came and, with the help of
four slaves who had done such work about the farm, began
the construction of the wagons. Household belongings
were sorted into rooms of what would be taken and what
would be sold; Bessie Lou wept uncontrollably over the
loss of her great cast-iron stove, saying no other would be
found to replace it.

Zelma, between tearful visits with her friends, super-
vised the selling and packing of her household belongings.
She retained an aura of resigned martyrdom, eating dinners
with her husband, speaking little, and continuing to bolt
the bedroom door each night. She excessively scolded the
house slaves and had Matilda beaten twice by Bessie Lou,
who scarcely laid her switch against the girl's back. Despite her irritability, she was never short with Vance and
spent even more time than usual with him on her lap. He
had spoken his first word, or she claimed he had, and she
was determined to teach him a multitude more immediately. Bessie Lou, watchful of such things, noted sadly
that her mistress never urged the child to attempt the
word "Papa."

Two days before departure, a letter came from the
senator. Dester tore the envelope open impatiently and
read:

My dearest Dester and Zelma,
I write this letter in haste so that it may reach you
before your departure. News has come from Messrs.
Monroe and Livingston in Paris, informing that they

are not only treating for New Orleans and surrounding countryside, but for the entire territory of Louisiana. Although the price has been settled at fifteen millions, they continue to treat over clauses in which Bonaparte holds firm. Do not fret. Agreement shall most certainly be reached. Mr. Livingston, although an optimist, feels the actual signing of the treaty shall be executed before the end of the month.

President Jefferson has consented that all inhabitants of Louisiana shall enjoy the same rights, privileges, and immunities as other citizens of the United States.

A question yet to settle involves entry of all French and Spanish vessels into any Louisiana port free of duty for a period of twelve years.

Bonaparte, the rascal, has already entrusted our plenipotentiaries with a document to be released on their return. His confidence astounds me. I have copied the document as it was received by President Jefferson. If anything should relieve your apprehensions, it should.

"Make it known to the people of Louisiana that we regret to part with them; that we have stipulated for all the advantages they could desire; and that France, in giving them up, has ensured to them the greatest of all. They could never have prospered under any European government as they will when they become independent. But while they enjoy the privileges of liberty, let them ever remember that they are French, and preserve for their mother-country that affection which a common origin inspires."

As you can see, Bonaparte is as much an optimist as to the signing of the treaty as our Mr. Livingston.

So, my beloved ones, go in peace, and with assurance that you are protected under the rights of this great land.

Remember me to my grandson.

Your Father.

Dester, pleased with the news the letter contained, hastened to give it to Zelma. She read it twice, perhaps searching for some message between the lines, then passed it back to him without comment. She busied herself over a box of Vance's toys that she was sorting to include in their own wagon or that of the slave children.

Dester, angered by her attitude, asked sharply, "Are you almost finished within the house?"

She answered without looking up at him, "I shall be finished here tomorrow." Then, nothing more to say to him, she called Bessie Lou and instructed her to distribute the old toys to the mothers of the slave children.

"There won't be no room for toys," Bessie Lou remarked. "The wagons are already full to bursting."

Zelma stared at her blankly for a moment. Then, drawing back her foot, she kicked the box of toys, spilling them onto the floor. Angrily, she stomped from the room, muttering that everyone was against her, her husband, her father—even her own damn house slaves.

Dester and Bessie Lou exchanged hopeless glances.

"Gather up the smaller toys, and see that room is found for them in the wagons," he told Bessie Lou. Then with a glance at the door through which his wife had disappeared, he turned and left the house.

Two days later, before the sun had dried the mist from the ground, James Moore, his wife, and overseer stood on the porch of the Granville farm, now theirs, and watched Dester Granville and his family, thirteen wagons, and forty-eight slaves depart for Louisiana.

"Damn fool!" Moore said and laughed. "Damn rainbow-chaser!"

CHAPTER FIVE

ZELMA, SNUGGLED DEEP into the plush feather mattress, woke and stared up at the strange, muslin-draped canopy of the bed. She suffered momentarily from disorientation. Then familiarity came rushing back to her. She, Bessie Lou, and Vance were staying at Madame Celine's fashionable boarding house in New Orleans, while Dester had gone up-country to their land. She turned and looked at the empty side of the bed. The night before he had gone she had given in to Dester's demands, and had, after the nights of rejecting him, actually enjoyed sex. Possibly because of the change in her attitude, Dester had been exceedingly gentle with her. He had been thinking of her satisfaction as well as his own, she now reasoned. She reached out her hand and touched the pillow where his head would have lain. Then, not wanting to admit to herself that she missed him, she got quickly from bed.

She threw back the lacy counterpanes and drew aside the damask draperies that barred the malodorous New Orleans night air from the room. The morning light through the outside shutters was making long shadows across the carpet. She pushed the shutters wide and stepped onto the balcony. She breathed deeply, and clutching handfuls of her nightdress, moved to the edge of the balcony and leaned against the iron railing. A thin layer of fog concealed the paving stones of the courtyard below. Only the topiary trees, enameled dark green with dew, rose into sight. The air was warm, almost heavy, and she felt moisture collecting on her cheeks. From somewhere up on the roof, a single bird began chirping in a slow, mechanical manner, and a low feminine voice drifted

37

up from the far end of the garden court where the carriage
house and kitchen closed off the house from the alleyway.
She stood listening to the song of undistinguishable words,
A lullaby? she wondered. *No, a love song.* She found the
thought pleasant. Closing her eyes, she let the song sweep
over her, through her. She felt oddly alive, excited; New
Orleans was nothing like she had expected it to be, and
although she did not like to admit it, she had begun to be
recaptured by Dester's dream. How long would he be
away? she wondered.

She had refused to leave New Orleans until a suitable
house had been built for her. She could not live like a
pioneer, a slave in the naked countryside. Had he expected
that of her? He had not said; he had merely gone away
and left her as she had requested.

The song ended, and Zelma opened her eyes. She
stepped back with a slight start. To the right where the
gallery bent to embrace the wing of the house, Emile
Faviere stood leaning against the frame of his open door.
He was fully dressed, in cravat and coat, even pale gloves,
his feet and lower legs lost to view in the low-lying fog.
He was gazing toward the back of the court, perhaps listening to the same mysterious song. He had not taken note
of her. She appraised him openly, as she had been unable
to do at dinner on the previous nights. He was strikingly
handsome, with his black hair and dark probing eyes. He
had only the slightest hint of an accent, and when he
spoke he used his hands in expressive gestures. He was
thin, moved with an appealing litheness, an awareness of
himself that encouraged awareness from others. Dester
had told her he was the son of their nearest neighbor,
Maurice Faviere. She had also learned from Madame
Celine that Emile Faviere was twenty-four, unmarried,
somewhat of a rogue, and given to drinking too much of
her valuable wines. He visited New Orleans once a month,
always hated leaving, and sometimes, when he extended
his stay, was called for by an older sister and two particularly burly slaves.

Afraid of being discovered on the balcony in her nightdress, Zelma quickly withdrew into the room. Thoughts of

Emile Faviere brought a blush to her cheeks, but in the murky reflection of the dressing table mirror, it was not detectable. She removed her mobcap and began unplaiting the single, thick braid of auburn hair. With slow deliberateness, she began to comb out her hair and to hum the melody she had heard on the balcony.

A glance at the tiny clock told her it was only half past seven. At home, things would have been well underway for the day, but here in New Orleans, people would not rise for another hour. These gay, exiled Parisians appealed to her. She liked their easy, carefree approach to life.

On impulse, Zelma rose from the dressing table and returned to the open doors. Standing well into the shadows, she peered diagonally through the opening toward the wing of the house where Emile Faviere had stood. He was no longer there. The door to his rooms was closed.

Down in the kitchen, a bell tinkled. A woman laughed and another called out orders. From the front of the house came the faint singsong calls of the street vendors.

Zelma returned to the dressing table and continued preparing her appearance for the day with particular care. When Bessie Lou came in to awaken her, she was already dressed and eager for breakfast.

"Isn't is a glorious day, Bessie Lou?"

Bessie Lou's eyebrows lifted with an unvoiced question. She moved to the bed and began to make it.

But Zelma's mood would not be spoiled. Gaily, she said, "So you're angry with me, are you? Over last night?" She moved across the room and touched the slave affectionately on the shoulder. "Don't be angry, Bessie Lou. I'm happy, wildly happy."

"Is being happy what made you drink too much wine at dinner last night?" Bessie Lou retorted.

"I only had two glasses of sherry," Zelma said.

"Three," Bessie Lou corrected. "More than one ain't proper for a lady."

Zelma, turning away from her, wandered back to the mirror for a final appraisal of her appearance. "At home, one is proper," she said, "but this isn't home. It's New

Orleans. Madame Celine had three glasses, too, and she's
very much a lady."

"French women have different standards," Bessie Lou
said knowingly. "Besides, if things I heard in the kitchen
are true, Madame Celine is certainly no lady."

"Kitchen gossip," Zelma chided. "She's charming.
There was certainly no one like her in Savannah."

"Not in *your* Savannah," Bessie Lou said in a whisper
that did not reach her mistress. Louder, she said, "And
that man, that Frenchman, you seemed to find him mighty
charming—and Master Granville only gone a few hours.
If this had been back home, I'd have. . . ."

"But this isn't back home," Zelma said firmly, her mood
being quickly dampened by the critical Bessie Lou. "I was
dragged away from *back home,* if you remember correctly," she said.

"A lady is a lady wherever she goes," Bessie Lou said.
"And don't you go letting these fancy foreigners tell you
that ain't so."

In another part of the house, Madame Celine was astir
earlier than usual. It was apparent, after the evening before, that scandal was in the making, and she did not intend to miss a single moment of it. *Mon Dieu,* excitement
was rare enough in this forgotten corner of the Empire. A
breath of scandal would remind her of her beloved Paris.

This young American girl was unpolished, naive. Ah,
but Madame Celine had detected *la force vitale* the very
moment Mrs. Granville had set foot over her threshold.
She had not clung helplessly to her husband's arm as did
so many of these mawkish American women but had
walked proudly beside him—no, almost as if she dared
walk ahead of him. *La!* A woman capable of interesting
actions, Madame Celine decided. Mrs. Granville's coquet-
tish exchange with Monsieur Faviere at dinner the night
before had been amusing, and Monsieur Faviere had been
receptive. Definitely scandal in the making.

A chubby, black girl, her face still swollen with sleep,
appeared in response to Madame Celine's bell-cord. The

strap of her apron drooped from her left shoulde. the hem of her serving dress was soiled.

Madame Celine looked at her disapprovingly but was in too high spirits to reduce herself to scolding. "Breakfast for me and Madame Granville, in Madame's chambers," she instructed. "The usual, I think, and perhaps a fish or two." She smiled slightly, remembering those barbaric breakfasts in London so many years ago. "Yes, two fish, fried crisp, for this American."

The girl left, and Madame Celine turned to view herself full-length in the standing mirror, approving of the heavy black silk dressing gown, disapproving of her washed-out countenance. She pulled a touch of oil to her eyelids and gave her cheeks two smart slaps to get the blood circulating. She then moved to her vanity for closer inspection of herself. There was a rustle of silk behind her, but she did not redirect her gaze in the mirror. She knew it was Pierrot emerging from her bed.

"*Bonjour, mon petit choux,*" she murmured. "Did you sleep well, my pet?" She did not expect an answer, in either French or English, because Pierrot was as mute as he was beautiful.

Pierrot's beauty made him irresistible to Madame Celine. She could never look at him without recalling that first day she had seen him, a bronze-skinned child, his near-naked body glistening with sweat on the slave auction block. The trader had told her the golden child was from Jamaica, not Africa, and she had suspected him immediately of being a mulatto. She had been so taken with his delicate face and slender body she had not even attempted to speak to him before placing her bid for his possession. She had not known until she had brought him home that he was a mute. *Ah, well, no matter. She knew enough endearing words for both of them.*

Turning on the bench, Madame Celine considered the naked boy who stood quietly, halfway between her and the bed. At fifteen or so, he was beginning to broaden at the shoulders, deepen at the chest. There was a delicate curve on the insides of his thighs, just above the knees, and another at the outsides of his calves. But it was to his face that her gaze kept returning, to his eyes, sleep-filled, now gray-brown smudges above the shiny, taut cheeks, and his narrow, pointed nose and unswollen lips. Soon, she thought, the blush of youth would leave him. Ah, unhappy day! A wave of gentleness swept over Madame Celine.

She extended her hand to Pierrot, and he approached soundlessly, bare soles treading the muting carpet. Tenderly, her hand traced the shallow ridge along the base of his chest, then trailed down over the smooth flesh of his stomach to his groin. The hair there was curiously silky and unmatted. Her breath came in quicker rhythm as she began to stroke his penis, coaxing it into a golden, pulsating shaft. When she heard him gasp, she quickly pulled the lace cap from her head and sent her unbraided hair cascading forward against his thighs, which were now straining and flexing in anticipation. She took him eagerly in her mouth, her head going back and forth until she felt the expansion and release deep within her throat.

Pulling back, she kissed the head of his ebbing penis and patted him affectionately on the buttocks. He smiled down at her, the sleep now gone from his eyes. She knew there were words of loved trapped within his speechless throat, words that she longed to hear but would be denied.

"Ah, *mon cher*," she said. "You are my prize, my angel." She patted him again and then turned away. To his reflection in her mirror, she said, "Now run along, my pet. I won't be amusing you today. I'll be spending my time with our new guest." Catching his gaze, she asked, "Do you find Mrs. Granville pretty? Prettier than I?"

Pierrot shook his head from side to side.

"Ah, men," Madame Celine said to her image after he had gone, "even those without voices find a manner of lying to you."

She took up her dyeing comb and began to color the gray hair at her temples.

Madame Celine patted her lips with a lace handkerchief and discreetly cleared the phlegm from her throat. Her dark eyes watched her young guest, who sat absently moving the food about her plate without interest. Madame Granville, she noted, looked exceedingly pale. "Are you ill, Madame?" she asked.

Zelma, brought out of her private thoughts, managed an unconvincing smile. "Nothing serious," she said. "Perhaps the change in climate."

"*Oui*, perhaps," Madame Celine murmured. "Or perhaps you are missing your handsome husband."

Bessie Lou, who had been on her way to the adjoining room to quiet the crying Vance, was brought up short by the mention of her mistress being ill. She studied Zelma with an appraising glance and was startled that she had not noticed her mistress's paleness earlier. A flurry of concern touched her. Despite Madame Celine's presence, she was about to speak to Zelma, when Zelma's eyes turned on her and silently commanded her silence. With a shrug, she left the two women.

"My husband often travels," Zelma told Madame Celine. "I am not a pampered wife who must have her husband about her at all times."

Especially not when your eye roams to such as Monsieur Faviere, Madame Celine thought. Aloud, she said, "You are not . . . what shall I say? . . . the typical American wife." Fearing her remark might be taken as other than a compliment, she laughed and quickly added, "You, I think, have a French soul. You are not a woman who smothers her man." She carefully folded her napkin and placed it beside her plate.

The image of Dester being smothered by anyone, herself included, amused Zelma. She laughed.

"Also," Madame Celine went on, "I think you are not a woman who would allow herself to be smothered."

Zelma sensed the remark was both a statement and a question, but not knowing what to reply, she merely smiled, averted her gaze, and continued to toy with her breakfast. If only she could tell Madame Celine how much she detested fried fish, she thought. This morning even staring at it on her plate brought a queasiness to her stomach.

"A pity you shall eventually leave our city," Madame

Celine said. "Once you've accustomed yourself to the
climate and noise, it is quite a nice place to live." She
sighed, remembering her own period of adjustment. It had
been worse then, smaller and less civilized. But then, she
had arrived from Santo Domingo with a company of
French and Canadian actors to give the first professional
dramatic performance ever seen in New Orleans. They had
established *Le Theatre St. Pierre.* How long ago? Eleven
years, she recalled. It seemed longer, at least three de-
cades. The theater had been closed within a few months
of its opening by the Spanish authorities because the actors
insisted upon singing French revolutionary songs at un-
expected points in their performances. She had not been
known as Madame Celine then. That had been before
marriage to Etienne, before he had died of a knife wound
in a street brawl and left her the inheritance of two houses,
this fine one and the other across town. What a surprise
that other house had been—*Mon Dieu!*—What a blessing
also! Zelma cut into her thoughts.

". . . stay in New Orleans rather than go to some farm
carved out of the wilderness," Zelma was saying. "I find
New Orleans exciting. It's unlike anything I imagined. I
should very much like to see more of it."

"Then you shall," Madame Celine told her. "I'm sure
Monsieur Faviere would be most happy to show you
around our city."

Bessie Lou, who had come back into the room cradling
young Vance in her arms, stood openly listening. Softly to
the child, but loud enough for them to overhear, she said,
"In Savannah, it wasn't proper for a married lady to be
seen in the company of a strange man, was it, my precious?"

Zelma felt the color rush to her face.

"Nor is it here," Madame Celine said before Zelma
could speak. She laughed. "Leave it to a devoted slave to
remind us of what's proper. I shall show you the city
myself—" she turned and glanced pointedly toward Bessie
Lou—"from the respectable vantage point of my carriage."
Turning back to Zelma, she added, "But, of course, I shall

be allowed to have a few friends in to meet you? Your husband would not object?"

"Of course not," Zelma assured her, anger at Bessie Lou still blazing in her eyes.

Madame Celine leaned back in her chair and, more to herself than to Zelma, murmured, "I'll invite Monsieur and Madame Carron. And Señor Salazar, you'll find him amusing. He's an artist with a most remarkable talent for. . . ." The planning of her guest list was interrupted by a tapping at the door.

A young slave girl stuck her head into the room and told Madame Celine there was a gentleman caller asking for her. "An emergency," she added.

"Yes. Very well." Madame Celine excused herself and departed.

As soon as the door had closed behind her, Zelma rose and spun in Bessie Lou's direction. "How dare you!" she cried. "You embarrassed me deliberately!"

"If reminding you of what's proper is embarrassing, then it was deliberate," Bessis Lou retorted. Vance, still cuddled in her arms, had begun to cry again at the sound of his mother's angry voice. She touched his cheek and began talking to him in a soothing tone, turning away from her mistress.

"You forget yourself!" Zelma told her, trembling. "Just because we're in New Orleans where almost half the niggers are free, don't you go forgetting your place!"

Bessie Lou glanced away from the baby for a moment, her steady gaze meeting that of her mistress. "I won't forget my place," she said quietly, "if you don't go forgetting yours." She walked out of the room, quietly soothing Vance in a singsong voice, and closed the door.

Zelma sank back into her chair at the table. Bessie Lou had been right, of course. She couldn't be seen flitting about New Orleans in the company of a strange Frenchman, but—damnit!—the idea was certainly appealing.

When Madame Celine returned, her expression was troubled. "La tragedie!" she announced. "Mon Dieu! A poor girl who lives in my other house died last night."

"Oh, I'm so sorry," Zelma said.

"Ah, well, yes." The older woman patted her red hair absently, pushing a loose strand back into the grasp of its comb. "She'll be buried today. Poor dear. I hate funerals, but I must attend. The other girls wouldn't. . . ." She bit her lower lip. "It needn't change our plans," she said, composing herself. "Funerals are short here, as they should be. If you'll attend with me, I'll keep my promise and show you our city afterward."

"Oh, but perhaps another time would be more appropriate," Zelma suggested. "After a funeral, you won't feel like being guide to a tourist."

"I promised to show you the city, and I refuse to disappoint you," Madame Celine told her. "At noon, then, Madame Granville."

"Oh, but—!"

Madame Celine turned in the open doorway. *"Oui?"*

"It's . . . it's just that I haven't the slightest notion where my black dress is packed," Zelma said.

Madame Celine smiled. "No reason for concern," she said. "Claudette, poor dear, always hated black. It wouldn't be respectful to wear it to her funeral. I must send Pierrot to locate Monsieur Faviere. He was fond of Claudette and will want to. . . ." The closing door cut off her words.

Zelma sat staring at the closed door, thinking, what a strange woman. What strange attitudes toward death and funerals. What a strange city—and how exciting!

Madame Celine and Zelma occupied one seat of the carriage, and Pierrot, wearing a gray suit with mauve trim, sat facing them. His back was straight, his eyes fixed unmoving on his mistress.

Zelma looked at the young, mute slave and thought that Madame Celine treated him somwhat like a favored pet. Although, she recalled, Bessie Lou said the kitchen slaves hinted at a more clandestine relationship. Nonsense, of course. Pierrot, as if sensing her thoughts, turned his eyes on Zelma, and smiled.

"Pierrot likes you," Madame Celine said, obviously pleased. "Isn't he precious? Those hazel eyes! And his *café au lait* color!" In a softer voice, still not soft enough to prevent Pierrot from hearing, she added, "There was definitely a white sailor in his family's woodpile."

Zelma averted her gaze from Pierrot's eyes and said nothing. The youth's presence, his inability to speak, and the way Madame Celine doted on him made her uncomfortable. Another discomfort was the color of her dress, a chocolate brown, the darkest in her wardrobe, with white lace about the bodice and cuffs, somber but definitely not her idea of the proper attire to wear to a funeral. She told herself not to be concerned. Madame Celine was wearing emerald green.

Zelma wanted to enjoy the ride, and to take in the sights of New Orleans, but within a few minutes they were clear of the shade trees surrounding Madame Celine's house and the temperature became oppressive. The sun seemed to burn directly through her parasol, and her body was baking inside the oven of her heavily starched dress. She glanced at her companion, but Madame Celine appeared unscathed by the heat. Pierrot, looking equally cool despite the direct sun, removed two fans from inside his coat, snapped them open, and leaned forward to fan his two ladies.

"How thoughtful of you, Pierrot, to have brought an extra fan," Madame Celine commented. *"Mon cher,* you are precious."

Zelma attempted to ignore the heat by examining the buildings they were passing. Most were made of stucco or brick, roofed with slate or tiles, Spanish style, built around patios or coutyards, like Madame Celine's. Farther back from the river, she had occasional glimpses of the homes of the middle or poorer classes. These were made of wood, with shingled roofs, many elevated on high posts. She commented on this to Madame Celine.

"Oui, it is necessary," the older woman said, "to keep the snakes and alligators out of the houses."

When they returned onto Chartres Street near the Cabildo, Zelma sat forward with a little cry, the oppressive heat forgotten.

"Ah, the pillories," Madame Celine said. She motioned

to Pierrot to have the driver stop the carriage. "I had a
friend, a fellow actor, who spent five days in one of those
contraptions," she told Zelma.

Zelma stared at the pillories in shocked fascination.

There were two, one now in use. A man's head and
hands protruded through the planks. Some boys were
hurling rotten fruit at him while they loudly wagered as
to which had the most deadly aim.

"My friend didn't object to the imprisonment as much
as the rotten missiles," Madame Celine went on with
amusement. "They reminded him of too many past performances."

"But—he's a white man!" Zelma suddenly exclaimed
as the man lifted his head.

"Oui. No doubt a thief," Madame Celine said. "That
placard around his neck reveals his name and crime and
the number of days he's to be exposed."

"But he's white!" Zelma repeated.

Madame Celine glanced uncomfortably at Pierrot.
"Crime is not restricted to the color of one's skin," she
said coolly. "Nor is the punishment." She gave the driver
a signal to move on.

Madame Celine's carriage was the last to arrive at the
cemetery. The graveside services had already begun, and
the minister, obviously put upon by the interruption of a
latecomer, paused in his sermon. Madame Celine waved
at the women gathered around the coffin and alighted
from her carriage with Pierrot's assistance. Then pulling
a lace handkerchief from her cuff, she took up her place
among the mourners.

Zelma spotted Emile Faviere standing to one side of
the little group, like a spectator who had stumbled upon
an interesting activity and had stopped to observe casually.
Feeling as much the stranger as he appeared, Zelma left
the carriage and approached him.

Emile smiled and bowed ever so slightly as she approached. His black hair had fallen down about his high
forehead and accented his dark, probing eyes. There was
the hint of a smile lurking behind the irises. "You're the
last person I expected to meet here, Mrs. Granville," he

told her. "Surely you had not made the acquaintance of our Claudette?"

"No, I had not," Zelma answered, and she explained that Madame Celine was combining the services with a sightseeing outing. She looked longingly toward the shade of a nearby tree, and Emile, sensing her wishes, led her out of the noonday sun.

"An uncivilized time of day for a burial," he said, "but here in New Orleans, they must get the dead settled as quickly as possible."

Zelma seated herself on a stone bench and collapsed her parasol. The heat was as intense in the shade as it had been in the sun. She opened Pierrot's fan and fluttered it before her face.

"The humidity is not so bad up-country," Emile told her. He had moved to the tree and was leaning against the base, watching her.

"Thank the Lord," Zelma murmured. The fan was useless, and she quit the movement.

"Of course, given the choice between the humidity and extreme desolation, I'd choose the humidity," Emile remarked. "Perhaps after a few weeks of plantation life, you'd make the same choice."

"Perhaps," Zelma said. "If the choice were mine to make."

"Not that I consider New Orleans the ideal place to be," he said as if she had not spoken.

"And what might the ideal place be, sir?"

"Paris," he answered quickly. "Six years in this wilderness and I'm still homesick. I miss the city of my birth, the friends of my youth." The distant expression that had come into his eyes vanished, and he smiled. "What is this effect you have on me, Mrs. Granville? I've only seen you twice before, and I'm already talking to you as if we were old friends."

"Twice before?"

"Last night at dinner," he said, eyes sparkling, "and this morning on your balcony."

"Oh!"

"Did you enjoy the Creole lullaby?"

"It was quite beautiful," she answered coolly.

"Oh, you're angry with me because I admit to seeing you in your chemise—or, as you Americans say, nightgown? Please don't be angry. You were, I think, also watching me. Besides, it is too hot for anger."

Zelma abandoned her pretense at anger and smiled at him.

"That's much better," he said. "You are very beautiful when you smile."

Her smile faded.

"Have I offended you again? Forgive me. You are apparently more strict with your compliments in Savannah than we are in New Orleans. Tell me, Mrs. Granville, what do you think of our city?"

"It's exciting and strange," she said.

"Strange, how?"

She told him about the white man in the pillory who was being pelted with rotten fruit by black youths.

"Not so long ago, he would also have been branded on the shoulder with a *fleur-de-lis*," Emile told her. "Being white, he'd be run out of the area. A freed black might be flogged, branded, and transported to the West Indies to be sold into slavery." He folded his arms across his chest, then unfolded them as if in a fit of indecision. Reaching above his head, he plucked a leaf from the tree and twirled it absently between his fingers. "What else do you find strange?"

"For another, that," Zelma said, nodding toward the small group of women standing about the grave. "Madame Celine told me the dead woman detested the color black, but regardless, I've never seen such brightly colored gowns worn to a funeral." Bright blue, pink, Madame Celine's emerald green; in comparison, her own brown gown with its white lace was fitting to the occasion.

Emile laughed. "That's because they are . . . well, very special women," he said. "Surely Madame Celine explained to you that. . . ."

Zelma had leaped to her feet before he could finish and pressed her fingers to her mouth in astonishment. The minister had closed his Bible and stepped back from the group. Two giant slaves, lifting the coffin as if it were weightless, had set it into the open grave where it had made a sloshing sound and was now bobbing above the surface. As she watched, the slaves climbed onto the lid, arms outstretched to keep their balance on the swaying box.

"The coffin will sink quickly if they've bored the proper number of holes in the bottom," Emile said.

Indeed, the top of the coffin had vanished, and the water was creeping up over the slaves' ankles.

"What a disagreeable way to be buried," Zelma murmured.

"In New Orleans, there is but a choice of disagreeables," Emile told her. "If not a watery tomb, then the corpses are encased in brick sepulchers and the sun bakes them. As for Claudette, I'm certain she would have preferred the water."

Zelma turned away as the Negro slaves sank up to their waists. The women mourners were separating, and Madame Celine, seeing them to their carriages, had been stopped by an elderly white man and stood talking with excited gestures of her hands.

"I hope," Zelma said with a shudder, "that burials up-country need not be so barbaric."

"You need only find a hill," Emile told her.

"Then indeed I shall," she said firmly. She changed her position on the bench so she faced away from the sinking coffin. She glanced at the Frenchman. "Madame Celine tells me you travel to New Orleans once a month."

"Yes. There is nowhere else to go," he answered. "I should go mad if I did not make these monthly excursions."

"If you are so unhappy with plantation life, I would think you would abandon it," Zelma told him candidly.

"Ah, but like you, I haven't a choice," he said. "You see, I am dependent upon my father, and he cannot be swayed in the matter."

Zelma shrugged. "At least you shall soon have neighbors to visit," she said.

"I seriously doubt if my father will be swayed there either," Emile said sadly. "Did you not know he wanted the land your husband purchased?"

"My husband did mention it."

"My father is not accustomed to losing what he wants," Emile told her. "He lost the land to your husband, and that makes him his enemy."

"Oh, but that is absurd!"

"A fitting word to describe my father," Emile murmured. "You will not find him a hospitable neighbor."

"I shall win him over," Zelma said confidently.

Emile looked at her doubtfully. "Ah, here comes Madame Celine to collect you," he said. He pushed himself away from the tree. "It was pleasant chatting with you, Mrs. Granville. I hope we shall have the opportunity again soon." He took her hand, pressed it lightly, and walked away.

Zelma turned on the bench and watched his departure. Passing Madame Celine, he touched the brim of his hat. He repeated the gesture as he passed the open grave with the upper bodies of the Negro slaves protruding from the watery depth.

"Ah, my dear," Madame Celine said excitedly, "something has come up to spoil our tour of the city. I am so sorry. I shall leave you my carriage and Pierrot to see you home." She glanced at Pierrot to make sure he understood. Then, with an apologetic smile she turned and hurried away.

After Madame Celine had climbed into the elderly man's carriage and sped away, Zelma opened her parasol and followed Pierrot back across the cemetery.

She didn't mind Madame Celine's "something" that had prevented a tour of the city. In the privacy of her rooms, she could shed her hot clothes and seek coolness in a cold bath. She might even instruct Bessie Lou in the use of Pierrot's fan. The thought of Bessie Lou's reaction amused her. She would have laughed aloud if it had not been too hot for the smallest unnecessary movement.

On the ride back to Madame Celine's, Pierrot sat

sullenly opposite her, apparently distressed at having been abandoned to this American's services by his mistress.

Zelma instructed the driver to bypass Chartres Street and the pillories.

CHAPTER SIX

MADAME CELINE RETURNED home in a state bordering on hysteria. Being a woman of a normally even nature, she could not handle extreme agitation and always, when it seized her, locked herself away in her room until it had subsided. Even Pierrot, sensitive to her moods, usually avoided her during these dark moments, but today, because he was feeling insecure and unloved, he climbed the trellis outside her window and slipped into her room unnoticed, to stand and wait for her to acknowledge his presence.

Madame Celine sat at the foot of her bed, her back to him, rocking to and fro with the fury trapped inside her. What to do? she kept asking herself. What to do? If only God had made her a man, then she'd know how to handle those who were out to get her. But then, if she were a man, they would have left her girls alone. Claudette would not have gone to her grave, and the other girls would not be threatening to revolt out of fear of joining her. Ponce, *le batard!* He didn't have the spirit of these new Americans—he wanted no competition.

The more she considered her problem, the more upset she became, so that when Pierrot, tiring of waiting for her attention, stepped forward and gently touched her shoulder, she sprang to her feet, startled. Before she could stop herself, her fury vented itself on the beloved youth. She called him names in French, English, and Spanish, and ordered him out of her room.

Crushed, Pierrot sank to his knees before her and attempted to clutch at her skirts.

"Get out!" she repeated and struck him across the face.

Her regret of the action was immediate. She saw the disbelief, the pain in Pierrot's eyes. A single tear streaked the *café au lait* colored cheek and caused her to plead for his forgiveness. But Pierrot, leaping to his feet with the agility of a cat, darted across the room and flung himself over the balcony railing.

Terrified, she rushed forward expecting to see his precious body broken on the cobblestones below, but the courtyard was empty. She called his name repeatedly, but he did not respond. *"Mon Dieu! Mon Dieu!* What have I done?" she wailed. Nothing, no one, meant more to her than Pierrot, and now she had caused him to run away. What would happen to him if he were found wandering about aimlessly? She well knew the punishment of a runaway slave. The idea of one precious hair on his precious head being hurt was more than she could bear. Trembling, she ran to instruct the entire household of slaves to abandon their duties and go in search of the boy, offering a reward to the one who brought him back unhurt.

Zelma, fresh from the bath, was sitting at her dressing table fixing her hair when Madame Celine knocked and then entered without waiting to be let in.

"I've done the most dreadful thing!" the Frenchwoman cried and collapsed in a heap of emerald silk on the bed.

Zelma turned from her mirror, and Bessie Lou, setting Vance down, shoved him into the other room and closed the door. She was not about to get secondhand from the kitchen slaves what would surely prove to be a choice bit of gossip.

Madame Celine stopped crying long enough to look up into the puzzled faces above the bed and explain, "I've struck Pierrot! I've made him run away!"

"Good Lord!" Bessie Lou exclaimed, snorting through her broad nose, and said, "This place is a madhouse. Master Granville leavin' us here was a mistake. I knew no good would come. . . ."

Zelma silenced her with a glance and sent her from the room, knowing she stopped to eavesdrop beyond the closed door. Then, smothering the humor she couldn't help but feel at the reason for Madame Celine's distress, she sat down beside her and attempted to quiet her with soothing remarks about Pierrot surely returning before nightfall.

Madame Celine sat up and dried her tears. Her face became angry. "It was that Ponce's fault!" she said.

"Ponce?" Zelma asked.

"That Spaniard who is trying to ruin me," Madame Celine told her. "Because of him, I was angry, and because I was angry, I struck Pierrot." The mention of Pierrot's name caused her lower lip to tremble anew and the tears to re-form in the corners of her eyes.

"Perhaps you should tell me about it," Zelma said.

Madame Celine seized her hands and held them. "If only I could, Madame Granville. I need a friend to talk to, but I've only had Pierrot, who can only listen and perhaps not even understand what I say." Her expression clouded over, and she turned her face away. "Ah, but what would you think of me if I told you my secrets? You are not . . . pardon me, a worldly woman. You would only turn against me and move from my house."

Zelma said, "I assure you I would not." She felt offended at being considered unworldly. "Of course, if you'd rather not—" She rose from the bed and returned to her dressing table. She pretended to occupy herself with a stubborn curl that refused to lay as she wanted it, but she was actually watching Madame Celine's reflection in her mirror.

Madame Celine needed a friend, but she did not wish to lose her tenant. Her financial future was perilous enough because of that bastard Ponce. This American's stay would be a long one if she remained until her husband built the home he planned. She needed the tenant fees to maintain her house and staff and to purchase clothes and trinkets for herself and Pierrot. Poor Pierrot! She sobbed quietly.

"My father being a United States senator, we entertained his constituents from all walks of life in our home," Zelma said casually, hoping this would make her seem worldly. She did not add on such occasions she and her sister, Zona, had been banished to distant rooms.

Madame Celine weakened. Her need to unburden herself overcame her reasoning. She concealed nothing, telling a silent Zelma how she had discovered her husband's source of income when she had inherited a house of prostitution, how she had managed to continue its operation and yet maintain a desirable position in the community as an upright citizen, and how Ponce, one of her competitors for the dollars of the Mississippi boatmen who poured in and out of New Orleans, now threatened her with ruin by having had Claudette killed to terrorize the other girls into leaving her employ for his. She ended with, "I shall lose everything. This house, my position—"

Scarcely above a whisper, Zelma said, "You mean the women at the cemetery were . . . ?" She let the sentence trail off, understanding why Emile Faviere had been surprised to see her attend the burial.

"*Oui*, my girls," Madame Celine said. "Good girls, too. The best in New Orleans." She rose and began to pace about the room, her small stature made even smaller by the stoop of her shoulders. "Now that Louisiana is part of the United States, Ponce knows that New Orleans will become a great port. He dreams to become the vice king by driving the rest of us into ruin. I am the first because he thinks I will surrender the easiest. I am only a woman in a man's. . . ." Her pacing stopped abruptly. She turned and stared questioningly at Zelma. "I have shocked you, have I not, Madame Granville? You now hate me and will seek other lodgings?"

"No," Zelma said hoarsely. "I . . . I'm not shocked."

Bessie Lou opened the door and stepped into the room, a smile of satisfaction playing about her lips. There, her face said, I told you so; now let's pack our things and follow your husband. You shouldn't have stayed behind.

Zelma tossed her a lofty glance. To Madame Celine, she said, "And of course I shan't seek other lodgings. I'm perfectly happy here."

Satisfied, Madame Celine resumed her nervous pacing.

"If only," she said, "I were a man. Then I'd know what to do."

"Why? What would a man do?"

"A man would seek retribution on Ponce," Madame Celine said. "He'd strike back, only worse, so his competitors would know he couldn't be pushed around."

"Worse? What could be worse than killing a woman, even if she's only a . . ." Zelma bit her tongue. "What could be worse?" she repeated.

"Mon Dieu! I don't know," Madame Celine said. "Maybe burning his house down." Her pacing stopped at the windows. She opened the shutters and stared down into the courtyard. Two kitchen slaves were scurrying about without direction, checking and rechecking the storage sheds for the missing Pierrot and the promised reward for his return. "Ah, what to do, what to do?" she said with a heavy sigh.

Zelma rose from the dressing table and turned to Madame Celine. "I think there is only one option open to you," she said matter-of-factly. "You must do as a man would do. You must burn this Ponce's house down."

Madame Celine's hand fell away from the shutters. "But I am only a woman! My capacity for violence doesn't go beyond . . ." her voice cracked . . . "beyond striking poor Pierrot."

"Then we must find a man who'll do it for you," Zelma told her.

Bessie Lou raised her hands in a gesture of exasperation. "I know you when you get that look," she said, "and I'm warning you. . . ."

Ignoring her, Zelma crossed to Madame Celine. "Perhaps a slave you trust," she suggested.

Madame Celine shook her head. "The only slave I trust is Pierrot," she said, "and even if he comes back to me, I'd be afraid he'd be caught and killed."

Zelma stared thoughtfully through the open shutter. As she gazed at the courtyard, she saw Emile Faviere entering the gate. While dropping the latch back into position, he turned and stared up at the house. At first, Zelma thought he had spotted them behind the shutter, but then she realized he was looking above them to the roof.

"Pierrot!" he called. "What are you doing up there? Come down before you fall, you little monkey!"

"Pierrot!" Madame Celine cried excitedly. "Monsieur Faviere has found Pierrot!"

Continuing to stare down at Emile, Zelma said, "He might also very well be the man to burn down a house."

But Madame Celine had rushed from the room to rescue Pierrot from the roof.

Madame Celine tossed Pierrot frequent reassuring glances of affection. Because of Zelma Granville, he was not allowed to eat at the table. He had to sit removed, hands folded on his lap, long legs tucked under his chair. When it came time to serve cognac, he would perform his one function for the evening, but only if Monsieur Faviere returned for dinner. Judging from the nervousness of the two ladies, who sat sipping wine and waiting, Monsieur Faviere's return was highly questionable. Pierrot did not understand the Frenchman's mission, but he knew it had something to do with a favor for his mistress, something only a man could do, and, since he had not been asked—a white man.

Madame Celine sighed, twisted in her chair, and said, "Surely he's been caught. *Mon Dieu!* Poor Monsieur Faviere. It's my fault! Mine!" She touched her bosom in a dramatic gesture meant to show she accepted all blame, even though it had been Zelma's idea to enlist the Frenchman's aid. "Tomorrow we shall probably find him at the pillories. *Mon Dieu!*"

Zelma heard the grandfather clock in the entryway strike the last of eight chimes. "Let's not commit Emile to the pillories quite yet," she said. "He isn't the type to be easily caught." Her second glass of wine was beginning to make her feel heady; the room was exceedingly warm, the air close. She touched her handkerchief to her brow, and because she did not want Madame Celine to see the worry in her own eyes, she looked across the room at Pierrot. She considered him a useless, lazy nigger and wished she had the authority to order him to waste some energy on the rope of the pukha. But she kept her silence, and the oblong ceiling fan remained motionless, giving no relief from the heat. She pushed her wine glass aside so it would not tempt her further. What would Dester say if he learned of this taste she had developed for wine?

"Monsieur Faviere does have the spirit of an adventurer," Madame Celine murmured, "but, dear, dear, I shall never forgive myself if he's caught. If that father of his learned that his crime was committed as a favor for me, well, I shudder at the thought of what he might. . . ." She broke off speaking at the sound of the outer door opening and footsteps hurrying across the entryway.

Both she and Zelma had risen from their seats when the doors burst open and Emile entered. There was a smudge across his forehead but no other signs of an ordeal. Excitement sparked in his dark eyes. Reaching behind him, he drew the dining room doors closed. The smile playing about the corners of his mouth vanished as he took the few quick strides that brought him to his place at the table.

"Ladies," he said and made a gesture for them to be seated. When they had done so, he seated himself, turned to Madame Celine, and said, "Shall we begin? I'm famished."

Choking back her questions, Madame Celine reached for the crystal bell, jangled it to signal the slaves to begin serving, and slumped back in her seat. "Well?" she pressed.

The taunting smile returned to Emile's face.

"You succeeded, didn't you?" Zelma asked him.

"I did," he told her. "Madame Celine, your competitor now has one house less. You have been avenged."

The tension went out of the older woman with a sigh, and she slumped even more in her chair. "And none of his girls were killed? And you won't be arrested for arson?"

Emile didn't take his eyes from Zelma as he answered, "None of the girls were killed, and, no, I don't expect to be arrested. I did, as we planned, arrange for your carriage to be seen in the vicinity." He pulled his gaze away from

Zelma and turned to the woman at the head of the table. "You did report it stolen at seven-thirty?"

"Oui," she said and glanced at Zelma for confirmation.

"I sent Bessie Lou to the sheriff with a note reporting the theft," Zelma assured him. The grumbling slave had returned and closed herself away upstairs with only young Vance to hear her complaints. Zelma knew Bessie Lou would continue her objections to the conspiracy later, but she did not want to dampen their victory by considering that now.

"Bon," Emile said, and it was the first time Zelma could remember hearing him revert to French. "Then only Señor Ponce will know the truth, and he won't be able to prove it. The three of us are one another's alibis. We were here enjoying a leisurely repast." He glanced across the room at Pierrot. "You remembered to instruct the slaves?"

"She did," Zelma answered. Her excitement had built to match his. "Do you really believe they'll come to the house?"

Emile nodded. "If I know Ponce, he'll run straight to the authorities and point an accusing finger."

"The bastard!" Madame Celine said without a hint of her usual accent. She pulled herself up in her chair as the slaves entered with trays. As instructed, the confused slaves began the meal with the entree. Madame Celine cast a critical eye at the plates as they were set before them. "It's a barbaric way to dine," she said, "but, of course, you were right, Zelma. If we're interrupted, we can't be found in the middle of our soup and expect them to believe we've been dining for the past half-hour."

Emile began to eat with relish, but both women stared down at their plates without appetite. "You must eat," he told them.

Zelma picked up her fork and forced down her first bite of meat. Possum—she detested possum almost as much as crisply fried fish for breakfast. To Emile, she said, "Are you going to give us the details of the fire?"

"If they would interest you," he said teasingly. He laughed at her expression of impatience. "It was quite simple," he said. "The house is one of those built on poles.

In the darkness, it was easy to coat the poles with fat and light them. The flames flared up the poles and caught the floor before I got back to the road."

"But the house must have been busy," Madame Celine said. "Two keelboats anchored this afternoon."

"I told you there were no deaths," Emile assured her. "I took time to yell a warning. There was ample time for anyone inside to save themselves, but not enough time to save the house."

Madame Celine shuddered. "I remember the second of the great fires," she told Zelma. "It was in December of 1794. It was started in a courtyard on Royal Street by children playing with flint and tinder. The flames were fanned by a northern wind and swept quickly through the city. Two hundred and twelve buildings were destroyed. My husband built this house on the ruins of a government building." She turned her attention back to Emile. "You don't suppose. . . ."

"There's no northern wind tonight," he told her. He caught Zelma's eye and winked. "There's no wind from any direction." He pointed up at the fan. "Could Pierrot possibly oblige us?"

Madame Celine motioned to Pierrot, who rose and began jerking the fan's rope.

"By the way," Emile said, "if the sheriff doesn't locate your carriage by morning, it's tied up near the market-place. You can arrange for one of the slaves to stumble across it while doing the marketing. That is, if it isn't stolen for real before morning. Your keelboat crews are an unlawful bunch." He laughed. "But I doubt that even they would set fire to one of their favorite establishments."

The worry had not left Madame Celine's expression.

"You should be happy," Emile told her. "You've had your revenge, and your business for tonight is going to be doubled."

Zelma averted her gaze at the mention of Madame Celine's business.

Madame Celine forced a smile to please him. "I am happy," she said. "And very grateful—to both of you. I am indebted to both you dear friends for saving me from ruin. If only I knew how to repay—"

A loud pounding on the outer door brought her up short. She caught her breath with a gasp and dropped her fork onto her plate.

Emile's eyebrows lifted. "So soon," he said. "Señor Ponce doesn't waste time." Shrugging, he continued to enjoy his meal.

"The smudge on your forehead," Zelma cried. She rose, dampened the corner of her napkin in the water glass, and went around the table to wipe away the telltale smudge.

Emile smiled up at her. "You're enjoying all this, aren't you, Mrs. Granville?" he said. "You find your part in our conspiracy to revenge Madame Celine exciting?"

"I do," Zelma confessed.

"It shows in your face," he told her. "I'll bet you would have liked to be with me when I set the fire."

Was he teasing her? She couldn't determine. She returned to her chair, and all three of them continued toying with their food while they waited for a slave to answer the door.

"I'm so nervous," Madame Celine murmured quietly. "I only hope my face doesn't give me away."

Emile smiled at her. "Pretend you're back in your old theater days," he told her, "and this is only a part you're playing."

Madame Celine considered this; apparently accepted his advice, because the nervousness suddenly left her.

Presently, there was a rapping on the dining room doors, and they opened to admit one of the slave girls. She said, "Some gentlemen to see you, Madame. I told them you were in the middle of dinner, but—"

"It's all right, Maudie," Madame Celine told her. She took a deep breath, rose, and went into the entryway.

Zelma could see three men through the open door. Two were tall and heavily bearded and wore clothes that had been blackened and stained. They did not remove their hats. The third man was the sheriff. He was shorter than his companions, fair complected, and carried his hat in his hand. He spoke softly so that his words did not carry across the entryway. He appeared embarrassed.

"The one with the scar on his right cheek is Ponce," Emile said. "The other is his brother." He sat back in his chair as if he had finally had enough of his dinner and turned to the open door with curiosity. "The sheriff is his cousin, I believe, and no doubt has financial interest in the house I burned."

"Shh," Zelma said.

"But if we can't hear them, then they can't hear us," Emile said with a smile. "Do you think it time we went to our hostess's rescue?" He pushed back his chair and rose without waiting for an answer. With Zelma on his arm, they moved into the entryway. "Good evening, gentlemen." He turned to Madame Celine, whose face was a mask. "Is there a problem?" he asked.

"Oh, *Mon Dieu*, Monsieur Faviere," she stammered with a display of distress. "Why they come to me with this is beyond comprehension. It seems Señor Ponce's house —one of his houses—was burned and—"

"And your carriage was seen beating a hasty retreat from the scene," the man with the scar blurted out angrily.

Zelma removed her hand from Emile's arm. "Madame's carriage was stolen," she said.

The sheriff's gaze turned to her questioningly.

"This is Mrs. Granville," Madame Celine told him. "She's my guest while her husband is establishing a plantation up-country" he added pointedly, "Mrs. Granville's father is a United States senator, a very important man in the capitol."

The sheriff nodded politely and gave his cousin a warning glance meaning he would not tolerate accusations until he had had the opportunity to question those present.

"We all know why she'd like to see my house burned," Señor Ponce pressed on.

"This is no place to discuss business," Madame Celine told him. "As for burning your house, my dear man, even if I had such inclinations, I have been here all evening, entertaining my guests."

"Then you had a slave do it," Ponce accused.

"A slave?" Madame Celine laughed. "The only male slaves I own are Elias, who is past sixty, and Pierrot, who is scarcely more than a boy." She nodded at the fancily attired Pierrot, who had appeared in the dining room doorway. "Neither of them are capable of setting a fire such as you described even if I had ordered them to do so. Besides," she added, letting anger fill her voice, "I am a gentle woman who would not even think of such male barbarism. As for my business, competition does not threaten me as it seems to threaten you, Señor Ponce." Her eyelids lowered. "Or do you accuse me for reasons other than competition?"

Señor Ponce glared at her, knew he couldn't mention Claudette's death, and said nothing.

"This has been such a distressing day," Madame Celine told the sheriff. "First my tenant's funeral, and now . . . now this outrageous accusation."

Zelma stepped forward and took the older woman's arm. With concern, she said, "Perhaps you should retire, Madame. I'm certain the sheriff now sees the ridiculousness of these charges." She looked to the sheriff for confirmation of her remark.

"Well," the sheriff said hesitantly, and he absently shifted his hat from hand to hand. A quick glance conveyed his position to his cousin. To Madame Celine, "Was your stolen carriage reported to my office?"

"It was my own slave who delivered the note," Zelma told him.

"Your slave? Why not one of Madame's?"

"My Bessie Lou has almost nothing to do," Zelma answered. "You know what idleness does to a slave. I don't want her to become lazy while we're waiting for my husband to send for us. I give her chores to do for Madame Celine."

The sheriff turned to Emile. "And you, you spent the entire evening in the company of the ladies?"

"I did," Emile answered.

"That's not like you, Faviere," Ponce said suspiciously. "I've never known you to miss a cock fight when you're in New Orleans or spend a quiet evening when there's drinkin' and women to be. . . ." He glanced at Zelma and did not finish his statement.

Emile laughed cheerfully. "I have been captivated by Madame Celine's other guest," he said and smiled at Zelma. "Who knows? This change in me might become permanent."

Zelma realized Emile was taking this opportunity to flirt with her openly, and she averted her eyes. Embarrassingly, his flirtation pleased her. She looked into Madame Celine's eyes and knew the older woman understood the attraction between them.

The sheriff directed his cousins toward the door with a nod of his head. "Forgive our intrusion," he said to Madame Celine, "but you understand, it's my duty to check out all accusations such as my . . . Señor Ponce made against you."

"Yes, yes, I understand," Madame Celine said with a wave of her hand. "Your cousin should not judge others by himself. I am not a greedy person. Since the United States has purchased Louisiana, New Orleans will double in size. There will be enough business to make us both rich. Competition is good for *l'ame*—ah, how to translate?"

"The soul," Emile supplied.

"Ah, yes, the soul," Madame Celine murmured. "Tell your cousin competition is good for the soul." She added. So that only Zelma, who was at her side, could hear, "If he has one."

After the sheriff had gone, Madame Celine burst into peals of laughter. "We've done it!" she cried. "Did you see Ponce's face? He knew I was responsible for the fire, and he knew it was revenge for Claudette! He didn't expect it from me—from a woman! He'll consider carefully before he tries to put me out of business again. By morning, the whole city will be talking. My girls will no longer be afraid. Ah, la, la, la!" She grabbed a surprised Pierrot and twirled him about the entryway in a dance of victory. He danced awkwardly, mouth open in silent laughter.

"I think I've earned a cognac," Emile said.

"Monsieur Faviere, you have earned a case of my best," Madame Celine shouted over her shoulder.

"A glass will do," Emile laughed. "And you, Mrs. Granville? Wil you join us in a cognac?"

"No, I think not," Zelma told him. "It's been an exciting day and I'm tired. I'll bid you both good-night."

"But it's so early," Madame Celine protested.

Emile took Zelma's hand and brushed his lips against it. When he lifted his head, his eyes met hers. "Goodnight," he said. "You're a worthy partner in crime—and a most beautiful woman."

Zelma drew her hand back a little too quickly for politeness, hoping that her eyes conveyed no encouragement for him. She kissed Madame Celine's cheek and climbed the staircase, aware that Emile was watching her ascent.

In her room, she leaned against the closed door and smiled unwillingly, remembering the sensation that had passed up her arm at the touch of Emile's lips on her hand. It was wrong, that sensation. She was a lady of quality, a married lady. She had known no other man than her husband, and she should not want to know one. Still, her mind filled with fantasies. She imagined Emile's touch on intimate parts of her body, his kiss and embrace.

Suddenly from the darkened corner of the room, Bessie Lou's voice broke into her thoughts, "A fine way for you to be acting. You were raised in the Lord's ways, and now you're conspiring with the Devil. I heard what was said down there in the hallway." She stepped out of the darkness and into the glow of the lamp. Her face looked pinched with worry and anger. "That woman is no more than a. . . ."

"Oh, hush, hush!" Zelma cried. She went to her vanity and began unhooking her dress. "Help me," she ordered.

Bessie Lou didn't move.

"Don't be angry with me," Zelma said with a little laugh. "I like it here in New Orleans at Madame Celine's. I feel . . . well, happy and young again."

"And actin' it, too," Bessie Lou told her critically. "Actin' like a foolish child, that's what you're doin'. If

Master Dester knew what was goin' on here, he'd send for us right away. And rightly so."

"Yes, but he doesn't know," Zelma murmured quietly. "And we're here for a long while, so why shouldn't I enjoy myself? I'll be trapped in that wilderness soon enough."

"Your only trap is yourself," Bessie Lou mumbled. She came forward and began to undo the hooks of Zelma's gown. "And don't go tellin' people I have nothin' to do," she said. "I haven't known a moment's idleness since your Papa gave me to you as a wedding present."

But Zelma had ceased listening. Her mind had returned to her fantasies.

Zelma awakened from a sound sleep and sat up in bed. The hands of the porcelain clock were coming together, midnight. Something, some unfamiliar sound had awakened her. She remained alert, listening, thinking that perhaps Vance had called out her name from the adjoining room.

She had returned her head to the pillows when the sound came again—something being thrown against the glass of the french windows. She rose, pulling her dressing gown about her, and moved to the windows. Peering out, she found she could not see beyond the railing of the narrow balcony. A small pebble struck the pane opposite her face, and she cried out, startled, and let the curtain fall back into place. The moon came from behind a bank of high clouds and bathed the courtyard in a silvery half-light. Zelma could make out the shapes of the topiary bushes, and then, when he moved, the shadow of a man.

She knew immediately it was Emile Faviere.

Another pebble struck the windowpane, and throwing open the french doors, Zelma moved out onto the balcony.

"What is it, Emile?" she whispered. "You'll wake the entire household."

"If you don't come down, I will wake the entire neighborhood," Emile called back. His voice unmistakably told her he had had too much to drink.

"You're intoxicated," Zelma accused. "Go to bed, Emile."

"Not without talking to you first." He stood with his

head thrown back, the moonlight reflecting off the paleness of his face.

"We'll talk tomorrow," Zelma promised him. But the idea of joining him in the courtyard for a midnight rendezvous appealed to her sense of the romantic.

"Not tomorrow. Tonight," the Frenchman pressed stubbornly. "Come down. Please. If only for a few moments."

Zelma felt herself weakening. What harm would there be in going down to talk to him? Still, if Bessie Lou or Madame Celine should discover them—

"If you don't come down, I'll come up," Emile threatened. He moved toward the trellis of climbing roses that ended at her balcony.

Zelma panicked. "No! I'll come down."

She slipped quietly from her room and into the darkened hallway, pausing outside Bessie Lou's door to listen for sounds of movement before descending the stairs. All was quiet.

When she entered the courtyard from the library, Zelma did not at first see Emile. He had stepped out of the moonlight and stood waiting in the shadows of the arches. He came up behind her, touched her arm, and Zelma, startled, gave a muffled cry of alarm.

Emile ignored her cry. "You *did* come down," he said excitedly.

"But only for a moment," Zelma told him. "Can you imagine what this would do to my reputation if one of the servants discovered me here with you in the middle of the night? I'd be branded a scarlet woman."

"In this house," Emile murmured, "nothing would be thought of it. The Puritanical American code of morals, which, I might add, exists nowhere outside this country, was thankfully not written into the Louisiana Purchase by your leaders." Emile stumbled slightly and clung to Zelma's arm to steady himself. "Forgive me," he said. "The excitement . . . the cognac . . . I am not quite myself."

Despite the warmth of the night air, Zelma felt a chill and pulled her dressing gown protectively about herself. Now that she was standing here in the darkness beside Emile, she knew coming down to meet him had been a mistake. His hand remained on her arm; she felt the warmth of his touch through the sleeve of her dressing gown, smelled the odor of liquor on his breath—sensed that his desire for her companionship went beyond conversation. "I'd best go back in," she murmured. "It's late, and I'm tired." She made as if to turn and reenter the house, but he refused to relinquish his grasp on her arm.

She glanced up at him and saw his teeth flash in the moonlight. "Tell me, Zelma, is it me you're afraid of? Or is it yourself?"

Zelma did not answer. She tried to pull her arm away, but the pressure of his fingers only tightened.

Emile laughed quietly, drunkenly. He pulled her into the curve of his body. He tried to kiss her, but she turned her head away, wedging her hands between them to hold him at bay.

"You are not a gentleman, sir," she said stiffly.

"I am the hero come to claim his reward."

"Reward? Reward for what?"

"You know for what," he said. "It was for you that I burned Ponce's house."

"And your reward was gratitude from both Madame Celine and myself," Zelma told him. She pushed away from him, although he did not relinquish his grasp of her arm. "I should think the pleasure the adventure gave you would have been reward enough. If you expect more—"

Emile pulled himself erect, shook himself as if to clear his head. "Yes, of course. Gratitude," he said. "Only a fool or a rogue would have expected more." He suddenly released her arm. Stepping away from her, he leaned against one of the arches, his back to her, and stood silently.

"One thing," Emile said.

Zelma turned, her hand on the door handle. "Yes, Emile?"

Emile pushed away from the arch and turned. His face was lost in the shadows. "Tell me," he said, "your flirtation with me . . . was it . . . was it just something to amuse yourself in your husband's absence?"

The frankness of his question stunned Zelma into silence.

Emile misinterpreted her silence. He came quickly forward, and before she could prevent it, swept her back into the cradle of his arms. He pressed her tightly against his body. His lips, because she turned her head away, found her cheek.

"No," Zelma protested. "Emile, please!" But she made no effort to free herself. When his lips again sought hers, she became submissive and did not attempt to escape his lingering kiss. *It was not merely flirtation,* she thought. *God help me, I want him! It's against everything I was taught to respect in myself as a lady—but I want him!* She clung to his neck, returning his passion, surrendering her guilt to the demands of her body.

When Emile broke the kiss, he buried his face in her neck and repeated her name several times as if unable to believe her response. "Come," he said. He took her hand and led her across the courtyard to his room.

Inside, Zelma stood awkwardly waiting while he removed his coat and boots. She had not felt more like the frightened virgin on her wedding night, nor had her nervousness mingled with greater desire for Dester. When the thought of Dester crossed her mind, her guilt returned. She closed her eyes and attempted to force the guilt away from her, but it would not leave her.

She did not open her eyes until Emile drew her to him. She buried her face in his chest and let him lead her to the bed. She felt him push her dressing gown from her shoulders, then her nightgown. Eyes downcast, she saw both articles settled about her ankles. Warm and caressing, his hands moved over her naked body. His head came down, and his lips kissed first one breast and then the other while his hands continued to explore, to promise gentleness, passion, a fulfillment of the desires of her body.

"Oh, Zelma," he said scarcely above a whisper. Sweeping her into his arms, he lay her on the bed as gently as if she were some precious, fragile object.

She watched through lowered lashes as he undressed—his cravat, blouse, and stocking. Hooking his thumbs into the waistband of his trousers, he rolled them down off his hips and pulled them free. Then, as if aware of her admiration, he stood for a moment exposed to her before reaching to extinguish the lamp.

The darkness settled about her. The draperies had been drawn against the moonlight, and there was not the slightest speck of light in the room. The springs of the bed groaned as Emile crawled beside her. The Frenchman's hands, more demanding now, continued their exploration of her nakedness. She turned her head to meet Emile's lips. The tension in her body began to subside, her breathing became as labored as Emile's. She whimpered and clutched at his head, her fingers lacing through his hair as he lowered himself over her.

She drove her head deep into the feather pillows with the pleasure of the sensation.

Emile forced her legs apart with his knees. He mumbled something in French, but she did not understand. He found her lips, kissed her, and then, as she lifted her lips to receive him, he penetrated her and forced her back against the mattress with a savageness he could no longer control.

It was almost dawn when Zelma slipped from Emile's bed, dressed, let herself quietly out into the courtyard, and crossed through the swirling fog to the main house. From somewhere around back came the noises of the slaves beginning their morning chores, pans clattering, singing. Beyond the courtyard walls, the first of the vendors had begun calling out their wares.

Zelma stopped in the library doors and made sure no slave was in sight before entering.

She reached her room, relieved not to have been observed, and crawled into her cold bed. She was exhausted. She had not slept, but lay quietly through the night, listening to Emile's heavy breathing. Sleep would not come. She bit her lower lip and turned her face into her pillow.

She imagined Dester and what her infidelity would do to him should he learn of it.

Guilt. Remorse. They were too high a price to pay for

a few moments of sexual pleasure. She would never again surrender herself to a moment of weakness—not ever again.

She had not yet fallen asleep when Bessie Lou came to awaken her.

CHAPTER SEVEN

DESTER OPENED HIS eyes.

The treetops seemed to make a funnel above him. The sky was beginning to lighten in the moments before dawn. He had slept alone on the hilltop in the clearing where the house was to be built. In the two weeks since he had left Zelma in New Orleans, he and the slaves had made a good amount of progress. The shacks for the slaves had been completed and the fields cleared and readied for planting. Still, he was impatient. The plantation house had to be started. Zelma's absence gnawed at him every night—and every morning when he awoke and did not find her beside him. It was absurd, of course, to think of her nestled next to him in his bedroll under an open sky; even, he realized, to consider her consenting to live in one of the slave shacks until the house could be built. She had been raised to luxury, the senator had seen to that, and was not a woman to be expected to forego those luxuries, even temporarily, although he would have been proud of her if she had insisted on accompanying him to the land instead of remaining in New Orleans. Zelma had the strong, pioneer spirit of her ancestors, he felt, but that spirit was sleeping because of her soft life. One day, when she saw that his —their—dream was realizing fruition, that sleeping spirit would awaken in her. What a woman, what a wife she would be then!

He folded his hands behind his head and stared up at the sky. Below the hill, the slaves had begun to stir. He could smell the smoke of the cooking fire and hear the women's chattering as they went about the task of preparing breakfast.

There was a noise among the trees, and thinking it was Jingo come to awaken him, he turned.

He raised himself to his elbows and waited, but no one emerged from the shadows. "Jingo, is that you?"

There was no answer.

An animal, he thought. Perhaps a cougar. One of the slaves had reported spotting one near the river. He reached for his pistol and cocked the hammer.

"No! Don't shoot, Master Granville!" It was a woman's voice, frightened.

"Come out then," he said, "where I can see you."

There was a snapping of twigs beneath her feet. A branch was pushed forward, and the slave girl Matilda stepped into the half-light of the clearing.

Dester eased the hammer down and returned his pistol to its holster. "What were you doing there spying on me?" he demanded. "Well, girl, answer."

"I . . . I wasn't spying," she said. "I was just walking."

"In the dark?" He knew she was lying.

"I ain't afraid of the dark," she murmured.

"Did you know there's cougars around here? A cougar would make a quick breakfast of a girl like you and still be hungry."

She glanced around at the circle of shadowy trees and stepped closer to where he lay as if seeking protection.

"Go on," he said. "Get down the hill. Tell Jingo to get the horses saddled, and we'll go hunting before breakfast."

She hesitated, seemed about to speak, then turned and ran off down the incline toward the slave shacks. Watching her go, Dester remembered Zelma complaining of her that she was sassy and independent. Amusing, he thought, since Zelma herself was both of those things.

He climbed out of his bedroll, stood, and stretched himself. The morning breeze was cool against his naked body, but he knew the heat would be intense long before noon. He pulled on his breeches and boots and flung his other clothes over his shoulder. Since his first day on the land, he had taken to swimming in the creek during the early hours. The water near the banks of the creek was filled with reeds and the mud on the bottom deeper than a man's calves, but farther out a strong swimmer could hold his own against the current. He came down the hill, skirting the slave shacks, and made for the creek.

He hadn't reached its banks before he stopped, puzzled, and cursed beneath his breath. The water was drastically down, the reeds growing out of mud. "Damn!" he shouted. "Goddamnit!" The creek was important to him. Only yesterday they had completed the floodgates for the irrigation ditches. The entire field they had cleared for planting was to have been irrigated from the creek. He turned and hurried toward the slave quarters.

Jingo had finished saddling the horses and was busy cleaning the rifles when he saw Dester hurrying up from the direction of the creek. He knew there was trouble. So, too, did some of the women who were gathered around the outdoor cooking pits. They abandoned their duties and reached Jingo at the same time as their master.

"Never mind the hunting," Dester said. "There's something damming the creek." He was pulling his arms into his shirt and hastily fumbling with the buttons.

"Maybe a tree," Jingo offered.

"Maybe," Dester said. "Whatever it is, we've got to find it and clear it away. We can't plant without water for irrigation." He glanced around and saw Africa emerging from one of the shacks. He called the giant's name and told him to saddle a horse for himself.

"How far upstream, I wonder?" Jingo murmured.

"Perhaps a mile, perhaps twenty miles," Dester said with irritation.

"Could be a landslide," Jingo mused. "Caused the creek to change its course. I've seen that happen often enough."

"If that's so, then let's hope it's a slide that can easily be cleared away," Dester told him. "We don't have time to dig irrigation ditches all the way from the Mississippi."

The gathering of slaves had grown. They began to mumble and argue among themselves over the reasons the creek might be going dry; some saying it was the Lord's will if His creek had changed course and that they ought to pray.

After Africa joined them with his horse, Dester picked out two of his best slaves and put them in charge of the field workers, and then the three of them, Dester and Jingo and Africa, rode away.

They followed the winding curves of the creek for almost an hour without finding the reason for the blockage. The land became unfamiliar, and Dester knew he and Jingo had not ridden over this section when they had first come to inspect the land. He didn't even know if they were still on his land or trespassing on Faviere property.

The answer confronted them when they rounded a bend and came across about a dozen slaves harvesting a rice field. Not one slave looked up at them. Dester saw why; a Negro overseer was riding around the dirt embankment that surrounded the field, keeping the slaves under his watchful eye. He carried a short-handled whip which had lashes four or five times the length of the staff. Judging from the backs of the slaves, the overseer was quick to use the whip if he felt they were not exerting themselves to the fullest.

Upon seeing them, the overseer, dug his heels into his horse's flanks and approached at a gallop.

Dester glanced at Africa, who was staring at the slaves through eyes that had narrowed to mere slits. His jaw was firmly set, the muscles in his neck bulging.

Dester understood. "They remind you of your former owner?"

Africa nodded.

"Faviere is probably worse than Moore," Dester told him. "Moore was an ignorant sonofabitch, but I understand Faviere is educated."

"Don't see the difference," Africa mumbled.

"Maybe there isn't any to them," Dester said, nodding toward the bent and lash-marked backs of the slaves, "but to me, it's somehow worse." He turned away from Africa as the overseer reined in his horse only feet away.

"You're trespassin' on private property," the Negro told them. "Monsieur Faviere doesn't take kindly to trespassers." He had drawn his whip up across his lap as if readying it for use.

"We didn't realize we were trespassing," Dester told him, "but I'm afraid I find it necessary. Something's blocking the creek."

"Then you'd be Mr. Granville," the overseer said. His white teeth flashed in a smile.

"That's right," Dester told him. "Your new neighbor."

"My employer say that one neighbor is one neighbor too many," the Negro said and laughed.

Dester returned the smile without humor. "I understand I'm not your employer's only neighbor," he said. "There's a family named Cole that moved in near the fork a few years ago."

"Cole's not a neighbor," the Negro said. "He's a small-time dirt farmer who'll never amount to much. He's only got about ten acres, and most of that's nothin' but swamp land."

"Then a man's only a neighbor to your employer if he owns equal or more land?" Dester said.

The overseer nodded. "Me, I don't care how many people crowd into the land," he said. "I only work it. I don't own it and don't want to. I can work for one man as good as the next. But I do follow orders from those I work for, and my orders is to keep all trespassers off this property."

"Meaning you expect us to turn around and ride away?" Dester said. "Without finding what's blocking the creek?"

"Meanin' just that," the Negro told him.

Africa stiffened in his saddle, and Jingo's hand went gently to the butt of his rifle.

Dester pushed his hat back on his head. "I'm afraid we can't do that," he said. "The creek water means life or death for my crop. I've got to find the blockage and clear it. I suggest you send one of your slaves to inform Mr. Faviere that I'm crossing his land. If I'd known it would have been necessary, I'd have come to him, but since I didn't, I'm proceeding without permission." He nudged his horse and rode past the overseer, Africa and Jingo close behind.

It was almost noon before they located the blockage. As Jingo had first suggested, it was a fallen tree, fallen by an axe across a well-chosen gorge. Smaller trees, logs, and debris had been thrown into the water behind it to dam the flow even more, causing it to reroute itself in a different direction.

They fastened ropes to the branches and with the aid of the three horses, managed to dislodge the blockage. The released water gushed down the creek bed and overflowed the banks.

"Faviere isn't goin' to be happy 'bout this," Jingo said, worried. "That water's goin' to rise above the banks and flood his rice fields."

"The bastard deserves it," Dester said. "No one but him could have ordered that dam made."

"I agree," Jingo said. "His reason seems clear enough too. Still, I think we should go back a different way than we came."

Smiling, Dester asked, "Is this another of your predictions or just natural worry that we'll be ambushed along the way?"

"Don't have to have the power of prediction to know there's goin' to be trouble," Jingo murmured. "Just better to go another way and avoid him for now. Let him cool down before you two meet."

"All right," Dester said to please him. "We'll go back a different way."

Africa made a grumbling sound in the base of his throat to make it understood that he would have preferred to meet Faviere while his own temper was still high.

Jingo took dried beef from his saddle bag and passed it around.

They ate as they rode.

On the ride home they didn't pass Faviere or see any of his slaves.

It was late afternoon when Faviere and a dozen of his slaves came riding down the road bordering Granville land. They reined up opposite Dester's make-shift bridge, and Faviere dismounted.

Dester was just arriving in camp ahead of the weary field hands. When he saw the group at the bridge, he walked down, stopping on his own side to lean against one of the supports. Then, in a gesture of proving he was willing to meet the Frenchman halfway, he strode to the middle of the bridge and stood waiting for Faviere to join him.

Faviere was a large man of short stature. At first glance, his bulk appeared to be fat, but closer inspection revealed him to be large-boned with solid muscle. He wore an unkempt beard flecked with gray that had not yet invaded his dark hair. His eyes, beneath bushy brows, were black, and now angry. He walked with a slight limp, favoring his right leg. His hands were small, almost feminine, and looked as if nature had been playing a game on him by attaching such small extremities to such a large body.

The overseer Dester had met that morning and what at first he took for a boy and then realized was a woman in man's clothes dismounted and followed Faviere onto the bridge. He had heard of the woman and knew she must be Faviere's daughter, Claudine. She took the hat from her head and long, dark hair fell about her shoulders. She was deeply tanned and could have been mistaken for a mulatto if her features had not been so fine. Her eyes were as dark and as angry as her father's.

Faviere stopped before reaching the middle of the bridge. "You've flooded my fields," he growled.

"I sort of thought that's why you'd come," Dester told him evenly. "I wasn't expecting a neighborly visit,"

"I've no time or inclination to be neighborly," the Frenchman said in the same angry voice. "I want to know what you intend to do about the damage you caused."

"Not considering myself responsible, I wasn't planning on doing anything," Dester said.

Faviere's daughter stepped up to her father's side. "It was you who broke up the dam," she snapped.

Dester nodded. "And your father who had it built."

"It was on Faviere land and. . . ." She was silenced by a glance from her father.

"I do what I want on my land," Faviere said. "That includes damming up the creek if I decide to."

Dester restrained his anger. Quietly, he said, "You don't

own the water no more than you own the sky and the air. If you dam the creek again, I'll break it up again. I don't care how many of your fields are put under water."

Faviere's face paled. He seemed about to unleash his rage but, suddenly glancing behind Dester, hesitated.

Dester turned and followed his gaze and saw that all his slaves had come down from the camp and were standing silently watching, waiting for trouble. Jingo and Africa stood in front of them, both with rifles laid across their arms.

"Helluva lot of niggers you've got for a new planter," Faviere said uneasily. He gave his daughter and overseer a signal with a toss of his head that sent them back to where they had left their horses. The anger was less evident in his voice when next he spoke. "Look here, Granville. You cost me money today by tearing out that dam."

"If I'd already had my crop in, you'd have cost me more by building it," Dester told him.

Faviere exhaled loudly through his flared nostrils. "The point is you didn't have your crop in, and it didn't cost you anything."

"It cost me and two slaves most of the day," Dester disagreed. "Time's the same as money. I figure my losses offset yours, and that we're even." *And you've learned your lesson,* he wanted to add but didn't.

Faviere stared at him through narrowed eyes. "You don't give a hoot in hell if you make me your enemy, do you, Granville?"

"I don't want any man as my enemy," Dester answered, "but I guess I'm not Christian enough to turn the other cheek and call a man friend when he's done something against me." He pushed himself away from the log railing of the bridge and stood facing the Frenchman. "If you've had your say, I've things to do," he said.

Faviere glanced back at his daughter and the overseer. He apparently disliked losing face in their eyes even more than not getting satisfaction from Dester. "I'm a reasonable man," he said, anger now completely gone. "There's a way you can compensate me for my fields, and it will not cost you anything."

"Oh? How's that?"

Faviere nodded toward the silent slaves. "That nigger there," he said, indicating Africa. "He's a fine specimen. Will you sell him to me?"

"No," Dester answered almost before the question was out of the Frenchman's mouth.

Faviere scratched his beard. "I need stock like that one," he said. "If you won't sell him, how about renting him out to me? I could use him for studding. That way I'd consider us squared."

"I don't sell slaves, and I don't breed them," Dester said sharply. "And I've already told you I consider us even. You built the dam, and I destroyed it."

Faviere's pretended good humor vanished. His small hands closed into fists. He mumbled beneath his breath in his native tongue. Then in English, he shouted, "If you're seen on my land again, you'll be shot, Granville!" He spun around to leave.

"Just a moment," Dester said. "We both depend on that creek for irrigation, Faviere. There's enough water there for both of us. If you try to cut me off again. . . ."

"What'll you do?" Faviere interrupted.

"I'll go above your land to the creek's source," Dester told him, "and do to you just what you do to me. If you dam the creek from my land, I promise you I'll reroute it aways from yours. Where will either of our plantations be then?"

Faviere stared at him coldly. "You haven't a plantation yet, American," he growled. "You've only got the land your friends in Washington helped you to get. Land that should have been mine. You'll be facing ruin within a year. Then all the land north of Plantation Bend will be mine." Laughing, he moved on to his horse, mounted, and dug his stout legs into the animal's flanks.

Dester watched until they were out of sight.

Then he walked back to the camp. The slaves followed behind him, chattering and arguing over the ruin the Frenchman had predicted for their master.

Jingo fell into step with Dester. "What's this Plantation Bend he was talkin' about?" he asked.

"The bend in the road there in front of my land," Dester told him. "The land north of the bend is considered the most fertile in the area. Faviere would like to have it all for himself. But he won't," he added firmly. "I'd die here rather than see that bastard own this land."

Jingo, remembering the vision he had had of his master's tombstone, felt a shiver run the length of his spine.

"In fact," Dester said, with a sudden laugh, "that's what I'm going to call my place. Plantation Bend. We'll even put up a sign so every time Faviere passes on the road to New Orleans he'll be reminded of his hollow threat."

Jingo said nothing.

Dester ate his evening meal in silence. Then he leaned against a crate of Zelma's belongings and watched the sunset. A longing for her spread over him as quickly as the redness of the setting sun was spreading across the western corner of the sky. But when the redness of the sky had faded, his longing remained. He thought of writing her a letter, but he told himself he could not spare a slave to deliver it. Actually, he knew it would be impossible to express himself in a letter. He looked around the fire and saw that Jingo was sleeping, his head down over his chest, and Africa, as was often his habit, sat staring into the flames of the fire, eyes unblinking and body immobile, as if he were made of some highly polished black stone and not of flesh and blood. Dester got to his feet, took up his bedroll, and climbed the hill to the clearing.

He did not know how long he slept, but something, some sound unfamiliar to the night, awakened him. The disturbance irritated him. He had been dreaming of Zelma, of her soft, pale flesh, her body beneath his. He raised himself to his elbows, still caught in the netherworld between sleep and waking. He was about to reach for his pistol when he saw the slave girl Matilda.

She stood motionless in the middle of the clearing,

naked, the moonlight bathing her in a silvery glow. Her clothes lay on the ground at her feet.

"What are you doing here?" Dester asked, but he knew. How long since he had slept with a slave girl? Not since he had been a boy discoverng his sexuality. Since marrying Zelma, he had had no need to slip from the house in the middle of the night and seek out willing companionship in the slave quarter.

Matilda moved, shifting her weight from one leg to the other. "I . . . I thought . . ." her voice quavered . . . "thought maybe . . . you'd want me," she answered.

Dester did not speak for several moments.

He was engaged in a mental debate with himself. He told himself he should order the girl away, express anger with her so she would never again approach him in this manner. Yet, seeing her naked, willingly offering herself to him, his physical need for a woman had been awakened. He was not the sort of man many of his friends in Savannah had been, using their prettier slaves for animallike lust, screwing them, and then beating them into promises of secrecy. Since his father had died and he had become master of their people, he had not demanded sexual gratification from any of the slave women. Before marriage to Zelma, he had gone into Savannah and sought satisfaction of his physical needs from the women whose profession it was to sell release to pent-up male passions. He was an extremely sexual man. Lust, once awakened in him, was not easily satiated. But he had abandoned his periodic trips into Savannah after he married Zelma. And he had channeled his energy into his work. He had taught himself to be gratified by his wife's ungenerous consenting to sex. His love for her caused him to remain faithful. And he still hoped she would one day awaken to her own sexuality, a smoldering sexuality that would match his.

"Do . . . do you . . . want me?" Matilda murmured scarcely above a whisper.

Damn Zelma, Dester thought. *Her place was here with him, not in New Orleans. If she had been here, he would not even consider—*

He reached out a hand to Matilda. "Come here," he told her. "I want you."

Matilda crawled into his bedroll, her body as cold as the night breeze against the warmth of him. A shiver of pleasure plaited along her spine as his rough hands moved down over her abdomen and between her thighs. Her own hands became aggressive. She reached for him, found and squeezed the hot solidness of his erection. She inhaled the maleness of him and felt heady. Whimpering, she opened herself to his probing fingers. Forgetting herself, she almost mumbled words of affection, of love. But she caught herself. The love she felt was forbidden. Even the fantasy of it was dangerous.

The weight of him as he rolled on top of her was crushing. She clung to his back, fighting for breath until he raised himself on his knees between her legs. She felt for him again, guided him toward her, and cried out as the largeness of him penetrated her. She let him set the rhythm; then, wrapping her legs about his thighs, she encouraged the savageness of his thrusts. Her broken fingernails dug into the flesh of his back. She kissed, bit at his ear lobes. Silently, she prayed for him to whisper endearing words—to even call out her name in his passion.

When he did make a sound other than the groans of passion, it was at his moment of completion.

He called out his wife's name.

Then, rolling off of her, he promptly fell asleep.

CHAPTER EIGHT

EMILE WAS TO escort Zelma and Madame Celine to the reopening of *Le Theatre St. Pierre,* with many members of her old troupe appearing, but the afternoon before the performance, two burly slaves arrived at Madame Celine's back door with a letter for the Frenchman. The letter was from his father and told him he had overstayed himself in "that city of sin and corruption." The letter also informed him that his return was expected immediately; and should he hesitate, the two slaves had been instructed to bring him home by force. Resigned and angry, Emile sadly bade both women good-bye and departed with a promise to see them again as soon as possible.

The women, dressed in their best finery, attended the theater opening together.

The play was ill-chosen, the performances dreadful. Madame Celine, not knowing what to say when she and Zelma were invited backstage, exclaimed to the leading actor, "Oh, my dear, what you did out there!"

The actor was fortunately egotistical enough to take her remark as a compliment. They drank champagne, toasted the new life of the theater under the Americans, and departed.

At home, Madame Celine invited Zelma into her drawing room for coffee. Zelma had been quieter than usual all evening and seemed troubled. Neither woman spoke until the coffee had been served. Then Madame Celine leaned back on her settee and stared at her young friend over the rim of her cup. "Emile is quite taken by you, I think," she said. She thought it was Emile's departure that was upsetting Zelma. "It is always a sad thing when an *affaire* ends. *Mon Dieu,* I've been through it often enough, *cherie.*"

"There was no affair," Zelma said stiffly. "Perhaps a moment of weakness on my part, a surrendering to temptation, but not an affair."

"Ah, but—"

"I told him an affair was impossible," Zelma interrupted. *"Impossible?"*

Zelma returned her cup to its saucer and set the coffee aside. "I am a married woman," she said as if that was explanation enough.

"Ah, *oui!* An American wife," Madame Celine murmured. "Is that why you've been so upset all evening, my dear? You find it difficult, this being married and wanting what you are taught is forbidden?"

"No. That has nothing to do with it," Zelma told her.

"Surely it wasn't the play. It was a disaster, but nothing to give you that long, sad face." Madame Celine sipped her coffee thoughtfully. "Perhaps," she suggested, "you are lonesome for your husband?"

This was closer to the truth. There had been no letter from Dester in the month since he had left her in New Orleans. Emile's sudden departure had intensified her loneliness. It weighed heavily upon her and brought on her mood. "I miss my husband, of course," she said. "It's only natural."

Madame Celine smiled. *"Naturel,"* she repeated. "I will confess something to you. When Monsieur Celine died, I spent one night crying, but I never missed him. Isn't that shameless of me? He was a good husband, and although the means were questionable, a good provider. He never beat me or demanded more of me than I was willing to give. Yet I didn't miss him." She shrugged her tiny shoulders. "I guess I didn't love him. Why else would I not feel his loss?"

"I do love Dester," Zelma said quietly. "At times, he's exasperating, but I love him."

"What man isn't exasperating?" Madame Celine murmured.

Zelma stared down at her coffee but was not tempted by

the strong liquid. "What do I know of men?" she said
more to herself than to Madame Celine. "There have only
been two men in my life. My father and my husband."

"Is that what's troubling you, my dear?" Madame Celine asked. "The discovery that you are not as worldly as
you imagined?"

"Not entirely," Zelma answered. But her month in
New Orleans had whetted her appetite for the gay, carefree life. Any day she expected Dester to appear and
whisk her away from the excitement; yet with the passing
of each day, she was also disappointed when he did not
come. A battle surged within her. She wanted him to return; yet her ultimate surrender to burying herself in the
country made her wish at the same time that he would not.

Emile had been a diversion, someone with whom she
could chat and flirt and prevent herself from considering
her problem. Until Emile, she had never had a male friend.
Emile, however, had expected more than friendship.
"Emile did try to make love to me," she told Madame
Celine.

Madame Celine laughed. "I am not blind, my dear. I
was expecting a *scandale,* at best. Ah, but I'm glad you
rejected him. The quickest way to lose two friends is to
have them engage in an *affaire.* You become an outsider
or a *confidante* whose usefulness ends with the relationship.
Besides, Emile is a handsome rascal, but a rascal all the
same. His father keeps him under his thumb and prevents
him from becoming his own man."

"Emile made me take a serious look at myself," Zelma
said on his behalf. "That's something I've managed to
avoid."

"And this depresses you?" Madame Celine pressed.
"This is what makes you so silent and *de mauvaise?*"

Zelma nodded.

"But why?"

"I'm not exactly pleased with what I see," Zelma answered truthfully.

"You are young and beautiful," Madame Celine said.
"You have a handsome husband who will one day be rich.
Your father holds an enviable position in Washington and

can grant you favors. Forgive me, my dear, but I do not understand this depression of yours."

"I am also spoiled and demanding and discontent because I do not know what it is that would make me happy," Zelma told her. Rising, she began to pace the room. Stopping in front of the windows, she threw open the shutters to the night air. "When I first met Emile, I thought what I wanted was another man, but the truth is I only wanted to engage in a flirtation."

"What woman does not enjoy flirtation?" Madame Celine said with a shrug. "What man also?"

Zelma closed her eyes and turned her face to catch a wisp of a breeze. The stays of her gown were cinching her waist too tightly; she reminded herself to have Bessie Lou attend to them before she wore it again. Returning to her chair, she tasted her coffee and found it cold.

"Dester is all the things I am not," she said. "He has a purpose to his life, his dream. I cannot accept myself as part of it. I don't know if I want to be. I love him, but I don't know if I love him enough to go willingly to that wilderness. I'm glad he left me in New Orleans, but there's not a night I don't feel guilt for not being with him." She fluttered her hands in an expression of frustration. "What to do, what to do?" she murmured with a sigh.

"I cannot advise you, my dear," Madame Celine said, "even if I presumed to do so. The dilemma is your own, and it is you who must make the decision."

"I've never been good at decisions," Zelma confessed.

"If I might offer an observation—?"

"Please."

"I think you are restless and discontent because you have excluded yourself from your husband's dream," the older woman said. *"Mon Dieu!* I hope you are not angry with me for saying this, but there is much of the child still in you, Zelma. I do not think this is entirely wrong. I am often accused of childishness myself. There should be some of the child in all of us, but there is a time when we must become more adult and do what we must."

"You mean, of course, to accept my duties as a wife?" Zelma said rather drily.

"What else can you do when the time comes?" Madame Celine said. "What are your alternatives, my dear? Would you return to your father's house and look for another man, one who is better than your husband?"

"There is no better man than Dester," Zelma said quickly, and the statement suddenly hit her like a revelation.

"Ah, but you consider him less than perfect because he has a dream that forces you to live in the country rather than the surroundings you are accustomed to? You would not have this discontent if he settled here in New Orleans or remained in Savannah?"

"I told you I was spoiled," Zelma said and managed her first smile of the evening. She had expected sympathy from Madame Celine, and instead she was being talked to as if by her own mother.

"I wish I was young again and facing this future you look upon so grimly," Madame Celine told her. "Ah, but why dream futile dreams? I am me and you are you. I will stay here in New Orleans and live as I am, because I must. You, also, will do what you must. You will put the childishness behind you and learn to become a planter's wife."

"As you said, what are my alternatives?"

"We are *les femmes,*" Madame Celine murmured. "We haven't the options of choice that a man has. We do not have their physical strength." She lifted her hands and clinched them into fists. 'How can these compete with those of a man?" She relaxed her hands and lay them quietly in her lap. "But we are survivors," she said, "if we learn to use our minds. Our strength lies there, in what many men call our silly heads. I used my head. That's why I am here in this grand house and those girls of Monsieur Celine's are across town lying on their backs to survive."

Zelma turned her head to conceal her flushed cheeks.

"When I was young, I saw the importance of pleasing a man with more than my body," the older woman continued. "I learned how to stimulate his mind as well. I can discuss politics and literature and history with intel-

ligence. I added those things to the knowledge of womanly
things. When I was a girl, I learned to make exquisite lace
from my *grandmère*. Many times when I was an actress
and stranded in some hostile city or country, I made lace
and sold it to survive. The other actresses who were less
wise were reduced to relying on the favors of men." She
rose from the settee, went to the highboy, and removed a
lace shawl. She carried it back and held it from Zelma to
examine. "This is the last piece I shall ever make," she
said. "My eyes are no longer good. One day I shall be
buried in it."

Zelma touched the lace and said, "It's magnificent,"
not because it was expected but because it was the finest
piece of lace she had ever seen.

"Do you sew, my dear? Do you create with your
hands?"

"I'm not good with a needle," Zelma confessed.

"Then you should learn. How could I have imagined as
a child that learning to make lace would one day save me
from starvation or prostitution?" She refolded the lace
carefully and returned it to its drawer in the highboy.
"Learn everything," she said as she returned to the settee.
"Learn sewing, learn your husband's business. When you
are busy filling your mind, there is less time for discontent.
Discontent is for the very young and the very old." She
reached for her coffee, decided she did not want it, and
jangled the silver bell at her elbow. "You will never find
happiness in indecision," she said. "Accept your fate as a
planter's wife," she advised reluctantly. "You must make
a scale of your mind and determine what is best for your
survival as a woman, not a girl. The gaiety of the cities
fades, and so does one's beauty. We all must eventually
rely on what we've stored in our minds to survive."

One of the household slaves knocked and entered, and
Madame Celine ordered a bottle of her best cognac. "Will
you join me, my dear?"

Zelma said, "Yes, a small one."

"Ah, that reminds me. I let Monsieur Faviere go away
without his promised cognac," the older woman said to

change the mood. "Perhaps when your husband visits, he would be so kind as to deliver it for me."

"If he visits," Zelma said in a near-whisper.

When the cognac arrived and she sipped it, the liquid burned her throat and settled warmly in her stomach.

"We have had an interesting *tête-à-tête*," Madame Celine said cheerfully. "I always regretted not having a daughter to share these moments with. Ah, well, I would not have made a good mother. I was always much too devoted to myself. That was my mistake, Zelma. Don't make it yours." She lifted her glass in the gesture of a salute and drained the contents in one quick gulp.

Zelma bid her good-night and left her in the drawing room with the dwindling bottle of cognac. In the entryway, she heard her ring the silver bell again and tell the slave to send Pierrot to her.

Tossing sleeplessly in bed, Zelma found her mood becoming even darker. She turned her face into the pillow and cried tears of frustration. She felt that something was changing within her, and she was not prepared for the adjustment. What was the change? Was she saying goodbye to her youth? Was it her lonesomeness for Dester that made her cry?

Frustration turned to anger at Dester for having uprooted her, causing this painful change in her.

All for a dream! His dream—not hers—of a gigantic plantation, their inheritance to their children and grandchildren and all the children to follow.

Bessie Lou, ever-alert, heard her crying and came to the bedroom door to inquire of the cause. "Are you ill?" she asked with concern. "Do you want somethin'?"

"I want to go home to Savannah!" Zelma cried. "I don't want to change! I'm afraid!"

Bessie Lou crossed to the bed. She took Zelma in her arms as she had often done when her mistress had been a girl and rocked her back and forth, saying, "There, there. There's nothin' to be afraid of. Bessie Lou's here. She'll protect you." She continued to rock, speaking in a singsong voice that eventually drove her mistress's fears away and allowed her to sleep. She tucked the quilts about her and crept quietly from the room.

Now unable to sleep herself, she lay listening to young Vance's rhythmic breathing. Somewhere beyond the courtyard a dog was barking. A horse neighed in the stable and kicked at its stall. Someone passed on the street, his heels clicking over the cobblestones. When the footsteps had faded, vanished, she turned onto her side and closed her eyes.

She hoped her master would return soon and take them away from New Orleans. It was a city that belonged to the Devil—and he could have it.

CHAPTER NINE

IT WAS MIDAFTERNOON when the caravan of wagons from New Orleans came lumbering down the road toward Plantation Bend. They were piled high with supplies to build the big house.

Matilda, always looking for an excuse to seek Dester out during the day, ran to the fields to tell him the supplies had arrived. He pulled her onto his horse behind him and rode back to the camp.

Because the makeshift bridge across the creek was not strong enough for the heavy wagons, they were unloaded on the road, and the slaves were given the task of carrying the supplies across and stacking them at the base of the hill. It was nearly dusk when they finished.

Dester, now that the supplies had been delivered and the house could be started, experienced a depression because Zelma was not there. As mistress of the house, he felt she should be present from the laying of the foundation to the final tile placed on the roof. Without her, the pride of accomplishment would wane. Besides, he had grown guilty about his affair with Matilda and wished to have no reason to continue it. As he strode around the stacks of supplies, comparing that delivered against his order, he suddenly flung the tally board to the ground and sent the startled boy who had been helping him to search for Jingo.

"Hitch the carriage," he told Jingo, "and follow me into New Orleans. I'm going after my wife!"

Jingo hid his pleasure behind the mask of his face. All the slaves was gossiping about their master and Matilda. The mistress's return would put an end to that. "Yes, sir!"

94

he cried and ran off to obey what he considered a wise and necessary order.

Matilda, who heard her master instruct the household slaves to clear out one of the shacks and set up his wife's bedroom set, was heart-stricken. She ran to the hill where she had known so many nights of happiness and flung herself wailing to the ground. She had always known she would eventually lose her status with the master, but not so suddenly, not so soon. The ravages of wanting him would now return to gnaw at her insides. The other slaves who were referring to her as "that uppity nigger" would gloat over her rejection, her anguish. They would shun her and make her feel like an outsider. Still, she had known the price she would pay for creeping into Dester's bedroll, and even if she suffered from now until she died, she would never regret it. She sat up, drying her eyes, and listened to Dester's horse's hooves clomping across the bridge. As they faded into the distance, she thought, *Maybe the mistress will refuse to return with him. She was stubborn and headstrong and too proud to live in a slave's shack, even temporarily.*

It was not yet daylight when Dester arrived at Madame Celine's door. His knock was answered by a sleepy-eyed slave who recognized him immediately and let him enter without a word. He told her to awaken Elias and have him attend his horse. Then, exhausted, he climbed the stairs to his wife's room.

Zelma shrank back from him as if he was a stranger who had invaded her bedroom.

"It's me. Dester," he told her and turned up the gas of the lamp so she could see him.

Still cowering, caught between sleep and waking, she said, "I know who you are. Why . . . why are you here?" The smile faded from his face. No welcome, no words of endearment, no delight at seeing him. Anger and concern mingled in the furrows of his brow and eyes. "I'm here to take you home," he told her.

"But the house. It can't be finished."

"It isn't even begun."

"But you promised! You said—"

The door burst open, and Bessie Lou and Vance stepped into the room. The child, crying, "Daddy, Daddy!" ran forward and leaped into Dester's arms. Bessie Lou remained in the open doorway, pleased because she had heard Dester's remark about taking them home.

"At least my son's happy to see me," Dester said to Zelma. He hugged the boy and asked if he had been good. "I'm taking you home," he told the child, and Vance laughed with excitement and delight. He motioned Bessie Lou forward, passed her the boy, and told her, "Jingo will be here with the carriage before noon. Can you have your mistress's things packed?"

"Packed and waitin' on the doorstep," Bessie Lou said and scurried away to begin the pleasure of packing.

Dester turned back to Zelma. "I'm sorry I can't keep my promise to leave you here until the house is finished," he told her, "but I need you with me."

"But how will I live? Where will I sleep?" she demanded. Tears had begun to form in her eyes, and she willed them not to overflow.

"You'll live with as much comfort as I can provide you," he answered without emotion, "and you'll sleep in a slave's shack with me until the house is completed."

Zelma stared at him in horror. "A slave's shack!" she cried. "You can't expect it!" She flung the quilts aside and sprang from the bed to confront him on her feet. "I won't! I won't!"

He remained silent and calm until her raving had spent itself. Then, he said, "I do expect it, and you will obey me. You're my wife, and your place is with me." He turned and moved across the room to the door. "Now I'll sleep until Jingo arrives," he told her. "Be ready when he does." He left and closed the door.

Madame Celine took the news of Zelma's departure with tears. She had become extremely fond of the young American and knew she would miss her as she had never missed another woman except her mother, and that was a long, long time ago. They embraced and kissed each other's cheeks and promised to write often. Madame Celine re-

mained in the doorway, waving and dabbing her eyes.
Behind her, Pierrot waved also, but with a smile of satisfaction; he would now have Madame to himself again.

As Zelma climbed into the carriage behind Vance, she
said sadly, "Today I say good-bye to my youth." She sat
with her back straight, her hands folded on her lap, and
looked neither to the left nor right as the carriage rolled
out of New Orleans and into the countryside.

Dester, preferring his horse to the crowded carriage,
glanced back at her and thought she looked like a martyr
going to her execution. Angry, he urged his horse ahead
and kept a distance between himself and the carriage for
the first hour.

When he fell back again, she had not altered her position to any noticeable degree. "Isn't the countryside beautiful, Zelma?"

"Yes, the countryside is beautiful," she answered without turning her head.

"It's even more beautiful at Plantation Bend."

She said nothing, just continued to stare at the back of
Jingo's head.

"Damnit! How long are you going to act this way?" he
shouted.

"I shall act as you instruct me to act," she retorted.
"You are taking me to a slave's shack so I shall conduct
myself accordingly."

Another hour passed, and she had slumped in her seat,
feeling faint from the heat and exhaustion.

"Do you want your smelling salts?" Bessie Lou asked.

"No," she answered. "I shall endure."

"And so shall we," the old slave murmured.

They stopped to rest and eat beneath a gigantic tree
with limbs that hung over the road, but Zelma refused
everything offered except water. She sat removed, feeling
the outcast, and watched them enjoy their meal. She had
to admit that the heat was more bearable in the country
than in New Orleans. A slight breeze, uninterrupted by
buildings and free of city odors, rustled the tree boughs
and gently touched her cheeks. She leaned back against
the tree trunk and closed her eyes.

She was deep in thought and near to napping when Vance suddenly ran to her and threw his arms about her legs. Startled, she pushed him away, saw the damage his greasy hands had done to her dress, and scolded him.

He ran crying into Bessie Lou's open arms and buried his face in her bosom. "Hush, my sweet," she said to quiet him. "Your Mamma didn't mean it. She's feelin' poorly."

Zelma called Vance back, took him into her lap, and began to sing to him as she had when he had been a baby and could not sleep. "Mamma will feel better soon," she promised him when his tears had stopped. Avoiding Dester's eyes, she added, "As soon as she adjusts."

They did not arrive at Plantation Bend until after dark. Zelma went directly into the shack that had been made up with her fourposter bed and a bureau, and closed the door.

Dester gave her an hour before following her inside,

She was sitting up in bed in a white nightgown, brushing her long auburn hair. When he entered, she lay the brush aside and slipped down beneath the sheet.

"You'll like it here if you give yourself a chance," he told her as he undressed.

'I am not a woman with a pioneer spirit," she said stiffly. "You should have determined that before you married me. In case you haven't noticed in all these years, I'm small and fragile. I am also at this moment humiliated at being brought down to this, sleeping in a slave shack with nothing but mosquito netting over the windows and cracks in the floorboards to let all sorts of insects crawl over me at night." Her lower lip began to tremble. "You should have married a stronger woman."

"It was you I loved," he said quietly.

"If you loved me, you would have left me in New Orleans until the house was finished.

"I couldn't. I needed and wanted you here with me." He crawled into bed beside her and took her in his arms. When his embraces and kisses became more demanding, she did not struggle as he expected but opened herself to him, giving herself without sound—and without passion.

He slept and then awakened, aware that she was no

longer beside him. He sat up and saw her standing in the open doorway, her white nightgown shimmering in the moonlight. "What are you looking at?" he asked.

"Our land," she answered without moving. "Our land in the moonlight. It *is* quite beautiful."

He felt his tension ease. "It's just as beautiful in the light of day," he told her. "Now come back to bed before you catch cold."

Still, she did not move. "There is something I must tell you, Dester."

He lay back against the pillows and propped his head on his hands, asking sleepily, "What is it?"

Quietly, she said, "I'm pregnant."

"You should have told me in New Orleans," Dester said. "If I'd known, I wouldn't have been so eager to bring you back until the house was built." He threw away the quilts and went to her. He slipped his arms about her waist. He held her gently, her head nestled under his chin. "I'll take you back, of course," he told her.

"No. You were right to come for me," she said. "I'm here. I'll stay."

"But—" He laughed. "You're an impossible woman, Zelma Granville!"

"An impossible man needs an impossible woman," she said and, turning, lay her head against his naked chest. Her arms encircled him, and she felt the hardness, the solidity of his back, and she felt secure. "Even though I don't always show it, I love you," she whispered. "Forgive me for today." She brushed her lips against the mat of blond hair on his chest and added, "And tonight."

He scooped her up in his arms as if she were a weightless doll and carried her back to bed.

In the morning before breakfast, they climbed the hill, and she stood with his arm about her shoulders while he pointed out a glint of sunlight through the distant trees and told her it was the Mississippi River. Ahead of them where the blueness of the horizon appeared to dip too low, that was the blueness of the Gulf of Mexico blending with the sky.

"Behind us, that's our land for farther than you can walk in a day," he told her proudly.

"And the Faviere plantation?" she asked. "Where is that?"

His mood darkened. "Follow the road for about three miles, and you'll come to it," he said. "But it'll be a road seldom used by us at Plantation Bend." He told her about the difficulty over the damming of the creek. "Claude Faviere predicted I'd be ruined within a year."

"Then Mr. Faviere doesn't know you," she said, hoping to restore his good mood. It appeared she'd have to hold Emile's gift of cognac from Madame Celine. "It's a pity. Our only neighbors, and to be enemies." From all she'd heard of the elder Faviere from Madame Celine and Emile and now from Dester, she was intrigued enough to want to meet him. There'd never yet been a man she'd met she couldn't win over if she set her mind to it.

"We have other neighbors," Dester told her. "Sam and Ginny Cole. They have a ten-acre dirt farm on the edge of the swamp."

"Then I'll go calling when I have time," she said, pleased that there was another woman within visiting distance.

From below the hill came the racket of a slave beating on a washtub to signal breakfast was ready.

"I'll start the house today," Dester said. "You'll be out of the slave shack and under your own roof before you know it." He indicated the view with a sweep of his hand. "Think of looking at this scene every morning for the rest of our lives," he said.

"You mean the house is to be built here?"

"Yes. In the clearing." He noted the expression on her face. "Why do you object? It's a perfect location."

Zelma was remembering the burial she had attended in New Orleans, seeing Madame Celine's girl sunk into a pit of muddy water. If the house was built on the hill, then the cemetery would be below. One day it would be her coffin the slaves would stand on to sink. "I'd prefer the house down there," she said, indicating the base of the hill opposite the slave shacks.

"But why?"

She knew she couldn't tell him her reason. He would laugh at her, ask what it mattered what happened to the body after the soul had left it. To her, it mattered. "I . . . I wanted beautiful gardens," she told him. "The slope of the hill wouldn't lend itself as well."

He looked at her, troubled. But he accepted her reason. "All right," he said. "The house shall be where you want it." He turned and saw Jingo coming up the hill to meet them. "It'll be easier also," he said. "The supplies won't have to be carried up." He pulled her into the curve of his body, and they walked down the slope to meet the loyal slave. Dester told him about the change in plans.

Jingo said nothing. Hadn't his vision already told him as much, the great white house below and the cemetery above?

"We'll begin immediately after breakfast," Dester told him. "You select the slaves to be taken out of the fields for the building."

Zelma did not have to wait for time to go calling to meet Sam and Ginny Cole. They came riding up the road to Plantation Bend in their rickety wagon, drawn by the echoes of hammering and sawing that carried across the land on the morning air.

Sam Cole was a tall, angular man with a skeletal frame. He wore an unkempt beard and had had a broken nose that had been badly set, or not set at all, which gave his face a twisted appearance. His eyebrows were dark and bushy, and beneath them, his eyes radiated a pinpoint of blue the color of china. His clothes, overalls and a printed shirt, were worn and multipatched, but scrubbed clean and faded from washing. He was, he said, a competent carpenter and offered his skill for the day as a neighborly gesture.

But it was on Ginny Cole that Zelma focused her attention.

She was almost as tall as her husband, only with a larger frame. She could not have been more than a few years older than Zelma, but time and circumstance had etched fine lines of age about her eyes and mouth. She wore her hair combed straight back from her face and twisted into a bun at the back of her head. Her dress was made out of a coarse cotton and the print was as faded from excessive washings as that of her husband's shirt. Her arms were deeply tanned, almost sunburned. Her hands were cracked by dryness and hardened by heavy work. Aware of Zelma's scrutiny, heavy lids closed over her eyes as she stared at the ground in discomfort. She was a shy woman, unaccustomed to the company of her own sex.

"I'm very glad to discover I have a woman as a neighbor," Zelma told her. "Until Dester told me about you and your husband, I was afraid there'd be no one to visit."

"The farm doesn't leave us much time for visiting," Ginny mumbled. "There's only been the Favieres, and they're not the visiting sort."

"So I've been told."

"Mrs. Faviere came by once," Ginny said. "Brought me some preserves. That was two years ago. I haven't seen her since." She glanced after her husband, who was walking away with Dester to consult the blueprints of the house. "I guess her husband stopped her from comin' again."

"What was she like? I've met Emile, but none of the other Favieres."

"Lonely," Ginny said. "Although Sam said I shouldn't, I felt sorry for her." She smiled, showing even white teeth. "Now if you'll excuse me, Mrs. Granville, I think the men are about ready to start to work."

"Oh, but I thought . . . I mean couldn't you and I spend the time chatting?" Zelma said.

"I came to work," Ginny told her.

"But surely it's men's work and we. . . ."

"I've been doing man's work all my life," Ginny said. "Besides, Mrs. Granville, I'm not much for chatting. Nothing really to say. Excuse me." She turned and walked away, glancing back briefly before she joined her husband.

Zelma, stepping back under the shade of a tree, stood watching. She noted, as Ginny Cole moved among the slaves and began carting the supplies to the site of the house, that she was a powerful woman. Her too-tight dress pulled over the bulge of her back muscles; she lifted and carried loads equal to the men, seemingly without a drain on her strength.

"Now that's a pioneer woman," Bessie Lou said from behind Zelma. "I never seen a white woman work like that."

"Hmm," Zelma murmured. She smiled to conceal an uneasiness Ginny Cole sparked in her, a sense of useless-ness. "It was nice of them to offer their help," she said.

"Mighty nice," Bessie Lou agreed.

"Well, since they've been so nice, I think we should prepare a special meal for them," Zelma told her. "Some-thing extra special."

"Don't think they're the sort for anythin' fancy," Bessie Lou told her mistress thoughtfully. "They're just plain folks. Probably wouldn't be comfortable with somethin' special."

"Nonsense," Zelma said. "Every woman appreciates nice things. Besides, it's the only way I know to show her my appreciation." She told Bessie Lou to leave Vance in Matilda's care and to assist her.

She had her dining room table and chairs taken from beneath the tarpaulins, waxed, and set up under the branches of a giant magnolia tree. "Use the lace cloth and linen napkins," she told the slaves, "and see if you can find the silver candlesticks my mother gave me as a wed-ding present." She spun around to Bessie Lou, her eyes sparking with excitement. "Do you realize this will be the first time I've entertained at Plantation Bend? Every-thing has to be perfect. Do you think we should risk the Limoges? I mean, since we're eating outside."

Bessie Lou looked concerned. She was glad to see her mistress happy, but she couldn't shake the feeling that she was making a mistake putting out all her finery for the Coles. "I don't think. . . ."

"Of course we'll use the Limoges," Zelma went on before the slave could speak. "Be a dear, Bessie Lou, and see to the venison. Absolutely no one fixes venison like you." She scurried away to supervise the unpacking of the china dishes.

Mumbling to herself, Bessie Lou went off to the make-shift kitchen to do as she was told.

It was nearing high noon when Zelma sent one of the boys to call Dester and their guests to eat. She surveyed the table a final time, decided it was as elegant as it could be made under the circumstances, and sighed with satisfaction. It was quite pleasant, really, dining under the magnolia. The tree's flowers gave off a fragrant aroma, and the branches shielded the table from all but tiny prisms of sunlight that danced across the crystal and china. A slight breeze blew in from the Gulf of Mexico and stirred the leaves above.

As she saw Dester and the Coles approaching, she anticipated their surprise at the trouble she'd gone to.

She knew instantly she had been wrong, Bessie Lou right.

Dester noticeably paled. He glanced at Sam Cole and his wife, embarrassed, and then met Zelma's gaze in a reprimand. Ginny Cole took a step backward as if she was ready to turn and flee. Only her husband's hand on her arm restrained her.

"A fine-lookin' table," Sam Cole said. But he, too, was uncomfortable. "We've never seen anythin' like this before, have we, Ginny?"

"No," Ginny said in a voice that was scarcely audible.

Bessie Lou, who had been standing behind Zelma, stepped around her and pulled out Zelma's chair. "You folks go on an' take a seat," she told the Coles. "Mrs. Granville, she went and took out all her fine things to show you how much she appreciates your comin' to help with the house."

Dester tossed Bessie Lou a grateful glance for trying to explain the elaborate table. "Sit there, Sam," he said. "And, Ginny, you over here." He pulled out the big woman's chair for her.

Zelma, a heavy weight crushing her chest, sank into the chair Bessie Lou was holding. Why hadn't she listened to the old slave? The Coles had never seen a table so elegantly set. It threatened them. She saw Ginny Cole staring at the arrangement of forks and spoons with confusion, and she bit her lower lip to keep it from trembling. Did they think she was making a joke of their simplicity? She dared not glance at Dester, for she knew she would read the answers in his eyes. She wanted to leap from her chair and run and hide herself, but Bessie Lou, always sensitive to her and anticipating just such an action, stood so that her great bulk prevented escape.

"I hope you folks like venison," the old slave said. "Solomon, who ain't more than thirteen, got himself a deer this mornin'."

"Maybe I could get Solomon t' teach me t' hunt," Sam Cole said with a little laugh. He was obviously trying to relieve the tension. "Myself, I haven't caught anything 'cept possums in the past two weeks." He reached carefully for the long-stemmed goblet and wet his lips with the cold water. "Do you like possum meat, Mrs. Granville?"

Zelma, half-listening, was aware of Bessie Lou nudging her arm. "Yes, very much," she lied.

"Maybe my Ginny can fix you a possum dinner one day," Sam told her. "She fixes a great possum stew."

Ginny smiled weakly and said nothing.

"That would be wonderful," Zelma said with forced enthusiasm. *She'll never have me in her house,* she thought. *I've shown her that there's too much of a gulf between us.*

She saw one of the slave girls approaching the table with the tureen of soup; it was their custom to serve in the French style. "Put the tureen on the table," she told the girl. "We'll serve ourselves."

The girl glanced at her mistress, surprised; then shrugged her shoulders and did as she was told.

The meal passed with only polite conversation. Every bite that Zelma forced into her mouth seemed to lodge in her throat. Sam Cole ate heartily, but his wife scarcely touched her food. She answered when spoken to but made no effort at conversation.

Zelma was relieved when the meal was finished, and

she was left alone at the table. Resting her elbows on the corner of the table, she lowered her face into her hands.

"Now don't go upsettin' yourself," Bessie Lou told her. "You made a mistake, but it was an honest mistake. The Coles will understand that you didn't mean. . . ."

Zelma pushed away from the table and ran to close herself away in private. She closed the door of the shack despite the heat and threw herself across the bed to unleash her tears. Bessie Lou came and pounded on the door, but she told her to go away. She spent the afternoon closed inside, crying and sweltering.

When Dester came near dusk, he pretended not to notice the heat inside the shack or her swollen eyes. He left the door ajar to catch the cooling evening breeze and sat on the foot of the bed to remove his boots. He had decided not to mention her mistake.

It was Zelma who brought it up. "I didn't mean to make them uncomfortable," she said. "I just didn't think beyond wanting to do something special for them."

Dester nodded his understanding. "I've hired Sam Cole to help me with the house," he told her. "He's a good carpenter."

"And his wife?" Zelma asked. "Will Ginny work alongside him everyday?"

"I think not," Dester answered. "At least it wasn't mentioned. They have two slaves. Ginny will probably stay home to see that they do their work."

"An excuse," Zelma mumbled.

"What was that?"

"She hates me! She think I'm pretentious, and she hates me!"

Dester poured water into the porcelain basin and began to splash himself. "I believe she did think you were making fun of their poverty and simplicity," he said. "Bessie Lou came over and talked to her, tried to explain you hadn't meant anything insulting."

"I don't need a slave defending me," Zelma cried.

Dester reached for the towel and rubbed himself vigorously. "No matter," he said. "You'll have another chance to win Ginny Cole over."

"You don't understand women," Zelma accused. "She'll never give me another chance. She'll be polite, but never friendly. The only woman this side of New Orleans except for the Favieres, and I've managed to alienate her on our first meeting!"

Dester laughed. "Don't be so dramatic," he told her. He came to the bed, stooped, and kissed her. "You'll think of a way of winning her over. I may not understand women, but I know you."

CHAPTER TEN

ZELMA'S DAYS WERE empty.

Until the house was built and she could take over its operation, there was little she could do to feel useful. One long day stretched into another. Restless, she began to look about for something to occupy her time.

When she learned the household slaves were to plant a vegetable garden, she announced she would assist them. One morning scarcely after the sun had risen, she appeared in a long-sleeved dress, a wide-brimmed hat, and gloves to protect her pale skin from the Louisiana sun and, with a cheerful wave to Dester, marched off to the fields in the midst of the silent, disbelieving slaves.

Her determination to labor lasted less than two hours. The sun burned through her cotton dress, perspiration drained into her eyes, her back began to ache. She sought the shade of the nearest tree and collapsed with a fan and a damp cloth across her forehead. When the slaves went back to the camp for their noonday meal, she went with them and did not return to the fields.

"If only there was something for me to do," she complained to Bessie Lou. "Something I *can* do."

Bessie Lou was sympathetic. "Solomon found a patch of blackberries when he was out huntin'," she said. "If you and some of the girls went pickin', we could do some cannin' and have cobblers through the winter."

Zelma leaped at the suggestion. "Papa took us berry-picking when Zona and I were girls," she recalled.

The next day, she and four of the household slaves let Solomon guide them to the blackberry bushes. The thorny branches were laden with the ripe fruit. When the first thorn tore the sleeve of her dress, her fond memories of that past outing vanished. She wanted to abandon the picking, but she knew Matilda and the other girls were watching her, expecting her to seek the shade of another tree as she had done in the fields. She bit her lip when the thorns pricked her hands and arms, but she continued until her buckets were filled. Her perseverance impressed the slaves, except for Matilda, who had become oddly silent and distant, and that night around the fires, they talked about their mistress's willingness to work at their sides. Zelma, however, declined to repeat the expedition the following day. Finding one of Dester's books on the growing of sugarcane, she retired to the top of the hill, and with the echoes of hammering and sawing from below making concentration difficult, she forced herself to read it from cover to cover. *Nothing you learn is wasted,* Madame Celine had told her.

She also decided to try her hand at sewing. She could tell she was going to be larger with this new baby than she had been with Vance. She unpacked her maternity clothes and proceeded to let out the darts. After repeatedly pricking her fingers, she sighed with exasperation and turned the task over to Bessie Lou.

"Since you wanted the house built below so you could have gardens, why don't you start hunting for small shrubs that can be transplanted?" Dester suggested.

Solomon begrudgingly followed behind her with the wheelbarrow for three days while she searched the woods for appropriate plants.

"You don't like doing this, do you, Solomon?" she asked him when they had stopped to rest.

"No'm," he said. "I'd rather be a hunter than a gardener."

"Well, I don't like it either," she confessed and laughed. "It's just that I haven't anything else to do."

Solomon rubbed the beginnings of a growth of hair on his chin and looked at her thoughtfully. "Then why don't ya just do nothin'?" he asked, puzzled.

"Would you like doing nothing?"

"No'm."

"Well, neither do I," she told him. "Everyone likes to have something to do, and to be good at it."

"I'm good at huntin'," he said.

"Yes, and I'm good at running a house." She sighed and rose from the boulder where she had been resting. "If the house is ever finished."

They found a fresh water spring with wild watercress growing in abundance. They picked enough for a salad and wrapped it in a handkerchief dipped in the cold spring water to keep it fresh.

Zelma pointed to a moonflower that was twining its way up the trunk of a dead tree. "I wonder if that would live through transplanting," she murmured.

Solomon looked at the closed flowers and said, "It looks dead already."

"That's because it blooms at night and closes during the day," she told him. "Yes, I think we'll try to transplant it. It'll be lovely growing along the porch."

Solomon, wondering why anyone would want a flower that bloomed at night when you couldn't see it, took the shovel from the wheelbarrow and dug up the roots of the vine. As he worked up a sweat over his digging, he hoped these days of being assigned to his mistress would soon end. The moonflower roots were deep, and the ground was becoming harder and more difficult to turn. His muscles continued to work for him, but his mind began to wander; he daydreamed of being free in the woods, stalking a deer, or try to flush grouse from their nests.

The tone of his mistress's voice calling his name startled him out of his daydreaming. He saw the sudden paleness that came over her face, and then he heard the noise in the underbrush. *The cougar!* he thought. He dropped the shovel and dashed back to the wheelbarrow, where he had left the rifle. He had cocked the hammer and was aiming in the direction of the sound when the branches parted, and Simon, the Faviere's overseer, stepped into the clearing.

The Negro stood looking at them, as startled by coming upon them as they had been by the noise he had been making. He was carrying a rifle across the back of his neck with his arms resting over the barrel and stalk.

A bad hunter to have made so much noise, Solomon thought.

Zelma relaxed and laughed nervously. "We thought you were some wild animal," she told the overseer.

The Negro continued to stare at them without speaking.

Zelma glanced at Solomon. "Lower that gun," she told him, "before it goes off."

"Yes'm." Solomon lowered the barrel, but he didn't take his finger from the trigger.

"What you doin' here?" the overseer demanded. "This here's Faviere property."

The hostility in the Negro's voice caused Zelma to take a step closer to Solomon. "Oh, we didn't know," she said. "I'm Zelma Granville and. . . ."

"I know who you are," the overseer said. His eyes went to the hole Solomon had been digging. "You're takin' what don't belong to you."

"It's only a moonflower vine," Zelma said, feeling her anger begin to replace her nervousness.

"If it's *only* a vine, why'd you want it?"

"Because . . . oh, this is ridiculous! I didn't know we were on Faviere property, but I'm sure the Favieres aren't going to miss a vine. I'm a friend of Emile Faviere's, and I'm certain he'd give permission to take all the vines I could find."

"It ain't his land. It's his father's," the overseer said.

"I know, but. . . ."

"I'm responsible for trespassers. Monsieur Faviere told your husband he'd have him shot if he caught him on his land again." Stepping toward the dead tree trunk to examine the hole Solomon had dug, the overseer staggered and almost lost his balance. He swung the rifle from his shoulder and jammed the barrel into the loose dirt to regain his footing.

"Likker'd up," Solomon murmured to Zelma.

The overseer's eyes narrowed to mere slits when he next glanced at Zelma and the young slave who'd dared accuse him of drunkenness. "I'll have to tell Monsieur Faviere about this," he growled.

"Do that!" Zelma said angrily. She turned to walk away, grateful that Solomon was with her and was still holding the rifle as if he'd use it if the need arose.

"Maybe Faviere'd be interested knowin' you was likker'd up," the young slave said. "One story begets 'nother."

"Solomon!" Zelma spun around, afraid the young slave would provoke the overseer into doing more than just threatening them. "That's enough!" she told him. "Let's go."

"Yes'm." Solomon backed away from the overseer, not taking his eyes from his face. When he reached the wheel-barrow, he hesitated.

Zelma realized that Solomon, if he struggled with the wheelbarrow, would have to put the rifle inside. The young slave obviously didn't trust the Faviere overseer and felt more comfortable for her and himself as long as he held the rifle in readiness. She glanced at the overseer's face and saw the hatred in his expression: he had pulled the barrel of his rifle from the loose earth and looked as if he would raise it at them if Solomon had not had the advantage. "I'll get the wheelbarrow," she said. The rough wooden handles dug into her hands, but she managed to turn it around and to push it up the slight incline. "Come on, Solomon!"

"Yes'm."

She glanced over her shoulder and saw Solomon backing up the incline close behind her. The overseer hadn't moved, was still glaring at them, calculating, she imagined, if he could be quicker with his rifle than the young slave. "I'll call on the Favieres about this," she shouted back.

The overseer didn't answer.

When they were a distance away, Solomon said, "I'll take the wheelbarrow now, mistress."

"Oh, but what if he follows us?"

"Too likker'd up to do that without us hearin'," Solomon said knowingly. " 'Sides, if he fired his rifle with the barrel full of dirt, it'd probably explode in his face."

Zelma relinquished the wheelbarrow. She pressed her
hands to her chest to quiet the beating of her heart.

"You scared?" Solomon asked.

"Yes. Very," she answered. "You could sense the evil
in that man."

"If he'd raised his rifle, I'd have killed him," Solomon
told her with bravado. "I'd have buried me one freed
nigger out here in the woods where nobody'd of found
him."

"Solomon, don't talk like that," Zelma said, an edge
in her voice because of her nervousness. "Thank God it
wasn't necessary." Glancing back at the underbrush that
fell into a thick curtain behind them, she stepped closer
to Solomon, still afraid the overseer would suddenly burst
out on them.

After a few minutes, her nervousness began to subside.
She glanced at Solomon and realized he was no taller than
she, a mere boy. She had been a fool to have wandered
so far from the camp with only a child for protection.
What would Dester say when he learned of what had
happened? He'd be furious at her and at Solomon. "We
won't tell anyone about this," she told Solomon.

"No'm."

"Faviere won't be told either," she said, more to herself than to Solomon. "He won't want his employer knowing he was drunk in the middle of the day."

Solomon looked at her doubtfully, but said nothing.

"What are you thinking?" Zelma pressed.

"The Frenchman knows all his freed niggers drink,"
the boy told her. "The drinkin' makes 'em mean, and he
wants 'em to be mean."

"How do you know?"

"I talked to a runaway from the Faviere place," Solomon told her. "He told me all about them people, says
the whites on that place are all devils, and the freed niggers are worse."

"That's not true," she said, thinking of Emile.

"Yes'm."

Zelma glanced down in the wheelbarrow and saw the
handkerchief of wild watercress. "Not much for our ef-

forts," she murmured. "I don't think we'll go out again for a few days." She laughed at the elation that came to the young slave's face. "You really love hunting, don't you?"

"Yes'm," he said with enthusiasm.

"And are you really good with that rifle?"

He nodded proudly. "The master taught me hisself."

They walked on in silence until the camp came into view. Then Zelma put her hand on Solomon's arm to stop him.

"Tell me, Solomon, do you think you could teach me to be good with a rifle?"

The boy looked at her, his brow furrowing as he was trying to determine if she was serious. Realizing she was, he nodded affirmatively.

"Then we'll continue to go out every day," Zelma told him. "We may even bring back a few shrubs. But we'll spend most of our time teaching me to use a rifle."

Nothing you learn is wasted.

Zelma could imagine Madame Celine smiling—with incomprehension. *"Mon Dieu, cherie!"*

"It's to be our secret," Zelma told Solomon. "You're not to tell anyone."

"Yes'm."

"I wonder if Ginny Cole is good with a rifle?" Zelma murmured.

Solomon realized no answer was expected of him.

Women, he thought, *were strange creatures.*

CHAPTER ELEVEN

ONE WING OF the house was completed, and Zelma began decorating almost before the final nails were hammered in and the glass set in the window frames. Her father had sent them a couch and two chairs in the French Empire style. She was not overly fond of the intricate carvings or the lion-footed legs, but the upholstery fabric was a rich blue silk, and she coordinated the drawing room around them.

In her sixth month of pregnancy, she became ill. Dester confined her to her room and sent to New Orleans for a doctor. A waste of money, she told him. The doctor, a sour-looking Frenchman with white hair and yellowish pallor, gave her a foul-tasting medicine and recommended she remain in bed for the next month. She consented to remain in her room for two weeks. Reading, writing letters, she passed the time like a prisoner awaiting the end of a sentence. She spent hours at the window, watching the other wing of the house build up and the yard she had wanted take shape under the careful supervision of Jingo and Solomon.

A letter from her father informed her that her sister Zona had met a young man who "has a great political future," and would be married on the first of the following month in a simple church service. As for himself, he had decided to run for an additional term of office. He was well, her mother was well—and they both missed her and were proud that she would once again make them happy grandparents.

A letter also came from Madame Celine.

Cherie,

Your letter found me well, physically if not mentally. New Orleans is rapidly changing, not, I think, for the best. Emigrés and their slaves pour in by the thousands. The city's resources are sorely strained. Rents and food prices have become astronomical. The newcomers quickly exhaust their incomes and add to the great number of poor and distressed already living here. It is nothing to see entire families sleeping in the streets, children huddled in doorways or on stoops. Elias is kept busy keeping the poor creatures out of my courtyard. We do what we can to feed them, but, *Mon Dieu!,* I am not a rich woman. Add to this the rumors that there have been several cases of yellow fever reported, and you will understand my anguish.

Some strident American voices are demanding that the English language and American practices replace the French. I no longer feel secure when I leave my door. The new government is talking of laws that will abolish cockfights, gambling, the sale of liquor and—well, I may find myself in a worse position than when you and Monsieur Faviere came to my rescue.

Speaking of Emile, he has not returned for his usual visit. I hope he enjoyed the cognac you so graciously consented to deliver to him.

I pray, *cherie,* that you come to see me after your child is born. I think of you often, my friend.

Adieu until next we meet.

Madame Celine.

Zelma called Bessie Lou and told her to find a boy to deliver something to the Faviere plantation. She had forgotten the case of cognac until reminded by Madame Celine's letter.

"I think you'd best ask the master about this first," Bessie Lou told her.

"Nonsense. There's no need to bother him."

Shaking her head doubtfully, Bessie Lou went away and came back with Solomon.

"Oh, not Solomon!" Zelma cried.

The boy, who thought of himself as his mistress's favorite since he had taught her the use of a rifle, looked hurt and confused. His smile faded and he stood, eyes downcast, and fingered the brim of his cap.

"You didn't say which boy," Bessie Lou complained. "And what's wrong with Solomon runnin' your errands? He volunteered hisself for anytime you needed him."

Zelma motioned Solomon to the chair beside her bed. "Solomon is too valuable to waste on such a menial task," she said. She was afraid the boy would run into the overseer they had met in the woods and be ambushed on his return. "I'd like Solomon to stay and keep me company while some other boy goes. Would you like that, Solomon?"

"Yes'm," he said, his smile returning.

Bessie Lou scurried away, mumbling and disgruntled.

"She'll be calling you my pet now," Zelma told the boy.

"I don't mind bein' teased," he said. In the slave quarter, he was already being called the mistress's pet nigger.

"How's your hunting going? Do you still go out every morning?"

The boy laughed, pleased she'd asked. He'd missed their outings together while he had taught her about rifles and flushing grouse and waiting patiently for wild game. " 'Cept for the master, I'm still the best shot on the plantation," he bragged. He lowered his eyes. " 'Cept the master and you," he added quietly.

"You don't have to flatter me," she told him. "I know I wasn't an apt pupil."

"Best woman with a rifle I've seen," he said proudly.

"Tell me what's happened to you since I've been imprisoned here," she told him.

He told her in detail about the last deer he'd killed. Then he said, "I ran into that Faviere overseer again."

Zelma sat up and took interest. "He didn't try to hurt you?"

"No'm. He didn't even see me," Solomon told her. "I was hidin' in the brush watchin' him."

"Where? You surely didn't go back to the spring."

Solomon was quiet for a moment before saying, "I had to get you that moonflower. Jingo and me, we planted it so the vine'll grow up the porch columns."

"That was thoughtful of you," Zelma scolded, "but it was wrong to trespass after we'd been warned. If he'd have seen you—"

"He didn't see me. No'm, he wasn't much interested in what was watchin' him. They got a place out there where they make their likker. I see them bring in the corn and get the fires to goin'. They use the spring water. Guess it makes it taste better, or somethin'."

"Well, I forbid you to go there again," Zelma told him sternly. "Do you promise?"

"Yes'm."

They chatted until Jingo came in search of Solomon. Before getting back to his yard chores, Solomon asked if he could visit her again, and she told him she would look forward to it every afternoon until she was well.

Bessie Lou brought in the boy who had been sent to the Faviere plantation. He was very nervous and had to be pushed out from behind Bessie Lou's bulk before he would talk.

"Tell her what you told me," the old slave instructed. She boxed him gently on the side of the head. "Go on."

"I . . . I did like ya told me," he stammered, looking at Bessie Lou instead of Zelma. "I . . . I drove the wagon right up to the front porch."

"You already told me your story," Bessie Lou said. She placed her hands on his shoulders and turned him around to face Zelma. "Go on, tell your mistress."

"Don't be afraid," Zelma encouraged. "Did you deliver the cognac?"

"No. . . . no'm. This here slave came out, and I asked t'see Mister Emile, and he went back inside t'call him. A bunch of slaves were watchin' me from the windows like they were all curious, and I . . . I was awful scared 'cause I heard what them Favieres are like. Devils, they call 'em."

"Never mind that. Did Mister Emile come out?"

"Yes'm. He was right pleasant and said to say thank you. You'd saved him from bad whisky. Then this other man comes out."

"His father?"

"I guess t'was. He kinda limped. Anyways, he asked where that case of likker come from, and when Mister Emile told him, he snatched it out of his hands and tossed it back into the wagon. Almost knocked me off the seat. He said he'd have nothin' in his house that came from the...."

"The what?" Zelma demanded impatiently.

The boy averted his eyes. "From the goddamn Granvilles, that's what he said. He told me to get my black ass off his property lest he feed me to his hogs."

"And Mister Emile?" Zelma asked. "Didn't he say or do anything?"

"He jest stood there kinda white like he had a big madness inside him that wouldn't come out," the boy answered.

"Your fancy French gentleman don't seem to be his own man," Bessie Lou said smugly.

Ignoring her, Zelma told the boy he'd done well and to go to the kitchen for a piece of apple pie as a reward. She lay back against the goosedown pillows and stared thoughtfully at the canopy of her bed. "I'd hoped Emile and I might act as liaisons between Dester and Claude Faviere," she said.

"A hope you might as well forget," Bessie Lou told her. "Ain't nothin' but trouble goin' to exist between these two plantations." The old slave began to busy herself by picking up the letters and books Zelma had scattered over her bed. "The creek's goin' down again. A little every day. Jingo thinks maybe the Favieres are buildin' up a lake that they'll one day let loose to flood us out."

"Oh, and what does Dester say?"

"He don't say nothin'," Bessie Lou told her. "He just looks at the creek every morning like he's measurin' the water and can't decide if it's the will of the Lord or the meanness of the Favieres." She stacked the letters and books within easy reach and started to leave.

"Oh, Bessie Lou. One more thing," Zelma called. "You sent Mati up with my lunch today."

"Yes, that one," Bessie Lou said gravely. "Is that why you hardly touched your food? 'Cause of somethin' Matilda said to upset you? You shouldn't pay any mind to her. She's sassy, but she's young. You won't get well if you let someone like Matilda keep you from eatin'."

"Yes, yes, don't scold me," Zelma told her. "It's just that I didn't know Mati had married."

"Married? Far as I know, Matilda ain't settled on any man," Bessie Lou said. "She's a wild one, that girl. She's not ready for marriage and children."

"But that's the point," Zelma murmured. "I'm sure she's pregnant."

Bessie Lou shook her head doubtfully. "I don't . . . I'll find out," she said. She went away to look for Matilda and came back half an hour later looking greatly distressed.

"Well?" Zelma demanded.

"She's pregnant all right," Bessie Lou told her.

"And the father?"

Bessie Lou, although she had dusted earlier, found a speck of dust on the bureau top which occupied her motions and allowed her to avert her eyes. "Wouldn't say who the father is," she said. "I told you she was a wild one. She probably don't know." She wiped her hands on her apron and wandered out the door.

That night when Dester came to bed, Zelma told him about Matilda's pregnancy. "I won't have bastards born on our plantation," she said. "It's something we never allowed in Savannah, and we're not going to change here. You'll have to make the girl tell you who the father is and arrange for them to marry."

Quietly, Dester murmured, "Yes, I'll do that."

He turned off the light and snuggled down in bed without kissing her good night.

Zelma lay sleepless because she had napped during the day. She was aware of his restlessness, his mumblings when he finally drifted into sleep, and she thought he was worried about the level of the creek and if there would be enough water to irrigate the crops tomorrow. How could she have imagined that it was Mati and her pregnancy that weighed so heavily upon his mind? The father of the slave's child could never marry her—Mati had told him that he was the father.

In the middle of the night, Vance crept from his bed and into his parents' room. He had heard the slaves talking about his mother, saying that she would soon give the master a second child. He had understood and had felt jealousy. He touched his mother's hair, whimpered until she opened her eyes, and then was delighted when she allowed him to crawl into bed with them. He curled himself up between his parents, the privilege of sleeping with them somewhat soothing his jealousy, and slept.

Zelma, once awakened again, could not return to sleep. She lay listening to the sounds of the night, the settling of the new house, and the rhythmic breathing of the two people she loved more than anyone in the world, and she wondered why she felt apprehensive.

Bessie Lou waited until the house had settled down for the night before slipping out the back door. Moving carefully, she walked around the base of the hill to the slave quarter. She picked out the shadow of the shack she knew to be Jingo's and went to tap on the door. Before her knuckles had struck the wood, she heard movement behind her and turned to see a shape approaching across the field from the direction of the creek. She squinted her eyes, studied the movements of the man, and knew it was the slave she sought. She went to meet him so they could talk away from the shacks.

"What are you doing out here?" he asked. Then, more urgently, "Is something wrong at the big house?"

"Nothin' we can do anything about tonight," she said evasively.

"Then what brings you down here after dark?" he asked.

"I've . . . I've got to talk to you," she answered.

Jingo led her to a wooden bench made by some of the children, tested it for strength, and then took her arm and helped her settle herself. He squatted on the ground beside her. When she did not seem ready to speak, he said, "The creek's gone down another couple of inches. I think that bastard Faviere is holdin' it back little by little until he's collected enough water in a lake to flood us out. Someone ought to go check it out."

"That they should," she said quietly. "But right now I've more on my mind than the creek."

"And what might that be?"

"Matilda," Bessie Lou said, almost spitting out the girl's name. "She's expectin' and she says the master's the child's father." She couldn't see Jingo clearly in the moonlight, but she felt him stiffen and heard him catch his breath. That was enough to answer the question she had come to ask. "It's true then," she said with a disheartened sigh.

"Everyone knows it's true except you and the mistress," Jingo told her. "It happened when Mistress Zelma was in New Orleans."

Bessie Lou folded her hands in her lap and laced her fingers together to stop their trembling. "I haven't shed a tear since the slave trader took me away from my mamma and papa," she said, shaken. "I'm too old to start weeping now, even though that's what I feel like doin'." She straightened her shoulders and held her head back to stop the flow of tears that had begun to collect in her eyes. "This'll kill the mistress if she finds out," she said. "I may be just a slave, but she's like my own daughter. I even asked her father to include me in her dowry when she married Master Dester." The tears overflowed her eyes despite the tilt of her head. They streaked down her cheeks and glistened silvery in the moonlight. "Oh, Lord, I don't want her to be hurt like this," she wailed. "If any other man would have hurt her like this, I'd have cut his heart out with a kitchen knife." She buried her face in her hands and cried freely.

Jingo lay a hand on the top of her gray head. "What's done can't be undone," he said, "but we can try to keep her from discovering the truth."

"How you proposin' to do that?" Bessie Lou asked, drying her tears on a corner of her apron. "Master Dester's not goin' to sell Matilda. That's not his way. He don't sell no slave that don't ask to be sold."

"Then we'll just have to get Matilda changed to the fields," Jingo said. "Keep her out of the mistress's sight."

"The mistress already knows she's pregnant," Bessie Lou told him. "You know she won't allow no bastards born among her slaves. Someone's goin' to have to marry that girl. Then, after the baby's born, how we goin' to hide a mulatto child? With no other white men been around, it'll be like hangin' a sign around that baby's neck."

Jingo stood and stretched his legs to get the circulation started again. "We've got a few months to worry about that," he said. "The thing right now is to make sure no one does any talking about the master and Matilda—especially Matilda. We'll find her a husband and get her taken away from the big house."

"She's not goin' to consent to marryin' anyone," Bessie Lou said knowingly. "That girl ain't never accepted her lot in life."

"I'll see that she does what she's told," Jingo assured her. "You leave that to me."

Somewhat relieved, Bessie Lou let him help her to her feet. "I'm gettin' old," she said. "I'll see Mistress Zelma through this, the Lord willin', but who's goin' to look after her when I'm gone? She ain't never growed up. She's still a girl in a woman's body, and she needs protectin'."

Jingo gave the big woman a gentle hug. "You'll be around to bury us all," he said.

"No. I don't want to be around to bury any of you," Bessie Lou said seriously. "If the Lord lets me live long enough to see Mistress Zelma become a strong woman, I won't ask for more."

"That you'll see," Jingo promised her.

"Is that another one of your predictions?" she asked. "Did you have a vision?"

"Yes, a vision," he said, but he offered no further information.

Taking Bessie Lou's arm, he walked her back to the kitchen door of the big house.

Matilda's marriage to Africa was a joyless occasion.

Because Zelma had a relapse, she could not attend, and Dester, looking solemn and uncomfortable, attended only because it was expected. He had given the slaves the afternoon away from their duties.

Matilda, in a final show of rebellion against the forced marriage, refused to change out of her field clothes. When the traveling preacher asked the ceremonial questions of *honor and obey,* she grumbled her answers and glared at the tall, muscular Negro at her side.

"I now pronounce you man and wife," the preacher told the couple and closed his Book with a smile of satisfaction. He'd done well this day, earned himself a dollar, and obviously saved the world from another black bastard.

Matilda walked away through the crowd of witnesses, ignoring the few who had the affrontery to wish her well, and disappeared into the shack she was to share with Africa. After the door slammed behind her, the slaves, relieved of tension and grateful the ceremony had been concluded without an expected scene from the bride, became more festive. The women began chattering and urging the men to the tables set up under the trees.

Dester declined the offer of food and walked back to the big house. The house was nearing completion. He only had a few more hours of work to finish off the interior of his study. He went inside and began to work in solitude, glad the sound of his hammering drowned out the music from the slave quarter that drifted over from the far side of the hill.

He had worked for about an hour when he heard Zelma calling his name. Something in the tone of her voice filled him with alarm. He dashed through the side door and looked up at her window.

She was leaning out of the open frame, her unpinned hair spilling down over the bodice of her dressing gown. "There!" she cried and pointed out toward the road.

Bessie Lou came out onto the porch, looked up at her mistress, and was about to scold her for being out of bed.

"I can't see anything," Dester called up at Zelma. "The shrubs are blocking my view. What is it?"

"A man, there on the road," Zelma called down. "He's hurt. He keeps stumbling and picking himself up."

Bessie Lou went to the edge of the porch and, shielding her eyes with her hands, stared out at the road. "A maroon," she called to Dester. "Probably shot by some slave bounty hunter." While she watched, the Negro stumbled and pitched into the ditch. He tried to get up, then lay very still. She saw Dester start for the road. "Shouldn't go out there alone," she called. "He may be crazy with pain an' fear." When the master didn't listen to her, she stepped down off the porch and hurried off to alert some of the men to the situation.

The Negro was brought unconscious across the bridge and put up in one of the shacks.

"The poor bastard's burning up with fever," Jingo said when he straightened from the cot. "There aren't any wounds."

"You don't suppose he's from the Faviere plantation?" Dester murmured.

"Not likely," Jingo said. "There's no welts on his back."

Some of the slaves who were standing in the open doorway laughed nervously.

"Well, when he's better, we'll have to contact the authorities," Dester said. "He's obviously a runaway, and I can't be responsible for hiding him whatever his reason for becoming a maroon."

The Negro on the cot groaned and opened his eyes. He had been conscious and listening. "Can't go back," he cried weakly. "Had to run away. Bells . . . bells drivin' me mad . . . had to run away from the bells."

"Where you from?" Jingo asked. "Who's your master?"

The runaway, sweat beading on his forehead and streaking down into his eyes, clamped his hands over his ears and cried, "New . . . New Orleans . . . still hear them bells . . . can't get away from 'em."

"Who's your master?" Jingo repeated. He took the Negro's hands and forced them away from his ears.

"My master's H. B. Trist," the runaway answered.

"The collector of customs?" Dester asked, surprised.

"Yes, sir," the Negro murmured.

"Well, we'll have to send word to him where you are," Dester told him. "If you've a legitimate grievance against your owner, you can bring it up with the authorities before they return you to Mr. Trist."

"Master Trist's dead," the runaway said. "Bells . . . they ringin' for Master Trist and all them other folks." He tried once again to cover his ears, but Jingo restrained him.

"What do you mean about the bells?" Jingo demanded.

"Funeral bells," the slave mumbled. His eyes were becoming glazed. "People dyin' so fast . . . faster than they can be buried . . . bodies bein' dumped in the river and . . . and the bells they never stop."

"Dying from what?" Dester asked.

The Negro didn't answer. He was again slipping into unconsciousness.

"Is it the fever?" Dester asked. Zelma had told him about Madame Celine's letter mentioning several reported cases. "Answer me, man! Is it the fever?"

"Yellow . . . yellow fever," the Negro mumbled. His eyes fluttered, closed, and he was still.

Jingo stooped over the cot. When he straightened, he said, "No need contacting the authorities now. He's dead."

One of the women slaves in the doorway screamed, "Yellow fever kill'd 'em! And my man touched 'em!" She ran off shrieking. The crowd in the doorway moved back from the shack, looking at one another as if to ask, *Did you touch him?*

Dester, brow furrowed, looked at Jingo for confirmation.

"Most likely the fever did kill him," Jingo murmured. He was feeling the same fear that was spreading through the other slaves, and through his master.

"Wrap the body in a tarpaulin and take it into the

woods and bury it," Dester said. "Cover it with lye and make some kind of marker so the. . . ."

The preacher who had married Matilda and Africa appeared in the doorway. "I understand there's been a death," he said. "I'd be glad to say a few Christian words over the deceased . . . for a small donation."

"Say the words if you want," Dester said. "He's a yellow fever victim, and we don't even know his name."

The preacher paled. Spinning about on his heels, he made quickly for his horse.

Dester walked back to the house.

Bessie Lou was standing on the porch, waiting. She'd heard the commotion but hadn't yet heard the reason. "By that wailin', I guess he's dead?" she said.

"Yellow fever," Dester told her. "There's apparently an epidemic in New Orleans. Now that runaway's. . . ." He cut off the sentence without completing it. "See that your mistress and Vance stay in their rooms," he instructed. "I don't want any slave other than yourself coming into contact with them. Is that understood?"

"Yes, sir," she said, trembling.

"And make up a bed for me in my study. Even I'll keep my distance until I'm certain I haven't been affected. In her weakened conditions, she'd never survive—" He looked up and saw Zelma at her window. Her expression told him she had overheard. "Just a precaution," he called up at her. To Bessie Lou, "When Jingo returns from burying the body, have the shack the runaway died in burned along with everything he might have touched."

Bessie Lou nodded her understanding. Within an hour, she had learned which of the household slaves had been around the fever victim and which had not. Those who might have been exposed were barred from the house. The few who remained were forbidden to set foot outside the door until they were told. She sent Solomon into the woods for special herbs and barks from trees known to have healing powers. Pots were set to smoking throughout the house. Before nightfall, a blue haze hung about the ceiling of every room, and the new wood absorbed the odors. She brewed sassafras tea and forced everyone, including Zelma and Dester, to drink it before bedtime. She added drops of turpentine to all food that left the kitchen and made every slave wash twice a day with the strong lye soap reserved for laundry.

The first Plantation Bend slave came down with the dreaded disease two days later. His name was Epps, and he was nearing his fiftieth year and was weakened by a respiratory illness he had had since a boy. He became unconscious and died in his sleep.

Twelve other slaves contracted the disease—five joined Epps in the corner of the cemetery plot atop the hill.

The dark clouds blew in from over the gulf and hid the afternoon sun. Darkness came early and with it the raindrops that stung and streaked the windowpanes. A deep, rumbling sound approached, grew louder, and eventually rattled the house with its fury. Lightning crackled and filled Zelma's room with a blinding glare.

She pulled herself up in bed and cried out, but her cries were deadened by the thunder. She fell back against the pillows, sobbing, biting her lips against her pain. She gathered her strength, waited until there was a lull between the thunder and wind, and called out again for Bessie Lou.

I'll die alone here, she thought, *with the storm raging outside and no one hearing me!*

Then she heard a decided creak on the stairs. She held her breath, waiting.

Bessie Lou had scarcely pushed the door open before Zelma cried,

"The baby's coming!"

The slaves moved excitedly in and out of her room, bringing water, linens, carrying news to Dester, who waited nervously below.

Zelma gripped Bessie Lou's hand, squeezing with each surge of pain and fighting the urge to scream.

"Breathe deep, baby," Bessie Lou instructed with anguish. "Don't hold back. Let the baby come."

Zelma's grip lessened as the pain subsided. Perspiration had streaked into her hair and straightened the natural curl; she could feel it sticking to the sides of her face. Her eyes felt sunken into her head; even they ached. "It's harder this time," she murmured. "The pain with Vance was nothing in comparison."

"It'll be over soon," Bessie Lou assured her.

"What if . . . if I die?" Zelma cried with sudden fear.

"Hush! You're not goin' to die."

But Zelma would not be stilled. "What if the baby's dead? Maybe the yellow fever—"

"Hush, hush, I say! Ain't nobody goin' to be dead around here! Not you, not the baby! Take your mind off that notion." She freed one hand and dabbed at her mistress's brow.

Zelma grabbed her hand and tried to force herself up on the bed. "I want to see Dester!"

"This ain't no place for a man," Bessie Lou firmly told her. "You don't want him to see your pain."

"Why shouldn't he?" Zelma cried accusingly. "He wants lots of children. Let him see what it costs me." She fell back, driving her head deep into the goosedown as a new surge of pain spread through her body. Tears rolled from the corners of her eyes, and her lips whitened from being pressed tightly together.

"Breathe deep!" Bessie Lou reminded her. "Open your mouth! Stop fightin' it!" Her voice was trembling, her own eyes watering.

When the pain ebbed, Zelma felt drained, too weak to face the next surge. She lay still, eyes wide, listening to the wind and thunder and thinking how auspicious that the baby had chosen the time of the storm to be born. She turned her head and looked up at Bessie Lou. "This will be my last child," she said. "I won't have another."

Bessie Lou understood what she meant.

The baby, a boy, was born at the height of the storm. Bessie Lou claimed the honor of the first gentle slap. She washed and wrapped the child and lovingly placed it into the curve of her mistress's arm. "He's goin' to be big and handsome just like his father," she said proudly.

Zelma examined the tiny head and hands and body and,

finding nothing wrong, kissed the baby's head and broke into tears of gratitude and relief.

Bessie Lou patted her head with affection. "Now I'll go tell the master," she said. She laughed. "There's goin' to be some celebratin' this night at Plantation Bend. Yes, siree! There's goin' to be dancin' in the slave quarter regardless of this here storm."

"Tell them the boy's name is Clayborn," Zelma said. "Clayborn Arnold Granville."

CHAPTER TWELVE

FROM THE DAY of his marriage to Matilda, Africa was a husband in name only. On his wedding night when he returned from helping Jingo bury the yellow fever victim and burn the infected shack, he found his bride asleep in bed. He undressed with anticipation, thinking that a marriage for the sake of his master had not been entirely without personal reward. But when he lifted the quilts to crawl in beside Matilda, she awakened with a cry of protest. Snatching a kitchen knife from beneath her pillow, she forced him to back away from his bed, telling him that she would never submit to his sexual demands. Should he overpower her, which she knew he could do if he attempted it, she promised to catch him asleep and plunge a knife into his heart.

Grumbling that he'd never force himself onto a woman who didn't want him, Africa made up a pallet on the floor. He lay listening to her breathing until the deep of night, when, cursing her, he vowed he'd rid himself of her after the baby was born.

He spent the following nights on the floor beside the bed. During the days, he was gentle with her but always was cautious not to say anything that would hint of his desires. She mended his clothes, kept the shack clean, talked with him—but she never went to bed without first making certain the knife was beneath her pillow.

A month before her baby was due, he moved out of the shack and slept in the nearby woods. His desire for her had become more than he could cope with. He became increasingly more quiet and moody and often was so deeply lost in his thoughts that he would not hear when people spoke to him. They understood his torment, but when anyone would broach the subject of Matilda, the big man's anger would be aroused. He would hear nothing against her. The slaves shook their heads in sympathy for Africa. Their dislike for Matilda grew, and they waited for the day of her comeuppance. And Africa waited for the day when Matilda would see reason and become his wife in more than name.

It was a late afternoon when Matilda went into labor. The woman who was always called for deliveries was working beside Africa in the fields when the girl from the big house came to fetch her. He followed the midwife back to the slave quarter and stationed himself outside his and Matilda's shack. Oddly, he felt as if it was his child causing the screams that came through the closed door. For the first time since he had come under ownership of Dester Granville, he felt resentment toward him. He willed this to pass, but he was less equipped to deal with the panic that replaced it. He loved Matilda, he who had never loved a woman—what would he do if she died? His own mother had died in childbirth—because, he had been told, he had been such a giant of a baby. He prayed to some god he could scarcely remember that Matilda's baby would be small; then, because he felt it could do no harm, he prayed to the Christian God of the white folks.

Africa was still sitting outside the hut when the slaves came in from the fields. One of the women stopped and said, "She's having a hard time of it, is she?" He glared at her, hating her for her smugness, her cruelty, and she hurried away.

A youth named Carley came over and sat down beside Africa. He didn't speak for a long while, just sat staring out across the meadow toward the creek and hoping his presence somehow conveyed his understanding.

The dinner bell sounded, but neither man made an effort to rise from the ground.

Finally, Africa rose and stretched his great limbs. He looked down at Carley and said, "I can't just sit here any longer."

Carley understood it was an invitation. "Where you wanta go?" he asked. "You feelin' like it, we could hike back through the woods."

"That's a waste of time," Africa told him. "If I'm goin' to do anything, I want it to be useful."

Carley got to his feet and slapped the dust from his trouser legs. "Whatever you wanta do," he said. He had always admired the big man and wanted to be his friend.

Africa stroked the stubble on his broad chin. "There's somethin' I've been wantin' to do," he said. "It's almost dark. After the sun's gone, why don't you and me follow the creek upstream and find out once and for all if that Faviere bastard's buildin' up a lake of water like they say?"

Carley felt fear grip his stomach muscles.

"You don't want to, just say so," Africa told him. "I'll go alone."

"No, no! I'll go!" Carley said. The idea of trespassing on Faviere land made the fear crawl up his spine, but he wasn't about to disgrace himself in the big man's eyes by giving in to it. "We goin' to tell anybody?"

Africa shook his head from side to side. "What they don't know they can't be accused of," he said.

They walked down to the creek and looked at the mud drying brick hard along the banks.

"Should be easy goin' if we stick to the water line," Africa mumbled.

They walked up the creek bank past the front of the house like two men out for an evening stroll. Mistress Zelma, Vance at her feet, and the new baby cuddled in her arms, was sitting on the front porch with Bessie Lou. The final rays of the sun was turning her dress a golden hue. Young Vance spotted them and pointed them out to his mother. Africa and Carley waved and walked on.

After the sun had gone, the going became rougher. The moon had not yet climbed high enough to be of any use to them. Judging from the speed with which the clouds were moving in over the gulf, they would hide the moon anyway before it rose high enough to shed any light down between the treetops.

"A good thing," Africa murmured as if reading Carley's thoughts. "If there's no moon, they won't be able to see us."

Carley's imagination told him when they'd crossed the invisible boundary line separating the Granville and Faviere properties. He fancied that even the atmosphere changed. The air felt heavier and reached his lungs laden with moisture, but that, of course, was because the rain clouds were now almost directly above them. In the last moments before the moon was completely hidden, he stumbled and pitched forward. When he regained his footing, he was covered in sludge and had to spit repeatedly to clear his mouth of foul-tasting slime. He wanted to vomit but knew that would betray his fear.

Africa came back to him. "You hurt?"

Carley said, "No."

"Can't be far now," the big man said. "The bastard wouldn't dam up water where it'd flood his own land when he broke it loose."

They found the dam just as the first drops of rain began to pelt the ground. Faviere had chosen well. Here the creek narrowed as it ran between two rocky hills. The dam was constructed of logs bound together on either bank with a large gate in the middle that could be opened or closed by a wooden wheel. The gate was half-closed. Behind the dam the restrained water had collected in a gully.

"How we goin' to destroy it?" Carley whispered into Africa's ear. "If we cut through them ropes, it'll take us most of the night."

"If we cut through the ropes, we'll achieve just what Faviere wants hisself," Africa said patiently. "All that water'd flood Plantation Bend. We're goin' to open that gate a little at a time until the water level's safe. Then we'll see 'bout cuttin' the ropes."

Africa walked along the tops of the logs to the center of the dam with an easy balance Carley knew he could not equal. The rain had already wet the tops of the logs, and they felt slippery beneath his feet. One miscalculated step and he'd either pitch over the side or into the dam

DARK DESIRES 135

to be sucked through the gate by the churning water. Arms
extended to either side, he inched his way along. When
he reached the center, Africa was already turning the large
wheel. The sound of the water grew louder as the gully
began to drain.

"Now we wait," Africa said.

They squatted, holding the wheel for support, and
waited until the water level went down enough for the
gate to be opened farther.

Carley turned up the collar of his shirt, although it did
no good. They were both soaked through and caked with
mud and slime. Africa was quiet, thinking that when he
returned to Plantation Bend Matilda would either have
had her baby or—

"I hear somethin'," Carley said, cutting into his
thoughts.

Africa cocked his head and listened. He heard nothing
except the patter of the rain on the water, the swaying
of the treetops in the wind. "Your imagination," he said
and went back to thinking about Matilda and wondering
if having the baby would change her.

He had turned the wheel twice more, and the level of
the creek was almost back to normal.

"We can cut the ropes bindin' the logs now," he told
Carley. "In the mornin', Faviere'll discover he only wasted
his time. I doubt he's foolish enough to build another
dam, not knowin' it'll just be knocked down again." The
big man gave a grunt meant to pass as a laugh. "This'll
be between just the two of us," he said. "We won't tell
the master or any—"

Carley saw the lights first. He stood so abruptly he
almost pitched off the top of the logs. "Jesus!" he cried.
"They're on both sides of us!"

Africa turned to look from one end of the dam to the
other. On one side, his lantern held so that the light
illuminated him, stood Faviere, his full head of hair and
beard giving Africa the impression of a great, angry lion.
At the other side, Simon, Faviere's overseer, looked
equally as menacing. Both men carried rifles, each backed
up by half a dozen slaves.

Carley's voice cracked as he said, "We're trapped!"

Africa looked down at the churning water. "Jump!" he said. "Quick! Jump!"

"Can't swim," Carley cried, terrified.

"Don't kill the big one if you can help it!" Faviere shouted. "I can use that black bastard for studding!"

The plantation owner's meaning was clear enough to the overseer. The giant was to be taken alive, the other one could be killed. He raised his rifle to his shoulder and fired.

There was a flash of light, an explosion. Carley cried out with pain and slumped forward into Africa's arms. "You . . . you jump," Carley groaned. "Save yourself." Then he became a dead weight.

Africa saw it was too late to jump. The water, reaching its normal level, had quit gushing through the gate. The creek below was shallow. If he jumped, he'd break his legs, at best become mired in the mud, trapped until they managed to get ropes around him and pull him out.

He placed his ear against Carley's chest and discovered the wound had killed him. He released his grasp and let the youth's body tumble off the top of the dam. It landed in the water with a splash and disappeared beneath the surface. Bellowing with rage, Africa crouched and waited for the slaves who were being sent out from either end of the dam to capture him. When they got closer, he could see the terror in their eyes. They had been given only clubs to face an enraged giant.

He flung the first two down onto the embankment below, and the others, screaming their fright, retreated to face the wrath of the overseer or their master rather than the black man who tossed them about as if they were weightless.

"Goddamn worthless niggers!" Faviere yelled. He knocked the last slave to leave the dam aside with a blow of his fist and stepped out onto the top of the logs. "You haven't got a chance," he shouted at Africa. "Either come off there peacefully or die. The choice's yours." He raised his rifle to his shoulder and took aim.

Africa looked from one side to the other. He saw

Faviere's daughter step up behind him. She was also carrying a rifle. It was merely a choice of facing the two rifles
of the Favieres or the one of the overseer. He placed his
hands atop his head as the slave traders had taught him
and edged his way toward the overseer.

"Get those chains around the sonofabitch when he
reaches you," Faviere shouted across the dam.

The overseer stepped away from the end of the dam so
he would have a clear shot at Africa if it became necessary. He yelled at the cowering slaves to ready the chains
and promised he'd shoot them as well if they didn't obey.

As he reached the end of the dam, Africa pretended to
trip and went down on his knees. As he expected, the
slaves rushed forward with the irons to catch him at a
disadvantage. He grabbed the first to reach him and flung
him backward into the overseer. The overseer's rifle went
off with the impact, but the ball went straight up into the
air. The overseer fell to his back, and his rifle fell away
from him. While he fumbled for it, Africa seized the
chains from a terror-frozen slave and struck out at the
lantern to douse the light.

Before the lantern shattered, there was a shot from
across the dam. Fire burned the muscles of Africa's arm.

"I hit him!" he heard Claudine Faviere shout.

He clinched his teeth against the pain in his arm, and
before the overseer could retrieve his rifle, Africa fled into
the darkness.

He did not stop running until near dawn. Then he collapsed on the side of a hill. He cleaned the wound on his
arm from a puddle of rainwater caught in a concave rock
and saw that the damage was not serious. He tore away
the tail of his shirt and bound it up. He sat staring out
across the valley, waiting for the sun to come up. When it
did, he saw a distant ribbon of smoke rising into the morning sky, and he knew it was from Plantation Bend. He also
heard the baying of dogs and knew they were on his trail.

He rose, took several deep breaths into his lungs, and
then turned and ran deeper into the wilderness.

He knew that Faviere would never catch him.

He also knew he could never again return to Plantation Bend and Matilda.

Carley's body was found the following day wedged against the supports of the bridge. Since the two had been seen together the night before, Africa's fate was assumed to be the same.

Dester, with Jingo and Solomon, searched the creek banks as far as his property extended without finding the big man's body. He returned to the house, wrote a letter to the authorities, and sent Jingo into New Orleans to deliver it.

"Nobody'll be coming," Jingo told him when he returned. "They said if you or some other white man didn't see the killing there's nothing they can do."

"So much for justice," Dester murmured. He went to the gun rack, loaded his pistol, and carried it with him from that day on.

The authorities did arrive one week later. They introduced themselves as representatives of the new territorial government of Louisiana and had with them a warrant sworn out by Claude Faviere and witnessed by his daughter and freed Negro overseer. *One slave called by the name Africa and an unidentified companion did knowingly and willfully trespass on Faviere property for the purpose of malicious destruction. When caught in the act of destroying valuable property, these slaves chose to fight rather than surrender. In the ensuing battle, the slave Africa killed three slaves owned by Claude Faviere. His companion was also killed. The owner of these renegade slaves is known to be Dester Granville.*

The sheriff, after reading the warrant, scratched his head and added, "Even after you make restitution, Mr. Granville, I'm afraid the hangin' order for your slave will still stand."

The two men conducted a thorough search of the grounds and slave quarters and departed with a warning that Africa would have to be turned in if he returned. Most likely, they said, he'd be caught in New Orleans trying to stow away on a ship bound for the West Indies.

Dester, going back into the house, said to Jingo, "At least we know he's alive." He added, scarcely above a whisper, "You'd best tell his wife."

Matilda took the news of Africa without comment or determinable display of emotion. Her baby had been born the night Africa had disappeared. She had named the boy Aaron after a father she could hardly remember. Aaron was light of skin, with hazel eyes and, she thought, the forehead and squared jaw of their master.

She expected Dester to come to look at the baby if only out of curiosity, but he did not. Bessie Lou came. She held the baby and looked at him with a sad expression in her eyes.

"He's a fine son," she said and passed the baby back to Matilda as she prepared to take her leave. "There's somethin' I have to tell you," she said. "Your baby's never to be allowed to come near the big house. Not now, maybe not ever."

Matilda, who was offering Aaron her breast, glanced up with defiance. "Who told you to tell me that?" she demanded. "Was it the master?"

"No," Bessie Lou admitted. "It wasn't him."

"Who then? Her? Did she find out? Is she the one who sent you?"

"She doesn't know," Bessie Lou answered calmly, "and if I can help it, she never will. I'm the one who's tellin' you I don't ever want her to see your baby if it can be helped."

"You have no authority to tell me my Aaron can't ever go near the big house," Matilda shouted. "You're just a nigger slave same as myself! Unless the master hisself tells me to the contrary, me and my Aaron will go and do as we please!"

The baby, frightened by his mother's angry voice, began to cry.

"Maybe I don't have no authority," Bessie Lou said with the same calmness in her voice, "but I promise you, if you bring your baby to the big house so my mistress can see it, I'll personally arrange to have him sold."

"You wouldn't do that?" Matilda challenged. "There

ain't a baby in the world you don't feel like you're its
nanny." But she looked into Bessie Lou's eyes and saw
the truth. The old slave never threatened lightly. She had
her mistress's ear—and thereby the power to make good
her threats. "All right," Matilda told her. "Your precious
mistress ain't ever goin' to see my Aaron's face." She
returned her nipple to the baby's greedy mouth and rocked
him gently back and forth as he fed. "And me?" she
asked. "I suppose I ain't ever supposed to come to the big
house either."

"You're a field worker now," Bessie Lou reminded her.
"You ain't got any cause to come to the big house unless
you're asked. Realize, child, I ain't got nothin' against
you. You've always been headstrong and kinda wild, but
you're not a bad girl." She glanced again at the feeding
baby, and her expression softened. "All babies are sent
by the Lord," she said. "Sometimes the reason ain't for
us to understand. Maybe little Aaron there's got a purpose
for bein' born we'll not live to know about, but I'm goin'
to see that purpose ain't to bring pain to my mistress. Not
in my lifetime anyway."

After Bessie Lou had gone, Matilda began to cry,
softly at first, then with loud, uncontrolled sobs that
brought some of the women to the door to peer in at her.

"Get your asses away from my door!" she bellowed and
flung the hairbrush from her bedside crate across the room
and into the yard. They moved away, laughing, and Matilda cried even louder.

The day before she was to go back to the field, Matilda
left Aaron with one of the young girls and walked around
the hill to the big house. She skirted the back to avoid
Bessie Lou and slipped in through the front door.

It was early and the house was quiet. Matilda knew the
morning routine, knew the mistress would just be rising
and alone in her room. She climbed the circular staircase
and rapped lightly on Zelma's door.

Thinking it was Bessie Lou with her breakfast tray,
Zelma called for her to enter. She was surprised to see
Matilda's reflection in her mirror. She turned away from
her vanity to face the young slave. She had awakened in

a particularly good humor and had difficulty coping with the sudden sadness Matilda's presence stirred within her. "I heard about your baby," she said. "I'm deeply sorry." They had told her Matilda's baby had been stillborn. "Your baby, then Africa—you've had more than your share of ill fortune."

Matilda nodded solemnly. Her gaze faltered, and she settled her eyes on the carpet as if drawing comfort from the intricate pattern.

"Are you back in the house to resume your duties?" Zelma asked.

"No'm," Matilda mumbled.

Poor girl, Zelma thought. The tragedies had taken away her zest. She seemed a mere replica of the sassy serving girl she remembered. "If you're not feeling well enough to return to the house—"

"I'm a field worker now," Matilda interrupted. She glanced up, then immediately back to the carpet.

"Oh, but that was to be near your husband, wasn't it?" Zelma said, recalling the reason she had been given for the girl's absence. "With Africa gone—" Zelma heard Bessie Lou's footsteps outside the door and was relieved. "Look who came to pay me a visit," she said cheerfully to the old slave and turned back to her vanity to finish pinning her hair.

Bessie Lou's eyes sparked with questions and concern. Still, she said nothing. She set her mistress's breakfast tray on the table in front of the windows and opened the curtains to the morning sun. "A beautiful day," she said, and her eyes went to Matilda to warn her that she'd best not make cause to change that statement.

"Mati's coming back to us from the fields," Zelma said, fussing with a stubborn strand of hair at her neck. "She'll be resuming her duties."

"But we have Dolly now," Bessie Lou said quickly. "We spent two months trainin' her, and you like Dolly, you said."

Zelma's hands paused atop her head. Thoughtfully, she said, "Yes, I do. She's very good with the baby."

"Then we won't be needin' Mati again," Bessie Lou told her, her eyes never leaving the young slave's face.

Zelma laughed. "We'll keep them both," she said. She rose and crossed the room to the table and sat down. "You're getting too old to keep up with Vance when he goes out of the house. I saw you running after him yesterday, and it was really quite funny." She flipped open her napkin and looked hungrily at her food. "Mati can take care of Vance. That'll leave you free for other things."

Bessie Lou's expression told Matilda she had better object.

"But if I'm not really needed," Matilda said weakly. "I don't object to the fields that. . . ."

"Oh, but you are needed," Zelma said firmly. "It's settled then. You'll take over the care of Vance starting tomorrow."

"Yes'm," Matilda said and hurriedly left the room.

Bessie Lou stared at the door so intently it appeared her vision passed through the wood and followed the departing Matilda down the staircase. "You'll regret this," she told Zelma. "You know how headstrong and sassy that girl is."

"She seems to have changed," Zelma reflected. "It must have been losing her baby and husband. She's crossed that fine line separating a girl from womanhood. I think she'll be good with Vance."

"I'd be better," Bessie Lou said stubbornly. "And I ain't too old to keep up with him like you said."

Zelma looked up from her plate and laughed. "You're jealous," she accused. "You're afraid Vance will like her better than you. Dear Bessie Lou, don't you know no one could take your place with Vance or me or Dester?"

It's not my place that girl's out to take, Bessie Lou thought. It's yours. Stupid, stupid girl! She only wants to be around the house so she can be near the master. And him only wishin' he'd never see her again to be reminded of his time of weakness. What'll I do with that girl? What?

Zelma heard voices and leaned forward to look down from the window. Dester was standing below talking to Jingo. The bright sun had drained all color from his blond hair. He carried a rifle and was dressed for hunting. *How handsome he is,* she thought. *How like him our youngest son will be.* Solomon came up leading three horses; they mounted and rode away.

Zelma sipped her coffee and stared at the lawn stretching away to the creek bank, the trees beyond swaying in a gentle morning breeze. "It is a beautiful day," she said quietly.

"I've seen better," Bessie Lou mumbled and went to make the bed.

Matilda soon discovered that being back at the big house did not achieve what she had planned. She saw Dester every day, but he never acknowledged her presence with the slightest glance or word. In fact, she felt he made a conscious effort to ignore her.

It struck her that he now hated her—or worse, refused to recognize that she existed at all. The nights they had spent together meant nothing to him. Neither did their son. She was a woman betrayed.

She had also offended the other slaves and had no friends among them. For the first time since his disappearance, she thought of Africa and missed him. She had only her baby during the nights and young Vance during the days for companionship. Desires were beginning to stir inside her again. She had the need of a man. She wanted Dester but could not have him, and none of the slaves were available to satisfy her needs.

The solution came to her one day when she had taken Vance for a walk. They had gone farther from the house than she had realized until she saw the slaves from the Faviere plantation working in a cotton field. She reached for Vance's hand and said, "We'd better go back."

The boy had been enjoying the exploration of strange territory. He tried to pull his hand free, complaining that he didn't want to go home now.

"All right," she told him. "A few minutes more."

She found a knoll where she could sit and watch the Faviere slaves at work and let Vance amuse himself at a nearby marshy pond by collecting the cast-off shells of snails. He ran back to show her each new find, laughing with excitement, and made a growing pile of shells to be carried home.

Matilda leaned back on her elbows and unbuttoned her blouse to feel the cooling breeze on her flesh. The slaves had finished picking the cotton from the far side of the field, and a few of the men had come to the near corner to begin stripping the laden plants. A tall Negro about her own age worked with his shirt off, the sinewy lines of his body glistening with sweat. As if sensing her eyes on him, he glanced up and saw her. Then, fearing the overseer would see him standing and gaping and come to apply his whip to his back, he continued with his work. Still he would glance at her fleetingly without interrupting his work.

Matilda smiled to herself. The next time she was sure the slave was looking at her, she waved. He concealed the return motion of his hand by shielding it from the overseer with his body. Matilda gestured for him to join her, wishing he would, but thinking he would not dare.

The Negro glanced in the direction of the overseer, who had turned away to admonish a lagging worker. He then spoke to one of his companions and nodded toward Matilda. When next the overseer turned away, he flung his near-empty sack of cotton into the shrubs bordering the field and dropped to his stomach to crawl beneath.

Matilda sat up, her heart pounding with excitement. She knew it was dangerous to be with the Negro working his way toward her through the tall grass. If the overseer missed him and came searching, he'd probably beat them. But the danger only added to her expectation.

Vance came running back with a handful of shells. He dropped to his knees and added them to the pile. "Pretty?" he said.

Matilda looked at the boy as if wondering what to do with him. "Real pretty," she told him. She picked up the shells and carried them nearer the pond and told him to make the stack there so he wouldn't have to walk so far. She then went back to the knoll, only the far side where neither the slaves from the field nor Vance could see them, and she waited.

She heard the slave crawling through the grass before she saw him. He had not seen her go behind the knoll. "Here," she whispered.

He was even more handsome than she had realized from the distance. When he crawled out of the grass to her side, he was smiling, revealing even, white teeth. He reached for her with an urgency she understood and slid his hands through the opening of her blouse to her milk-swollen breasts.

"I ain't never given myself to a man that I don't know his name," she said. Before he could offer his name, she clutched at his head and brought it down to her body. As his mouth worked at her nipples, she stared at his head and saw the tiny flecks of cotton lodged in his hair.

His hands were tugging at her long skirt, hoisting it about her waist. She lifted her buttocks and responded to the touch of his hands along her inner thighs. She moaned when he entered her and wrapped her legs about him to urge him to deepest penetration. He became quick, rough, his hard body slamming into hers with such force it threatened to wind her. She closed her eyes and pretended it was Dester inside her; Dester's hot, panting breath in her ear, his hands kneading her breasts.

She heard Vance cry out, but it only momentarily drew her attention away.

The Negro on top of her suddenly groaned; his entire body became rigid, tensed by the sensation of climax. He pulled out, drove himself into her, and she could feel the expansion and release of his completion.

He became a dead weight on top of her, crushing her. She wedged her hands against his shoulders, pushed gently, and he rolled off her onto his back in the grass.

"Mati! Mati!"

The terror in Vance's voice reached her.

She sat up, struggling with her skirt and closing her blouse.

The Negro opened his eyes. "Your master's son?"

Matilda nodded.

"Sounds hurt," he said, and he, too, sat up.

"Just a crybaby," she murmured. "He's always fallin' and bruisin' hisself and cryin'."

She stood and peered over the knoll.

Vance was running to where he had last seen her, clutching his forearm with his hand. Tears had streaked his cheek, and his eyes were wide with fear. "Mati." His voice was oddly weaker, different. He stumbled and fell to his knees.

Matilda panicked. She ran over the top and down the far side of the knoll. The Faviere slave reached her as she was lifting Vance into her arms. The boy was extremely pale, his eyelids heavy. "What is it?" she cried. "What's happened to you?"

Vance looked up at her through half-closed lids. "My arm," he murmured. "It hurts, Mati. Please make it stop hurting."

The Negro pulled the boy's hand away from his arm and two small puncture marks were visible on the tiny forearm. "Snake," he said. "Probably cottonmouth."

"Something . . . in the grass," Vance told them with failing voice.

Matilda screamed. She threw back her head, and her anguish cut through the quiet of the afternoon air. The slaves in the field stopped their working, and the overseer, forgetting them, came running.

The Negro took Vance from her arms. He pulled a small piece of shiny metal from his trouser pocket and made a gash over the two puncture marks. He covered the wound with his mouth and began sucking at the blood and poison. If he was aware of the overseer standing over them, he gave no indication. He spit blood and saliva and poison onto the ground beside him; once, twice, three times. Then he stopped and looked down at Vance. The boy was very still and pale. He bent and placed his ear against the small chest, listening for a heartbeat.

When he straightened, he said, "He's dead!"

Matilda, refusing to believe him, pulled the boy's body into her arms. "Can't be dead! Can't be!" she cried. "Don't let him be dead! Please don't let him be dead!"

But when she touched her lips against Vance's cheek, she could already feel it cooling.

The overseer poked the Negro with the handle of his whip. "Get back to the fields," he ordered.

The slave hesitated, gave Matilda a helpless look, and walked away.

"Better take the boy back to his father," the overseer told Matilda.

Matilda had become very still. Vance's body had slipped from her arms and lay crumpled at her knees. His eyes and mouth had opened in death, and his eyes seemed to stare at her accusingly, his mouth to shout silent recriminations for her neglect. She reached out her hand and closed the eyelids. "I can't take his body back. I can't ever go back," she said steadily. "If I do, they'll kill me."

The overseer stared down at her thoughtfully for several moments. Then he motioned the slave he had sent away back to them. "Take the boy's body to where they'll find it," he instructed. "Somewhere away from our property line. The woman'll stay with us."

CHAPTER THIRTEEN

When Matilda had not returned with Vance by dinner-time, Zelma was annoyed but not unduly concerned. Matilda was known for her inability to judge time.

"A mistake bringin' that girl back to the house," Bessie Lou grumbled.

Zelma ignored the complaint. She finished eating and went out onto the porch. The sun was warm, and no longer concerned with retaining the paleness of her skin, she sat in the porch swing and turned her face up to the warm, tanning rays. Her gaze fell on the moonflower vine. How quickly it grew. It had already entwined itself around the columns and was reaching out across the inside of the porch roof. The blooms were closed tightly, waiting for the diminishing of the sun to unfurl their beauty. The vine awakened a sense of security in her, a kind of thoughtfulness. Like herself, the vine had survived transplanting and was flourishing. Time had made it strong, and yet it retained its beauty. Time, she hoped, would also make her stronger, make her belong to Plantation Bend as the moonflower now belonged to the porch. Sighing, she closed her eyes and allowed herself to drift into a half-sleep.

The slamming of the door awakened her.

Bessie Lou stood looking at her, worry creasing her brow. "That girl ain't returned with Vance yet," she said. "It's past time for his nap and him not even eatin'."

Zelma rose from the swing and stretched herself. "You worry too much," she said. But she, too, began to sense a twinge of concern.

"I'm goin'to send some of the boys to look for them," Bessie Lou mumbled. "No tellin' where that girl's taken him. I'm goin' to give her a piece of my mind whether you like it or not."

"I'll speak to Matilda," Zelma told her. She had seen Matilda and Vance cross the yard earlier and disappear among the trees. "You can send out the boys if you want," she said. "I'll also look for them." Stepping off the porch, she walked across the yard in the direction she had seen Matilda and Vance take earlier.

Bessie Lou's voice calling for the boys followed Zelma in among the trees.

Zelma walked for some distance before stopping and calling, "Mati! Vance!" Her only answer was a gentle rustling of the treetops in a high wind. A gull flew overhead screeching. From off in the distance of the house, a dog was yapping, probably chasing at the heels of the boys as Bessie Lou dispersed them in search of Matilda and Vance. Zelma cupped her hands to her mouth and repeated her call, "Mati, Vance, where are you?" Her twinge of concern increased when her calls repeatedly went unanswered. Unless Mati and Vance had worked their way around toward the canefields, they could not help but hear her. Unless—she recalled her own experience of meeting the Faviere overseer when she and Solomon had accidentally wandered beyond the property line. "Mati! Vance!" Her voice became edged with panic. "Answer me! Vance! Answer your mother!"

She heard the shouting of the boys from behind her as they ran through the trees calling Matilda's name. They were making a game of it; laughing, shouting, more laughter, teasing the dog.

Zelma moved on ahead. She had had very little exercise since Clabe's birth, and the strain was beginning to show on her. Her chest was heaving, her steps faltering. Loose twigs snagged at the hem of her skirt and almost pulled her down. She paused, hand going to her brow as she peered around at the underbrush as if expecting Vance and Mati to spring suddenly out at her, laughing over their game of hide-and-seek.

The boys caught up with her. When they bounded through the bushes and came across her, their laughter ceased instantly. They recognized the concern on their mistress's face and felt guilty for having made a game of their searching.

Zelma forced a smile, convincing herself her panic was uncalled for. "We'll spread out," she told the boys. "I think they're playing with us. But we'll find them." To return them to their game mood, she added, "Whoever spots them first wins one of Bessie Lou's gooseberry pies."

"The whole pie?" one of the boys asked in disbelief.

"Yes, the whole pie. All to himself," Zelma answered. She waved the boys to spread out in a semicircle.

They had gone only a short distance when one of the boys cried out.

The cry struck horror into Zelma's heart. It had not been a cry of jubilation, of excitement over winning the promised reward. The cry was one of terror. She ran in the boy's direction, shoving away branches that reached out toward her face, yanking her skirt free from snagging twigs with no regard for the rending tears.

She broke through the bushes into a clearing and was brought up short, her worst dread becoming a reality.

In the middle of the clearing lay the remains of a decaying log. In the fork of its gnarled branches lay the body of her son.

Zelma leaned heavily on Dester's arm as they climbed to the clearing atop the hill.

Gulls had come in from the gulf in search of food and were circling, screeching above the treetops. Their sounds mingled and became part of the sobbing and wailing of the slaves.

Zelma did not hear the gulls, or the slaves, or the words of encouragement Dester whispered into her ear.

They offered her a chair when she reached the clearing, but she refused it. She stood peering out from behind her black veil with eyes seeing but not fully comprehending.

The Coles were there, dressed in their best Sunday clothes, and all the slaves. Bessie Lou had gone down on her knees and had her hands clasped before her. Her lips were moving, but there were no words. Her heavy cheeks were wet and shiny in the sunlight. There was a preacher reading from the Bible. He kept glancing at Zelma, possibly realizing his words fell on deaf ears. When he closed the book and stepped aside, two slaves came forward and lifted the tiny coffin off its stand.

To Zelma, it was like a dream, an unreality, this scene. Her chest felt curiously leaden as if she wore a great, heavy shield about it to keep out the pain that was shrieking to get inside. A voice inside her head kept repeating, *Must keep the pain at bay! If it reaches you, the sense of unreality will be shattered. The child in that coffin will become "your" child, your Vance. Reality will kill. Must keep the pain at bay!*

The two slaves went down on their knees to lower the coffin into the ground. Their arms and shoulders disappeared into the hole, but regardless of their efforts to touch the coffin to the bottom, it slipped from their grasps and gave off a thudding sound as it struck. The slaves straightened and retreated with apologetic looks.

Zelma realized all faces were suddenly turned to her. What did they expect of her? What ritual did this dream demand? The small coffin had nothing to do with her. She was only an observer, an intruder into cruel fantasy. If she kept the pain away long enough, she would awaken without being scarred. When the dream ended, she would draw her two sons to her bosom and love and protect them, and memory of this nightmare would pass.

Dester stepped away from her to the edge of the grave. He was pale in his dark suit. Grief was etched about the hollows of his eyes. He bent and scooped up a handful of earth and dropped it into the opening. He turned to Zelma and extended his hand, and she realized she was expected to repeat his action.

She came forward as if some quirk of her body prevented her knees from bending. Her hand reached out toward the mound of earth, but she could not lower herself to reach it. Dester scooped up a second handful and transferred the dark, damp dirt into her hand. He gave her his arm to help her closer to the open grave.

She peered down into the blackness and could see the

lighter surface of the coffin staring back at her. *At least,*
she thought, *there is no water. My Vance will not rest in
a watery grave.*

The earth left her hand and struck the intruding wood.
The hollow sound beat against her ears like a dirge, made
her aware of Bessie Lou's wailing and the sobbing of the
slaves. The protective shield about her chest and mind
shattered.

With a scream that tore up from the very depth of her
being, she attempted to fling herself into the grave of her
son.

The following week Dester met Sam Cole on the road
between his farm and the river.

The dirt farmer carried a rifle over one shoulder and a
gunny sack over the other. His hands and arms were caked
with earth. Seeing Dester, he stopped, dropped the gunny
sack, and wiped the sweat from his brow. "You don't object to my hunting on your land, do you?"

"Hunting for what?" Dester asked.

"Ginseng," Sam told him. He nodded down at the heavy
gunny sack. "It's how I keep body and soul together when
the crops aren't good. Sell the ginseng roots to the phar-
macist in New Orleans. He, in turn, sells it to the traders
for shipment to China, I hear. The Chinks make medicine
out of the roots."

"No, I don't mind," Dester told him.

Sam squatted down in the middle of the road to rest his
weary legs. "How's the wife?" He hadn't seen Dester since
the day he had carried Zelma down the hill from the cemetery after burying their son.

Dester's brow creased. Zelma seldom came out of her
room. She would not allow Clabe out of her sight, would
let no one attend to him except Bessie Lou. She had lost
one son, and she intended to be overly protective of the
other. It was not good for her—or the boy, Dester realized,
but he had been unable to reach her. "It'd be helpful in your
wife would pay Zelma a call," Dester told the farmer. "She
needs another woman to talk to."

Sam nodded his understanding. "I'll tell Ginny," he

said, emphasizing the word *tell*. His wife, he suspected, would refuse to visit their neighbor unless he forced her. Zelma Granville was too grand for Ginny's taste.

"I'd appreciate it," Dester told Sam.

They talked for a few moments about planting, about the Favieres, who were expanding their fields of rice to the border of their land, and then Dester, judging the time with a glance at the sky, bade Sam good-bye and went back to his chores.

Ginny Cole never paid a visit to Plantation Bend, and the next time Dester met Sam, he didn't mention it.

Zelma's grief began to wane. She stopped locking herself in her room with Clabe and started once again to join her husband for supper. After a month, she visited the hillside cemetery and brought flowers for Vance's grave. Grass had already begun to push up through the rich, dark soil.

PART TWO

CHAPTER FOURTEEN

THE PLANTATION FLOURISHED during the next years.

Dester built a road from Plantation Bend to the Mississippi River and a dock where the flatboats could tie up because it was more economical transporting the sugarcane downriver to the New Orleans refineries than carting it overland. When the flatboats would be required by weather to tie up overnight at the Plantation Bend dock, Zelma always invited the captains to dinner.

On one occasion, she suggested to a captain that his crew might be allowed to come ashore for the night.

The captain almost choked on his wine. "You apparently know nothing about flatboat crews," he said. "They're the roughest and toughest breed of men to be found in all of this country. Letting them come ashore would be inviting disaster. Only three things interest them, drinking and fighting and, well . . . " he looked across the table at Dester and winked, "there's the fleshpots of Dixie when we tie up along Tchoupitoulas Street."

"Dixie?" Zelma questioned.

"New Orleans, m'am," the captain explained. "Dixie is the nickname given the city by the rivermen."

"However did you come by such a name?" she asked.

"From the ten-dollar notes the banks of New Orleans printed up," Dester explained before the captain could answer. "One side of the notes is printed in English and the other side in French. *Dix* is the French word for ten. Right, Captain?"

The captain nodded. "Proper pronunciation of French isn't a skill of the rivermen," he said. "Collectively, they call the notes 'dixies' and for some reason applied the name to the city as well."

Zelma repeated the name several times with amusement. "It's catchy," she concluded. "And it'll give me something to add to my next letter to my friend Madame Celine."

The captain looked startled. "You know Madame Celine, Mrs. Granville?"

Dester explained that his wife had occupied rooms at Madame Celine's house when they had first arrived from Atlanta.

The captain turned rather pale.

Smiling, Zelma said, "Not that house, Captain."

The riverboat captains were the only guests to Plantation Bend, and Zelma always looked forward to their visits. Dester made infrequent business trips to New Orleans, but being a man not given to gossip, seldom brought back more than a smattering of news. Zelma's main source of connection to the outside world came from her father's and Madame Celine's letters.

Her mother had died the year after Clabe had been born, and her father had retired from politics. He returned to his Savannah plantation and lived a quiet life until his friend James Madison took over the office of president from Thomas Jefferson in 1809. He wrote:

Madison has stepped into a veritable hornet's nest. American grievances against England grow daily. The western frontier accuses the British of stirring up Indian warfare. The English and French blockades remain in effect. The Republican party, insensible to the fact that we are not prepared for war against a nation which is prepared, is putting pressure to bear on the president to have Congress sign a declaration of war. Madison is for keeping the peace, but the war party grows, and war psychology prevails under the eloquence of Henry Clay of Kentucky and John Calhoun of South Carolina, who are incidentally now being called the "young war hawks." Madison has asked me back to Washington as an advisor.

Although I am not in the best of health, I cannot
refuse his request.

Closer to home, Ginny Cole had given birth to daughters
in two consecutive years and named them Victoria and
Vienna. When Victoria was born, Zelma, who had become pregnant and suffered a miscarriage, had the baby
clothes and quilts sent over to her neighbor. The slave
who had taken them brought them back with a polite note
saying they were not needed. When Vienna was born, Zelma
repacked the gifts and sent them over again. This time,
the slave brought back two jars of preserves and a thank-
you note.

Claude Faviere's wife died of pneumonia. According
to gossip from the slave quarter, the now white-headed
Frenchman had ridden into New Orleans the day following her burial and returned with a new wife who was a
year younger than his daughter, Claudine. The new wife's
name was Lilith, and some slave who could read con-
sulted his Scriptures and announced that Satan's wife's
name had also been Lilith. It was rumored the woman had
coal-black hair and coal-black eyes and wore nothing
except coal-black dresses. The slaves who had been
brought from Savannah remembered the Frenchman had
been called "The Devil." The name was rechristened, and
women told stories about his evil deeds that made their
children tremble whenever the Faviere carriage passed on
the road.

In 1812, Louisiana was admitted as a state. That same
year, on June 18, war was declared on England.

The Americans expected to take Canada with one run
and a dash. Instead, the defeat was inglorious. General
Hull led the attack with two thousand men and was
forced back by a handful of British and Indians, losing all
the Michigan territory.

Spring of the following year, Zelma received a letter
from her father telling her he was coming for a visit. She
detected something strange in the letter; it lacked his usual
chattiness, and he did not ask after the health of his

grandson. As the day of his arrival drew nearer, she became more apprehensive.

She was in Dester's study teaching Clabe from the new books she had ordered from New Orleans, when she heard the carriage clatter across the bridge.

"Grandpa!" the boy shouted and ran from the side door to meet the carriage.

Zelma closed the books and went through the house to the entryway. She stopped briefly to appraise her appearance in the hall mirror, patted her hair into place, and then dashed through the door with excitement that surpassed her son's.

The senator was climbing out of the carriage with the aid of the coachman. It had been ten years since Zelma had seen her father, ten years that had turned him into a very old man she hardly recognized. When he reached the ground, he stood badly bent and relied heavily on his cane. His hair was completely white and thinning, and his once fleshy face was gaunt and badly wrinkled. Only his eyes remained unchanged, alert and intelligent, and now sparkling with laughter as he greeted his grandson.

Zelma gave her father and Clabe a moment together before running forward and throwing her arms about her father. She was crying, saying, "Papa, Papa, Papa," over and over again and covering his cheeks with kisses. When at last she stepped back, controlling her joy, she saw that there was also moisture in her father's eyes. "Papa, I'm so happy to see you." She called instructions to one of the slaves to fetch Dester in the fields. Taking her father's arm, she started to lead him toward the porch.

"But wait!" he said, laughing. "I didn't come alone. Aren't you going to greet your sister?"

Zelma was speechless. When she turned back to the carriage, Zona was stepping to the ground.

Where time had dealt badly with her father, it had been a friend to Zona. The once plump and rather plain younger sister that Zelma remembered was now a woman of striking beauty. She wore a blue silk dress in the latest fashion with a hat to match, the color accentuating the blueness of her eyes.

Zelma left her father's side and ran to embrace her sister.

Both were still weeping from the happiness of their reunion when Bessie Lou shouted from the porch that the senator had best come in out of the noonday sun.

Exhausted from their trip, both the senator and Zona retired to their rooms to rest after greeting Dester.

Alone, Zelma said to Dester, "He looks ill, doesn't he?" She hoped he would disagree with her.

Instead, he said solemnly, "Yes, he does, Zelma. He should have stayed in Savannah and not gone back to Washington at President Madison's request. At his age—"

"Oh, but maybe he just needs rest," she interrupted, not wanting to hear more. "I'll see that he's kept quiet, and Bessie Lou can nurse him back to health."

"Bessie Lou is not a miracle-worker," Dester murmured and dropped the subject.

To the senator, Bessie Lou's dinner was a miracle.

She had prepared all his favorite dishes as she remembered he liked them. She had inspected the table numerous times before giving her approval to the grumbling staff, and she would have done the serving herself if she had not learned to mistrust herself with the heavy trays. Instead, she stationed herself by the door and inspected every plate that left the kitchen, sending back anything that did not please her critical eye.

Zelma, anticipating that her sister would wear something striking to dinner, had gone through her wardrobe of gowns she had not worn since New Orleans and selected one of emerald green. The only jewelry she chose to wear was her wedding band and a small emerald pendant inherited from her mother. The gown was a bit snug at the bodice and waist and smelled of mothballs and lavender sachet.

"You look lovely," Dester complimented.

When Zona came down the spiral staircase in a stunning blue gown of Empire design, Zelma wished she had conquered her feminine vanity for competition. In comparison, her gown was outdated, a relic. But her jealousy only lasted an instant. She came forward, complimented and kissed her sister, and led her into the drawing room, where Dester and their father were discussing tactics of war.

"Winchester's defeat at Raisin River by the British was a disaster," the senator was saying. "The wounded were abandoned and massacred by the Indians. We may take York, but I seriously doubt if Montreal will fall. We have a year, perhaps years, of fighting ahead. . . ." He broke off speaking when his daughters entered the drawing room. He appraised them proudly. "Tell me," he said to Dester with a wink, "have you ever known a man to have two more beautiful daughters?"

"Never," Dester flattered.

The senator's gaze went to Clabe, who had been sitting at his feet listening raptly to talk of the war. "Or a more handsome grandson," he said. Leaning forward, he ruffled the boy's hair.

"You haven't lost the flattery of a politican," Zelma teased.

The senator laughed and nodded affirmatively to the decanter of whiskey Dester was offering. Rest had not dissipated his weariness. The whiskey, his third, was relaxing him. Before he had finished it, however, Bessie Lou came to the door to announce dinner.

During dinner, they chatted about Washington society and Dolly Madison's prominence in the social functions at the White House.

"But why not?" Zona said. "She certainly had practice since she acted as first lady during Jefferson's administration as well."

The senator smiled good-naturedly. "As you can see," he told Dester and Zelma, "the women of Washington are no less envious of the charming Mrs. Madison. They clamor to be on her guest lists but continue to sharpen their tongues at her expense. My daughter is no exception."

"I consider all Washington society a bore," Zona said flatly. "I would never have become active in Washington society if William. . . ." She stopped speaking in mid-sentence and glanced questioningly at her father.

Zelma caught the quick negative turn of his head. The apprehension his last letter had awakened in her returned. They were keeping something from her. Perhaps it had been ten years since she had seen them, but she knew them well enough to understand the exchange passing between them. But what? Something they both felt had to be presented at the proper time and in a delicate manner. Something, she reasoned, that had to do with Zona's husband, William Porter. She decided to wait and not question them. Her father had a way of creating the appropriate circumstances to present a delicate announcement.

That time came after Clabe had been sent away to bed and Bessie Lou had served the coffee.

The senator lit up his pipe and said that he would enjoy a brandy.

Zona, who also knew her father well, knew that the moment she was dreading was at hand. She visibly stiffened in her chair.

"I suppose," the senator said, "you've been wondering why I didn't inform you in my letter that Zona would be accompanying me."

"I'm delighted, of course," Zelma told him, "but the thought did cross my mind."

"The truth of the matter is your sister feels she can no longer live in Washington society. I'm afraid a delicate situation has turned into somewhat of a scandal." The senator sipped his brandy and set the glass aside.

Zelma glanced fleetingly from her father to Dester to Zona. Her sister's eyes were riveted on her coffee cup, the muscles in her thin neck standing out as if she was clinching her teeth. To her father, Zelma said, "Zona was involved in a scandal, Papa?" The tone of her voice conveyed her disbelief.

"A delicate situation that your sister turned into a scandal," the senator said with a weary sigh. He absently ran his index finger about the rim of his brandy snifter.

Zona looked up. "What Papa is trying to tell you is that William divorced me," she announced.

"Divorce!" The news so startled Zelma that the word came out as a shout. She saw her sister recoil as if struck. "Forgive me," she said. "It's just . . . just that I was shocked."

"Of course, you were," Zona told her with a forced laugh. "Shock is always the first reaction when someone hears. Then the snickering and gossip begin." She waved her hands in a gesture of dismissal. "I understand it's fashionable in Europe. Bonaparte saw to that when he divorced Josephine. But Washington isn't Paris." Her lower lip began to tremble. "We're very backward in Washington," she said. "A divorced woman becomes a scarlet woman. That's what I am—a scarlet woman!"

"Please, Zona," the senator said. "Let's save the emotionalism until after this discussion." He drained the balance of his brandy and looked grateful when Dester rose to refill his snifter.

"But . . . but I don't understand," Zelma said. She turned to her sister. "Why did your husband divorce you, Zona?"

"For the same reason Bonaparte divorced Josephine," Zona answered. "I'm . . . I'm barren. William wanted children, lots of little Porters to flatter his ego and carry on his name." She covered her face with her hands and wept quietly.

"I don't blame any man for wanting children," the senator said, "but, to me, marriages are made in Heaven. If a couple is unfortunate not to be blessed with offspring, they should consider it the will of God and make the best of it."

Zona stopped weeping and pulled her hands away from her face. Her eyes were brimming and reddened. "Make the best of it!" she said mockingly. "If William couldn't have the best of any situation, he merely turned away from it and looked elsewhere."

The senator went on as if she had not spoken. "This is the first divorce in my family or in the families of any of my friends," he said. "William is an ambitious man, and like many ambitious men, is somewhat of a scalawag. His eye is on a political appointment, and he felt that the image of a childless marriage was detrimental."

"But that's absurd!" Zelma cried. "Look at all the famous men in government who do not have children."

"William plans to be more famous than any of them," Zona said. She laughed again, bitterly. "He's already made me the most notorious woman in Washington." She glanced at her father. "Sorry, Papa. Of course, I'm exaggerating."

"Yes, you are," the senator said gravely. "Much of the notoriety could have been avoided."

"I made matters worse," Zona explained to Zelma and Dester, "by following William to one of his rendezvous and making a scene. The young lady he was meeting so discreetly on the side turned out to be the daughter of one of Father's fellow senators. The news was all over Washington before morning. Only William wasn't the villain. I was."

"No point in going into all that now," the senator told her crossly. "Zona's problem is this. She can't remain in Washington, and she refuses to return to Savannah and face her friends."

"A woman in disgrace cannot go home," Zona murmured.

"I was hoping," the senator said, "that you might welcome her here at Plantation Bend until things blow over."

"Things will not blow over," Zona said firmly. "I'm a branded woman."

"Nonsense," her father retorted. "You're dramatizing again. You're only in the limelight until the next scandal comes along, and in Washington, my dear, scandal is as common as political debate." The old man turned to Dester. "We should not have imposed as we did," he said, "by anticipating your welcoming your wife's sister into your home, but frankly I was at my wit's end. If their mother had been alive—"

"Zona is welcome at Plantation Bend for the remainder of her lifetime," Dester interrupted.

"Yes, yes, of course she is," Zelma added.

"Thank you," the senator said, obviously relieved.

Zona was again staring at her cup. "The remainder o

my lifetime," she murmured. "It almost sounds like a sentence."

The senator remained at Plantation Bend for two weeks. He rode out to the fields with Dester, examined the crops, talked to the slaves, and had a much needed rest. Under the sun, his pallor left him, and color returned to his cheeks. He even managed to get around without his cane. It was apparent, however, that by the end of two weeks he was becoming impatient to take his leave.

"President Madison needs me in Washington," he told Dester and Zelma the day he decided he must depart. "I am but an old man who is of little help, but he relies on me for what I can do. I can't abandon him now that I know Zona is safe here with you."

The following morning, the carriage was brought to the front door shortly after breakfast. The senator, who had gone into the kitchen to speak to Bessie Lou, came out with a basket of food she had prepared for his trip. He shook hands with Dester, kissed his daughters and grandson, and waved until the carriage had rolled out of sight.

Bessie Lou was waiting in the entryway when Zelma and Zona returned to the house. She was clutching a small package in her hands. Holding it out to Zelma, she said, "The senator gave me this, but I can't accept it."

"What is it?" Zelma asked without taking it.

Bessie Lou opened the flap and showed her the emerald ring that matched the brooch Zelma had inherited from her mother. "Your mother's ring," the slave said. "He said she'd of wanted me to have it."

"And she would have," Zelma said sincerely. "Keep it, Bessie Lou, as a remembrance."

"I don't need nothin' to remember your mother by," Bessie Lou told her, "and it's much too fine for me to wear." She pushed the ring case toward her mistress.

"No, it's yours," Zelma said, refusing the ring.

Bessie Lou stared at the case for a moment. "Then I'll save it until Master Clabe marries," she said. "It'll be my present to his bride."

Zelma did not want to remind Bessie Lou that Clabe

was now only nine years old. The old slave was in her mid-sixties. "It will be a nice gesture," she said.

The next news they had of the senator came in a letter from President Madison. The senator had died in his sleep three nights after returning to Washington. The president expressed the country's loss, his own as the senator's friend, and told them the senator had been buried with honors beside his beloved wife.

With her father and mother dead and Zona at Plantation Bend, Zelma's final ties with Savannah were broken. If there had been any restraints about accepting Plantation Bend as her home, they vanished. Her roots were firmly planted.

Zona took over Clabe's tutoring. She had a limited knowledge of French and Latin, and when the boy had absorbed all she knew, they taught themselves together from the books Zelma had ordered from New Orleans.

"Why Latin?" Dester asked Zelma.

"Why not?" she countered.

"He should be learning about the earth and sugarcane and how to barter with the refineries."

"He shall," she assured her husband. "There's time for you to teach him those things. We're both young. There's time."

But Dester was stubborn and finally managed to steal his son away from French and Latin books for the morning hours. He taught him to ride and hunt. He explained about soil condition, and the importance of not exhausting the land. Much of what he taught was lost on the boy, and he knew it, but he continued just the same. Losing Vance and then Zelma's miscarriage had made him realize that he would probably have no more than one son. He was determined to pass along everything he knew to Clabe so that when the time came he would not be ill-prepared for the operation of the plantation.

It worried Zelma that Clabe, between his sessions with Dester and Zona, was not given enough time to himself to do as he pleased. He was a child, and she did not want the days of his childhood taken from him. She already recognized the seriousness in her son's eyes, the lack of laughter

in his voice. She understood the intensity with which both
her husband and sister approached the boy's education;
Dester because he was determined his son should know
everything about the plantation, and Zona because teaching kept her mind off her own troubled nature. She decided she would aproach them both and take away part
of the time the boy spent with them. If necessary, she
would tell them she wanted her son to spend more time
with her, his mother. Let them think she was jealous if
they would.

Clabe had not yet returned from his time with his
father when Zelma went down to the study to speak to her
sister.

Zona had the books open on the desk and was already
consulting the lesson she planned for the day. "Otherwise," she explained, "Clabe learns faster than I and becomes bored."

Zelma took a seat by the window and glanced out at the
sky. It had been clear during the morning but was now
clouding over. She could feel rain in the air and hoped it
would not be a storm. There was not a storm that didn't
remind her of the night Clabe was born and how she had
convinced herself she was going to die. "It's going to rain,"
she said absently.

"*Pleuvoir,*" Zona translated.

Zelma smiled. "You were always good at your lessons,"
she remembered. "I always felt so stupid in comparison."

"I had to be bright," Zona said without looking up from
her book. "You were the beautiful one. It was my only
way of competing."

"I never thought of us as having competed with each
other," Zelma told her. "Why did you consider it necessary to feel competitive? Our parents always treated us
equally."

"That's true," Zona said. "But then other people paid
more attention to you." She closed the book and leaned
back in her chair. She made a pyramid of her hands and
touched the tips to her chin much like one in prayer. "By
other people, of course I mean boys."

"I don't remember," Zelma said.

Zona laughed. "It hasn't been that long ago, Zelma."

"It seems like a lifetime."

"Perhaps that's because your childhood was a happy one," Zona suggested.

Zelma's brow furrowed. "Implying yours was not?"

"Not particularly."

"I can't believe you'd say that," Zelma told her, thinking she was just being dramatic. "I know you don't believe it."

"You mean you wish I hadn't admitted it to you," Zona said. "I was plump and almost ugly. I was introverted, a wallflower, insecure with anyone outside the family. All the things you were not." Rising, she walked across the study, her silk skirt rustling about her legs, and stopped at the window beside Zelma's chair, looking out. "You never really took an interest in me," she said quietly. "I was always just someone who was there, the sister who existed in your shadow."

"That's not true," Zelma objected. "I've always loved you. Always."

"But why?" Zona asked. "Because I'm your sister, and you're supposed to love your sister? Not certainly because you know me or ever really tried to." She turned away from the window and looked down at Zelma. Seeing her hurt expression, she said, "I'm not saying this with malice. I'm merely stating a fact I've become acutely aware of since coming to live at Plantation Bend."

"I've done something to offend you," Zelma thought aloud.

"No, you haven't," Zona said with a sigh.

"Then why are you accusing me like this?" Zelma demanded. "Haven't I made you feel welcome here?"

Zona bent down beside Zelma's chair and took her hand. "Dear, dear Zelma," she said. "It's what you haven't done that makes me realize we're almost strangers. As a girl, I always wanted to share my thoughts and feelings with you, but I never could. I can't now."

"I admit I was preoccupied with myself when we were young," Zelma said reflectively, "but now—Zona, you have to understand. I've been at Plantation Bend for almost ten

years. I've not moved in Washington society going to teas
and parties. For ten years, my only communication with
other women has been through letters. I'm no longer preoccupied with myself, but I now have my family and my
home. It's not that I have no interest in you as you suggest.
I love you. I love having you here with me." She took
Zona's hands and held them tightly. "I assume you mean
by what I haven't done is not pressing you to talk about
William and your divorce."

Zona said nothing, but her expression told Zelma she
had struck the truth.

"The subject seemed so painful for you," Zelma went
on, "that I wanted to wait until you came to me. You see,
Zona, that display at the dinner table the night of your
arrival, your bitterness and hatred of your husband, I knew
it was all a sham."

Surprised, Zona cried, "You knew?"

Zelma nodded. "I understand you'd come to Plantation
Bend to more than escape a scandal. I knew you'd come
to try to get over loving the man who divorced you."

Zona buried her face in Zelma's lap and began to weep.
"Oh, dear God, Zelma," she cried. "I love him so much.
I'll never get over him. Never."

Zelma gently stroked her sister's head.

Clabe knocked on the study door and came in without
waiting to be invited. He saw his mother and aunt, both
weeping, and turned to creep out again.

"No, wait," Zelma told him. "Your Aunt Zona is
anxious to give you your lessons." She knew she would
not have to request Clabe spend less time with lesson to
allow him time to play. She understood that she and her
sister had discovered one another, and Zona would now
spend more time with her. To Zona, she said, "We'll talk
more after your lessons."

Zona dabbed her eyes with her handkerchief. "Thank
you," she said. Smiling, she turned to her nephew. *"Bonjour, Monsieur* Granville."

"Bonjour," Clabe answered, looking dismally at the
raindrops beginning to streak the windowpanes. By the
time his lessons had ended, the rain would be heavy, and

he wouldn't be allowed to go play with his new friend, Aaron.

"Carriage comin'," Bessie Lou called up the stairs.

When Zelma glanced out her window and saw the bright yellow parasol and the Negro in matching yellow coat and hat, she knew who her surprise visitor was.

"*Cherie!*" Madame Celine cried as Zelma emerged from the house. "You seem determined not to come to New Orleans, so I've come to Plantation Bend."

The two women embraced.

"You haven't aged in all these years," Zelma told Madame Celine as she took her into the drawing room. "You look the same as you did the day Dester took me away."

"Ah, *cherie,* a beautiful lie," the Frenchwoman said gratefully. "But I have my mirror and the reflection in Pierrot's eyes to tell me the truth." Removing her gloves, she moved to the sofa and seated herself. Pierrot had entered behind them and stood awkwardly just inside the door. Since Zelma did not offer him a chair, Madame Celine motioned him to seat himself across the room on the window seat. "You don't object to Pierrot remaining in the room, do you, *cherie?*"

"Of course not," Zelma told her, although she would have been more comfortable had he not. She glanced at the mute Negro. He had, of course, lost his youthfulness, but he had developed into a striking man. Despite the trip, his yellow coat and beige trousers looked freshly pressed.

"Come, *cherie,*" Madame Celine said, patting the cushion beside her. "It's so good to see you. Are you well? Where is that handsome husband of yours? And the son you rave so much about in your letters? Who was the other woman I caught a glimpse of in the upstairs window?"

Zelma sank to the sofa beside her friend and laughed at the barrage of questions.

"Ah, one thing at a time," Madame Celine said. "First, tell me about yourself."

"I am well," Zelma said.

"And happy?" the Frenchwoman pressed.

Zelma looked at her thoughtfully for a moment. "Yes," she answered. "I am happy."

The old woman smiled. "Then that discontented girl who occupied my rooms has gone away?" she said. "Good."

"She went away because she didn't have time to be discontent," Zelma said. "Would you like. . . ."

Zona appeared in the doorway, was motioned into the room, and introduced to Madame Celine. She somewhat paled at the sight of the Frenchwoman's overly bright gown and heavily painted face, but hiding her shock, she was polite and said she'd have tea prepared.

Scarcely had Zona left the room than Madame Celine lay a hand on Zelma's arm. "I think more than tea will be required to remove the dust of the road from my throat," she said and winked.

"As a matter of fact, I think we have some of your favorite cognac," Zelma said. She excused herself and went into the kitchen to tell Bessie Lou to open the case of cognac they had been unable to deliver to Emile. "Forget the tea," she told Zona. "I'll have a glass of sherry."

Zona, who was getting out the china, turned away from the cupboard. "That woman," she said, "she's . . . she's . . ."

"A very nice lady from New Orleans," Zelma said with a smile. "Perhaps later she'll consent to visit your French class. It'll give you and Clabe an opportunity to test your fluency with the language." She turned to Bessie Lou. "If memory serves me correctly, I believe Madame Celine likes possum. And, oh, yes. Fried fish for breakfast."

Bessie Lou grunted. "It'll be better than we got in New Orleans. I'll guarantee that."

As Zelma returned to the drawing room, she heard Madame Celine speaking in a low voice to Pierrot. So as not to surprise them, she caused her heels to click noisily across the polished floor. Judging from Madame's Celine's expression and Pierrot's downcast eyes when she entered, Zelma thought Pierrot had been receiving a scolding.

"Ah, *cherie*. Pierrot was just going outside to take advantage of the country air," Madame Celine said rather stiffly.

Obediently, although begrudgingly, Pierrot rose from the window seat and left the room. The outer door closed behind him with a bang.

"He's a darling," Madame Celine said with a sigh. "Part of his charm comes from his boyishness." She sipped her cognac and dismissed the subject of her mute slave, or so Zelma thought until she said, "One is fortunate to have loyal slaves during these troubled times. Don't you agree, Zelma?"

Zelma nodded. "Our people have always been loyal."

"Then you're luckier, *cherie,* than the planters at St. John the Baptist Parish," Madame Celine told her. "You heard, of course?"

Zelma had not.

Madame Celine told her about a slave insurrection in that parish. The terrified planters and their families had fled to New Orleans. "The federal troops and the entire city militia were mobilized. Oh, *cherie!* It was dreadful, the roll of those drums, the fear of having our throats cut during our sleep."

"How many Negroes were involved?" Zelma asked, wondering why Dester, who must have heard, had not told her.

"Hundreds," Madame Celine answered. "Of course, they didn't stand a chance against the military. Those that were captured were tried and executed. Their heads were displayed on poles at the Place d'Armes as a warning to the remainder of the slave population. And this war, *cherie! Mon Dieu!*"

"We are well away from it at Plantation Bend," Zelma said. "Since my father's dead, what news we hear of the war comes from the riverboat captains who tie up at our dock."

"It is not wise to feel too safe, *cherie,*" Madame Celine told her knowingly. "I'm sure those planters were caught unaware when *their* slaves rebelled."

"Our people are happy," Zelma said with assurance.

"There'll be no insurrection here, and I seriously doubt if the war touches us at all."

"Pray you are correct, *cherie*." Draining her cognac, Madame Celine rose and began to pace the drawing room. "I have been evading the real issue of my visit," she said quietly. Her pacing came to a halt by the window, and she stood for a moment staring out at Pierrot, who had retreated to the shade of the nearest tree. "The truth is, Zelma, I am ruined!" She glanced over her shoulder, her eyes filling with moisture that threatened to spill down her heavily rouged cheeks. "My business, my savings, they're all gone."

Zelma was shocked. "I don't understand. Your letters .... you mentioned nothing about. . . ."

"These things cannot be written in letters," Madame Celine said gravely. "Besides, *cherie,* it all happened so quickly. One day I was fine, and the next I was facing poverty." She returned to the sofa, sat down, and took Zelma's hands. "Señor Ponce waited all these years for revenge," she said, "and he finally managed through some political maneuver to have my house . . . business closed. My girls who wouldn't consent to work for him were driven out of the city. *Mon Dieu!* That was not all. I had invested in a company exporting goods to Europe. The English sank two of the company's ship and they went bankrupt." She released Zelma's hands and drew a lace handkerchief from her cuff to dab at the corners of her eyes. Rising again in a burst of nervousness, she resumed her pacing. "I've sold my jewelry, the furnishings from my home—even most of my wardrobe." She stopped, eyes blazing. "What ghouls they were!" she cried. "Those women who wouldn't even speak to me on the streets poured into my house in droves to pick and barter over my clothes."

"I'm . . . I'm so sorry," Zelma told her. "If there's anything I can do. . . ." She suddenly felt a genuine need for the sherry she had held untouched.

"Folie!" Madame Celine cried. "I must begin again at my age. All I have left is my home—and that bare—and

one slave girl too incompetent to sell. And, of course," she glanced toward the window, "Pierrot."

Zelma swallowed a mouthful of sherry to steady herself. "You want me to . . . to buy Pierrot?" she managed.

"Oui, cherie! I couldn't turn him over to the slave traders! Not Pierrot!" Madame Celine cried, "I couldn't bear the thought of some crude bully's whip cutting into his precious back. *Mon Dieu. Mon Dieu!"* She shuddered as if the mere thought brought her pain. "Pierrot is a prize, a treasure. Only a mistress of quality would appreciate him. Naturally, I thought of you first."

"And when you thought of me," Zelma said, "what price did you consider?" She didn't even blink when Madame Celine mentioned a price three times the slave's value.

Sensing her reluctance, Madame Celine went on nervously, "What I intend to do, *cherie,* is to bring only the best and most beautiful girls into my own home. Discreetly, of course."

"Of course," Zelma murmured.

"I will claim the most prominent gentlemen among my clientele. Then even Señor Ponce's manipulations cannot touch me." Returning to the window, Madame Celine's eyes once again moistened as she stared out at Pierrot. "If you buy Pierrot, it will make my new venture possible. Also, if you buy him, I shall not, I think, feel the guilt I would suffer if he went elsewhere. Sometimes I do not blame the slaves for insurrection. Sometimes I think the entire system is . . ." she waved her hand in a gesture of confusion . . . *"tragique!"* she said.

Zelma excused herself, went to her room, and returned with a small metal box. She counted out the proper number of gold coins.

Madame Celine, as if touching the coins would somehow insult their friendship, opened her purse and let Zelma drop them inside. *"Merci.* Oh, *cherie,* what a friend you are! This is the second time you have saved me." Her excitement clouded over. "But don't you have to consult your husband? Will me not be angry if you buy a slave without his consent?"

"The money is mine," Zelma told her, "from my mother. What I do with it is for me to say."

Convinced, Madame Celine snapped the catch of her purse closed.

"One thing," Zelma said. "I do not wish to purchase Pierrot."

"But . . . but I do not understand!" Madame Celine cried, instinctively clutching her purse to her as if Zelma was about to demand the return of the gold coins.

"I would not dream of taking Pierrot from you," Zelma explained. "So, dear friend, I'd like you to consider the money a gift."

"Oh, no! Never! I could not accept it! I did not come for charity!"

"An investment, then," Zelma suggested. "You may repay me when . . . whenever."

Those terms were acceptable to Madame Celine. She kissed Zelma's cheek, sat back with a sigh of relief, and asked if she might have another cognac.

Zelma refilled her glass and helped herself to a second sherry.

"Have you seen or heard from Emile?" Madame Celine inquired.

Zelma told her that she had not, that only hostility existed between the plantations, and that Emile had made no effort to visit her.

"He comes very infrequently to New Orleans now," Madame Celine told her sadly. "He drinks more heavily and spends all his time on the riverboats. Poor Emile. He confessed that the only thing making his life on his father's plantation tolerable was his mother, and now she's gone and his father has taken another wife."

"Did you know the new Mrs. Faviere?" Zelma asked, curious.

"*Oui, cherie,*" Madame Celine assured her, lowering her voice as if afraid of being overheard. "She was a bond-woman. A sweet, simple girl whose fate was bound up by a ruthless father who used her to satisfy his debts. Monsieur Faviere saw her cleaning floors at Tremoulet's Coffee House and took a fancy to her. He bought out her bond,

sent one of the waiters for a preacher, and married her
right there. One of my girls acted as maid of honor, so I
learned all the details. New Orleans talked of nothing else
for days." She bobbed her head. "It's no wonder Emile
comes to New Orleans less often. Men make fun of him
for having a mother younger than he."

They chatted for almost an hour. Then Madame Celine
began pulling on her gloves.

'But you're not going?' Zelma asked her. "I expected
you to spend the night at least."

"Oh, no, no, I cannot, *cherie,*" Madame Celine told her.

"But it's such a long ride. You must rest. . . ."

"No, *cherie.* There is no time for rest. I can rest after
our business is paying us profits." Determined not to be
detained, she rose and reached for her parasol. "I shall
keep you informed," she said as Zelma saw her out onto
the porch. "Who knows? This investment of yours may
make both of us very rich women." She called to Pierrot,
who rose reluctantly and came forward expecting her to
bid him farewell. "You won't be staying with Madame
Granville," she told him happily. "Madame Granville has
most graciously saved me from ruin without taking you
away from me."

Pierrot, unable to express himself in words, waved his
arms and began to dance about the two women as they
moved toward the carriage.

"Enough," Madame Celine told him, although his an-
tics obviously pleased her. "Stop being the buffoon. There's
a gift for Madame Granville under my seat. Get it, please."
Pierrot drew a box from beneath the seat, handed it to
Madame Celine, who passed it on to Zelma. "Something I
very much want you to have," she said as she kissed
Zelma's cheek. Pierrot helped her into the carriage, and
the coachman's whip snapped above the horse's heads.
"Adieu, adieu!" Madame Celine called, and she waved
until the carriage crossed the bridge and was hurrying
away toward New Orleans.

Zelma opened the package when she returned to the
house. Inside, she found the exquisite white lace shawl
she had admired those many years ago at Madame Ce-

line's, the shawl the Frenchwoman had told her she would be buried in.

When Dester learned of Madame's Celine's visit and Zelma's investment, he laughed until tears came out of his eyes.

Zona, drawn from the study, came to peer into the drawing room at her sister and brother-in-law. She saw Zelma white-faced and Dester laughing with more humor than she imagined him capable.

Zelma had begun to laugh also.

"Has everyone gone mad?" Zona cried. "What's happened? Tell me."

"Your sister," Dester laughed, "has just become part owner of a New Orleans brothel."

Zona's expression told them she found nothing humorous in such jesting.

CHAPTER FIFTEEN

In August of that year, the British sailed into Chesapeake Bay and landed four thousand soldiers to launch an attack on Washington. They took the capitol and burned the federal buildings. When news of the defeat spread to New Orleans and Dester picked it up from the rivermen, he traveled into the city and purchased additional rifles. Anticipating an attack, he saw that those slaves who were capable were trained in the use of firearms. He convinced Zelma this was necessary. He told her there might be a time when she would be thankful for their training.

That time came in early January.

Solomon was tracking deer and had been brought near the banks of the gulf. He crouched patiently in the heavy underbrush, waiting for the animals to reveal themselves by the snapping of a twig or the rustling of a branch. It was early morning, and a light mist was falling. The quiet was broken only by an occasional gull circling above the treetops. Unmoving, Solomon waited and daydreamed of Dolly, whom he had recently begun to court. He wanted marriage and a steady woman and perhaps a child or two. . . .

A movement through the tree limbs caught his attention and brought him back to the present. He raised his arm and carefully moved a branch for a better view. Coming out of a bank of fog offshore was the mast of a British ship. As he watched, a second ship appeared out of the fog. Both dropped anchor in the deep water offshore.

Solomon's heart began to race, his pulse pounded at his temples. He let the branch snap back into position and leaped to his feet. Startled, a buck and his doe, which had been standing less than fifteen feet away, bounded off through the thicket. Solomon ran in the opposite direction in equal panic.

He ran at an unfaltering pace, leaping over fallen logs and holes, and bounded across the bridge into the yard with his lungs ready to burst. Laying his rifle against the side of the porch, he staggered breathlessly to the signal bell. The pounding of blood against his eardrums almost drowned out the alarm. When the faces of the household slaves began to appear at the windows, he stopped ringing the bell and slumped down to the ground. He was only vaguely aware of his mistress and her sister appearing in the open doorway in their dressing gowns, or of Dolly running across the lawn toward him.

Dester came riding in from the fields at a gallop, Jingo close behind. He rode into the cluster of slaves, and they stepped back from Solomon.

"The British have dropped anchor in the gulf . . . two ships," Solomon told him, still breathless.

Dester glanced at Zelma. He reached down and pulled Solomon onto his horse behind him and shouting for Zelma to call the slaves in from the fields and arm them, rode off with Jingo to investigate Solomon's report.

Zelma found herself left with panicked slaves milling and screaming around her. She did her best to restore order, having to strike out numerous times to silence terrified screams. She finally managed to drive the household slaves into the house. She sent Clabe to bring the workers in from the fields and hurried inside to unlock the gun room.

Pale and sobbing, Zona stuck close to her heels. "We should hide! A bunch of armed slaves aren't going to hold off an attack! Please, Zelma! Let's run into the woods and hide!" she sobbed.

"No!" Zelma shouted.

"Oh, God! We'll be slaughtered like lambs!" She became more and more hysterical, until Zelma was forced to slap her across the face. Stunned into silence, Zona stared at her, hurt and trembling and choking with fright.

Zelma turned to Dolly. "Take my sister to my room and stay with her." Zona began sobbing anew. "Zona, please control yourself," Zelma said. "We're not going to be slaughtered. I doubt the British are interested in the plantation. They might not even come ashore." But Zelma knew her doubt was revealed in her voice despite her effort to prevent it. She impatiently waved Zona and Dolly away and began passing out ammunition to Bessie Lou and two girls, instructing them to separate it into small sacks of twenty rounds each.

When the slaves arrived from the fields, Zelma saw the panic in their faces, and it frightened her. Training to use a rifle was one thing but the using of it was another. Encouraging them as best she could, Zelma situated an armed slave at each downstairs window and sent the others to conceal themselves in the trees along the creek bank. She sent the women and children into the woods with two armed men to protect them and told them not to return until they heard the all-clear signal.

Then they waited.

Dester, Jingo, and Solomon peered out from behind cover of the underbrush. The bank of fog had begun to lift, and they could see the activity aboard the two British vessels.

"Soldiers," Dester observed.

As they watched, the crew began lowering the longboats.

"They're comin' ashore," Solomon murmured.

Dester nodded. "It looks as if the British are planning a surprise attack on New Orleans. They're probably landing soldiers to march in from behind the city and will sail into the harbor while our soldiers are holding them off." He turned away from the gulf and sat quietly thinking. Finally, he said, "The rivermen told me Andrew Jackson was in New Orleans with a small army. We've got to warn him."

"I'll go," Solomon volunteered.

Dester shook his head negatively. "You're a crack shot with a rifle," he said. "I'll need you at Plantation Bend."

He turned to Jingo, and the loyal Negro nodded his understanding. "Go then," Dester told him. "Take both horses. One will never make the ride without collapsing. Tell Jackson what we've seen here. He'll know what must be done." He patted the Negro on the shoulder and wished him God's speed.

"Soldiers are loadin' into the boats," Solomon announced.

Dester rose from the embankment. He knew there would be no hope of the soldiers bypassing his plantation. To reach the road to New Orleans, they'd have to emerge from the underbrush across from Plantation Bend. He watched Jingo ride away with his favorite stallion in tow.

"Let's go," he told Solomon. He glanced over his shoulder and saw the longboats moving away from the ships. "At a run!"

When they neared the house, Zelma came out onto the porch. She had her hair tied away from her face with a kerchief and was holding a rifle, an ammunition sack slung over her shoulder. On either side of her, rifle barrels protruded from the windows. Her brow was drawn with concern.

"They're coming ashore," Dester told her gravely. "I don't see any way of avoiding attack on the plantation."

Zelma nodded her understanding. "Every man you trained has been armed and given twenty rounds of ammunition," she told him. "I sent some into the trees along the creek bank. The others are inside the house."

He reached for the rifle she carried. He did not know Solomon had long ago trained her in its use. He thought it was meant for him. Zelma surrendered it reluctantly, slipping the ammunition sack from her shoulder.

"Except for the house slaves, I sent the women and children into the woods," she said as she followed him back into the house.

Clabe, his eyes wide with excitement, was crouched at a front window beside one of the armed slaves. He came running to his father. "May I fire a rifle, Papa? Please!"

Dester nodded his approval, and Zelma paled.

"No!" she cried. "He's just a boy!" She reached for her son to draw him protectively to her, but he evaded her grasp.

"I'm not a boy!" he cried defiantly. "Papa taught me the rifle! I'm not a boy!"

She glanced pleadingly at Dester, but she saw that he was not going to deny their son on her account. An image of her first son's burial flashed before her eyes, and she began to tremble. She watched Dester load and pass a rifle to Clabe, and she bit her lower lip to keep from crying out her objection.

Clabe ran to the window where Solomon had positioned himself and crouched down beside him, emulating the slave's stance and fixing his gaze on the underbrush across the creek where the enemy was expected to emerge.

Zelma grabbed Dester's arm. "If anything happens to him, I'll never forgive you!" she whispered vehemently.

He removed her hand from his arm without speaking and moved away to give last-minute instructions to the slaves.

Zelma went into the kitchen and saw all the household slaves crouched along the walls except for Bessie Lou. The old woman was busy at the stove setting pots of water to boil. The calm attention she paid to her task was belied only by the frightened expression in her eyes.

"We'll need bandages," Bessie Lou told Zelma matter-of-factly. "I'll have the girls tear some of the linen into strips."

"Perhaps we should wait," Zelma said. "Maybe there won't be a need ... maybe. ..."

"Can't be any fightin' without someone bein' hurt," Bessie Lou said. She lifted the round plate from the stove top and shoved additional wood onto the flame. She glanced at Zelma, and her expression became firm. "Don't go breakin' down in front of them," she whispered, indicating the terrified girls crouched along the walls. "It'll be bad enough controllin' them once the firin' starts. If they see you're not afraid, it might shame them into keepin' their wits about them."

Zelma steadied herself. "Clabe's at one of the win-

dows!" she told Bessie Lou. "Dester wouldn't deny him
using a rifle!" She turned away so the girls couldn't see
the tears of concern welling up in her eyes.

Bessie Lou opened her mouth to speak, thought better
of it, and went about her chores. She left the stove and
went into the back room and returned with a stack of
freshly washed linen. She dropped them onto the harvest
table and called to the girls to gather around her. Then
she began instructing them in tearing the linen into strips
for bandages.

Glancing up at her mistress, she asked, "You want to
help us?"

But Zelma had other ideas of how to keep her mind
off her fears. "No. I'll help with the ammunition," she
said, leaving the kitchen.

She hauled the crate of ammunition from the gun room
and dragged it across the entryway and into the drawing
room, where both Dester and Clabe had positioned themselves. Her draperies had been torn from the windows and
lay in a heap before the great fireplace. Chairs and tables
had been pushed aside. One of her prized porcelain
figurines lay shattered on the edge of the carpet. She began
sorting the ammunition into sacks in the event additional
rounds were needed after the attack began.

"There they are!" she heard Clabe shout.

Zelma ran to crouch beside Dester, who was staring
out beyond the creek. At first, she saw nothing. Then a
glimpse of red showed through the green underbrush.
"There are so many!" she cried when the redcoats began
emerging onto the road.

"Get back out of the line of fire," Dester told her. To
the slaves, he said, "Don't shoot until they start across the
bridge. If they're beyond the bridge, you'll be wasting
your ammunition." He raised his rifle to his shoulder and
checked the sights.

Zelma crept back away from the window and stationed
herself in the "v" of the fireplace and wall where she
was protected but could still keep Dester and Clabe in
sight. She noted Solomon glancing in her direction. He
smiled encouragement, and she managed a weak smile

in return. Reading her concern, the Negro tapped Clabe's shoulder and motioned for him to keep himself more protected by the window frame.

"Damnit!" Dester cried.

The first shot had been fired by one of the slaves hidden along the creek bank. He had hoped he had taught them enough about tactics for them to wait until the British were either on or over the bridge so they'd be caught in the crossfire.

"Too anxious," Solomon mumbled, and he cursed beneath his breath.

Zelma saw the sweat begin to bead on Clabe's forehead. He impatiently wiped one hand on his trouser leg and returned it to grip his rifle tightly, waiting for his father's signal to begin firing.

The explosion of rifle fire began and increased until Zelma covered her ears with her hands.

"Now!" she heard Dester shout, and the drawing room became a den of noise.

The smell of gunpowder filled the room. One of the windows was struck and glass shattered across the floor. Even above the noise, Zelma could hear Zona's screaming from upstairs. She hoped Dolly had enough sense to keep her away from the windows. Creeping out from against the fireplace bricks, Zelma dragged the ammunition behind her, crawling from one man to another and depositing additional rounds within easy reach. She stopped behind Clabe and peered over his shoulder.

The British were in the yard, using the trees and shrubs to conceal themselves. She saw flashes from the metal buttons of their uniforms, from their rifles. As they fired their guns, small clouds of gray smoke materialized in the air and were gobbled up by the gulf breeze. A soldier's body lay sprawled in her flower bed, another's dangled from the bridge railing. A wounded slave she recognized as Freddie, the blacksmith, shirtless and with redness spreading along his black torso, was trying to crawl into the safety of the cattails lining the creek bank.

Zelma spun about as a piercing scream filled the drawing room. The slave beside Dester had fallen back from

the window, clutching at his face. He writhed on the floor
in agony. She crawled to him, but he was dead before
she reached him. She pulled his hands away from his
face, but his nose and half his face had been blown away,
and she could not tell who he was. Sickness rose up inside her stomach. She turned away and vomited.

"You're wasting your shots!" Dester bellowed angrily
at the slaves. "Take aim, damnit! Take aim!" Panic and
the fear of defeat had crept into his voice.

Zelma heard the rifle balls zipping above her head.
All the glass of the windows had been shattered. She had
crawled through some of the splinters, and they had torn
through the fabric of her skirt and slashed her knees. The
air was now heavy with gunpowder and chips of wood
torn from the paneling.

"Solomon! Get around to the side of the house! Hurry!
The study! The bastards are. . . ." Dester's words were
cut off by a volley of explosions.

Solomon, motioning another slave to take his place
beside Clabe, scampered across the drawing room and
through the door. When Zelma glanced up, she saw Clabe
following Solomon. She yelled at him to stay behind, but
he did not hear her or he deliberately disobeyed. He
vanished into the entryway.

Picking up the dead slave's rifle, Zelma followed.

Two slaves lay sprawled on the entryway floor. She
did not take time to see if they were dead. She reached
the open door of the study and peered inside. Solomon
and Clabe were crouched side by side at a far window,
firing into the yard.

Again Zelma could hear her sister's hysterical screaming. She glanced at the stairs, calculated her chances of
reaching the second-floor landing, and then, hoisting her
skirts in one hand and clutching the rifle in the other, she
took the steps two at a time.

Zona and Dolly were in the middle of the bed, clinging
to one another in their terror. The window had been
shattered and the thin curtains were billowing into the
room.

Zelma went to the two women. Pulling them apart,

she grabbed her sister by the shoulders and shook her roughly. "Stop it! Stop it!" she shouted.

Remembering Zelma's previous slap, Zona's screams turned to whimpering. She reached out for Dolly as if expecting the young slave girl to protect her from her sister as well as the fate she anticipated at the hands of the British. But Dolly, wide-eyed, backed against the wall and remained pressed there as if caught in the flowery grips of the wallpaper.

Zelma pulled Zona to her feet and forced her to sit on the floor behind the bed and away from the window. She motioned the mute-frightened Dolly to join her sister. "Keep her quiet even if you have to gag her!" she instructed.

Turning, Zelma was about to leave the room when she heard a scraping noise just outside her window. She stepped against the wall and moved quietly toward the frame.

The red-sleeved arm of a British soldier was just appearing over the edge of the porch roof. He had somehow managed to evade the rifles of the slaves below and had used the moonflower vine to hoist himself up the porch columns.

Zelma moved back to the bed and crouched beside Zona and Dolly. She aimed the rifle over the mattress and waited.

"I told you we should have hidden in the woods!" Zona cried. "Oh, God! We'll all be . . ."

"Shut up! Damnit! Shut up!" Zelma told her through clinched teeth and nodded toward the window. The soldier's shadow had appeared across the bottom of the curtains.

Zona, seeing the shadow, choked back her hysteria, and a fright so complete seized her that she felt almost in a state of forced calmness. The fate she had anticipated was upon them. Only Zelma and her rifle stood between them and death. They were doomed!

Zelma drew back the rifle hammer.

The soldier moved the curtains aside with the barrel

of his rifle and peered inside. He was young. His eyes were wide, alert, and cautious.

Oh, Lord! she thought. *If only I could scream for him to go away! If only——!* She felt Zona and Dolly stiffen beside her and saw the young soldier put one leg through the window into the room.

She willed her hand to be steady and gently squeezed the trigger.

Her rifle ball caught the soldier in the chest just as he was straightening up. With a cry of astonishment and pain, the impact propelled him backward. He went through the window and crashed onto the porch roof.

Zelma avoided Zona's and Dolly's surprised gazes and fought the renewed sickness rising up from the pit of her stomach. She knew if she showed her true feelings their hysteria would return. She choked down the bile in her throat and crept to the window. The soldier lay sprawled on his back, an arm and leg twisted beneath him, giving him the appearance of a cast-off straw doll. Beyond the porch roof, the British were edging closer to the house. She dropped to one knee as Solomon had taught her, and fired.

Below in the kitchen, Bessie Lou stood at the stove. The iron was beginning to glow red and didn't need more wood, but she added more for something to do. She had taken the iron plate off the top when one of the girls at the harvest table screamed. Spinning around, she saw the British soldier through the glass of the back door. He had peered inside and seen only the slave women. Confident, he had lowered his rifle and was reaching for the doorknob.

Bessie Lou drew back her arm and flung the stick of stove wood.

It shattered the glass in the surprised soldier's face. He fell back screaming onto the floor of the back porch. His screams were silenced by one of the girls who ran from the table and through the shattered door before Bessie Lou could stop her. She seized the soldier's rifle and brought the butt down against his head. The impact sounded like a melon being dropped to the floor.

The girl stared at the soldier and the bloody butt of his rifle. Then, looking back at Bessie Lou, she cried, "There's one who'll not hurt any. . . ." A rifle ball tearing into her back silenced her forever. Like a puppet without a spine, she crumpled onto the soldier she'd killed.

Bessie Lou, screaming for the girls to help her, up-ended the long harvest table. They dragged it in front of the door and used the heavy chopping block to wedge it there. "Keep 'way from the windows," she warned. She pulled down the rack of butcher knives and selected the most lethal for herself. *I never thought I'd die anywhere but my bed,* she thought. She placed her free hand over her chest to quiet her racing heart. She wasn't aware that her lips were moving, that she was speaking, but the girls heard her and echoed her words: "Lord, though I walk through the valley of the shadow of death. . . ."

Solomon heard the British signal retreat and saw the soldiers begin to fall back from the yard to the bridge. "I don't understand," he told Clabe. "They had us. They had us good. Why'd they retreat . . ." he scratched his head thoughtfully . . . "unless they was afraid of losin' more men they need at New Orleans?"

Not questioning the reason, Clabe shouted, "We won! We won!" He dashed out of the study to collide with his mother, who was just coming down the staircase. The sense of manhood he had felt during the battle crumpled as he saw his mother's blood-soaked skirt and haggard expression. He stared at her speechless, suddenly feeling helpless and stricken.

Zelma drew him into her arms. "I'm all right," she assured him. She began to cry with gratitude that he had not been injured or killed. She was crushing him against her, saying, "My big man. I'm so proud of you, so proud," when she became aware of Solomon standing in the drawing room doorway.

The Negro had a strange expression on his face that registered terror in her heart she had not known during the attack.

She pushed Clabe away from her and moved to the

drawing room door. Dester was slumped against the
windowsill, a pool of blood collecting about his knees.

Her anguished scream tore through the house. Everyone came running into the entryway.

One of the slaves went to Dester, bent over him, and
lay his hand on his chest. "He ain't dead, mistress!" he
shouted. "He ain't dead!"

But within the hour, Dester Granville died of his wound
without gaining consciousness. Bessie Lou and Dolly
washed him, dressed him in his finest Sunday suit, and
had him laid out on the entryway so the slaves could file
through and pay their final respects to their master.

The British siege of Plantation Bend had claimed the
master and eleven slaves.

It wasn't for three days, when Jingo returned, that
news of the Battle of New Orleans was known. The British
had attacked with ten thousand men, but Andrew Jackson
had defeated them with half that number. The futility of
the battle and the incident that had cost her her husband
was never known to Zelma—the War with England had
already ended and the Treaty of Ghent had been signed;
but the news of peace had not reached either side before
the battle.

When Zelma returned from burying Dester beside her
first son in the hilltop cemetery, she locked herself in her
room and refused to open the door to anyone.

CHAPTER SIXTEEN

WHEN BY THE third morning Zelma still had not unlocked her door, Bessie Lou, who had not managed the stairs in a long while, sent Dolly to fetch two of the strongest field hands. When they came, she was waiting at the foot of the staircase and instructed them to deposit her bulk on the second-floor landing. Laughing, they picked her up and deposited her outside their mistress's door.

Bessie Lou knocked firmly and demanded to be let in.

"Go away! Leave me be!" Zelma cried.

Bessie Lou turned to the two muscular slaves. "Knock the door down," she told them.

The two Negroes looked at one another in dismay, not knowing if they dared obey.

"Knock it down!" Bessie Lou repeated sternly.

Still, they hesitated.

"Go on! Do as I say! Do you want your mistress to die in there? If anyone'll be beaten, it'll be me," she assured them.

The two slaves nodded. They struck the door with their shoulders at the same moment, hitting it with such force it was completely torn from its hinges and sent flying into Zelma's room. Bessie Lou stepped through the open frame.

Startled into a bolt upright position on the bed, Zelma sat staring at the severed door. She glared at Bessie Lou and fell back against her pillows. "I'll have you flogged for this," she said weakly.

"Not until I've had my say," Bessie Lou told her. She moved to the bed and sat down on the edge of the mattress. She looked at the dark circles about her mistress's

191

eyes and shook her head in sympathy. "You've got to
eat," she said. "Ain't nothin' goin' to be accomplished by
your starvin' yourself."

"I don't want to eat," Zelma mumbled. "I just want to
be left alone!"

"I can't do that," Bessie Lou told her. "You've got
more than yourself to think about now. This plantation's
your responsibility."

Zelma turned her head away. "I've given this land too
much already," she wept. "My son! My husband! I won't
give any more!"

Grabbing Zelma by the shoulders, Bessie Lou pulled
her upright, her old eyes blazing with anger, and shook
her violently. "You listen to me," she said. "This plantation was the master's dream—for you and his children
and their children. If you let it crumble now, you're
shamin' his memory. You've gotta put aside your grief,
child."

"Don't tell me my duty!" Zelma cried. She tried to
shake herself free, but Bessie Lou's grip was too strong
for her.

"You'll listen 'cause you know I'm right," Bessie Lou
persisted. "You can't let your son's future and your husband's dream be buried in that grave with him, child.
You'd never forgive yourself. You'd . . ."

She broke off speaking when Zelma threw herself into
her arms, buried her face in her bosom, and began sobbing
without control. Her anger at her mistress waned. Fighting
to hold back her own tears, she cuddled and rocked Zelma
as she had done when her mistress had been a child. "Let
it all out," she whispered. "Let all the pain out."

Zona and Clabe appeared in the doorway, but Bessie
Lou motioned them away. She waited until Zelma's weeping subsided and then gently persuaded her back against
the pillows.

"Your people are frightened," she told Zelma. "They're
whisperin' that Plantation Bend'll be sold to Faviere and
them with it 'cause the master's death took the spirit out
of you. There's talk of runnin' away rather than be sold
to that French devil. Jingo ain't goin' to be able to keep

order much longer. Unless you pull yourself together and show them it ain't so, you won't have enough slaves to work the fields."

Zelma dried her tears on the corner of the linen. "What can I do?" she asked helplessly. "I'm only a woman. A woman can't possibly run this plantation."

Bessie Lou took her mistress's hand and patted it affectionately. "Remember when your friend Madame Celine came to you with a problem? You told her she must do as a man would do? That's what you must do now, child. The slaves respect you, and there's Jingo to help, but you've gotta take charge. You've gotta keep this plantation together until your son is old enough to claim his birthright." She released Zelma's hand and got laboriously to her feet. "That's what the master would expect of you," she said, "and that's what you must do."

Slowly, weakly Zelma made her way downstairs to join Clabe and her sister for breakfast. She avoided glancing at the walls where the splintered paneling would remind her of Dester's death, and she refused to go into the drawing room even though Bessie Lou assured her it had been put back in order. She ate without conversation, scarcely tasting her food.

She returned to her room and then, in the afternoon, she dressed for riding. Meeting her sister on the stairs, she asked where Clabe had gone. She knew Zona was full of questions about their future, what would they do? would they return to Savannah? and she was grateful she held them for another time.

"Clabe is probably with his friend in the slave quarter," Zona told her. "Do you want me to send for him?"

"No. I'll go for him myself," she said. "Bessie Lou told me our people need to see me." She instructed Dolly to find Solomon and have two horses saddled, and then she left the house.

Clabe was in the dirt yard before the slave shacks. She called his name several times before he looked up. Some of the women came to their doors and peered out at her; she nodded in their general direction.

Clabe came running to her and stood kicking the toe of his boot in the dirt, not knowing how to express the grief they shared over his father's death.

Dizzied from the heat and her three days of fasting, Zelma moved to one of the benches beneath the trees and sat down. Clabe sat beside her, and she took his hand. "We've a great responsibility ahead of us," she said quietly, and he nodded without fully understanding. *He's so young to have his youth snatched away,* she thought. Gradually, she decided. She would give him the burden of responsibility a little at a time until he was older. Until then, the strength would have to come from her. "I thought we would ride out to the fields," she told him.

"Like Father and I did," he murmured, and she recognized the pain in his voice evoked by the memory.

"Yes, like you and your father did," she told him. "Our people need to see us."

"Why?"

"Well, because . . . because it's our duty to them," she answered. "It's up to us to show them things have not changed."

Clabe looked at her thoughtfully for several moments. "But they have, haven't they?" he asked pointedly. "Will you sell Plantation Bend to Faviere?"

"No, I promise you I shall not," she assured him. "Even if it had to be sold, I'd never sell it to your father's enemy." Not wanting to pursue the subject further, she turned her attention to Clabe's friend, who had moved away to one of the shacks and was sitting in the doorway watching them. It suddenly struck her that the boy was a mulatto. "What's your friend's name?" she asked.

"Aaron," Clabe answered.

"I don't remember a. . . ." She waved for the boy to come to her, but he hung back as if frightened. "I'd like to talk to your friend," she told Clabe. "See if you can coax him to me."

"He's afraid," Clabe told her.

"Of me? Why ever would he be?"

Shrugging his shoulders, Clabe walked over to the shack,

stood talking to his friend for a minute, and then returned with him in tow.

The boy bobbed his head stiffly in the gesture of a bow. He was, Zelma judged, about her son's age, although slightly shorter and thin of frame. His coloring was similar to Madame Celine's Pierrot, what she called *café au lait*. He had large, almond eyes and finely chiseled features. His fear of her was obvious in his expression and the manner in which he stood before her ready to sprint into a run.

"You have no reason to be frightened of me, Aaron," she told him quietly.

The boy lowered his gaze and stared uncomfortably at his bare feet.

"Who's boy are you?" she asked. When he didn't answer, she asked teasingly, "Don't you know your mother's name, Aaron?"

"No'm," the boy mumbled.

Zelma concealed her shock. "Then who takes care of you?"

"Miz Ruth and Miz Naome taken care of me long as I can remember," Aaron answered.

"But surely Ruth and Naome have told you your mother's name," Zelma pressed.

"No'm."

"Nor your father's?"

"No'm."

Zelma stared at the boy, confused. To her knowledge, there had been no bastards born at Plantation Bend— and certainly no *mulatto* bastards. The only white men in the area were Claude and Emile Faviere and Sam Cole. An occasional riverboat captain—unless one of the rivermen had crept ashore against orders while his flatboat was tied up at the dock. But then, she remembered, the dock had not yet been built when the boy was born.

Solomon came around the side of the hill, leading two horses. Aaron leaped at the excuse to escape the steady gaze of his mistress and ran to pat the two mares.

Zelma and Clabe rode through the fields. Clabe sat stiffly in his saddle not knowing what was expected of him, while his mother nodded and spoke to their people as if the tragedy of her husband's death no longer gnawed at her insides.

Upon seeing his mistress and young master in the fields, Jingo felt a stirring of pride. He knew what each smile, each friendly word of assurance demanded of her. The effect upon the slaves was as he had hoped. They ceased their grumbling and whispering and went back to their work with renewed dedication.

As they rode back to the house, Zelma turned to Clabe and asked, "Do you remember most of what your father taught you?"

Clabe nodded that he did.

"Then you must make use of what you learned," she told him, "and learn even more from Jingo. You are the master of Plantation Bend now. Together we must finish what your father began. One day this must be the biggest plantation in all of Louisiana."

"Does that mean I'll have longer classes with Aunt Zona?" he asked.

"No," Zelma told him. "Your classes with your Aunt Zona have come to an end. You will spend that time with Jingo in the future." Looking ahead, she added, "Perhaps in a couple of years, you'll go to New Orleans for a more formal business education."

She noted that the prospect did not seem to excite him.

"May Aaron come with me?" he asked.

"Perhaps," she answered.

That night as she was retiring, Zelma asked Dolly what they did with the clothes her son outgrew.

"Packed away so they'll be ready if there's another son," the girl answered and bit her lip at the blunder.

"They'll be no other son," Zelma said quietly. "Tomorrow, I want you to distribute Clabe's outgrown clothes to the boys of our people. See that some of the nicer ones are given to the boy Aaron." Then suddenly it became clear as she remembered Matilda. "He's Matilda's son, isn't he?" she asked.

Dolly nodded.

"And his father?"

Zelma learned the truth from Dolly's startled expression.

After the mistress and Clabe rode away, Aaron wandered back to Naome's stoop and sat down. He felt heavy in the chest and weak in the knees. He'd known it was bound to come someday, his meeting Mistress Granville, but he had expected it to be different. It was his fault, his fear and shyness, that had made the meeting go badly.

His greatest surprise upon meeting Mistress Granville was her curiosity about his mother. Until today, he had thought that something limited only to himself. Glancing over his shoulder at Naome, who was sweeping the floor of her shack, he asked, "Miz Naome, where'd I come from?"

"You'ze come from an egg, that's where, boy," she said and then began singing as if his question had not been important.

It was always the same when he questioned any of the slaves—some silly answer that made no sense and made him feel as if they were laughing at him. "I mean how'd I come to Plantation Bend?" he persisted.

The old woman didn't interrupt her sweeping, but at least she abandoned her song to answer. "One of the men folks found ye," she said. "He kicked over this rock, and there ye was as pretty as ye please. Brought ye back to me, he did, and I raised ye best I could, and that's how ye came to Plantation Bend, and I don't wanta hear no more questions." She stopped sweeping to catch her breath, sighed, and went on with her cleaning and singing.

Grumbling, Aaron left the stoop and wandered around behind the shacks to the wood. He found his favorite tree, where he spent so much of his time, and shimmied up the trunk to curl up in the triple fork that resembled a giant mother shell.

It had been here at the tree that he had always imagined his meeting with the mistress would take place. She'd come wandering along below and glance up and see his legs dangling between the forks of the branches. Laughing, she'd tell him he reminded her of a young bird that had

outgrown its nest and was afraid to fly. "Come down,"
she'd call, and he'd scamper down the trunk and bow to
her. Her blue eyes would widen with recognition. She'd
draw him to her, smothering him with kisses, and tell him
he was her long lost son. She'd promise to love him best,
more than Clabe, from that day on—just like the story
of the prodigal son in Miz Naome's Book.

Now that their meeting had taken place and did not
resemble his daydream, Aaron knew he would have to
abandon it, although it had always given him such pleasure. The answer to his identity did not lay with the
mistress. He'd have to look elsewhere for answers. Maybe
one day, he thought, he'd find one of the older slaves in
a talkative mood, perhaps their tongue loosen by forbidden whiskey. Then he'd ply them with questions. Why
were his parents never spoken of? Why was his skin so
much lighter than theirs? Why had he never been allowed
to go near the big house? Why was he ordered to stay
out of the mistress's sight? Why?

He thought again of Mistress Granville and how he had
often hidden and watched her in the yard of the big house,
her wide-brimmed hat protecting the whiteness of her
skin against the darkening rays of the sun. Without the hat,
her skin would have soon been the color of his. She, too,
would have been trapped, an outsider caught between
the two peoples of the plantation.

Without willing it, his old daydream returned. Only
this time there was a difference. When it reached the point
where he scampered down the tree to bow to the mistress,
she stared at him with her cold, blue eyes and asked,
"Who's boy are you?" She laughed at his hurt expression,
and her image popped like a bubble in his mind.

Aaron sat up so abruptly he almost slipped out of the
fork of the tree. Shaken, he realized he had been sleeping,
dreaming—and his cheeks were now covered with tears.

CHAPTER SEVENTEEN

IT WAS AN early morning in spring.

Zelma had awakened very early and had ridden into the fields to talk to Jingo about that day's flatboat shipment to New Orleans. When she returned to the house, she saw Zona slip from the front door and run across the yard to meet her at the hitching post.

"Emile Faviere's inside," she announced with excitement. "He's been waiting for almost an hour."

"Emile," Zelma murmured, her mind racing back in time to conjure his image. "Whatever would bring him calling after all these years?"

"He's so charming," Zona whispered, "and so handsome."

"That he *was*," Zelma recalled. She absently patted her hair, now streaked with gray along the temples, as she crossed the yard and entered the house. She discarded her hat and gloves and riding crop on the entryway bench and threw open the drawing room doors.

Emile, standing at the window, had apparently been watching as she had ridden up and stood talking to Zona. He turned, smiling, and hastened across the room. He took her hand, brushed his lips against the top, and held it longer than gallantry required. "Zelma," he spoke her name scarcely above a whisper, and then repeated it twice more. He released her hand at her gentle urging. "You haven't changed," he told her. "You're as lovely as I have always remembered."

The compliment brought an involuntary laugh from Zelma. "You haven't changed either, Emile. You're still the chivalrous Frenchman who so charmed me in New Orleans so long ago."

The physical change in him astonished her. To have remembered him so young, his face without the fine wrinkles about his eyes and the gray flecking his black hair, and then to suddenly be confronted by him and see the flaws of age, the slight paunch visible under his coat, the bent of his shoulders, the liver spots on his hands. She felt as if she had witnessed the very quick aging of a young acquaintance. Not that he had not retained his handsomeness, he had. But physically he did not seem the same man she remembered. Even his eyes, which had always attracted her with their expression of zest, seemed dulled by time.

"I see you've been served coffee," she said and crossed to the sofa. She sat down and felt the sides of the pot. It was still warm. She poured herself a cup, sipped, and savored the rich flavor. "I hope my sister properly entertained you while you were waiting."

"She did," Emile assured her. "And in my own language."

Suspecting Zona was listening outside the doors, Zelma said laughingly, "French with a southern accent. I'm sure you told her it was most charming and didn't correct her grammar."

Emile detected the hint of a biting tone behind her words, but chose to ignore it. He moved to the sofa and indicated he'd like permission to sit beside her.

"By all means," she told him.

He sat on the very edge, resting his right elbow on his knee, and continued to stare at her.

Zelma felt discomfort beneath his gaze. Was he considering the marks of time on her face as she had on his? No, not Emile. His gallantry would forbid it. She averted her gaze and continued sipping her coffee.

"I would have called sooner," he said, "but I thought it only proper to wait until you had shed your mourning attire."

"I did that after three days," she said coolly. "A woman

with a plantation to run can't be hampered by traditional mourning garments."

"Yes, of course. I understand."

They lapsed into an awkward silence.

Emile was first to speak, asking, "Have you heard from the flamboyant Madame Celine?"

"We correspond," Zelma answered and offered no further information about the woman through whom they had met.

"I seldom get into New Orleans anymore."

"So she told me."

"It isn't the same as before," he said. "As when we first met."

She realized there was nothing she could politely do to prevent him from launching into a recounting of those days. She listened quietly as he recalled Señor Ponce and setting fire to his house. He finished by saying, "You were so magnificent, so naive." He discreetly lowered his eyes. "We, you and I . . . we almost— Do you ever reminisce about those days, Zelma? Think of what might have been had you been less devoted to your . . . ?"

"No," she said to stop him, hoping Zona had abandoned her eavesdropping. Of course, it was a lie. She had often wondered how her life would have been changed had she abandoned herself to an affair with Emile. But it had been a long time since she had considered this.

She set her empty cup aside and turned so she faced her visitor. "I'm no longer naive, Emile," she told him bluntly. "Why, after all these years of being my nearest neighbor, have you decided to come calling?"

Her straightforward question rattled him. He had come to Plantation Bend expecting to find the same Zelma he had known in New Orleans, but the woman beside him was no longer the flirtatious, gullible, and indecisive female he remembered. He had thought his task would be an easy one—reestablishing their acquaintance, a little charm and flattery, a brief courtship—she was, after all, a lonely widow left with the impossible task of the plantation. He had expected her to welcome his attentions, so had his father. The old man was counting on it, demanding it of him in exchange for his financial freedom.

"Zelma, I . . . I have always wanted to call on you. It's just that my father . . . your husband . . . because of their feud, my father forbade it."

"Have you never gone against your father's wishes?" she asked pointedly.

"Well, I. . . ." He changed position uncomfortably.

"Dear Emile," Zelma said, smiling. "I know exactly why you've come. I realized it the moment I entered the drawing room. You're here at your father's insistence, isn't that so?"

Emile stared at her and said nothing. He had paled, and beads of perspiration appeared on his forehead.

"Your father most likely said, 'Ah, the planter is dead, and you, Emile, you once knew the widow in New Orleans. Get yourself over to Plantation Bend, woo the Widow Granville, claim her hand in marriage, and her land will be mine.'" She paused, then went on, "Is that the way it was, Emile?"

A muscle at the corner of Emile's mouth began to twitch violently. "You don't think very highly of me, do you, Zelma?" he stammered. "I certainly didn't expect hostility, not from you."

"No, you expected a grief-stricken woman who would look on your sudden reappearance as a godsend," Zelma accused. "Her rescuer from loneliness and incapability of managing a large plantation. Perhaps that would have been me at one time," she said. "I am disappointed in you, Emile. There have been times in the past eleven years when I have had need of friendship. You were so close, and yet you waited until you'd something to gain from me before calling at Plantation Bend."

"I can still be your friend, Zelma," Emile pleaded.

"No. No, you cannot," Zelma told him. "I could not have a friend such as you. When you came here, you had agreed to this scheme of your father's. If I had been the woman you expected, you would have succeeded in gaining title to our land through marriage. What were you to have done then? Transfer ownership to your father?

Give my son the crumbs of Faviere charity? What kind of friend would attempt such a betrayal? No, we cannot be friends."

Suddenly unable to remain seated beside Emile, Zelma rose and walked to the window, where she stood staring out at the children of the slaves who were playing along the creek bank. "Claude Faviere will never gain ownership to Plantation Bend," she said quietly, "not while I'm alive."

She heard Emile rise, felt his eyes on her, but she did not turn.

"You may not believe me, but I'm glad," he told her. "I'm genuinely pleased he's lost this one thing he wanted most."

"And what have you lost by failing him, Emile?" Zelma asked.

"Nothing worse than usual," he answered. "Financial freedom. My release from bondage to my father. Perhaps my . . . manhood." The floorboards creaked with his weight as he crossed to the doors. He opened them, hesitated, glanced back at her over his shoulder. "I wish to God I had been different," he said. "We truly could have been friends, if not lovers. You're one hell of a woman, Zelma Granville."

Zelma remained at the window and watched him ride across the bridge. Instead of turning left toward his father's plantation, he took the road to New Orleans.

Two weeks later, a letter from Madame Celine informed her that Emile Faviere had been killed in a duel.

CHAPTER EIGHTEEN

WITH CLABE NO longer taking lessons and Zelma busy from sunrise to sunset with the operation of the plantation, Zona found herself hard-pressed to occupy her time. She became weary of plantation life and longed for the excitement and glamor of Washington. She wrote letters to several of her friends, discreetly inquiring if the scandal of her divorce had blown over. Only one bothered to answer, and she, abandoning discretion for blatant gossip, wrote of nothing except William Porter and his new wife, the parties she'd seen them attending, William's popularity brought about by a speech attacking President Madison's foreign policies, the new wife's charm and sophistication. Zona tore the letter into shreds and was too depressed to come down to dinner.

She began taking long walks alone. Finding a grassy knoll or secluded meadow, she would sit for hours reading books of poetry, especially enjoying and rereading *The Prisoner of Chillon* by Lord George Gordon Byron, the poet who had become the rage in England and was gaining popularity in America as well. If she wasn't reading, she lay gazing up at the clouds, dreaming of herself as a prisoner of circumstance who would soon escape the boredom of Plantation Bend. She tried her own hand at poetry but found she had no feel for meter or choice of words. She did write one short poem titled "The Divorce," which pleased her but also awakened all her old agonies.

"We'll go into New Orleans to the theater as soon as I can get away," Zelma kept promising her, but she knew that unless Zelma could combine business with pleasure they'd never make the trip.

One day when Zelma and Clabe left the house without even having breakfast with her, her depression reached its peak. She wandered aimlessly from room to room interrupting Bessie Lou and Dolly in their chores. She tried to nap, to sew, and finally, taking a dog-eared book of poetry from the study shelf, she left the house for her solitary trek through the woods.

It was a warm, humid day. She had worn a light muslin dress with lace at the throat and arms so she might feel the slightest cooling breeze. Unlike Zelma, who had abandoned womanly fashions because they hindered her work, Zona still preferred her skirts made with the full twelve yards of fabric. The full skirts often became awkward during her walks, catching on limbs of shrubs. This day, because her thoughts were elsewhere, she walked farther away from the house than she realized. She did not see the long runner of blackberry bush that reached out across her path until the thorns caught at her skirts. Startled so abruptly from her thoughts by the tugging, she spun around with alarm and entangled the fabric all the more. The book of poetry slipped from her hand, and the spine broke as it struck the ground.

She cried out. Then she reached down to disengage the briar from her billowing skirts, but only pricked her fingers, drawing blood. Each way she turned only ensnared her more. She cried out again in frustration, fought back her panic, and then forced herself to stand quietly and consider the puzzle of releasing herself without shredding her dress. Tht thought occurred to her that if she could manage the fastenings alone she could step out of her dress altogether and thereby make it easier to disengage herself from the thorns. She was alone in a secluded section of the woods, and there would be no one to see her in her slips and corset.

Persistent, she finally managed the fastenings behind her neck, pushed her dress down over her naked shoulders, and stepped out of it. The billowing skirt collapsed and lay caught in the briars like the castoff skin of some colorful reptile. She bent and methodically began to separate the fabric from the clinging thorns.

Some sound unfamiliar to the woods touched her
senses, and she froze, listening, a sense of danger causing the plaiting of fear along her spine. Her gaze swept
the surrounding trees and bushes. She spotted a squirrel
scampering along the bough of a nearby tree. A hawk
was circling above, its wings spread as it glided with the
air currents. There was nothing more. She attributed her
alarm to her frazzled nerves and continued disengaging
her skirt.

The next sound was easily identifiable—a man's amused
deep-throated laughter.

Zona sprang to her feet and turned.

A white man and three slaves had stepped from the
cover of the underbrush and stood watching her. Although she had never met him, she knew from listening
to the descriptions of Plantation Bend slaves that the
white man was Claude Faviere. His great mane of white
hair made mistaking him impossible.

Zona grabbed for her dress and pulled it up to cover
herself. The fabric, still caught in the thorns, ripped and
the dress pulled free. She stepped back, clutching it about
her.

"What have we here?" Faviere said mockingly. "I believe we've caught ourselves a wood nymph, and on my
property, too."

Zona choked back her fright and cried, "How long
have you been watching me?"

"Since before you caught your skirts," the Frenchman
answered and laughed at her expression.

"You are not a gentleman, sir!" she cried. "A gentleman would not have taken advantage of the situation by
spying on me!"

One of the Negroes, whose position of authority she
noted by the whip hanging from his belt, turned to the
laughing Frenchman and said, "She dares criticize your
manners—and on your own land."

Faviere's amusement faded. "You're right, Simon," he
said angrily, "but then what would you expect of someone from Plantation Bend?" His eyes narrowed as he

stared at the trembling Zona. "You're not the widow. Who are you?"

"Her . . . sister." Zona began struggling with the fabric of her dress, fumbling for the hem so she might draw it over her head. "Please, Monsieur Faviere, you and your slaves turn around so I might get into my dress." When he made no effort to do so, just continued staring at her, Zona repeated the request in French, hoping he would be impressed enough by her command of his language to comply.

The Frenchman only laughed at her. "She speaks French like a trollop from the Left Bank," he told the Negroes, and they joined in his laughter.

Zona flushed with indignation.

"Perhaps she *is* a trollop," Faviere went on, encouraged by her obvious anger. "Perhaps it runs in the family. Her sister, that grand Widow Granville, once lived with a keeper of whores in New Orleans."

"Who else 'ceptin' a whore'd marry a bastard like Dester Granville?" the Negro with the whip asked with a smirk.

"No one speak of my sister like that!" Zona raged. "Especially no nigger!"

The Negro's jaw stiffened. His hand went to his belt and clutched at his whip.

"Simon's got a murderous temper," the Frenchman told Zona. "He's quick to use the whip, that's what makes him a good overseer." He turned to the Negro. "But you've never whipped a white woman, have you, Simon?" he asked teasingly.

"No, sir."

"Still, we've got to do something about her, don't we? I mean, it isn't as if we haven't warned people from Plantation Bend to keep off my property." Eyes narrowing, he looked back at Zona, stroking the unruly growth of his beard as if trying to reach a decision.

Zona's fear pushed her anger aside. "I . . . I didn't realize . . . I wouldn't have . . . deliberately trespassed," she stammered.

"Do you think we should take her word for that and let her go?" Faviere asked his overseer.

The Negro didn't answer. He knew by the tone of the Frenchman's voice he was not expected to.

"No, I think not," Faviere said. "We've been too lenient as it is. Perhaps the Widow Granville won't be the stubborn fool her husband was. Perhaps she'll learn a lesson from her sister's mistake." All amusement and teasing had gone from his voice. He was entirely serious.

Panicked, Zona glanced over her shoulder in the direction from which she had come. She would never be capable of outrunning the Negroes. If she screamed, she was too far from Plantation Bend to be heard. She had no alternative except to brave it out against the despicable Faviere. "You wouldn't dare let him use that whip on me," she said, her voice quavering. "There wouldn't be a white man alive who wouldn't seek you out and vindicate me."

"No, not the the whip," Faviere agreed. "The whip would leave its marks."

"This has gone far enough!" Zona cried suddenly. "If you mean to terrify me, you've succeeded! You've had your sadistic amusement!"

But Faviere had turned to his overseer. Ignoring her, he said, "I'll leave you here with her. It's not for me to plant suggestions, but we did determine the Widow Granville and her sister were trollops, didn't we, Simon? A trollop's good for only one thing."

Winking at the Negro, he turned to walk back into the underbrush from which they had emerged only minutes before. "I'll be getting home," he said, "where my loving wife and daughter will swear I've been all day."

"Monsieur Faviere!" Zona cried. "You can't mean—! Monsieur Faviere! I beg of you—!"

The Frenchman pushed through the branches, and they snapped back into position behind him.

Zona saw the three Negroes begin to advance on her. Shrieking, she dropped the dress she had been holding against her body and, spinning about on her heels, broke into a run.

She had only gone a few yards before they reached her. Strong hands caught at her arms, her hair. Fingernails dug into her flesh as a hand was wedged inside her corset. The garment gave with a splitting sound. Pleading, she felt herself being lifted off the ground. Her slips were torn away. She wrestled one arm free and dug her fingernails into the nearest face. The overseer cried out, cursed, and struck her. Her senses reeled as pain mingled with her terror. She was aware of being thrown to the ground, of the pebbles and twigs cutting into the naked flesh of her back and buttocks. One of the Negroes held her arms, the other her legs.

"Oh, please don't!" she begged. "Dear God, don't do this!"

The overseer snarled instructions. Her legs were spread. He dropped between them on his knees and began unfastening the buttons on his trousers.

"Kill me instead!" Zona shrieked. "I'd rather be dead!" She twisted and bucked as he lowered himself over her. She whimpered, stunned, as he struck her again to still her. And as he stabbed savagely into her, she was mercifully claimed by a blackness that blotted out pain and terror.

Only Zelma's chest moved with her quick, anguished breathing. She sat alone in the study, her hands gripping the arms of the desk chair with force that caused her knuckles to whiten. Her lips were drawn tightly together, her eyes, unblinking, staring into the space of the room without seeing.

Upstairs, Zona had shrieked herself into exhaustion and was now sleeping. At her bedside, Dolly had been left weeping and muttering to herself like one who had taken leave of her senses. She had been instructed to call her mistress if Zona should awaken.

Bessie Lou appeared in the study doorway. Silently, she entered and moved about the room, lighting the lamps. She glanced at Zelma, could find no words to express her feelings, and crept quietly away.

They had been holding dinner, waiting for Zona, when

one of the boys had come running around the house as if being pursued by the devil. He had been too excited to speak, pointing and making a gurgling sound in his throat as he indicated the woods.

Zelma had followed him, frightened of whatever she might find. She had come upon Zona, huddled beneath the low-hanging branches of a willow tree, naked, bruised, clutching the shreds of her slip about her loins. Zona had been in shock, her eyes glazed, blood trickling down her chin from a cut on her lip.

Almost an hour later, after they had brought her to her room, washed her, and put her to bed, Zona began emerging from her shock-induced silence. First, there had been hysteria, then tears—and then the explanation. Then a renewed seizure of shrieking had eventually brought on exhaustion and sleep.

Shaken beyond tears, Zelma had come downstairs to the study to nurse her pity, her anger, her hatred alone. When she could think beyond her emotions, she considered what must be done.

Bessie Lou returned with a tray of food and coffee. Without being asked, she slipped into the chair across the desk from her mistress. "What'll you do?" she asked. "Will you send to New Orleans for the authorities?"

Zelma glanced up as if just becoming aware of the old slave's presence. "It would only be the same as before," she murmured. "Besides, you heard Zona say that bastard said his wife and daughter would swear he hadn't left the house all day. It would only be her word against his."

"But it was the black men who raped Miss Zona," Bessie Lou reminded her. "It'd be a white woman's word against three slaves."

"A freed black man," Zelma reminded her. "And Faviere would protect his overseer as well as himself."

"But somethin' has to be done," Bessie Lou protested. She began to rock back and forth in the chair, wringing her hands. "If somethin's not done, won't be a woman who'll sleep nights," she mumbled. "You know how the people talk about Faviere bein' a devil. Miss Zona's assault'll make that a real fact to them. If only the master was alive. He'd know what was to be done."

Zelma reached for the coffee pot and poured herself a cup of the strong liquid. "Something will be done," she assured Bessie Lou. "My sister's not going to be beaten and raped and go without being revenged." She sipped her coffee, her eyes above the rim of her cup returning to their fixed, unseeing stare.

It was late when Zelma climbed the stairs and went to her sister's room. She dismissed Dolly and took up a vigil beside Zona's bed. During the night when her sister tossed and cried out in her nightmares, Zelma held her, spoke to her gently, and soothed her back into a peaceful sleep.

The next morning, Zelma came downstairs early, told Dolly to forget her other duties and stay at Zona's bedside, and waved away Bessie Lou's insistence that she eat breakfast. She went into the gun room and loaded a rifle. Leaving the house by the side door, she crossed to the storage shed and emerged moments later with the wheelbarrow. She went inside again, came out with a rope, put the rope and her rifle into the wheelbarrow and moved away into the woods.

She returned that night, sat quietly, preoccupied through dinner. Then she went up to her room and slept for three hours before joining Zona.

The second and third days she repeated the same procedure.

News of their mistress's odd routine quickly spread from the household to the field slaves. They shook their heads and conversed in whispers, saying both their mistress and her sister had been pushed beyond mental endurance by the devil Faviere.

Clabe heard the rumors spreading among the slaves. Sitting across the table from his mother at supper, the possibility of her slipping into madness struck him like a blow in the chest. His appetite left him, and he sat staring at the food on his plate, wondering what he must do. When he decided he must speak to his mother as discreetly as possible about the rumors of her mental condition, he looked up and discovered she had already left the table.

The next morning when Zelma moved away from the house with the wheelbarrow, he waited until she was out of sight, and then followed her. He knew when they had crossed into Faviere property because his father's stakes with a now-faded piece of red cloth brought back memories of the day they had paced off the boundaries. He thought to call out to his mother but realized she was moving with deliberation and knew her destination.

Zelma rolled the wheelbarrow into a cover of the underbrush and proceeded more cautiously. When she heard the sound of the spring, water running over rocks, she looked about for her hiding place and slipped beneath the overhanging branches of a cluster of saplings. From inside, she could see the spring without being seen. She sat down in the matted grass and rested her rifle across her lap. Today would be the day, she felt instinctively. Since she had taken up the vigil, neither Simon, the Faviere overseer, nor any of the slaves had come to tend their still. But it was there, recently in use. She had found it with difficulty her first day, and soon, someone would come to care for it.

She glanced at the sky to determine the time. If no one arrived within the next hour, she would have a long wait until noon. She knew the overseer would not be free of his duties until then if he did not come in the morning. She settled down to wait.

The sun was shifting between the treetops, melting the dew from the ground and foliage as it spread its rays. The air was already heavy with moisture, promising another humid day.

She had been in her hiding place less than a quarter of an hour when she heard movement through the underbrush. She pulled herself erect, pulse racing, and ran her hand along the barrel of her rifle to the cold metal of the trigger guard. Quietly, she changed her position from sitting to crouching, never taking her eyes from the underbrush surrounding the clearing of the spring. The sound of movement became increasingly louder. Then she saw the flash of blue fabric through the wall of branches and leaves.

When the Faviere overseer emerged into the clearing, Zelma was holding her breath, her heartbeat pounding at her temples.

Today! she thought with satisfaction.

The overseer was wearing a faded blue shirt, open at the neck to reveal a mat of black hair on his chest, and shoved into the waistband of his trousers, he carried a pistol. His whip dangled from the right side of his belt. He was not so tall as she remembered him, but then that could have been due to the distance he stood away from her. After stepping into the clearing, he stopped, like some animal expecting a trap, and let his gaze sweep the surrounding foliage.

When his gaze moved toward where she hid, Zelma had a moment of panic. What if he detected some flash of coloring from her clothing as she had with him? But his gaze moved on uninterrupted until it had completed a full circle. His body seemed to relax. The hand that had rested on the handle of his pistol fell away to his side. He moved to the spring. Cupping his hands, he caught water in them and bent his head to drink.

It was then, while he could be caught by surprise, that Zelma sprang from concealment, her rifle raised, ready to fire.

The overseer spun toward her, his comprehension instantaneous. Eyes widening, he took a step backward, and the top of his boot disappeared beneath the surface of the pool. He held up his hands, palms toward her, as if they would ward off a deadly rifle ball. "No! Miss Granville, no! I was only . . . I was obeyin' orders, Miz Granville! Swear to God!"

Zelma did not need to speak. Her hatred for him was expressed in her eyes. Before he could plead with her further, she eased back the trigger. Just before the explosion, she shouted, "For my sister!"

The impact threw the overseer backward. He landed in the spring water pool with a loud splash. When he rose to the surface, his body turned slowly, until it came to rest, facedown.

Zelma moved to the pool's edge and stood staring down at the dead overseer. Blood reddened the water about his head and shoulders. Laying her rifle aside, she waded into the water, grabbed the fabric of his shirt, and tugged him onto the bank. She rolled over the body and saw that her shot had caught him at the base of the neck and killed him instantly. His eyes were open. She turned away from the vacant stare.

Going back to where she had hidden the wheelbarrow, she rolled it forward, tipped it beside the body, and bent down to push the overseer into its bed.

"Mama."

She cried out in terror, not hearing the word, only the sound of a voice, and fell back onto her haunches. "Clabe!"

The boy stood less than six feet away from her. He was extremely pale. "I . . . I followed you," he stammered, looking at the dead overseer, not at her.

"Clabe, you shouldn't have. . . ."

"Is he the one who attacked Aunt Zona?" the boy asked before she could complete her reprimand.

Zelma nodded.

The overseer's body had rolled against her. She placed her hands against his back and pushed it away.

Clabe, his color returning, came forward to help her. "Why're we doing this?" he asked after they had succeeded in getting the body into the wheelbarrow bed and then righting it. "Why don't we just leave him here?"

"Because I don't want his body found," Zelma answered.

Clabe looked puzzled. Still, he decided not to question her further. He grabbed the handles of the wheelbarrow and followed behind her as she led him farther into the woods.

He was sweating heavily when she finally stopped and motioned for him to set down the wheelbarrow.

"This is the edge of the swamp," Zelma told him. "We've circled around to the back of our own property."

She came back to the wheelbarrow, bent, and took the whip from the overseer's belt. "I'll need this," she said without explanation. She tugged the rope from beneath the body and told Clabe to bind it firmly to the wheelbarrow while she looked for stones.

Once loaded with stones, it took both of them to maneuver the wheelbarrow. They pushed it to the edge of the solid ground and gave it a final shove.

Zelma watched it sink, and the slime spread back over the surface.

Turning away, she picked up the overseer's whip and Clabe the rifle, and they walked back to Plantation Bend without speaking.

Solomon was at the house when they returned.

Zelma ordered him to saddle her horse.

Recognizing the whip in his mistress's hand, Solomon, in mute silence, hurried to the stables to obey. When he came back leading her horse, she was waiting at the hitching post, her arms resting about her son's shoulders.

"Please let me do this for you," Solomon said.

"Or me," Clabe said.

Zelma smiled at both of them. "It's something I must do myself," she told them quietly.

Solomon helped her into the saddle, and she rode away without glancing back.

When she approached the Faviere plantation house, Zelma saw the front door open. Faviere and two women appeared on the porch and stood watching her. Zelma did not take the opportunity to satisfy her curiosity about Faviere's wife and daughter. She fixed her gaze on the Frenchman and was only vaguely aware of the two women on either side of him.

As she reined up in front of the long porch, Faviere stepped forward.

Their eyes met and locked.

No words were needed.

Zelma flung the overseer's whip at the Frenchman's feet, and he stepped back as if it were some poisonous reptile. One of the women uttered a little cry of recognition.

Zelma turned her horse and rode home to Plantation
Bend.

Zona's mental condition improved learning the fate of
her attacker. Her lucid moments grew increasingly longer
until she was seldom caught staring into space with a
blank expression on her face. She dressed and came
downstairs to take her meals with Zelma and Clabe. In
the beginning, she remained quiet and ate with downcast
eyes, but they finally coaxed her into their conversations.
They could not, however, manage to bring a smile to her
lips no matter what the topic, no matter how extreme
their efforts.

She adopted certain eccentricities. She had all of her
fashionable dresses packed and stored and would wear
nothing but drab muslin prints with high necklines and
loose-fitting bodices. Her world was confined to the house
and the front porch, and if one of the male slaves happened to appear, she'd retire to her room and lock the
door until convinced he had gone. Fearing to be alone
for a moment, she had a cot moved into her room and
arranged for Dolly to sleep there.

Zelma thought these things would pass with time. Then
one night she awakened to find Zona sitting in the darkness beside her bed, her white dressing gown silhouetted
in the moonlight streaming through a part in the draperies.

"What is it, Zona?" Zelma asked.

Zona hesitated. When she finally spoke, her voice was
distant and oddly calm. "It's ironic, isn't it, Zelma? William divorced me because I couldn't have his children."

"You mustn't think of that now, dear," Zelma told her
patiently.

"Oh, but I must," Zona said scarcely above a whisper. "You see, Zelma, I'm pregnant."

CHAPTER NINETEEN

TIME AND EVENTS moved rapidly in the next months.

On a chill winter morning, Bessie Lou awakened and discovered she could not lift her head from her pillow. There was a curious numbness in her arms and legs and a dull, heavy pain in her chest. She heard the kitchen staff milling about beyond the door of her small room. She tried to call out to them but found she had no voice. Words formed in her mind, but her tongue would not form them or her lungs force up the needed air for utterance. She lay waiting, knowing the Lord was calling her. She felt no fear. She was old, tired, and had only clung to life these past few years out of a protectiveness of her mistress. She had seen what she had one-time told Jingo she wished before dying—she had seen her mistress mature into a strong-willed woman.

When Bessie Lou did not appear in the kitchen at her usual time, Dolly tapped lightly on her door and looked inside. She immediately sent one of the girls to awaken their mistress.

Zelma arrived in time to kiss the dying slave's cheeks. She took Bessie Lou's hardened, wrinkled hands in her own and held them, choking back her tears because she knew the old woman would not want them. She forced herself to talk about her future plans for the plantation and Clabe, as if Bessie Lou would be part of them.

Smiling crookedly, the old woman sighed with what seemed to be contentment and closed her eyes forever.

stole whiskey from the Faviere still and plied older slaves with his questions. That same night, after learning the identity of his parents, he vanished. Three days later, when Naome was about to report him as a runaway, he reappeared on her stoop, hungry and sullen. He avoided Clabe for several days but was finally seen again in the young master's company.

One day the two boys encountered a Seminole raiding party while hunting. If it had not been for Aaron's alertness and cunning, they would probably have been captured and killed. Saying he owed his life to his friend, Clabe insisted upon the ritual he had heard was a custom among the Indians. They cut their wrists, held them together to let the blood mingle, and became "blood" brothers.

Zelma traveled to New Orleans for a meeting of the planters. At first, they laughed at her, but in the end, she won their respect and was instrumental in obtaining an increase in the price of sugarcane. Sugar became Louisiana's most important crop. Planters from other states continued to emigrate. The *Louisiana Gazette* carried an article claiming New Orleans to now be the third largest city in America.

The night Zona's child was born, a boy with light-colored skin and Negro features, she tried to smother it with a pillow. The baby was taken to the slave quarter and given to Naome, who named him Jojo and loved him as if her own.

A few weeks later, Dolly appeared in the doorway looking extremely upset. When she had gone to Mistress Zona's room to awaken her, she had found the bed unslept in, a letter propped against the pillows. Dolly had never learned to read, but she had instinctively understood the letter's content. It was not difficult to determine with Mistress Zona's bureau and closets emptied.

Dolly had sent for the stable boy, and he had told her that Mistress Zona had awakened him during the middle of the night and ordered a carriage hitched. He had loaded her things aboard and driven her to the Mississippi dock, where he had waited with her until the first flatboat bound for New Orleans had stopped for her just after dawn.

Zelma took the letter from Dolly and tore open the envelope. She read the contents of the letter without comment. Folding it, she returned it to its envelope and leaned quietly back in her chair.

"Your Aunt Zona has left us," she told her son. "I pray to God that wherever she goes she finds happiness."

Happiness for Zelma, she had come to realize, was here at Plantation Bend with her son and her memories.

PART THREE

CHAPTER TWENTY

PLANTATION BEND WAS ablaze with lights. Pigs roasted over open pits in the backyard. Laughter from the big house mingled with that of the slaves, as did the two distinctly different forms of music.

It was a time of celebration, the most joyous event at Plantation Bend since Clabe Granville had been born. Today, at age twenty, Clabe had been married, and the festivities were lasting well past sundown.

In the enormous drawing room, Zelma gazed across the room at her daughter-in-law. She had not taken the opportunity for such an appraisal before the wedding; she had been too intent on seeing it through, had prayed every hour of every day that nothing would delay or stand in the way of her son's marriage. She had considered it his only salvation.

The past three years had been unkind to Clabe. The last year the most unkind. Only a wife could save him from his fits of depressions which had been dragging him deeper and deeper into himself and away from his duties. She had feared losing him; indeed, she had almost lost him to suicide. When, two weeks before, he had come to her and announced his intention of marrying Vienna Cole, Zelma had, much to his surprise, encouraged the match, although only eight short months before she had vehemently objected to his proposal of marriage to Vienna's sister, Victoria.

But now Victoria was dead—and it was her younger sister who had led the prominent and wealthy Clabe Granville to the altar.

Vienna was eighteen and pretty enough. Although too

thin to please her mother-in-law, she had good bone
structure and hair as blonde as her husband's. Her cheeks
were now flushed by high color, and her eyes sparkled.
She used her hands too expressively and had an uncanny
way of staring directly into the eyes of anyone who spoke
to her. She did not walk well, often appearing to lope
rather than glide across a room. These unfavorable traits
Zelma attributed to the girl's upbringing; Sam and Ginny
Cole had remained the poor dirt farmers they had been
on their first visit to Plantation Bend long before their
daughter's birth. They had been unable to afford proper
tutors.

Still, Vienna had a certain charm, no doubt about it,
and had managed easily enough to capture Clabe's attentions. . . .

Zelma's thoughts were interrupted by a guest who
touched her arm and exclaimed, "She's simply lovely,
Mrs. Granville. A pure delight, I'm sure, for both Clabe
and yourself."

"Yes, lovely," Zelma murmured.

She didn't understand the twinge of jealousy that suddenly tugged at her heart. Clabe had been her entire
life since his father's death, and now she was giving him
over to another woman, a mere girl of eighteen. She
asked herself if any woman would ever give him as much
as she had?

She had objected to his marriage to Vienna's sister,
Victoria, and fate had dealt them both a brutal blow by
claiming the girl's life. She had been made the villainness
by denying Clabe marriage to the first woman he had
chosen, and so he turned away from her after the accident.

Now all of that was behind them. Clabe was married.

Although Zelma could have hoped for a daughter-in-
law from one of the more prominent Louisiana families
now settling the area, she would accept the wife Clabe
had brought her. Vienna would have to be accepted and
taught the proper ways of presenting herself as a lady,
a lady who would one day be the mistress of Plantation
Bend.

Zelma stood back and turned her attention to her guests. She knew most of them by sight, none well, except, of course, Madame Celine, who had traveled from New Orleans for the occasion and was now circulating among the guests, resembling a colorful butterfly in her yellow gown. Pierrot stood in a corner observing, smiling, and drew confused glances from the guests, who were trying to determine this fancily dressed slave's function since he made no effort to serve refreshments. Pierrot was oblivious to their curiosity. His gaze followed Madame Celine lovingly as she flitted from guest to guest.

Zelma spotted Sam and Ginny Cole, smiling, alhough nervous and obviously ill at ease in the rich Granville drawing room. They were hovering beyond the crowd which had formed about the newlyweds. Sam Cole had become even more gaunt with age. His hair was salt and pepper, and he had a slightly mischievous glint in his eyes. Ginny had become less hefty, her face now revealing the bone structure which enhanced her daughter's appearance. Her forehead was heavily lined from work and worry, as well as the torment she had suffered over the death of her eldest daughter. The thin smile on her lips kept appearing and fading and reappearing as if only kept there by concentration, which she found difficult to sustain. The gown she wore had obviously been hastily made by inexperienced hands and was ill-fitting. Still the color, a medium blue, suited her well. She wore no jewelry, probably choosing to wear nothing rather than the poor trinkets in her collection. Her hair, the color of sun-bleached earth, had been pulled back from her face and swept up at the nape of her neck. She held a champagne glass but had not touched the bubbling liquid. Her other hand lay gently on her husband's arm.

Zelma considered the parents of the bride, remembering the day they had met and how she had offended Ginny. As she crossed the drawing room to speak to them, she wondered how best to approach them with the plan that had occurred to her after Clabe had announced his intentions of marrying their daughter.

Zelma took Sam Cole's hand but directed her statemen′

to Ginny. "I've never seen a more handsome couple. Vienna is lovely."

Ginny Cole's smile became genuine. "Yes, that our Vienna is," she said proudly. "And your Clabe's a handsome gent, Zelma. I'd of set my sights on him if he'd been around in my day."

"Looks exactly like his Papa," Sam offered.

Despite the compliments to Clabe, Zelma could not help wondering, as she had wondered for the past few months, if the Coles harbored any secret resentment for her son.

Dismissing this from her mind, she turned her attention to Sam Cole. "I know it's improper to discuss business during such an occasion," she said, "but I've been giving serious thoughts to something that concerns the both of us."

"And what might that be?" Sam asked, puzzled.

"I know your plot of land is small and . . . and part of it is unusable." She had almost said, "and scarcely yields enough to feed and clothe you."

"Aye, small it is," Sam told her. "Next to the Granville plantation, it's like comparin' Louisiana to the whole of the continent of North America. And part of what I do own can't be used. The swamp waters rise durin' the rains and don't fall back till after plantin' season. We don't get much out of it other than vegetables for cannin'."

"Well, we have several acres joining your property that have been left idle," Zelma went on.

Sam Cole nodded. "Good land, too," he said.

"I was wondering if you would like to cultivate that land," Zelma said and added quickly, "and pay me a small percentage of your profits, of course? It's doing us no good standing idle. Something should be done with it."

Sam's eyes sparked with excitement. "Well, I . . . I can't . . ." He glanced at his wife in his confusion.

" 'Course, he would," Ginny told Zelma. "He's been lookin' at that piece of land since we moved in." Her eyes said that she understood Zelma's true reason behind the offer. Handing her husband the full champagne glass, she said, "I can't take a likin' to this, Sa▮ you fetch me some punch?"

Taking her glass, Sam hurried away.

"What you did was kind, Zelma," Ginny said. "Given the chance, Sam can make somethin' of hisself yet. A man's never too old. I understand the reason for your offer. Sam don't. But he will. All he can think 'bout now is that land he's been eyein'. When it does hit him that you did it 'cause you don't want your son's wife's kin goin' 'round like we must, he might get sore, but he'll get over it. Our Victoria's death hit Sam awful hard. Workin' a new piece of land'll help him get over it faster."

Zelma said nothing.

"We never got along," Ginny went on quietly, "and that was probably a lot to do with me. I didn't understand your fancy ways. Maybe I was also a little jealous."

"That was all in the past," Zelma said.

"Yes, t'was," Ginny murmured. "But I want you to know I've come to respect you. Not many women could do what you done with this plantation."

"Necessity breeds ability," Zelma said.

"Somethin' else I'd like to say to you. I saw you watchin' our Vienna from across the room. You were takin' stock of her, and I can't blame you for that. Vienna's a high-strung girl, always has been. She don't take kindly to criticizin'. A lot of her ways need changin', but . . . well, I guess what I'm tryin' to say to you is go gentle on her, and you'll get the best results. If you don't she'll be as stubborn as a mule that ain't been worked."

"I understand," Zelma told Ginny. "Thank you for advising me."

"I hope I didn't give you any offense."

"No, no, of course not," Zelma assured her.

Sam returned with his wife's punch. "About that land," he began.

But Zelma stopped him. "We'll discuss it tomorrow, Sam. Suppose you come to see me around noontime?"

"I'll be here."

"Now, if you'll both excuse me." She smiled at Sam and

Ginny and turned her attention to the newlyweds. As soon as the well-wishers had thinned out about them, she came forward. She brushed her daughter-in-law's cheek lightly and then turned to Clabe. "We should take your bride out where she can be seen by our people," she told him.

Clabe nodded.

Vienna, laughing nervously, asked, "Just be seen by them? Do you mean I'm not to talk to them?"

"Most certainly talk to them," Zelma answered with a smile, adding, "if you've anything to say to them, my dear."

Vienna glanced at Clabe, but his expression was frozen and gave no indication that she had made her first mistake with his mother. You didn't leave your guests to go out and socialize with the slaves. At home, her father owned only two slaves, Old Harry and Putt, and they were almost treated as members of the family.

Zelma began to lead the couple across the crowded drawing room, and Vienna, clinging even more tightly to Clabe's arm, followed, her gaze fixed on her mother-in-law's straight, proud back.

Before they reached the drawing room doors, they burst open, and the slave Vienna knew as Jingo stood in the open frame. He had an odd expression on his face as his gaze swept the crowded room in search of his mistress.

Zelma stepped forward. "What is it, Jingo?"

"Pardon me, m'am," the slave said, "but news that you'll want to hear just come from the Faviere plantation."

Zelma's eyebrows arched noticeably as they always did at the mention of Faviere's name. Something inside her tightened. She felt her throat constrict, and her breathing become labored. "What news?" she asked, almost without expression.

"Faviere's gone and died," Jingo blurted. "His heart burst, they tell me, while he was ragin' at his wife." The unfathomable expression Jingo had worn upon throwing open the drawing room door now appeared on the faces of both Zelma and Clabe.

Jingo stepped back through the doors and closed them behind him.

Madame Celine rushed to Zelma's side. *"Cherie,"* she whispered. "If you don't get that smile off your face, your guests are going to think you're demented."

Zelma, struggling to control her expression, turned and faced the wedding guests. She stood quietly for a moment, listening to them whisper about the Frenchman's death. Then she said, "We can't let this news dampen the spirits of such a happy occasion." She took a glass of champagne from the tray of the passing Dolly and lifted the glass in the gesture of a toast. "To the happy occasion," she said and drained her glass.

Clabe knew—and Victoria suspected—that the happy occasion she toasted was not theirs, but the death of a long-time, hated enemy.

Clabe slipped away from the house and climbed the hill behind. He knew if his mother missed him she would be furious, if Vienna missed him she would be frightened and confused. Still, he had to be alone, if only for half an hour. He hated parties, always had, and his own wedding was no exception. He would have liked to have spent a few minutes talking to Aaron, but Aaron, he suspected, like most of the other slaves, would be half-drunk and more than likely screwing some girl in one of the sheds. Since he couldn't be with Aaron, the next best thing was to be alone to sort out his thoughts.

In the half-light of the moon, the tombstones and granite slabs of the Granville cemetery had a silvery, incandescent quality. Clabe wandered among them, the graves of his father, the brother he had not known, Bessie Lou, and in a distant corner, smaller and crowded together, the graves of slaves who had not obtained Bessie Lou's status with the family. His father's and brother's graves occupied the center of the clearing, side by side, leaving room for those to come, for his mother, himself, and now his wife and, if they were fortunate, their children and grandchildren. The cemetery, he thought, would one day be a testament of their lives, of

the history of Plantation Bend. Much would be told by
the dates and inscriptions. Much would remain untold.
There would be those, mostly among the slaves, who
would whisper about this last, unfortunate year of his
life when they read his stone markings in years to come,
but the truth of Victoria's accident and his attempted
suicide would never be known by anyone other than
Aaron. Already the gossip and rumors had begun to die
down. The wedding should finish them off altogether.

Clabe seated himself on the edge of his father's great
stone slab. The night wind was cold for spring. He turned
the collar of his wedding coat up about his neck and
shoved his hands into his pockets. From below the hill
came the sound of music, the wild, excited, and abandoned
music of the slaves mingling with that of a waltz from
the big house. A carriage, the lantern bobbing like a
firefly, moved away from the house at a leisurely pace.
Clabe watched it until it disappeared around a bend of
the road and wished the other guests would follow the
example.

His thoughts turning to Vienna, he smiled. She was two
years younger than Victoria, not as pretty, but more
than merely attractive. She had the attitude of wanting
to please him, and when she looked at him, he recognized
a childlike love in her eyes. Whether that love blossomed
or died would depend on him. By God, he would try!
He had not chosen her, as his mother might accuse, for
the purpose of spiting her. And it was not as their friends
and neighbors suspected, that he had chosen Vienna because of her resemblance to her dead sister. That resemblance had actually caused him to hesitate. He had had
to convince himself that the personalities of the two sisters
had been distinctly different; only then had he proposed
marriage. If more than a little of Victoria had survived
in Vienna, he would have looked elsewhere for a wife.

Their courtship had been startlingly short and was probably creating further gossip, but that was as it had to
be. He needed to begin rebuilding his life, and delay
would have only made it more difficult. His only surprise
had been that his mother had so readily agreed to the

match, and with a girl who did not possess the breeding and background to match their own; a girl she no doubt classified as scarcely above white trash, or called a "swampbilly." He anticipated problems between them, but not immediately. His mother was too clever for that. She would wait, she would watch, she would begin slowly to meddle and needle his new wife, telling herself the girl had to be molded into the proper image of the mistress of Plantation Bend, her own image.

Clabe did not fear for Vienna. He knew she was made of strong stuff, high-spirited, with real grit. She might— and he hoped—give his mother one helluva time of it. His mother would soon discover a similarity between herself and Vienna that she probably did not suspect. He recognized the qualities of his mother in Vienna.

Clabe was brought out of his thoughts by approaching laughter. He started and peered into the darkness of the tree-covered slope. The laughter grew louder, and he could hear the twigs snapping beneath slow, faltering steps. He did not want to be discovered alone in the cemetery on his wedding night. Because of all his recent troubles, he was already thought to be slightly eccentric, like his Aunt Zona had been. It was whispered that Victoria's death had made him a bit demented. To be found as he was now, having deserted his new bride for the solitude of the cemetery, would only rekindle the gossiping and whispering among the slaves. Rising, he moved hurriedly under cover of a nearby oak and clung to the shadows, watching.

Aaron and a young slave girl named Pearl came out of the darkness and into the moonlit cemetery. It was forbidden for them to be there except under orders of clearing away the weeds or decorating the graves with flowers, but that would not deter Aaron. Althought he played his part of the obedient slave during the day, away from the watchful eyes and under the cover of darkness, he was his own man. He was, after all, the master's friend, and that, in both his and Clabe's eyes, gave him special privileges, an unspoken right to disregard minor plantation rules. He was now slightly drunk, as was evident by his staggering gait and the manner in which he clung clumsily to Pearl's waist.

Pearl was no more than fourteen, although she looked older and was one of Dolly's household helpers. Because of the climb up the hill in the darkness, she had tucked the front hem of her skirt into her belt. Her legs were thin and dark against the paleness of her white cotton petticoats. Her hair was tied in a kerchief, and her elastic bodice pulled down low enough about her breasts to insure her an angry smack across the cheek if discovered by Dolly or her mother. Pearl stopped suddenly and, because she had been half-supporting Aaron, almost sent him sprawling to the ground.

Aaron stumbled for his footing and cried, "What's it, girl?"

"This place," Clabe heard her answer. "We ain't suppose t' be here." There was a tremor of fear in her voice.

"So who's goin' to know?" Aaron demanded drunkenly. "Everybody's busy with their own celebratin'."

"It's creepy. 'Specially in the moonlight," Pearl said. "I don't wanta stay!"

"Hell ya don't!" Aaron, now taking her firmly about the waist, drew her forward to the center of the clearing and sank with her onto the edge of Dester Granville's great slab. "Ya wants what I got, and I'm awantin' to give it to ya even worse," he said with thick tongue.

The girl struggled against him, although weakly. "Somewhere's else," she protested. "Not here! I don't wanta do it here! This here's a sacred place. I feels like we'ze bein' watched."

"By who?" Aaron demanded.

"By those who's under these here slabs," Pearl answered truthfully. "This here's old Master Granville's slab we're sittin' on. My mama told me he didn't take to ways that were again' the Good Book."

"Your mama don't know nothin'," Aaron told her. "He was a man just like any other." He laughed almost angrily. "I could tell you a story."

" 'Bout him?"

"Yeah. About him," Aaron answered .

"Somethin' you heard from Master Clabe?"

"I ain't tellin'," Aaron said.

"Well, keep your stories to yerself," Pearl told him indignantly. "I'm still not stayin' here."

She tried to rise, but Aaron pulled her back to him. Holding her with one hand, he reached the other into the bodice of her dress and exposed a small, firm breast. His head came forward, and the stillness of the night was broken only by his groaning and drunken slurping.

Clabe wanted to leave them, but he knew if he went down the side of the hill they would hear his going. He shifted his weight quietly from one leg to the other and waited them out. He saw no harm in watching Aaron's success with Pearl. A few years ago, they had even taken the same girl; Aaron first, then him, as a sign between them of their friendship. It had almost been a ritual, like the time they had become "blood" brothers. Clabe no longer remembered the girl's name, only that that summer had been his awakening to sex. How many girls had he and Aaron shared before their companionable chain of adventures had been broken by him going after the white girls in New Orleans? Twenty, maybe thirty. It seemed so long ago; before Victoria—before Vienna.

Aaron pulled Pearl onto her back on the cold slab. Her skirt was raised even higher, and her underthings pulled carelessly about her knees. Aaron was fumbling to draw himself free of his trousers. His breathing was loud with passion. He raised himself above Pearl, but Pearl, crying out suddenly, closed herself to him.

"Damn ya, girl!" Aaron cried in frustration. "Whatsa matter with ya?"

"I don't wanta do it!" Pearl yelled.

Aaron cursed her. "It ain't 'cause yo haven't done it before," he growled. "Them boys talk. Why ya don't wanta do it with me?"

" 'Cause lotsa reasons," she answered, offended. " 'Cause of this here place, and 'cause girls talk same as boys. 'Cause them girls say you'ze too big and too rough with 'em. They say you treat 'em like you'ze a white man and they'ze nothin' but colored trash. And 'cause I'm afraid of ya, that's why!"

"Then why'd ya go and agree to come up here?" Aaron demanded. "Ya knew what I wanted." When she didn't answer, he pulled her back beneath him, accepting her silence as a renewed decision for submission. He struggled to position himself a second time, but at the crucial moment, Pearl suddenly pushed at him, catching him off guard and toppling him off the grave slab onto the hard round.

She sprang to her feet, pulling at her clothing, and made a dash for the path.

"Goddamn nigger prick-teaser!" Aaron bellowed as he struggled to his feet, fuming. "I'll see ya whipped!"

"Ya'll see no such thing," Pearl called from the darkness of the trees. "I ain't in ya care, halfbreed! I ain't no grovelin' field girl!" Her voice faded as she ran down the hill toward the slave shacks and the protection of the other slaves.

"Bitch prick-teaser!" Aaron grumbled angrily. "I'll see ya whipped all the same," he called after her.

Clabe, realizing Aaron's frustration, chuckled to himself. He would have come from beneath the tree then to chide his friend on his bad luck, but as he was about to step from the shadows, he saw Aaron turn, his loins thrust forward, his hand working furiously at his groin. Clabe froze in midstep, staring in horrified fascination as Aaron unleashed the fluids of his passion onto the gravestone of Dester Granville.

Zelma, seeing the last of the guests to the door, turned to her daughter-in-law, whom she had left standing behind her, but found Vienna gone. Thinking the girl was too frightened to find herself left alone with her on this first night, Zelma smiled to herself. Then, calling Dolly, she sent her to summon Jingo back to the big house.

As she went to the study, Madame Celine emerged from the drawing room. She was slightly intoxicated and leaning heavily on Pierrot's arm. "A lovely party, *cherie*," she said. "Who would have thought so many would have traveled so far to celebrate your son's wedding?"

Zelma laughed. "Plantation Bend, except for the Faviere plantation, is the biggest in the area," she said. "All the planters want to keep on our good side. They plan their crops, marketing, almost everything from our examples."

"Ah, you're now a woman of power, *cherie,*" Madame Celine told her. "We both are, in our different ways." She winked, laughed, and let Pierrot guide her to the stairs. As she ascended, she continued talking to herself. "Who would have thought when the Americans bought Louisiana that there would have been over five hundred and thirty plantations located here in so short a time? Amazing, these Americans. Do you know, Pierrot, I no longer miss Paris?"

Zelma watched them until they reached the second-floor landing and turned down the hallway out of sight.

Jingo found his mistress in the study, sitting behind the massive hardwood desk they had brought from Savannah so many years past. He was thinking of those days more lately, especially tonight, seeing the mistress in her emerald green dress, the big house ablaze with lights and guests. His vision of long ago had been fulfilled.

Although Zelma showed the strain of the long day, there was a smile playing about her lips and excitement in her blue eyes. "So Faviere is dead," she said with satisfaction.

Jingo nodded. "One of his slaves brung the news," he told her. "Said his master was screamin' at his wife, and her pregnant, when he grabs his chest and lets out a bellow like a stuck pig. Said the old bast. . . ."

"It's all right," Zelma told him when he cut off the statement. "You may call him a bastard if you like."

"Said the bastard fell on the floor, twitching like a chicken with its head cut off. Then he became awfully still. Missy Claudine, she went up to her father and felt his neck and told them he was dead."

Zelma, who had listened greedily to every detail, rose from behind the desk. She went to the sideboard, took down a bottle and two glasses. She poured and then passed one to Jingo.

The slave hesitated.

"Go on," Zelma told him. "It isn't every day that the Lord deals out His justice. He was damned slow in the case of Claude Faviere." She drained her glass and set it onto the desktop. "I'm glad I lived to see that Frenchman sent into hell."

"Yes'm," Jingo agreed. "That man couldn't have gone nowheres else." He touched the liquor to his lips, wet them, and licked the cognac away with his tongue.

"You looked troubled," Zelma observed.

"Yes," Jingo said.

"Is it something about Faviere you haven't told me?"

"No'm. It's the creek," Jingo told her. "I noticed it's gone down since this mornin'."

Zelma stared at him thoughtfully for a moment, remembering the incident with the creek during their first year at Plantation Bend. Finally, in dismissal, she said, "I'm sure it's nothing, Jingo. After all, Faviere's dead. Maybe a natural blockage upstream that'll clear itself by tomorrow."

"Yes'm," Jingo said doubtfully. He finished his drink and bid her good-night.

Vienna had slipped from the drawing room while Zelma had been bidding farewell to the last of the guests. Clabe had not returned from wherever he had slipped away to, and Vienna had no desire to be caught in conversation with her mother-in-law on her first night at Plantation Bend. She was more wary of the older woman than frightened by her. She did not want to be made to feel the usurper on her wedding night. She wanted no emotion to cloud the night ahead of her—her first night with Clabe.

In her bed chamber, Vienna changed into a flimsy nightdress her mother had hauled from a secret box of paraphernalia, explaining she had worn it on her own wedding night some twenty-odd years previously. "It'll strike any man's fancy," she had promised, somewhat embarrassed. "Even a man as grand as Clabe Granville."

Vienna turned inspectively in front of the gold-framed mirror. She had never seen such a seductive piece of attire, not even in the fashion magazines Victoria had once brought home from New Orleans and kept hidden beneath her mattress.

Vienna's image clouded. "There," she scolded herself. "I've done it! I've let myself think of Victoria!" She had promised herself to keep her thoughts away from her dead sister, away from Clabe's first choice of a wife, but she had failed. The nightdress had done it, that and the champagne. Now the memories and her doubts about Clabe flooded over her in a wave. Dejected, she crossed the room and sank onto the thick goosedown mattress. Leaning her head against the bedpost, she closed her eyes.

Vienna knew what people were saying, what Victoria's friends were whispering among themselves. They were saying she had taken advantage of her dead sister's memory in trapping Clabe. Why else would a man like Clabe Granville marry beneath himself? With Victoria, they had considered him smitten by love. With her, it had been entrapment. She had not the beauty or the charm of her sister. She was tomboyish. She rode a horse like a man, pitched hay, and, if called upon by her father to do so, could even slop the hogs and chase the cows. More like a boy than a lady, she had been seen many times paddling a pirogue down the creek, returning with a string of fish for the family's evening meal. Even her sister had laughed at Vienna, remarking that her "little sister" would never hook a man unless with a fishing pole.

Now Victoria was dead, and Vienna had a man—Victoria's man—and the vines not yet covering Victoria's grave.

Vienna had loved Clabe Granville long before he had come courting her sister. At fifteen, she had taken to hiding herself near the Granville property line and watching through the foliage as Clabe, tall and proud on his horse, the sunlight glistening off his golden hair, had ridden about the fields to inspect the work of his slaves. She had

looked upon him as a man to be worshiped. She had
dreamed of him, fantasizing herself his woman, his wife,
or sometimes when she thought him unobtainable, his
mistress. No other man had been able to force him from
her thoughts. She had refused to date the boys who had
asked her, determined that if she could not have Clabe
Granville she would remain a virgin, an old maid like her
Aunt Helen, who lived in New Orleans and supported
herself by taking in boarders.

Vienna had written long and love-filled letters each
night to Clabe, only to burn them the following morning.
She had filled her diary with his praises, had spied on
him at every opportunity. Once, drawn to the creek by
sounds of male laughter, she had seen Clabe swimming
naked with the mulatto slave she had heard him call
Aaron. Sitting his horse as master of Plantation Bend, she
had loved and admired him; naked, she had worshiped him
all the more, and she, who had never known a man, desired him, longed painfully to feel his embrace, to experience the passion of her first, and surely lasting, love. Sight
of Clabe wading from the water, the sun on his wet body,
his powerful chest and arms, his dangling sex—all had
caused her heart to race to the point of bursting. Dazed,
she had leaped to her feet to run, and he had looked up
and seen her. His white teeth had flashed in a smile. Making no effort to conceal his nakedness, he had thrown
his head back and laughed at her, calling for her to join
them. She had fled, mortified by his discovery, his intrusion
upon her secret world.

That had been the day before Victoria had gone to
New Orleans to visit Aunt Helen. Vienna had not left
the farm for several days. Not only had she been occupied
by her own and Victoria's chores, she had had no desire
to meet Clabe again so soon. When, after a week, she had
gone again to the Granville property line to spy on him,
he had not appeared. After three days, she had become
bold enough to question one of the slaves, and the girl
had told her her master had gone to New Orleans to bargain over the sugarcane crop.

Victoria had returned, somehow changed by her trip.

She had been less critical and even given to occasional kindnesses, which was unlike her. She had met a man, a gentleman. *What man?* Vienna, she had answered mysteriously, would see in due time.

Due time was less than a week. The gentleman who came courting Victoria had been none other than Clabe Granville.

Vienna's world had crumbled. Her fantasy-lover, now a regular caller at the Cole farm, had seldom paid her the slightest attention. He had belonged to her sister—how and why, she would never understand—but she had resigned herself to the blow fate had cruelly dealt her, and she had retreated into herself to suffer the agonies of lost love and jealousy. She had become even more determined to cling to her chastity. She had dreaded Clabe's visits. When he and Victoria had been carelessly left alone, she had fretted and burned with envy.

They had been alone the night of the fatal accident.

Victoria, given to frequent colds and maladies that Vienna always considered excuses for shirking her chores, had been ill with another of her fevers. She had been confined to bed, moody and irritable, and Clabe had been allowed to go in alone to cheer her up. Vienna had sat in the outer room brooding. She had listened to their laughter, had hated them both for the happiness which had been denied her. She had been silently cursing them when she had heard the sudden explosion of the pistol and had been the first to reach Victoria's door.

She had found Clabe standing beside her sister's bed, his sun-darkened face dreadfully pale. In one hand, he had held one of Victoria's stockings with his pistol bobbing inside the hole-blown toe. Victoria, silent and still upon her bed, had had a small red spot on her forehead which had begun to spread, then streak down over the bridge of her nose into the hollows of her eyes.

"It . . . it was . . . an accident," Clabe had stammered. "I was trying to amuse her . . . I . . . I dropped my pistol . . ." he had held up the stocking to Vienna in disbelief . . . "dropped my pistol into her . . . stocking . . . and . . . and the handle struck the seat of the chair." He had released the stocking, and his pistol had clattered to the floor at his feet. "My God!" he had cried. "I've killed her! My God, my God! I've killed Victoria!" He had flung himself across Victoria's lifeless body, and it had taken both the Cole slaves to remove him after the doctor and the justice of the peace had arrived.

Vienna had been as devastated by her sister's death as Clabe had been. And she suffered not only over Victoria's death but over its effect on Clabe as well. The tragedy had changed him. He no longer rode in the fields or swam in the creek. Guilt and grief had kept him confined to the immediate plantation house and yard. She had once glimpsed him from the road, and she had cried all that night. He had appeared old and beaten, a shell of the man she knew him to be. The next day she had heard that he had attempted suicide, had rigged a noose about the limb of an oak tree on the hill behind the slave shacks. If one of the darkies had not cut the rope before he had thrown himself off the limb, he would have been dead too.

How long ago it now all seemed to Vienna, and yet it had only been a few short months before. How surprised she had been when Clabe, not quite himself still, but with color in his cheeks and life sparking behind his blue eyes, had called again at the Cole farm, had called to court her, eventually to propose marriage.

Now Clabe Granville's wife, alone on her wedding night with him God only knew where, Vienna wondered if despite her love she had made a grave error. Would she be capable of adjusting and living with the knowledge that she had been his second choice? Would she be able to keep the image of Victoria from haunting her? From coming between them? Would she? These were questions she could not answer.

Vienna rose from the bed and paced about the strange room. The slave girl who had been assigned to her, a girl of fourteen named Pearl, had unpacked and put her things away. Vienna paused to examine the dressing table, expensive, highly polished wood with carved drawers and gold handles. Her handmade comb and brush and carnival bottles looked cheap and out of place on its top. The closets were enormous, her dresses scarcely occupying one corner. The floor beneath her feet was thickly carpeted in Oriental wool. She was accustomed to bare planks. The bed was the largest she had seen, the mattress the thickest, the covering a sky blue silk brocade. She faced the strangeness of the room—and she faced it alone, without Clabe.

How could he have done this to her? How could he have left her alone on their first night? What possible errand could have been so important as to have called him away from her? Hadn't she been more than agreeable in delaying their New Orleans honeymoon trip until the plantation could spare him? Had he not expected and understood her fears? Did he not desire her as she desired him?

This thought caused her to stop her pacing abruptly. She came back to the bed and sat down, the image of Victoria again flashing before her mind's eye. *He still desires Victoria,* she thought. *I'm but a poor second whom he'll take when the need drives him to me.*

No, no, no! It can't be! Neither God nor Clabe would have been so cruel!

She was about to collapse across the bed in tears when she heard footsteps on the stairs. Already accustomed to the sound of Clabe's step, she poked nervously at her hair and willed her eyes not to overflow and betray her.

She was standing quietly before her vanity mirror when he entered. She turned to him, smiled, but made no move toward him. She wanted him to come to her.

And he did.

Clabe took her in his arms, and the fears which were plaguing her began to subside as he whispered, "You are lovely, Vienna. Lovely. And you're mine." He lifted her and carried her to the bed and laid her gently between the fresh linen. As he began to remove his clothes, he said, almost inaudibly, "I promise you, I'll try to be a good husband."

Vienna closed her eyes and waited to feel him beside her.

CHAPTER TWENTY-ONE

MADAME CELINE CAME downstairs to breakfast complaining of a headache. *"Mon Dieu, cherie,* wine is lethal at my age." She slipped into her chair and managed to smile at Vienna. "And where is the new husband this morning?" she asked.

Before Vienna could answer, Zelma said, "Clabe had to be in the fields just after sun-up." She glanced at Vienna, who had scarcely said more than half a dozen words since joining her at the table. "There won't always be such a demand on him," she told her daughter-in-law. "It's just that this is a crucial time in our planting."

"So he told me," Vienna murmured.

"It's barbaric, this plantation life," Madame Celine said. "Early to bed, early to rise—" she pushed her plate away with a grimace—"no time for young lovers to spend together. I remember when I married Monsieur Celine. We spent four days and nights. . . ." She caught Zelma's expression and let the sentence trail off.

"They'll get their honeymoon," Zelma said. "As soon as the planting is finished, Clabe intends to take Vienna to New Orleans for a week."

"Then you must come visit me, *cherie!*" Madame Celine insisted. "I'll show you a side of our city you haven't . . . well, I'll show you the city."

Vienna smiled weakly. She toyed with her food, but did not eat.

"You seem troubled, Vienna," Zelma said.

"Perhaps, like me, it's the wine," Madame Celine suggested.

"Yes, the wine," Vienna said. She pushed back her

chair and rose. "Excuse me. I'm going back to my room." She quickly left the breakfast room. In the entryway, she closed the doors and leaned back against them. She could hear Zelma and Madame Celine clearly.

"Perhaps *l'amour* was . . . ah, well, disappointing for the poor girl," the Frenchwoman said sympathetically.

"You base too much importance on love," Zelma chided her.

"*Cherie!*" Madame Celine cried, surprised at Zelma's statement. "What can be more important to a woman than *l'amour?* No, no, don't answer me. Your answer may make sense, and I'm too old to be confronted by so startling a possibility."

Zelma laughed.

"Perhaps, *cherie,* your Clabe has spent too much time with my swans to please an innocent duckling," the Frenchwoman said.

"Clabe? One of your customers? Why haven't you told me this before?"

"If I told my clients' wives and mothers about their visits, I'd soon be out of business," Madame Celine answered.

Vienna had turned away from the breakfast room door just as Jingo came into the entryway from outside. Ignoring his greeting, she ran up the stairs to her room, where she let her tears flow.

Jingo knocked and entered the breakfast room when he heard Zelma's acknowledgement. " 'Scuse me," he said. "But could I talk with you, mistress?"

Zelma sighed. "I can tell by your face there's a problem, Jingo," she told him. "What is it? Has the creek gone down farther?"

"No'm," Jingo said, awkwardly glancing at Madame Celine. "I think you should come to the slave quarter. Somethin' there's needin' your attention."

"Something my son can't handle?" Zelma asked.

"Somethin' I think you'd want to handle yerself," Jingo told her.

Zelma knew that Jingo would not have come to her

unless he had good reason. She folded her napkin and rose.

"Don't bother about me, *cherie*," the Frenchwoman said. "As soon as this coffee revives me, I must pack."

Upstairs, Vienna glanced out of her window and saw Zelma and Jingo crossing the yard toward the slave quarter. She watched until they disappeared from view around the corner of the house. Then she moved back to the bed and sat down. She turned and stared at the crumpled sheets, at the imprints she and Clabe had left side by side in the goosedown mattress.

Too much time with my swans to please an innocent duckling, Madame Celine had said. It was not her pleasure that concerned her, not entirely. Clabe had made love to her last night. He had whispered all the terms of endearment she had expected, but innocent as she was, she had understood that he had found little pleasure in her. He had made love to her *because* it was expected, not out of desire. It had been as if a third person had shared that bed with them, a third person who had inhibited, taunted them out of their pleasure—Victoria.

Vienna leaned her forehead against the bedpost and closed her eyes. Aloud, she said, "He married me, but he still thinks of Victoria. I have a ghost for a rival. It's not fair, not fair!" Footsteps outside her door silenced her.

There was a gentle rapping, and Madame Celine opened the door. She looked at Vienna and then glanced about the room. "*Cherie,* surely things are not so bad as to make you start talking to yourself." She came in and closed the door. Moving to the bed, she sat down beside Vienna and took her hand. "Don't fret, child. Love between a man and a woman is often not right in the beginning. Patience and practice make it better. Take the word of one who knows. As you Americans say, much water has flowed under the bridge since my first lover, but I remember how. . . ."

She stopped speaking as Vienna turned and buried her face tearfully against her shoulder.

"There, there," she said, stroking the young woman's head. It should be Vienna's mother or Zelma in her posi-

tion now, she thought. She was not one to advise an innocent girl. She decided she would speak seriously to Zelma
before departing.

When Zelma and Jingo rounded the curve of the hill
and the slave quarter came into view, Zelma saw a group
of women and children crowded about a Negro sitting
beneath one of the trees. As she approached, they parted
for her, and the Negro rose to greet her.

Zelma was brought up short as recognition struck her.
"Africa!"

The giant black man smiled at her. "Yes, Mistress
Granville, It's me. Africa."

"We assumed you . . . you were dead or captured by
some slave trader," Zelma told him, still shaken by his
sudden appearance at Plantation Bend.

"No'm," Africa's short-cropped hair was now gray.

"But where have you been all these years? How have
you lived?"

"I've been in the Army, mistress," Africa answered.
Always one to say as little as possible, he knew Zelma
had noted his new ability with words. Not only was he
no longer hesitant to speak but he spoke with almost no
sign of the accent expected of a Negro.

"The Army?" One of the women had brought a chair
for her mistress. Zelma sat down and motioned Africa
to do the same. "I didn't know they took Negroes in the
Army," she told him.

"Yes'm," Africa said. "Not many, but they do take
some. They're taking more all the time. Won't be long
before there will probably be an entire regiment of black
men."

"I still don't understand," Zelma confessed. "How could
you become a soldier when you're a slave?"

"Forged papers saying Master Dester had freed me,"
Africa confessed. "For six months, I worked for a white
man who was good at copying official documents, and he
paid me by making up my papers."

"I see," Zelma said. "That night when Carley was
killed and you disappeared, what happened?"

Africa, who had already told the slaves, repeated his story.

"We suspected," Zelma said when he had concluded. "But why . . . why did you risk coming back? You must have known there would be a warrant sworn out against you by Faviere. If you're caught even now, you'll be hanged, and there's nothing I could do to stop them."

Africa told her candidly he had come back because he had never gotten over missing Matilda.

Zelma glanced at Jingo to confirm that the big slave had been informed of Matilda's disappearance.

Africa interpreted her glance. "They've told me all that's happened," he said gravely. "I'm sorry about Master Dester and. . . ."

"Yes, thank you," Zelma interrupted. "The point is, Africa, it's illegal for you to be here without my turning you in to the authorities. I don't understand why . . ." she glanced once again at Jingo ". . . why you didn't come and go without my ever knowing."

"You had to be told," Africa said, "because I don't want to go, mistress. I want to stay at Plantation Bend."

"Believing that someday Matilda will return just as you did?" Zelma asked.

Africa averted his eyes and did not answer.

"I don't say this to destroy your hopes," Zelma told him, "but I seriously doubt that Matilda's fate as a runaway has been as fortunate as your own. I can't even honestly tell you how I would react if she did return to Plantation Bend."

Africa nodded his understanding. "I still want to stay," he said, "if you'll allow it."

Zelma stared at the big man thoughtfully, remembering how fond of him Dester had been, how he would not now be in this situation if he had not been trying to help them. She was aware of the interest of the women and children surrounding them. They were practically holding their breaths waiting for her answer.

"Claude Faviere *is* dead," she said, more to herself than to Africa. "If you were careful not to be where you could be seen from the road. . . ." Smiling, she rose, her decision made. "You may stay," she told Africa.

The women and children gave a cry of triumph and began talking excitedly.

Zelma raised her voice to speak to all of them. "Not one word of this must be mentioned to any of the Faviere slaves," she said. "You must tell your husbands and sons when they come in from the fields. I know they gossip with Faviere's people when they're working near the boundary lines. They must say nothing about Africa returning. Is that understood?"

There was a chorus of, "Yes'm."

"Thank you, mistress," Africa said and gave her a quick bow of gratitude. "I'll do the work of three men," he promised.

"One will do," Zelma told him.

As Jingo walked with her back to the big house to pick up the shipment orders, Zelma glanced at him and asked, "Do you think I made the right decision, Jingo?"

The slave looked troubled. "It ain't for me to say, m'am," he answered respectfully.

It was obvious to Zelma that Jingo had not agreed with her decision. I hope for Africa's sake, it was the right one, she thought.

Madame Celine was waiting for her. Her carriage had been brought to the front porch, and Pierrot was loading the luggage aboard. "*Cherie*, I want to talk to you." She took Zelma's arm and led her far enough away from the carriage so their conversation would not be overheard. "It's about your daughter-in-law," she said. "The poor girl spent half an hour crying on my shoulder, but when I questioned her, she refused to tell me her problem."

Zelma glanced fleetingly up at Clabe and Vienna's bedroom window. "She'll come to me when she's ready to discuss it," she said.

"*Oui, cherie*," Madame Celine agreed and added pointedly, "if she thinks you approve of her and are her friend."

"Is there any reason for her to think otherwise?" Zelma asked coolly.

"You must answer that question yourself," Madame Celine told her. "I suppose it is not easy to turn one's son over to another woman after having him to one's self through his young life."

Zelma felt herself stiffen. "Are you accusing me of being a possessive mother who won't let her son go?"

"*Cherie,* I love you too much to accuse you of anything," Madame Celine answered. "I am only saying that after all Clabe's been through it may be upon your shoulders to make his adjustment to marriage as easy as possible." The old eyes narrowed as she estimated just how far she could go without offending Zelma. How many young men such as Clabe frequented her house? Young, handsome, rich men whose marriages were failures because they only understood the sort of women they must pay for, love that could be bought with a few bank notes, men whose wives fell short of the image of their mothers. She knew from listening to her girls that Clabe Granville was an ardent, demanding lover. "Ah, *cherie,* perhaps it is nothing serious. Perhaps the first morning after the first night, *oui?* You know, I only want Clabe and Vienna to be happy? I think of him as a grandson." She stood on tiptoes to brush her lips against Zelma's cheek. "*Adieu, cherie.*"

The memory of her own post-marriage confusion and upset flashed through Zelma's mind as she followed Madame Celine back to her carriage. She thought that the problem between Vienna and Clabe was probably more complex, something to do with his difficulty in adjusting to the loss of his first fiancée. Still, Madame Celine had reminded her of her duty. "I'll speak to Vienna," she promised, "and to Clabe."

"*Bon,*" Madame Celine replied. "The poor girl's own mother does not have . . . well, the sophistication perhaps to handle so delicate a problem."

She gave Pierrot her hand, and he assisted her into the carriage, climbing in behind her with a farewell nod at Zelma. "*Conduire!*" Madame Celine shouted at the coachman, and she waved as the carriage lurched and moved away.

Zelma did not keep her promise to talk to Clabe and
Vienna. Perhaps the task was too difficult. But Vienna's
moodiness seemed to improve, or at least she concealed
it, so Zelma contented herself by thinking that if there
had been a problem between the couple, they had solved
it themselves without her interference.

The following month, word came through the slave
grapevine that Faviere's young widow had given birth to
a daughter and named her Paulette. The creek continued
to dry up a little each day, the mud inching inward from
the banks and baking in the hot sun. Before it reached
a danger to irrigation, however, the water ceased receding
and ended Zelma's concern. The planting of the crops
completed, Clabe prepared to take Vienna to New Orleans
for their postponed honeymoon.

The day before the couple was to depart, Zelma called
Vienna into the study. She offered her a glass of wine,
but Vienna declined. Zelma motioned for her to sit down;
then she opened the desk drawer and drew out a small
package.

"You didn't know our Bessie Lou," she told Vienna.
"Although I loathe the expression, she was my mammy.
When I married Clabe's father, she stayed with me." She
absently fingered the package, remembering. "I don't
think I loved her any less than my own mother."

"Clabe has mentioned her," Vienna said.

"Bessie Lou wanted this given to Clabe's wife," Zelma
told Vienna and handed her the package. "I give it to you
now with Bessie Lou's love and blessing."

"It's lovely," Vienna said as she removed the emerald
ring.

"It came to Bessie Lou as a remembrance of my
mother," Zelma told her. "There's a brooch to match,
which I also want you to have."

Vienna slipped the ring on her finger and stared at it
admiringly. She could not, however, keep the thought
from her mind that the emerald ring would have been
something to elate Victoria. By right, she thought, it

should be Victoria sitting here now, Victoria receiving
Bessie Lou's belated love and blessing.

"I thought you'd want to wear it in New Orleans,"
Zelma said. "Also, while you're there, I'll give you the
name of a seamstress who once made my gowns. Have
Clabe or Madame Celine take you to her shop. Tell her
who you are, and she'll show you only the best fabrics.
Have half a dozen dresses made for yourself. You'll need
them for entertaining."

Where Zelma had expected a spark of excitement in
her daughter-in-law's eyes, there was only that same old
expression of resigned indifference.

"My sister Victoria loved gowns and jewelry," Vienna
said almost tonelessly.

"Don't all women?" Zelma murmured.

Vienna stared at her for a moment without speaking.
Then she said, "No, we don't. My mother never cared for
beautiful clothes or jewelry. Neither, really, have I." She
slipped the ring from her finger and returned it to its package. "Of course, I realize that as Clabe's wife I must present the proper image expected of the wife of a rich
planter. I also expected you. . . ."

"Go on," Zelma urged when Vienna seemed reluctant
to continue.

Vienna visibly steadied herself for what she was to say.
"I also expected you to guide me," she said, "since my
own mother is as foreign to this sort of life as myself and
doesn't know what's expected of me, but I'd . . . I'd rather
you didn't guide me under the pretense of pleasing me.
You're sending me to your seamstress because you know
she'll not allow me to select tasteless fabrics and styles
that will embarrass Clabe and you. I know you don't approve of me, not as your son's wife. As my papa would
say, 'Let's run the flag all the way up the flagpole.' We
both know where we stand, so no half-truths or pretense,
please."

Zelma leaned back in her chair. Vienna's bluntness only
vaguely jolted her. Quietly, she said, "I see that after weeks
of brooding silently about the house you've at last found
your tongue. All right. Borrowing from your father's alle-

gory, let's not keep the flag of truth at half-mast. My son needed a wife. He chose you. My approval or disapproval is inconsequential. You *are* his wife. I'll afford you all the respect that goes with the marriage. Agreed, you have an image expected of you. Yes, I did recommend my seamstress for the exact reasons you named, but—" she leaned forward over the desktop—"is there any reason I can't also have pleasure in guiding you and expect you to find pleasure in it as well? After all, it is more than the image that is important to me. You're the one who'll make my son happy or unhappy. You're the one who'll bear his children, my grandchildren. Unlike my friend Madame Celine, I do not believe that love is all-important, or all-conquering. There's more to a marriage." She stopped talking long enough to wet her lips with wine. "What I'm telling you, Vienna, is that I would like us to be more than mother-in-law and daughter-in-law. I'd like us to be friends. I'd like to help you, guide you, if you prefer that expression. If I started off by giving you offense, I'm sorry."

Vienna had gone rather pale.

"If you and Clabe don't find happiness in your marriage, it won't be because I haven't tried to help you adjust to his way of life," Zelma added. "We have that in common, our desire for him to be happy. It's enough for the beginning of our friendship, isn't it?"

Vienna nodded. "I'm sorry for . . . for sounding hostile toward you," she told Zelma. She felt a compulsion to unburden herself about Victoria, about the ghost she felt that was threatening her marriage to Clabe, but she could not bring herself to broach the subject. Rising, she forced a smile to her lips. "Friends?" she said.

"Friends," Zelma assured her.

Vienna left Zelma in the study and returned to her room to complete the packing for the trip to New Orleans. *Love is not all-important, or all-conquering,* Zelma had told her. To Vienna, it was of prime importance. If she could be assured of having Clabe's love, then the difficult adjustments to plantation life would become a challenge she'd meet willingly. If only she could believe he loved her and not the memory of Victoria.

Perhaps in New Orleans, she thought. Perhaps on their honeymoon in a strange city, she would evade Victoria's image long enough to determine her chances of happiness.

But that night at supper, a planter from downriver arrived in time to join them for coffee. And the honeymoon was canceled.

"It's the river pirates that brought me," he told them. "They've sunk another flatboat, robbed and killed the passengers and crew. That's three this month. When we start shipping our crops downriver, we stand to lose enough to bankrupt us. Something's got to be done." He glanced from Clabe to Zelma to Vienna, expecting them to agree with him, which they all did. "That's exactly what we're going to do," he continued. "Tomorrow."

"And exactly what are you going to do?" Zelma asked.

"A man from every plantation is joining us," the planter answered. "We're going to rid ourselves of those bastards once and for all. Naturally, we knew you'd want to join us, Mr. Granville, being the only white man at Plantation Bend. That's why I came."

Clabe glanced at Vienna, his expression clouding over.

Zelma saw Vienna's disappointment. "My son was leaving for his honeymoon tomorrow," she told the planter. "Is it imperative that he join you?"

"Well, now, Mrs. Granville," the planter said, "every other plantation and farm along the Mississippi being represented, I don't think Plantation Bend not doing its part will sit right with some of the men, considering it's the biggest and richest of them all." He glanced at Vienna. "You'll pardon me, m'am. I don't mean to mess up your honeymoon. I know what those things mean to a woman."

Clabe reached across the table and covered Vienna's hand with his own. "One more day postponement?" he said. He was asking her for permission to do what the other planters and farmers expected of the master of Plantation Bend.

Vienna nodded. "One more day," she said. She laughed.

"That'll give me the opportunity to change my mind again about what to take with me," she said. She glanced at Zelma and saw her mother-in-law's expression of approval. *Duty comes first!*

"We'll be sure to get him back to you by tomorrow night," the planter told Vienna. "We don't want to stand in the way of a honeymoon, no'm, but we do want these pirates caught."

When they finished their coffee, Clabe and Zelma went into the drawing room with the planter to listen to the plans for catching the river pirates.

Vienna went up to her room to wait for her husband.

Clabe left the house the next morning without waking Vienna. Aaron met him at the stables, and they rode to the Plantation Bend dock, where the other planters and farmers had made arrangements to pick up Clabe at dawn. It was the planters' plan to rally upriver and take a regular flatboat back down to New Orleans past an island they thought to be the pirates' stronghold.

There were eleven men and one woman on the journey upriver.

Clabe looked at the woman with surprise.

"Claudine Faviere," Sam Cole whispered into his son-in-law's ear.

Clabe judged Claudine Faviere was about his mother's age. She wore men's trousers, a faded shirt opened at the throat, and a heavy woollen jacket. Her boots were caked with mud because she had hiked through the woods to the river and had not used the road belonging to Plantation Bend. She removed her hat, and her hair, unlike Zelma's, was not streaked by gray. Instead, on the right side of her head was a narrow band of completely white hair that contrasted startlingly against the black.

"They say her father hit her there when she was a girl, and the blow took the color away," Sam Cole murmured. "She's a hard-looking one, that woman, truly her father's daughter."

Claudine Faviere, glancing in their direction, called out to the planter in charge, "I thought you said no niggers."

She indicated Aaron. "What's he doing here? A mulatto's still a nigger."

Clabe felt Aaron stiffen beside him. He grabbed his arm to restrain him from speaking.

"That's Mr. Granville's nigger," the planter answered. "He ain't goin' to be doin' any shootin' though." He looked at Clabe to make certain he understood. Since the pirates were suspected of being runaway slaves, no Negroes were expected to fire on their own people or, to be more specific, to be trusted with a rifle while the white men were pitted against them.

Claudine Faviere met Clabe's eyes, her own stare becoming hate-filled when she was told who he was. "What's the matter? Mr. Granville too grand to carry his own rifle?" she asked loud enough to be heard by the entire group. Laughing, she picked up her gear and moved to the far side of the boat to make it clear she wanted nothing to do with a Granville.

"The feud didn't end with her father's death," Sam Cole murmured. "At least, you now know that, Clabe. Better not let the bitch get behind you when the shootin' starts."

"She'd better not let me catch her near the edge," Aaron said beneath her breath, "or she'll go overboard."

They disembarked above the mouth of the Red River and were joined by the crews of a dozen flatboats, making their number total in the seventies. There were many small boats tied up along the shore, men having gathered from all points along the river. There was almost a carnival atmosphere as crewmen and planters met and exchanged conversation and moonshine. Bet sheets were passed around and a dollar collected from each man. The full amount collected was to go to the man who killed the most pirates. Clabe was about to refuse when he saw Claudine Faviere watching him with an interested smirk. He put in a dollar for himself and one for his father-in-law.

The single flatboat gave a hoot of its whistle, and the men began to board. They hid in the cargo box, pressed shoulder to shoulder, the planters appalled by the drunken

vulgarities of the rivermen in the presence of Claudine
Faviere. But she did not mind, on occasion joining them
with obscenities of her own. Not far downriver, they all
became hushed, waiting.

The boat sat low in the water and gave the appearance
of being heavily loaded with cargo. The small crew visible
above was working with obvious difficulty.

"Reminds me of when we staked that lamb out last
year to catch us that cougar'd been killin' Ginny's and
my animals," Sam Cole told Clabe. "Now I know how
the lamb felt."

"You've got it backward, Sam," one of the planters told
him. "It's the pirates who's the lambs."

A shadow appeared through the opening of the cargo
box. "We're approaching the island," a crewman told
them. "I'll stamp hard on the deck when those bastards
start to swarm us."

"If they start to swarm us," Claudine Faviere said. "We
could repeat this for weeks without any results." She
waved away the jug of moonshine offered her by one of
the rivermen.

She had scarcely stopped speaking when the signal
sounded above their heads.

Their silence turned into a pandemonium of shouts and
cheers as the men in the cargo box rushed onto the decks
to meet the pirates' attack.

Clabe saw canoes and skiffs swarming the flatboat, about
forty pirates, both white and black men. Caught by surprise and unable to turn their boats in retreat, the pirates
were not only outnumbered but at a disadvantage. Rifles
began to explode. Pirates screamed, the planters and
rivermen cheered. The current carried away some of the
bodies. Only a lucky few managed to escape. When the
fighting ended, some sixteen pirates were dragged onto the
flatboat from the water, a couple already half-dead from
their wounds.

"What'll we do with them?" Clabe asked the planter
in charge. "Will we take them to New Orleans to be
hanged?"

"The hell you say!" Claudine Faviere shouted. "The

bastards'll get the same treatment they gave their victims. An eye for an eye! Or don't you believe in justice at Plantation Bend, Granville?"

A shout of approval went up from the other planters and rivermen.

Clabe, Sam, and Aaron withdrew to the front of the flat-boat.

Lots were cast until ten winners, Claudine Faviere among them, were chosen. Armed with rifles, they stationed themselves atop the cargo box. The captured pirates were blindfolded and forced to walk the plank in deep water. As the poor bastards rose to the surface, sputtering and attempting to remove their bonds, the riflemen, urged on by the cheering of their companions, picked them off in the water.

Claudine Faviere was presented with the prize money and toasted repeatedly by the rivermen until the flatboat anchored to set her ashore near her plantation. Laughing, she slipped overboard into the shallow water and waded ashore, waving back at the cheering rivermen.

"She enjoyed it," Clabe told Aaron. "I've never seen anyone enjoy killing as much as that woman."

Sam Cole, leaning over the railing, thought Clabe was speaking to him. "Aye," he said, repeating, "she's her father's daughter."

It was after dark when Clabe and Aaron rode into the stables at Plantation Bend. Clabe bid his friend good-night and hurried to the house, expecting Vienna to be waiting for him.

He was told by Zelma that his wife had retired early with a headache. Dolly prepared a cold supper for him, and he was forced to relate the incidents of the day to his mother as he ate. When he finally climbed the stairs to his bedroom, he found the lamp burning low and Vienna asleep. He undressed and slipped into bed without waking her. Exhausted, he fell asleep almost immediately.

When she heard his heavy breathing, Vienna turned onto her back and opened her eyes. She had only been faking sleep, childishly punishing Clabe for having abandoned her on the day of their honeymoon. She stared across the darkened room at the shadowy stack of their luggage, and she felt guilty. What was one day more or less? Tomorrow night they would be in New Orleans, alone, in a strange room. Tomorrow night when Clabe made love to her, she would make certain it was with desire and passion. She raised herself to her elbows and stared down at Clabe's head, dark against the white linen, and she felt her love for him surging through her veins. Since their wedding night, they had never gone to sleep without bidding one another good-night, without him holding her—making love to her—although she felt her identity became lost to him during lovemaking. She felt a need for him now. Stretching out her arm, she ran her hand through his blond hair.

Clabe mumbled, stirred, and then called out a name in his sleep.

Vienna snatched her hand away, trembling. She remained motionlessly poised on her elbows for several moments as if some quirk of her muscles had locked into position and prevented her from ever again reclining. Then, choking back her sobs, she threw the quilts from her and rose from the bed. She went to the chaise longue, pulled the afghan about her, and snuggled down into the goosedown cushion to muffle the sound of her crying.

The name Clabe had called out in his sleep had not been hers. It had been "Victoria!"

When he awoke the next morning, Clabe found their luggage unpacked. Puzzled, he dressed and came downstairs looking for Vienna and was told she had gone off riding before breakfast. He summoned Pearl, his wife's personal slave, and asked if she had assisted in the unpacking. The girl told him she had not, but her mistress had informed her before leaving the house that they would not be going to New Orleans.

When Clabe approached Zelma, she was as puzzled by Vienna's cancellation of the trip as he was.

"Didn't she say anything yesterday? Was she angry?" he pressed.

Zelma told him, "No." It had been a particularly pleasant day. They had gone riding after breakfast, had visited Vienna's mother, and had spent the afternoon planning Vienna's new wardrobe.

Refusing breakfast, Clabe ordered his horse saddled. He was too confused and angry to wait until Vienna returned. He learned from the stable boys which direction his wife had taken, and he rode off.

He found her horse grazing alongside the dock road. Vienna was sitting at the edge of the dock, staring out at the river. She did not turn when she heard him ride up or when his footsteps sounded noisily across the dock planks. He sank down a few feet from her, his legs dangling over the side.

"You shouldn't go riding alone," he said quietly.

Vienna didn't answer, just continued to sit and stare at the muddy water of the Mississippi.

His anger faded. "The Indians attacked a family upriver last month," he told her. "Renegade white men lead bands of savages along the riverbank hoping to lure the flatboats in to the shore." One of the Indians' favorite tricks was to dress up in American clothing and cover their faces with flour. Pretending to be white men in distress, they'd hail the flatboats from the river's edge, pleading for help. When the flatboat crews came to their rescue, they were captured, the crews murdered, and the cargoes stolen. Now that the rivermen had become familiar with this practice, the savages were turning their attention to the smaller farms and roadways.

Vienna glanced at her husband. "How did it go with the pirates?" she asked without real interest.

Clabe told her of what had happened, omitting the gory details. He concluded with, "I'm sorry about the delay of our honeymoon, but I don't understand why you canceled it altogether."

"I decided it was a useless trip," Vienna answered bluntly.

"Useless? I thought you were looking forward to it," he said. "I know I was. It's been months since I've been to New Orleans."

Vienna found a small stone wedged between the dock planks. She pulled it free and flung it into the water, staring at the ripples. "You called Victoria's name in your sleep last night," she told him without meeting his gaze.

Clabe didn't question her statement. Hadn't he had nightmares about Victoria ever since her death? Only since his marriage had he found enough peace to sleep through an entire night without the nightmares waking him bathed in a cold sweat. "I must have been dreaming," he murmured.

"Do you also dream of Victoria when you're awake?"

"What are you alluding to, Vienna?"

"Just this," she answered. "When we're making love, I feel you forget it's me beneath you. It's. . . ."

"That's absurd!"

". . . it's Victoria," she finished.

"That's not true," he assured her. "Vienna! What kind of a man do you think I am?"

"An unhappy one," she said bluntly. "It's Victoria you loved, not me. Victoria haunts you. She haunts me. It's almost as if she hadn't died. Sometimes her presence in our bedroom is so strong I expect to see her standing over our bed staring down at us." She turned her head away from him. "I had hoped Victoria's memory would fade," she said. "That she'd leave us in peace. Leave you so I stood a chance of replacing her, but last night when I touched you and you called out her name. . . ." Her voice broke, and she was forced to hesitate while she regained control. "I knew it was hopeless," she went on. "That's why I canceled the honeymoon," she told him. "I couldn't go to New Orleans knowing I was only a poor substitute for my sister."

"Vienna, you're wrong," Clabe said in a near-shout. "If I called out Victoria's name, it isn't because I want her back from the grave. I love you. I married you. Victoria belongs to the past. We can't let her ghost stand between us."

Vienna turned to him then, her eyes near overflowing. "Can you deny a day doesn't go by without your thinking of her?" she demanded.

In all honesty, he couldn't. There was not a day when he did not visualize Victoria lying upon her bed, the tiny red hole in her forehead put there by a bullet from *his* gun. He had been her murderer, and he was destined to relive the horror, the torment of it by constant flashes of recall in minute detail. Isn't that inability to force Victoria from his mind what drove him to attempt suicide? "I didn't love Victoria," he told his wife, and he could see by her eyes that she felt he was lying. "It's you I love. You must believe that!"

Vienna grabbed the dock post and pulled herself to her feet. She stood staring down at him, her chest hurting. "I can't," she told him. "Victoria had you first. She still has you. She's holding you from the grave, and there's nothing I can do to fight her." Before he could say anything further, she ran from the dock, mounted her horse, and rode quickly away.

Clabe watched until she disappeared from view. He wanted to go after her, but the knowledge that he couldn't convince her he did not, *had not,* loved her sister without confessing the entire truth kept him on the dock. He knew if he told her the entire truth about himself and Victoria he would lose Vienna forever. He stared down at the muddy river water and thought how hopeless was his situation. A keelboat moving upstream from New Orleans sounded its bell in greeting, but Clabe, not hearing, did not give the expected wave in return.

That night, Vienna turned away from him in bed and lay stiffly facing the wall.

Clabe remained awake long after her steady breathing told him she slept. He stared at the patterns the moonlight created on the ceiling, listened to the neighing from the distant stables. He closed his eyes, opened them, visualizing, as Vienna had suggested, Victoria standing over their bed.

When Vienna awoke in the morning, she was told by Pearl that Master Clabe had left for New Orleans shortly after sunup.

CHAPTER TWENTY-TWO

It was September 10, 1830, Zelma's birthday.

As she rose that morning and sat before her mirror fixing her hair, it struck her with surprise that she was now forty-seven years old. Leaning into the glass, she closely inspected her face. Even if the lines about her eyes and mouth were not now deepened by concern over Clabe and Vienna, her face reflected all of her forty-seven years. She felt suddenly older, extremely tired. Turning away from her mirror, she completed the arrangement of her hair.

As she came downstairs to breakfast, Zelma hoped none of the others remembered her birthday. Celebration was out of the question. How could she celebrate when she was so preoccupied with the problem of Clabe's absences, the operation of the plantation? Having taken on the greater burden of Plantation Bend after Dester's death, she had hoped that after his marriage Clabe would have assumed his duties. Now with him in New Orleans more than at home, she had returned to spending most of her days and part of her nights devoted to the duties Clabe should have assumed. She was no stranger to hard work, but now, at forty-seven, her energy level had waned. If it had not been for Jingo and Africa, she doubted if she would be capable of holding the plantation together.

She had attempted to speak to Clabe, but he had become instantly angered and warned her not to meddle in his life. Vienna was no more talkative, so Zelma remained virtually in the dark concerning their marital problems.

Zelma prayed Vienna's pregnancy might bring the couple back together. She didn't even know what Clabe's feelings toward his pending fatherhood were, but she hoped that once the baby was born his philandering would cease. If he would not acknowledge his responsibility to Plantation Bend and his wife, perhaps a child would tip the scales in their favor.

That morning when she saw the riders crossing the bridge, Claudine Faviere among them, Zelma knew there was to be trouble. The only question in her mind as she came out onto the porch to meet them was the nature of this new calamity.

Claudine Faviere and two of the riders approached the porch, where Zelma waited. The others rode off toward the slave quarter. Comprehension struck Zelma, but it was too late to sound the alarm.

"Mornin', Mrs. Granville." Zelma recognized the sheriff even before he pushed back the lapel of his coat to display his badge of authority.

Zelma nodded a stiff greeting. Her gaze went to Claudine Faviere, meeting a cold, sneering stare. "What brings you to Plantation Bend?" she asked the sheriff, still holding the Frenchwoman's gaze.

The sheriff fumbled in his coat pocket and drew out some papers. "A matter of a warrant," he said.

"A warrant?" Zelma pretended surprise but saw she was not bluffing Claudine Faviere. She turned her full attention to the sheriff. "Why did your men ride into our slave quarter?" she demanded.

"Because of the warrant," the sheriff answered and waved the paper at her. "This here warrant was sworn out against a Granville slave name of Africa."

"Yes, I remember," Zelma told him, "but that was a long time ago, Sheriff. The slave was a runaway." The door opened behind Zelma. She glanced over her shoulder and saw Vienna emerge. Dolly and Pearl peered from behind her in the doorway.

"Seems this here runaway's been seen by Miss Faviere," the sheriff continued. "She came to fetch us to see that the sentence of hangin' is carried out." He stuffed the warrant back into his coat pocket, his eyes narrowing as he stared down at Zelma. " 'Course, the slave could be back and you not know 'bout it, Mrs. Granville. If you did know, I'm afraid there'd be grounds for a penalty against you or your son."

"Damnit, Sheriff!" Claudine Faviere shouted. "She knew! Can't you see she's been hiding the murdering black bastard?"

The sheriff turned to Claudine and said crossly, "That's no language for a lady, Miss Faviere. Nor is it language I'll tolerate bein' used in front of ladies." He turned back to Zelma and Vienna. "My apologies, ladies."

"The hell with your apologies!" Claudine snapped. "You came here to hang a nigger. Not to sweet talk the bitch that's been hiding him!"

"Miss Faviere, I warn you—!"

"I'll be with your deputies searching the shacks," Claudine yelled. Yanking on her horse's reins, she dug her heels into its flanks and rode off at a gallop toward the slave quarter.

"I'm sorry 'bout this, Mrs. Granville," the sheriff told Zelma with sincerity. "That woman's no lady."

"You have a remarkable grasp of the obvious," Zelma said.

"Everyone knows there's bad blood between your two families," the sheriff said, ignoring Zelma's remark. "Still, the law's the law, and it's my lot in life to see it's enforced. If that slave's found, we're goin' to have to hang him."

Vienna moved forward to Zelma's side and put her hand through her mother-in-law's arm. She knew how much Zelma depended on Africa, knew what the slave had been risking in remaining at Plantation Bend. Zelma's calm exterior was belied by the trembling Vienna felt through their contact.

Zelma steadied herself. "Sheriff, what if there were extenuating circumstances? If I signed a counterwarrant against the Favieres . . . ? Could there be a trial?"

"Already been a trial, m'am," he answered. "The slave was tried, convicted, and sentenced in his absence. All that's left is catchin' and hangin' him." He swung down off his horse and handed the reins to his deputy. "I take it,

Mrs. Granville, that's an admission of the slave being here?"

"My mother-in-law said 'What if,' Sheriff," Vienna inserted. "She didn't say the slave had returned. After all, whoever heard of a runaway returning after so many years?"

"I sure haven't," the sheriff admitted, "but Miss Faviere swears she seen the bast . . . slave. She said he was unmistakable because of his size and build. Ah, well, if he's here, we'll find him."

Pray God Africa had enough time to escape, Zelma thought.

A commotion from the slave quarter brought Zelma and Vienna to the end of the porch.

It had taken four men to restrain Africa. They were dragging him around the bend of the hill toward the big house, Claudine Faviere strutting ahead of them with a smile of satisfaction.

"Oh, God!" Zelma cried and clung tightly to Vienna's arm.

"Sheriff," Vienna shouted above the noise, "what if we pay for the three slaves Africa was accused of killing?"

"Yes, yes! We'll pay double, triple their value!" Zelma pleaded.

The sheriff, removing his hat, scratched at the side of his head. "That'd be up to Miss Faviere, ladies. She's the injured party. If she'll agree. . . ."

"What's up to Miss Faviere?" Claudine demanded as she approached. She glanced from the sheriff to Zelma with a triumphant smirk. *My victory this time,* her expression said.

"These ladies offer to pay triple the value of those slaves this Africa's accused of killin' ," the sheriff told her, "if you'll forget the warrant."

Zelma and Vienna saw the spark of greed in the Frenchwoman's eyes, and they thought for a moment she would agree. Africa had been dragged up behind her. The men had managed to tie his arms but continued to hold him as if the ropes were not sufficient. There was a gash above Africa's right eye, blood oozing down along the side of his face and onto his faded gray shirt.

"Five times their value!" Zelma cried out in desperation.

Africa, blinking away the blood in his right eye, looked at his mistress gratefully, remembering another occasion as a young man when her husband had bartered him away from a cruel master. But this time he was not hopeful.

Claudine Faviere laughed at Zelma's stricken expression. "Maybe this nigger means more to you than just a slave," she suggested mockingly. "Maybe he satisfies other—"

"That'll be enough!" the sheriff blurted angrily. "Will you take their offer or not? Seems more than fair," he added, hoping he and his men would be spared a hanging execution, " 'specially considering the escalated value of slaves nowadays compared to when. . . ."

It was Claudine's turn to interrupt. "It isn't a question of value," she announced. "It's a matter of justice. No, no, I won't accept your offer," she told Zelma firmly. "The nigger'll hang, and I intend to be the one to slap the horse out from under him."

Zelma knew she was defeated. Scarcely above a whisper, she said, "If it was a matter of justice, you wouldn't be here, Claudine Faviere. You and I both know why Africa was on your land in the first place."

Smiling, the Frenchwoman motioned for the sheriff to take away the captured slave. "That tree across the bridge will do," she said. "We'll leave the bastard hanging there as a warning for the other Granville people of what'll happen if they trespass on Faviere land again."

The sheriff nodded solemnly.

Claudine turned to one of the deputies and asked him to bring her the whip from her saddle horn.

"We'll have no whippin'," the sheriff told her.

"I'm only going to use it on the horse the bastard sits on," she assured him. She took the whip from the deputy, making certain Zelma saw; only the two of them understanding her insistence on using the whip that had belonged to the Faviere overseer.

As they started to drag him away, Africa shouted at the sheriff, "May I have a word with . . . my mistress, sir?"

The sheriff looked at the stricken Zelma. To Claudine's disapproving glance, he answered, "Yes."

Zelma, with Vienna still supporting her, stepped off the porch and walked up to the Negro. Defeat and anguish had filled her eyes with tears. The sheriff's men became hushed.

Africa showed no fear on his strong, dark face. For her benefit, he even attempted to smile. "Mistress Zelma, may I beg a favor of you, please?" he asked.

"Yes, anything," Zelma wept.

"Should Matilda . . . should my wife ever come home to Plantation Bend, mistress, will you promise me you'll welcome her back?" Africa requested. He nodded his head toward the slaves who had gathered in horrified silence. Aaron was standing in front of the group. "She may come back someday because she'll never overcome the need to see her son. When she does. . . ."

"She'll be welcomed," Zelma promised.

"Tell her I . . . tell her. . . ." He could not bring himself to finish the statement. He had been a private person in life. Facing death could not make him express his emotions for the woman he had loved.

"I'll tell her," Zelma assured him with understanding.

"Thank you, mistress."

Zelma turned away as they dragged the Negro across the yard and the bridge to the giant maple tree beyond the creek bank. "Dear God!" she cried and covered her face with her hands.

"Come inside," Vienna urged and tugged gently at her arm.

"No!" Zelma said strongly. "No." She pushed Vienna's hand away and pulled herself to her full height. "One doesn't bid farewell to a friend by hiding away in one's house," she said. She wiped the corners of her eyes dry with the lace of her cuffs. "That's what Africa is. My friend. We both knew that day he returned why he sent Jingo to fetch me. His papers made him a free man. He could have lived safely in New Orleans and paid the river-

men to make contact with our people and inform him if
Matilda returned. He didn't need to come to Plantation
Bend. I understood that. He came because he knew I
needed him." Scarcely audible, she added, "If only my
son were half as devoted."

With Vienna at her side and the Granville people behind her in mute silence, Zelma stood and faced the distant maple tree with its gnarled branches and brightly
colored autumn leaves.

Vienna saw her mother-in-law's lips moving, but she
heard no further sounds and did not know if Zelma was
praying or merely mouthing her anguished helplessness.

They stood, motionless and hushed, until after Claudine
Faviere had slapped the horse from beneath Africa and
the rope had snapped his powerful neck.

After the Frenchwoman, the sheriff, and his men had
ridden away, Zelma sent half a dozen men to cut down
the dangling body and told them to prepare a grave on the
hill.

Then she went back into the house and up to her room.

Vienna, staring up from the foot of the staircase with
concern, became aware of Dolly at her elbow.

The housekeeper had icing across the front of her apron.
"I'll send the birthday cake to the slave quarter for the
youngins," she said. "This ain't no day for celebratin'."

CHAPTER TWENTY-THREE

A LOG WAS pegged into the ground for a sidewalk. Negro convicts, burdened by iron collars and heavy chains about their ankles, were cleaning the ditches on either side of the street. The stench from the garbage and unnameable refuse they were shoveling into vats caused Clabe to quicken his step.

He had become a familiar figure along the New Orleans sidestreets, as he had in the fashionable cabarets and gambling houses and bordellos. People no longer called him Monsieur or Mr. Granville. He was now known by merchants and casino owners and bordello girls alike as just *Clabe*. Strangers were told he was a rich planter, an entrepreneur, a white slave trader, whatever came into the locals' minds when they were asked. He went nowhere without a wave, a handshake, a smile, for he dropped a bundle of banknotes nightly in the casinos, was generous with his women, and bought them expensive gifts from the merchants. Still, behind their friendliness, he knew their true opinion of him. The casino owners considered him an easy mark, the merchants a fool who'd pay twice an item's value, and the bordello girls—they thought he was sweet and thoughtful and troubled, and impotent. He would pay for their bodies and spend the night merely talking. On his frequent visits to New Orleans, he drank too much, gambled too much, spent too much money.

"Mon cher," Madame Celine had told him, "you have become a creature of excesses. No good, no good! You'll not find peace of mind in excesses."

Of course, the old woman had been right. He hadn't needed her to tell him. But if not in pampering his excesses, then where? He was hell-bent on a course of self-destruction. It was not the same as when, after Victoria's death, he had tried to hang himself, but it was suicide all the same, slow and agonizing. He was destroying himself physically and mentally. He wanted Vienna, their marriage, more than anything. Yet, each time he left New Orleans and returned home determined to convince her of his love, he no sooner came into her presence than his guilt overcame him. He would lock himself away in an upstairs back room until he had sweated out the alcohol. Then he'd come back to New Orleans and the vicious cycle of excesses.

This trip he had left Vienna at Plantation Bend even though her time of delivery was near. Last night he had toured the casinos and lost heavily. He had become drunk and ended up at one of the pleasure palaces outside the fashionable Vieux Carré. The girl he had selected had been a quadroon, with gray green eyes and skin coloring only slightly darker than his own. Her name was Daphne.

Because she worked for her uncle above Canal Street in New Orleans' most sordid section, Daphne had not known about the strangeness of the handsome blond gentleman she had taken to her room. She had immediately begun to undress, slowly, teasing him with her body as she knew men enjoyed. When she had stripped down to her last flimsy garments and Clabe had not responded, she had suspected the bad fortune of having landed one of the weirdos who had been banned from the Vieux Carré bordellos. She had had such men before, men who had wanted to beat her or for her to beat them, or worse. She had learned through experience that such men were generally white and rich and handsome, were kind to their children and gentle with their wives, and only came to her section of town when their pent-up, degenerate desires became insatiable. Clabe was certainly white and handsome and, judging from his clothes, rich. She had been about to call for her Uncle Pepe to have him removed from her room when he had suddenly covered his face with his hands and burst into racking sobs.

Daphne's fear had melted. She had never seen a grown

man cry, never heard such anguish as came from the blond stranger sitting hunched over on the edge of her bed. She had called Pepe and told him to bring a bottle. "And not that rotgut you give to the river swine!" She had forced Clabe to drink half a glass of whiskey. Then, gently pushing him back on the bed, she had sat beside him, stroking his brow, speaking to him as if he had been one of the three children she had left at home with her husband.

He had quieted, slept.

When he had awakened, she had fed him coffee and a foul-tasting paste she told him was made of a root known only to the Creoles. "It cures not only the body but the mind as well," she had told him.

"Now," she had said when he had finished, "you shall talk." It had been more of a command than a request. "The root does not work on the mind unless you talk," she had told him with an expressive gesturing of her hands. "So you talk. I listen."

Perhaps it had been the effect of the root, perhaps his trust in the compassionate Daphne, but Clabe found himself relating his most hidden thoughts. He hid nothing from her. He told her the truth about Victoria and about the guilt he felt when he was with Vienna. When he had finished, it was midafternoon, and he had talked for over five hours.

Daphne raised the window shades, and the bright sunlight streamed into the dingy room. Turning from the window, her hands on her hips, she stared down at him and smiled. "Tell me now," she said. "How do you feel?"

Clabe had had to admit he had not felt better in over a year. He felt curiously unburdened.

"So why can't you tell all this to your wife?" Daphne had asked.

"I . . . no, I couldn't."

"And why not, I ask you? You told me, a stranger who doesn't love you, who isn't going to be the mother of your child. Why not your wife? If she loves you, she will understand. If she does not—" she shrugged her kimono-draped shoulders—"you are no worse off. If you go on as you say you've been doing, she will hate you anyway You are a gambling man, no? Then you must play the best odds, my friend. Those odds are for confessing all you've told me to your wife."

"I . . . I just don't think I could. I even doubt if I'd have been so open with you if it hadn't been for your Creole root."

Daphne had thrown back her head and laughed. "There was no Creole root, my friend. Only a trick one of the Voodoo queens taught me. It's like the use of a *gris-gris,* the most feared of Voodoo magic. You have to believe in it, or it does not work. What you ate was mashed up turtle with a seasoning of herbs. You opened yourself up to me because you wanted to. You also want to be open with your wife, so convince yourself you will be, and then go and do it."

Clabe had left Daphne with as much gratitude as he could express and as many banknotes as he had had in his pockets.

Now as he turned off the sidestreet, his steps quickened. He practically ran from Madame Celine's gate to her door. His knock was so urgent, so demanding, the old woman answered it herself.

"Clabe! Come in!" She stepped back for him to enter.

"No, not this time," he told her. "I need a horse. Mine was stolen. I have to get home to Plantation Bend. Vienna's due to have our baby any day, maybe even today. I owe it to her to be with her."

"Mon Dieu!" Madame Celine cried happily. "Take two horses! Ride them both to death if you'll get home sooner!" She turned and called excitedly over her shoulder, "Pierrot! Mr. Clabe Granville needs a horse to go home! Quickly! Before this grasp of sanity deserts him!"

When Clabe reached Plantation Bend, he could not see Vienna immediately. She had gone into labor the hour before. He stationed himself outside their bedroom door, pacing, listening to her groans of pain, the excited chatter of his mother and Dolly and the midwife. Once when he could bear Vienna's cries no longer, he pounded on the door and demanded to be admitted. The thought had struck him with sudden horror that Vienna might die in childbirth.

Zelma appeared at the door. She came into the hallway, pushing him back away from the door. Her eyes were angry and tired. "You can't go in now," she told him firmly. "And stop that pounding! You'll only succeed in upsetting her more." She waved him away down the staircase. "Wait in the study. I'll call you the moment the child is born." Pointedly, she added, "Have a drink, two drinks!"

"I won't drink again," Clabe murmured as he retreated, but his mother had already turned to go back into Vienna's room and had not heard him.

He went to the study and continued his pacing. The mantle clock ticked past the minutes. An hour had gone by when there was a tapping on the french doors, and he looked up and saw Aaron. *Thank God,* he thought. *Someone to talk to.* He crossed to the doors and threw them open. "Come in, Aaron, come in!" He took his friend's arm when he hesitated and practically pulled him into the room.

"Just wanted to know if the baby's been born yet," Aaron told him. "Everyone's waitin' to hear before they go to bed."

"No, not yet," Clabe said. "I'm glad you came. I need someone to wait this out with me."

Aaron looked uncomfortable.

"What is it, Aaron? You have other plans?"

"Matter of fact, I do," Aaron confessed. "Pearl and me, we were plannin'—"

He'd never have done that a year ago, Clabe thought. He'd never have put one of his women ahead of me. He'd even alienated Aaron. "Oh, I understand," he told the slave. "I guess it's something a man has to wait out by himself anyway." He turned away so the disappointment wouldn't be seen.

Aaron hesitated. He moved to the doors and opened them to the cool night air. Without turning, he said, "Are you back to stay this time, Clabe?"

"Yes," Clabe answered without time to consider. "I'm back to stay."

"Good," the mulatto said. "Maybe it'll stop now."

"Maybe what'll stop?" Clabe asked.

"Jingo was waitin' to talk to the mistress tomorrow after the baby came," Aaron told him, "but I might as well tell you now that you're back for good. In the past two days, we've had three runaways."

"Runaways?" Clabe was plainly shocked. Runaways at Plantation Bend were unheard of. "Are our people so unhappy then?"

"They don't feel secure, if that's what you're askin'," Aaron said. "They can see the strain on the mistress. See how things are beginnin' to fall down. Some say the plantation'll be rundown beyond savin' by the time you. . . ."

"Go on," Clabe demanded. "Finish what you were going to say."

"Before you become a man," Aaron said. He turned and met Clabe's gaze. "Of course, they don't understand about what's been eatin' you. They think it's because . . . oh, hell, I don't know what they blame, Clabe. But now that you're back you can prove them wrong. About the plantation goin' to ruin, I mean." He backed awkwardly through the door. From outside, he said, "I'm glad you're back. Glad you've come to your senses." Then he was gone, swallowed up by the darkness of the night.

Clabe stood thoughtfully for several moments contemplating a feeling he had received from Aaron. He felt Aaron somehow resented his return. But why?

He did not have time to consider it fully. He heard footsteps on the stairs and rushed from the study to confront his mother as she descended the stairs.

"A boy," she said proudly. "Almost seven pounds."

"And Vienna?"

"She's fine," Zelma assured him.

Clabe started past her on the stairs, but she put out a hand to restrain him.

"Give them time to get her ready to receive you," she told him. "I told her you were here and anxious." Her eyes probed those of her son. "There's something differ-

ent about you," she said. "Some subtle change only myself and maybe Vienna would realize." Her hand tightened
on his arm. "Are you ready to forget whatever this foolishness is that's been driving you, Clabe? Is that what I see
in you?" Her voice was pleading with him to confirm her
question.

"I'll talk to you after I've talked to my wife," he told
her. "If she can forgive me, then I. . . ."

Dolly appeared at the top of the stairs. "You can come
up now, Master Clabe."

Zelma took her hand away from her son's arm, and he
rushed up the stairs.

Vienna lay propped up against her pillows, pale and
exhausted. Her hair, which had lost its natural curl during the last month of her pregnancy, had been combed back
from her face and twisted into a bun at the back of her
head in the manner often worn by women twice her age.
But on her, it emphasized her youthfulness. In the crook
of her arm, she held the bundled baby.

She was staring at the child when Clabe opened her
door and entered. She did not turn her head to look at her
husband until the midwife, congratulating Clabe on his fine
son, gathered up her paraphernalia and left them. Then
she turned and focused her attention on him, clearly expecting him to be intoxicated as he generally was for days
after returning from his debaucheries in New Orleans. It
surprised her that he looked sober.

"I've agreed to name our son after his grandfather," she
told him quietly, "unless, of course, you object to the
name."

"No, I don't object," he said, not questioning which of
the baby's grandfathers she meant. He approached the bed
as she pushed the blanket away from the baby's face for his
inspection. He stared down at the tiny, reddened head, the
glow of the bedside lamp glistening on the dome of fuzzy,
colorless hair.

"Dester Granville," Vienna murmured. "Your mother
says she already sees his resemblance to you and his grandfather. You may hold your son if you like."

The suggestion of his holding so fragile a being as his

son startled him, and he confessed as much. It occurred to him that it would take time to adjust to his fatherhood—if he was allowed that time for adjustment. "Vienna, I must talk to you."

Vienna brought the blanket protectively back about the baby's head. "Tomorrow," she said without considering the urgency in his voice.

"Tomorrow I may have lost my nerve," Clabe said persistently. He dragged the straight-back chair from her vanity to the side of the bed and sat down before she could object. "Vienna, I know what a bastard I've been to you," he confessed. "I've not only been torturing myself but you and my mother as well. Self-destruction is one thing, but when it's allowed to affect those you love, it's. . . ." He stopped speaking as she turned her head away, a stricken expression on her face.

A silence fell between them.

Clabe felt his determination waivering. He knew what she was thinking, that he had no right to pretend to include her in "those you love."

Vienna broke the silence. "If you're going to attempt to convince me it's me you love and not the memory of my sister, I want you to know it isn't necessary," she told him. "I've given it a lot of thought, Clabe. I had no right to demand what you were not capable of giving. I won't ask that of you again. All I do ask is that you accept the responsibility of Plantation Bend for our son's benefit. Someday he'll be master here. I don't want his birthright to come to him in ruins. He inherited his grandfather's name. Let him also inherit his dream."

"You would go on living with me as my wife, thinking I did not love you?" he asked incredulously.

"I would," she answered honestly.

"For our son?"

"Yes, for our son, but not entirely for him. For myself also. You see, regardless of your being haunted with love for my sister, I still love you."

Clabe leaned forward and clasped her hand. He felt its warmth, trembling, and he pressed it to his lips. "Vienna, there is something I must tell you that will be very painful to both of us," he said quietly. "After I've told you, you may do as you choose. You may wish to never speak to me again. You may decide to call the authorities and have me arrested."

Vienna pulled her hand away from his grasp. "I thought you sober," she said accusingly, "but I now see you're having another of your drunken delusions."

Stunned by her statement, Clabe could only stare at her questioningly.

"I've heard your rantings and ravings when you've returned from New Orleans and locked yourself away to rid your body of alcohol," Vienna explained, fighting the emotion in her voice. "I've stood outside your door at night and heard you cry out in fear of arrest, even hanging. At least then you were crying out from a drunken nightmare. Now I see you've progressed to the same nightmares while you're awake. Oh, Lord, Clabe! Did you love her that much?"

"No, I didn't," Clabe answered evenly.

Vienna's eyes registered disbelief as they always did whenever he denied the accusation. She was about to turn away again, not wanting to accuse him of lying even through some expression she could not prevent.

"I didn't love Victoria at all!" Clabe cried. "I loathed her!" The words tore from his throat in a shout brought up from the very depths of the guilt he had lived with since that fatal night over a year past.

Vienna, stunned by the vehemence of his outburst, stared at him as if unable to comprehend his meaning.

"It's true," Clabe said, fighting for control of his voice. He still could not stop the violent trembling of his hands or the fluttering inside his chest. He averted his eyes, unable to meet her gaze. "I never loved your sister," he repeated. "Believe me, Vienna. There was never a less lovable woman than Victoria. The ghost of her that stands over us isn't because I loved her."

Vienna's continued silence brought his eyes back to her face. She was still staring at him as if not comprehending his meaning.

"Don't you understand?" he cried. "It's my guilt that

has allowed her to stand between us! Not love! Dear God, not love! I wanted her dead! When it happened, I said a prayer of thanks!" Clabe heard the door open behind him and knew his mother had entered, had heard, and was probably frozen into immobility by shock of what he had said—as was Vienna as comprehension flooded over her.

"You . . . you can't mean . . . you . . ." her free hand came to her throat, and Vienna pressed at the muscles as if attempting to revive the vocal cords that were failing to respond to the commands of her brain . . . "you can't mean you . . ." finally, she managed to spit out the word, *"murdered* Victoria! You can't mean that!"

Zelma moved to the foot of the bed and into Clabe's line of vision. "No, of course he doesn't mean that," she said. "Do you, Clabe?" When he didn't answer, she said, "He doesn't know what he means. He's obviously had too much to. . . ."

Clabe raised his hand to silence his mother. To Vienna, he said, "Victoria was trying to force me into marriage. We used to meet in the fields and go to a place on the creek bank where we couldn't be seen. We'd been meeting for over a year. There was no emotional involvement on my part. There never could have been. I'd told Victoria as much. She said she didn't care. We'd keep the relationship strictly sexual. She wasn't as innocent as everyone suspected. She'd slept around since she'd been fourteen, had even slept with old man Faviere, or so she told me."

Zelma, paling considerably, had sunk onto the foot of the bed as if strength to remain standing had been more than she was capable of sustaining. "Clabe, maybe you'd better not. . . ."

"I didn't like Victoria. I actually disliked her. But you don't have to like a woman to—I didn't feel I was taking advantage of Victoria since she was more than willing and had a passion that equaled my own. My only concern was that her father or one of his slaves would catch us on the creek bank. I made Aaron stand guard to warn us if anyone came along. I wasn't about to be shot or horse-whipped or forced into a shotgun wedding for doing what both Victoria and I wanted. I didn't. . . ."

Almost inaudibly, Vienna whispered, "I . . . I don't want to hear . . . any . . . more."

"You must let me finish!" Clabe said firmly. "I've kept this bottled inside me for too long and look what it's done to us." Clabe rose from his chair beside the bed. Moving to the window, he pulled back the draperies and looked out into the darkness. From around the bend of the hill, he could see the glow of an open fire from the slave quarter. He knew they were celebrating the birth of his son.

"Victoria had made her plans from the beginning," he said, his back to his wife and mother. "She thought that by pretending indifference she'd spark my interest in more than sex. She was childish and vain and spoiled. She thought it inconceivable that a man who knew her body intimately would not also love her."

"Victoria thought every man loved her," Vienna recalled quietly. "I thought so too."

"When she began to talk of marriage, I started meeting her less often," Clabe continued. "When she persisted, I would have stopped seeing her altogether except she threatened to tell your father I raped her. Aaron, too. I knew Aaron would be found guilty without benefit of anyone believing me. No one could have stopped his being hanged, or worse. A slave accused of molesting a white woman is doomed from the moment the accusation leaves her mouth.

"I kept putting Victoria off about marriage, hoping like a fool that some solution would present itself. Maybe she'd meet another man who was more receptive to the idea of marrying her, maybe her father would go broke on that dirt farm of his and have to move away, maybe she'd . . . she'd die. The more she pressed, the more desperate I became. I despised her. I didn't want to marry a woman I detested, a woman I knew was after one thing only, to make a rich marriage and escape the poverty she'd been born into. Yet I didn't want to risk Aaron's life by refusing, or the scandal I'd bring down on my family and myself.

"I promised Victoria when I made a trip to New Orleans I'd make a decision while I was away. She was very sure of herself. 'Then when you get back, you can start courting me in a proper fashion,' she said. 'But we'll make it a short courtship. I want to be married and out of that stinking swamp before summer.'

"I guess with me away she became less secure in her hold over me. She managed to convince her father into letting her visit her aunt in New Orleans. I don't know how she knew where I was staying, but she came directly to Madame Celine's and confronted me. She told me she was pregnant with my child. I knew she was lying and I told her so. We argued and she finally admitted the lie. She threatened me again with accusing Aaron of raping her. I told her I'd give her money, enough for her to live in New Orleans in style until she met another man, one she didn't have to blackmail into marrying her. She laughed at that and told me it wasn't enough. She wanted to be the mistress of Plantation Bend. 'I can put on the airs of a great lady as well as your mother,' she said. I told her it required more to become a lady than she was capable of learning in her lifetime. She began to scream and throw things, and Madame Celine and Aaron came to see what was happening. When she saw Aaron, she started to make accusations against him then and there. The only way I could stop her was to agree to her demands.

"When I returned to Plantation Bend, I began to court her as she demanded. That's when I got to know you, Vienna. I'd seen you watching me in the fields and at the creek, but I never thought of you as anything other than Victoria's tomboy sister until I was forced to spend those evenings at your father's house pretending to be love-stricken over Victoria.

"Victoria recognized my interest in you, and it infuriated her. She couldn't understand how I could be taken by you when she was so obviously endowed with all the attributes a man would want in a woman while you were her opposite. Her vanity made it impossible for her to see beyond the physical.

"That last night I was supposed to ask her father for her hand in marriage. She had planned to pretend to be ill so I could call him into her room away from her mother, whom she thought might demand a longer courtship. I pleaded with her again to accept money and not force me into a marriage I didn't want. . . ."

Clabe glanced toward the bed, but Vienna was not looking at him. Her eyes were closed, her jaw firmly set, and the veins at her temples standing out, strained. She rocked the baby back and forth.

"You were in the next room," Clabe went on. "We had to keep pretending we weren't arguing. She kept laughing between her biting threats, but the laughter wasn't only for your benefit. She was openly laughing at me, at my helplessness. She called me a weak fool, told me she'd always known she would win with me. Any man who'd consider the fate of a mulatto slave over his own welfare was a natural loser.

"My first instinct was to strangle her. I'd never felt such repulsion for a human being. I wanted her dead. It seemed the only way to save myself and Aaron. My hands were trembling so violently I almost couldn't control them. I reached for her, and she laughed at me, slapping my hands away. I stepped back from the bed and drew my pistol. I wanted to kill her. God, how I wanted to kill her! But I couldn't. I couldn't squeeze the goddamned trigger.

"She looked at me oddly, without fear. She didn't stop talking, threatening me, laughing at me. I felt so foolish standing there holding my pistol. I meant to kill her, but I couldn't, so I began to act the buffoon to cover up my real intentions. Her stockings were draped across the foot of the bed frame. Like a child inventing some game to amuse himself, I picked up one of her stockings and dropped my pistol inside. She asked what the hell I was doing. I didn't know, except I'd seen a salesman in one of the New Orleans bordellos demonstrate the strength of his silk stockings to the whores by dropping his pistol inside and slinging it around the room without putting a run in it.

"But when I dropped my pistol into her stocking, the barrel struck the seat of the chair. There was a loud explosion. Victoria continued to stare at me with that same threatening expression. Only she was dead. There was a small hole at her temple that began dripping blood.

"What I'd done struck me with full impact when you appeared in the doorway. Everything after that is unclear. I remember your parents' horror, your screams, your father's two slaves bringing me home, but most of all I remember Victoria's dead eyes staring at me. From that night on, they've stayed with me, haunting me, accusing me. Finally, to escape them, I tried to hang myself. I was becoming demented."

Clabe moved laboriously back to the chair beside Vienna's bed and sat down wearily, drained by his confession. "If I hadn't seen you passing on the road one day and had my feelings for you awakened—" He lowered his head. His elbows rested on his knees. He buried his face in his hands. "But after we married," he went on, his voice muffled, "Victoria continued to haunt me. Haunt us. For two entirely different reasons. Me because of guilt I couldn't confess for fear of losing you. You because you misinterpreted my guilt as a tragic love for your sister that I couldn't get over. It came to the point when I knew that either way I was going to lose you. Victoria had won after all. She was right. I was a natural loser."

Clabe stopped talking. He continued to sit, slumped forward, his face buried in his hands, his shoulders and back moving in jerking spasms of anguish he could not let out.

The heavy silence in the room seemed like an abyss into which his confession had hurled them.

Vienna found her voice. "But you didn't murder her, Clabe," she said. "It was an accident. You said yourself you couldn't pull the trigger."

"But don't you see? I intended to kill her. That's why

I took out my pistol. The intention was there. I had murder in my heart. I wanted her dead, and I killed her."

"But by accident," Vienna repeated. "You couldn't have known the barrel of your pistol was going to strike the chair. You couldn't have known it was going to go off and kill her." She extended her arm and lay her hand gently on her husband's lowered head. Her eyes were moist with tears. "Forgive me, Clabe, for ever doubting your love for me."

Zelma rose from the foot of the bed. She took the baby from her daughter-in-law and left the room as her son was lovingly drawn into an embrace.

CHAPTER TWENTY-FOUR

IT WAS LATE afternoon. The morning had been bright and warm, but around noon the clouds had blown in from over the gulf and given the day a gray overcast. Still darker clouds on the horizon promised rain before nightfall.

Zelma was in the drawing room with Dester. Her grandson had celebrated his first birthday that day, delighting at the single candle Dolly had lighted on his cake. Of the multitude of presents, he had singled out a brightly painted horse Solomon had carved for him, and he was now playing with it on the floor at her feet.

Vienna returned from having taken the other presents to her son's room and seated herself on the sofa with her needlepoint, a talent that still evaded Zelma. She was in the third month of her second pregnancy and had made the announcement during Dester's birthday dinner. Clabe, who had promised to return from the fields for the occasion, had not kept his promise. Vienna had made the announcement anyway.

When a horse approached and reined up at the hitching post, Vienna's fingers paused momentarily with their needle.

"You're not angry with him, are you?" Zelma asked. The couple had been happier than she could have wished for in the past year.

Vienna glanced up at her and smiled. "No, I'm not angry, Zelma," she said. "But I shall pretend to be. My husband is becoming a bit too lax with his promises."

Zelma knew her daughter-in-law was referring to another promise Clabe had failed to keep—another trip to

New Orleans that had had to be canceled. "One day you'll have that honeymoon," Zelma told her. "One day." She picked up her grandson, realizing as a pain creased her back that she was now at an age when she must take caution with lifting. Not only was her back given to strains, she had less power in her hands, and her legs tired easily. As she balanced Dester on her knee, she thought that she must find work again to occupy her mind and body. The past several months with Vienna taking charge of the house and Clabe taking the responsibilities outside, she had had a well-deserved rest from a hard routine, but it was time for her to become active again.

She heard the footsteps along the porch outside. Before Clabe could join them, she said, "I checked the accounts this morning. Do you know he managed to increase the shipment of cane by twenty percent this season?"

"And says he'll increase it by another twenty percent next season," Vienna said without looking up from her needlepoint. There was as much pride in her voice as there had been in her mother-in-law's. "But don't flatter him until I've been allowed to make him squirm for a few moments."

"If it'll amuse you, I promise not. . . ."

A knock on the outer door caused Zelma to stop speaking.

"It isn't Clabe after all," Vienna said, more to herself than Zelma. She lay her needlepoint aside as she heard Dolly crossing the entryway to answer the knock.

Both women were staring expectantly at the door when Dolly opened it.

"A colored man to see you, mistress," the slave said.

Since the slaves called them both 'mistress,' Zelma asked impatiently, "Which of us does he wish to see, Dolly?"

"I don't rightly know, m'am," Dolly answered apologetically. "It's that colored man from New Orleans that don't have no voice."

"Pierrot?" Zelma set Dester back on the floor and rose from her chair to go meet Madame Celine's "precious" slave. As she walked across the drawing room, she realized she had begun to tremble. She had never known Pierrot to be away from Madame Celine's side. Perhaps the old woman was dying.

Pierrot was standing just inside the door. He had abandoned his fancy, colorful clothes for a drab gray coat and trousers typical of what was worn by the Negroes who were sent out of the city on errands. Any clothes other than these would have been an invitation to the robbers and Indian marauders who watched the roads.

The smile that spread across Pierrot's face upon seeing her told Zelma she had been mistaken in suspecting tragic news of Madame Celine. It still puzzled her that her friend would risk her beloved Pierrot to errands that could have been performed by a slave capable of only the most menial duties. If Pierrot had brought a letter, it had to be of extreme importance.

"Hello, Pierrot. You've ridden just ahead of the storm." She motioned for Dolly to take the Negro's coat and hat. "I'll have Dolly fix you food and coffee," she told the mute.

But Pierrot shook his head in refusal and indicated with his hands that he must leave immediately. He removed an envelope from his pocket and handed it to Zelma.

She recognized Madame Celine's pale blue stationery.

Pierrot, not waiting for her to open the envelope, gave a quick farewell nod of his head, and left. She heard his footsteps hurrying across the porch toward the hitching post.

When Zelma went back into the drawing room, her face was extremely pale.

Vienna, thinking her mother-in-law might faint, rose and came quickly to her side. "What is it, Zelma?" she asked with concern.

Zelma handed her the note from Madame Celine.

Cherie,

You must come at once! Quite by chance I have found your sister Zona. I will not take the time to

relate the circumstances. I will only tell you that she
is here with me and needs you.

I am sending Pierrot with this message because I
know he will not tarry in his haste to return to me.
                                                    Madame Celine

Vienna had scarcely finished reading the note when
Zelma, gaining control of herself, crossed to the drawing
room doors and shouted for Dolly to come to her. Her
complexion had regained some of its color, but she still
appeared shaken and trembled noticeably.

"We must go at once," she murmured. Without waiting
for Dolly to appear, she started for the stairs to begin the
urgent packing. "Have Dolly send for Clabe," she instructed over her shoulder. "Tell her to have the carriage
hitched and brought around. Make certain the stable boys
don't forget the lap robes. We're going to be caught in
the middle of the storm."

As if to confirm her statement, a distant roll of thunder sounded over the gulf.

Zelma paused halfway up the staircase, turned, and
looked down at Vienna. "Since Clabe refuses to carry
a pistol, have Solomon load one and slip it into the side
pocket of the carriage door. Also have him see that the
coachman is armed. A storm isn't going to hinder the
robbers, only make their occupation uncomfortable."

Vienna nodded her understanding of the hastily given
instructions.

"And Vienna?"

"Yes, Zelma?"

"If you choose to accompany us, I suggest you leave
Dester in Pearl's capable care," Zelma told her. Without
waiting for a comment from her daughter-in-law, Zelma
hurried on up the stairs. Taking command of the hasty
arrangements kept her from crumbling with anxiety over
the seriousness of Zona's condition. *Here with me, and
needs you,* Madame Celine's letter had said. The fact
that Zona had been found in New Orleans astounded her.
She had always suspected her sister of having returned to
Washington. Imagining Zona had found a measure of

happiness in the society she had loved and had been self-exiled from because of scandal had eased her own worry.

Despite the fact that the windows were closed and all flaps securely tucked in, the moisture found its way inside the carriage. It beaded on the interior of the roof and dripped down onto their hats and shoulders and fur lap robes. Because she could not ride backward without becoming ill, Zelma sat facing Clabe and Vienna. She had not spoken since they had left Plantation Bend but had sat staring thoughtfully from the windows until the rain had begun to streak the panes. Then she had stared down at her gloved hands, flinching with each clap of thunder, closing her eyes with each flash of lightning.

The condition of the road had forced the Negro coachman to slow the horses. As it was, they were having trouble with their footing in the mud and slime, and he feared an accident. He knew his passengers were being mercilessly jostled, but he could not help that. A trip in such weather was white folks' craziness. He loved Mistress Zelma, so he reasoned she had good cause for risking the lives of her prize horses, and herself. He hunched his head down into the collar of his greatcoat for the little good it did him against the rain, and wished he had had the foresight to bring a jug of the moonshine some of the boys had stolen from the Faviere still. He thought, seems the closer we gets to New Orleans the harder the rain. Wouldn't surprise me none if we round the next bend and discover there's no road at all. Just one big lake of rainwater. He wished this were so. Then they could turn around and go back home, and he could dry his bones with a fire and a drink and leave for New Orleans tomorrow, if the Lord's will hadn't washed that city of the devil into the gulf. He wondered again at his mistress's reason for a trip made dangerous by the storm, shrugged his wet shoulders inside his coat, and urged the horses on as fast as he dared.

Even a storm of less magnitude was enough to make the streets of New Orleans impassable. The black, loamy

soil became greasy and slippery. Water and debris overflowed the drains and choked many streets.

When the carriage came to a halt, Zelma opened the
window and stuck her head out into the rain. The water
stood a quarter of the depth of the wheels. Ahead, an
abandoned carriage had been overturned by the current
of the water and was blocking the street. The coachman
leaned around and peered down from above. Seeing Zelma,
he climbed down and waded back to the window.

"Water's gettin' deeper, mistress," she shouted above
the wind and rain. "I don't think the horses'll make it."

Zelma looked at Clabe. "What shall we do?" she asked.
"It can't be more than a few blocks to Madame Celine's."

"How long since you've been to New Orleans, Mother?
It's no longer the small city you remember. We're a good
two miles from Madame Celine's, and we've the worst
section to pass through. Even the locals don't go out at
night in a storm." Pushing the lap robe from his legs,
Clabe opened the door and climbed out to join the Negro
in the calf-deep water. His coat was instantly darkened
as the rain soaked through to his skin. "We'll lead the
horses as far as we can," he shouted at the coachman.
He looked back at Vienna and his mother with concern.
He'd seen carriages caught in the current of the flooded
streets in the past, overturned, the occupants drowned
before they could escape. "If you feel the carriage tipping,
get out!" he yelled. "On the side against the current!"

Zelma nodded her understanding. She pulled the door
closed as Clabe waded forward to take the horses' reins.
Changing her seat, she sat beside Vienna, taking her
daughter-in-law's hand in hopes of lessening her fears.

"Perhaps we should get out," Vienna suggested, shaken.
She clung to Zelma as the carriage lurched forward.

"We'll make it," Zelma assured her. "When we reach
Madame Celine's, you won't even be aware of the storm.
Her house is built on a knoll and the floors raised off
the ground in case the water should rise higher than
customary."

Vienna leaned forward and used her hand to wipe the
mist from inside the windowpane. The rain was falling in

sheets so heavy she could scarcely see the lights from the houses lining the streets. The oil street lamps swung madly from the projected arms nailed to wooden posts. Debris floated past the carriage, sometimes striking the wheels with a clattering sound. When they reached a cross street the current became stronger. Vienna was terrified that Clabe might loose his footing and be carried away in the current, and the coachman would be too occupied to notice and come to his assistance.

They continued slowly for almost a mile, the storm not letting up.

Zelma pushed down the window, and the rain and wind struck her face as she leaned out. She shielded her eyes with her hand and peered into the watery darkness. She could see the vague shape of Clabe or the coachman struggling with the reins of the terrified horses. In front of them, the middle of a cross street had been transformed into a churning river. Zelma became aware of Vienna at her shoulder, leaning out and peering around her head.

The carriage began to groan. The vibration and grinding of the wheels as they were forced sideways brought a scream from Vienna.

"Out!" Zelma cried. She flung open the door, but the wind tore it out of her hand and slammed it back into its frame. Panicked, Zelma screamed, imagining them trapped inside as the carriage tipped into the flood water. She knew Clabe couldn't hear her scream above the storm. She turned to Vienna. "Help me!" she shouted.

Both women put their weights against the door. They forced it open enough for the wind to catch it and slam it back against the side of the carriage. The water was now halfway up the wheels.

Zelma helped Vienna down into the churning water, clinging to her until she found support on the slippery bottom. Clabe turned and saw them abandoning the carriage and came back to help. Just as Zelma found her footing on the street bottom, the carriage groaned, skidded sideways, and overturned. The coachman fought to free the horses, succeeded, and then came back to help Clabe, who was trying to support both women.

Zelma was grateful for the Negro's strong arm. Her clothes were drenched and heavy, threatening to weigh her down into the water. She struggled out of her coat since it was soaked through and useless and was only hindering her, and it was carried away in the current. She motioned for Vienna to do the same.

"A high street!" Clabe yelled and pointed ahead. Vienna pulled into the protective curve of his body. He led them down the center of the flooded street, afraid if they veered too much to either side they would stumble into the deep drain trenches. Off in the near distance there was a rumbling sound, crashing, screams. He could sense his wife looking up into his face. "A building's collapsed," he said tonelessly.

Zelma lost her footing and stumbled. She cried out as she fell. The coachman clung to her arm but also lost his footing from her sudden lurching forward, and both went down. She tasted the sudden rush of muddy water in her mouth and fought desperately to raise her head above the surface. Her hands touched the bottom, slime oozing through her fingers. She felt herself slipping, her skirt and petticoats caught in the current and dragging her along beneath the water.

Then there was a mighty yank on her arm. The coachman's fingers dug into her flesh as he snatched above the surface and steadied her against the current.

She coughed and sputtered and spit out slime. The Negro lifted her from her feet and crushed her against his chest as he moved ahead as quickly as he dared to catch up with Clabe and Vienna, who had not even been aware of their near disaster.

They reached the high street without further incident. Here the water was shallow and the current less fierce. Zelma told the coachman to put her back onto her feet. In a sudden flash of lightning, she saw the flooded street down which they had just made their way. The water was reaching into the raised doors of the houses. In her own panic, she had been unaware of other people. She saw them now before the white glare of the lightning faded; men and women in the one-story structures trying to reach the safety of the taller buildings. She thought that even Madame Celine's well-planned house would be flooded if the storm did not subside quickly.

Indeed, Madame Celine's courtyard was already under water, and the water rose steadily along the base of the doors.

The little Frenchwoman herself answered their urgent pounding.

"Mon Dieu!" she screamed when she recognized the mud-covered Zelma. She pulled her friend into the entry-way. Closing the door behind the group as if it would hold the floodwaters at bay, she shouted for Pierrot and her household slaves, and started giving excited orders.

Pierrot lead Clabe and Vienna to an upstairs room. He saw that they had hot water and towels and hurried away in search of dry clothes for the couple.

Madame Celine took Zelma to her old room. With no regard for the damage to her own emerald green gown, she began helping her friend from her soaked, muddied clothing. *"Mon Dieu. Mon Dieu!"* she kept crying. "Pierrot returned after the water had begun to rise," she said excitedly. "I thought you'd have turned around and waited until after the storm. *Mon Dieu!* This is my fault!" She answered the door to the slave girl with water, took it, and filled the basin. "I'll find you clothes while you wash," she said and hurried away to check the closet of one of her girls she judged to be about Zelma's size.

When she returned, Zelma had washed herself and wrapped the bed-covering about her shoulders. She accented the petticoats and dress Madame Celine had brought her, and gratefully allowed the slave girl to assist her in dressing while Madame Celine vanished again to return with a bottle of cognac.

Zelma rinsed her mouth with the strong liquor to rid herself of the dreadful taste of the slime she had swallowed. She spit into the basin and then dropped wearily onto the chaise longue to finish the cognac.

Madame Celine perched nervously on the edge of the facing chair. *"Cherie,"* she cried. "I have sent for the doctor, but I doubt if he can be found, or will come if he is." Trembling, she snatched the handkerchief from her cuff and dabbed nervously at her eyes.

"I don't think we need a doctor," Zelma told her old friend. "We're shaken, but none of us is hurt. Thank God."

"Not for you, *cherie!*" Madame Celine cried. "For your sister. She is worse."

"Zona!" Zelma rose and set the cognac aside. "Where is she? I must go to her."

"I put her in my room," Madame Celine said, rising. "I will take you to her, of course, but she is now sleeping. The sedative the doctor left should keep her out until morning." She moved out of the room with Zelma close behind.

Clabe and Vienna appeared in the hallway at the sound of the women's voices and followed them into Madame Celine's apartment. Because no other men's clothing could be found, Clabe was wearing one of Pierrot's bright yellow suits, and Vienna was in one of the girl's dressing gowns with collar and cuffs of red-dyed ostrich feathers. Zelma thought how ridiculous they all looked as she moved past Madame Celine to the bed.

The bedside lamp was burning on a dim flame, but still Zona's appearance was visibly shocking to Zelma. The woman on the bed only vaguely resembled the sister she remembered. Zona's face was heavily lined, colorless, aged well beyond her years. Her hair had gone gray, had been dyed and not kept up, so that the crown of her head was almost white in contrast to the tinted dark strands of hair fanned out on the pillows. Wrinkled, heavy lids were closed over her eyes, her eyebrows reshaped in the fashion of women of the low-class bordellos. The flesh of her face was stretched tightly over the hollows of her bones. She looked skeletal, more dead than alive.

Zelma clamped a hand over her mouth to choke back her sobs. Turning away from the bed, she leaned into her son's shoulder, scarcely hearing Madame Celine as she said, "I only found her by merest chance, Zelma. I arrived early at the theater and was amusing myself by watching the crowd arrive. There was a disturbance in the parquet." Madame Celine's voice lowered, and she averted her eyes to the woman on the bed, obviously finding it difficult to continue.

Zelma pulled away from Clabe's shoulder. "Go on," she said.

"Well, *cherie,* there was a . . . a drunken woman creating the disturbance," Madame Celine told her. "She was arguing with her escort. A river boatman who had apparently brought her against his wishes and felt as ridiculous as he looked in the required full dress coat and white gloves. The commotion grew steadily worse as others joined in. You know how seriously the New Orleans audience takes their theater? I had taken one of my girls with me to improve her mind. We leaned over the box to watch the ruckus. The theater manager was trying to evict the riverman and his drunken ladyfriend before the mayor and his guests arrived. I thought the woman was somehow familiar, but I couldn't place her. I assumed she was one of those who'd worked for me in the past and now that she'd lost her beauty was working above Canal Street. *Mon Dieu!* It is too often the fate of these women." Madame Celine, as if suddenly too weak to continue standing, sank to the edge of the mattress beside Zona, and looked up at Zelma. "My girl confirmed my suspicions, told me the woman worked for Señor Ponce. The couple was thrown out of the theater, and I sat back to enjoy the performance and to put the incident from my mind. Only I couldn't. Something about the woman's face kept haunting me."

"It . . . it was Zona," Zelma said scarcely above a whisper.

Madame Celine nodded. "It didn't strike me until the last act when the heroine was . . . was attacked. Naturally, I was horrified. I told myself it couldn't be. The woman had only somehow reminded me of your missing sister. To satisfy myself, I sent a man who frequents my house to Ponce's to get information on the woman. When he came back and told me her name was Zona, I went myself to see her. She was as you see her now. The riverman had beaten her. She was ill and had a raging fever, and, *cherie*—she was dead drunk. The proprietor told me she was that way for the last time as far as Señor Ponce was concerned. He'd been ordered to throw her out into the street."

Zona moaned and turned her head on the pillow.

Madame Celine took the cloth from the bedside table and mopped her brow. "I brought her home and called the doctor and sent Pierrot to you," she concluded. "This evening when the storm was raging, the poor dear started raving, demanding whiskey, cursing us when we refused her."

Zelma came to the bedside, took the damp cloth from Madame Celine, and leaned down over her sister. "I'll take care of her now," she said. She touched Madame Celine's cheek with her fingertips. "Thank you," she told her.

Madame Celine and Clabe and Vienna quietly crept from the room.

Outside, the storm continued to rage, the floodwaters to rise. The night was passing slowly.

Zelma sat on the bed and held her sister. *I'll take you home to Plantation Bend,* she vowed silently. *I'll nurse you back to health. Oh, Zona, Zona! If only you had not run away.*

She heard the excited cries of the slaves below as the floodwater began seeping into the house from beneath the doors. Madame Celine's voice joined them as she shouted instructions for certain items to be taken to the second floor to be saved. There was scraping sounds from the drawing room below the rooms where she sat with Zona as furniture was being dragged and pushed about to save the expensive carpets.

The house suddenly gave a great groan, shuddered, and then settled as if with a deafening sigh.

Zelma moved Zona's head from her lap onto the pillows. She went to the window and looked out. The rain had slackened, but there were now waves of water sweeping along the flooded streets. The waters of the gulf had joined those of the Mississippi in the destruction of the city. The side of the house from which Zelma looked out

was not afforded protection from the waves by the walls
of the courtyard. The house groaned more loudly with the
impact of each new wave. The cries below from Madame
Celine and her household grew more excited, panic-strick-
en as the water level rose inside the house.

With a final glance to make certain Zona had not
been awakened, Zelma left the room. She was not aware
of how long since she'd been left alone with her sister,
but she imagined Madame Celine had shown Clabe and
Vienna to their room. Knowing Clabe's exhaustion and
the depth of his sleep, she thought that he might not be
aware of the increasing dilemma of the floodwaters. As
she went to knock on her son's door, she saw Pierrot
coming up the stairs laden down with the new draperies
Madame Celine was trying to save from destruction.

Clabe and Vienna appeared in the hallway before
Zelma reached the door of their room. Judging from her
son's eyes, Zelma thought he must have been sleeping and
had been awakened by a terrified Vienna.

"The water's rising," Zelma told the couple. "We must
help Madame Celine save what we can."

They had reached the stairs when the entire house suddenly seemed to be knocked from its foundation. Zelma
was thrown to the hallway floor, Clabe and Vienna into
the wall. There was a chorus of noises, splintering wood
and shattering glass, screams and a thundering crash that
seemed to have no end.

When Zelma pulled herself to her feet, Pierrot was
rushing past her down the stairs. Vienna was clinging to
Clabe in stunned silence. Except for the cries from below,
even those now very faint, a deadly silence had replaced
the pandemonium of noise. "See to Madame Celine!"
Zelma shouted at Clabe. As he disengaged himself from
Vienna's frightened grasp and hurried down the staircase,
Zelma ran to check on Zona.

Before she reached the room where she had left her
sister, Zelma felt the cold, wet wind on her face. She
stopped in the doorway, too sickened to even scream.
There was a great gaping hole in the side wall through
which the wind and rain poured in. Where the heavy,

fourposter bed had sat was another hole. When the wall
had collapsed, the timbers of the floor had given way,
plunging the bed and most of the other furniture through
to the drawing room below.

Vienna appeared behind Zelma. She tood one look at
the disaster and pulled her mother-in-law away from the
doorway before more of the floor collapsed and took
them with it. Zelma would not allow Vienna to restrain
her upstairs. She went below, wading through the knee-
deep water, pushing debris from her path as she made
for the drawing room.

Before she reached the doors, Clabe appeared with the
limp body of his aunt in his arms. Zelma did not have to
be told her sister was dead. She saw it in her son's eyes,
in the lifeless, crushed body draped across his arms.
"And . . . Madame Celine?" she asked.

When Clabe did not answer, staring at her with a
stricken expression, she pushed past him through the
drawing room doors. Amidst the destruction, she saw the
frantic Pierrot tearing through a pile of rubble to uncover
a half-buried figure in emerald green silk.

They waited upstairs in the protected side of the house
until morning. The storm passed shortly before dawn and
constant checking proved the floodwaters had begun to
subside.

When it was light enough, Clabe left Vienna and
Zelma. When he returned, he told them he had found
horses and a long-bedded wagon used for transporting
produce to and from the marketplace. If they used only
the high streets, he told them, there was a possibility they
could get out of New Orleans without serious difficulty.

Vienna pleaded they remain until the floodwaters had
subsided more, but when Clabe explained the looting and
killing that would surely follow the disaster, she quickly
changed her mind.

Clabe found their coachman and told him to take his
aunt's body down to the wagon and cover it with a tarpaulin so his mother would not have to look at it. As

the Negro was carrying Zona's body away, Clabe asked Zelma, "What about Madame Celine?"

Zelma shook herself as if coming out of a trance. "We can't leave her here," she said. "We'll take her with us and bury her at Plantation Bend."

Clabe nodded his approval.

Pierrot had carried his mistress's body into the adjoining room after they had brought it from the drawing room, and he had spent the balance of the night closed up inside with her. The only sound Zelma had ever heard from the mute had been his tortured, agonizing cries of grief which had not stopped until after sun-up.

Clabe went into the room to get the Frenchwoman's body.

He came out quickly, his face exceedingly pale.

"What is it?" Zelma asked him.

Pierrot had curled up in bed beside Madame Celine, mourned her until sunrise, and then he had slit his own throat.

CHAPTER TWENTY-FIVE

THE RETURN RIDE to Plantation Bend found no one in the mood for conversation. The coachman kept glancing over his shoulder at his passengers, three of which were wrapped in tarpaulins. On several occasions, it was necessary for all of them to climb out of the wagon to push the wheels out of the mire. When they reached home, it was afternoon. Too late, Zelma told Clabe and Vienna, to change before burying their dead. Dolly and Pearl helped with the washing and dressing of Zona and Madame Celine. As the elderly Frenchwoman was laid in her coffin, Zelma remembered the lace shawl Madame Celine had given her years past and brought it to wrap about the tiny shoulders.

The slaves had scarcely finished digging the three graves when the coffins were carried up the hill. Since there was no preacher, Clabe read from his mother's Bible.

Zelma stood quietly by, as if this new tragedy was more than she could fully comprehend. Both she and Vienna were drawing stares from the slaves because of their brightly colored, mud-spattered dresses. As Zona's coffin was lowered into its grave and the slaves moved to Madame Celine's, Zelma heard the sound of horses crossing the bridge. She turned and looked down the hill and saw the sheriff and three of his deputies approaching the house. She motioned for Solomon to go down to meet the visitors and inform them she and her son were on the hill.

The four men, hats in hands, made the climb and stood quietly by until the burial rituals were completed. The sheriff had not been to Plantation Bend since the hanging of Africa, and he glanced questioningly at Zelma to judge his welcome. She nodded stiffly.

Clabe, passing the Bible to his mother, approached the four men. Zelma heard the sheriff tell him there had been an Indian raid upriver, an entire farm family massacred. They had been out of New Orleans during the flood and had heard about it from one of the riverboat captains. The report given was that over fifteen hundred houses had been flooded. The number of lives lost was not yet known.

Zelma and Vienna joined the group of men. Zelma had decided she must invite them to supper. Before she could make the invitation, the sheriff turned to her and bowed slightly.

"A funny thing," he said. "With that storm and the Mississippi overflowin' its banks, the creek in front of Plantation Bend's at midsummer level."

Clabe and Zelma exchanged quick glances.

"Claudine Faviere," Zelma murmured. She turned to the sheriff. "Sheriff, you once were forced by duty to hang one of my slaves."

"Yes'm, I'm sorry about. . . ."

"Will you now perform another legal duty?" Zelma interrupted. "One not for, but against Claudine Faviere?"

"If she's broken the law, Mrs. Granville, I'd of course be obliged to do my duty." He turned the brim of his hat in his hands. "But I've no intention of bein' drawn into the feud between your families if there's been no laws broken."

"Claudine Faviere has dammed up the creek just as her father did years back when Africa tried to save Plantation Bend by opening the floodgate. I'm sure it's her intention to make good her father's threat to flood our land. What better time than when the water's at its highest level? With the Mississippi overflowing and the flood in New Orleans, how would we prove the destruction was an act of maliciousness?" She lay her hand on the sheriff's arm. "Unless," she finished, "you went with us now and saw the creek had been deliberately dammed."

The sheriff turned his gaze on Clabe for verification of his mother's accusation and request. "All right," he concluded. "It's our duty. My men and I, we'll ride with you to the Faviere plantation to confront Miss Claudine. I must warn you though. If the creek's been blocked by natural causes, we're all goin' to look like fools. Maybe worse."

"I can assure you, Sheriff, we are not going to be made to look like fools." Zelma turned to Solomon and Jingo and instructed them to saddle horses for her, her son, and themselves. Then, with a final glance and a silent farewell to the three open graves, she turned and hurried down the hill to change into her riding clothes.

As the Faviere plantation house came into view, the sheriff reined up his horse. Pointing, he shouted, "Look there!"

A column of black smoke was rising from the back of the large house. Slaves could be seen hurrying from their quarters and forming a bucket brigade from the well to the backyard.

Zelma heard one of the men yell, "Fire!" Then, with everyone else, she was urging her horse into a gallop. They dismounted in the yard just as Claudine Faviere came running from the front door, her arms filled with account books and papers. The Frenchwoman paid not the slightest attention to Zelma or Clabe. She had no time for feuds at this time.

"That crazy witch!" she shouted at the sheriff. "She's set the house on fire and locked herself and her daughter in her room!"

Zelma motioned Jingo and Solomon forward to join the water brigade. Sliding from her horse, she started for the house at the heels of her son. The sheriff and his deputies had already disappeared inside.

As Claudine emerged from her study with another armload of papers, she saw Zelma. She came to an abrupt halt, eyes blazing, she screamed, "Get out of my house! Out!" She flung the papers to the floor and made for Zelma.

The sheriff restrained her by grabbing her arm. "She's goin'," he promised and nodded for Zelma to leave.

Zelma glanced up the staircase. She could see Clabe on the second-floor landing. He and another man were trying to break down a door, apparently to reach Claudine's stepmother and half-sister.

Claudine followed her gaze. "Him, too!" she bellowed. "I don't want any help from a Granville! Let that crazy bitch and her daughter burn! Get those Granvilles out of my house!"

Zelma heard the door splintering above. Clabe disappeared inside the room. Smoke swirled into the hallway and spread along the ceiling. Hurrying through the door, Zelma retreated to the hitching post and tried to quiet the excited animals. She stood helplessly watching as slaves and deputies made repeated trips to the front yard, depositing articles saved from the house and returning for more.

Presently, Clabe came running onto the porch carrying a bundle. He looked about, saw his mother, and hurried to her. "The child," he said and passed the girl into her arms. "Her mother got away from us and ran back into the rooms." He turned to reenter the house.

"No, Clabe!" Zelma screamed. "You've done what you can! Stay with me!" She was afraid the enraged Claudine would see him inside the house and use her pistol on him. That he was helping did not alter the fact that he was a Granville.

Not hearing or deliberately ignoring her, Clabe ran across the porch and back inside the burning house.

The smoke was becoming heavier. Flames, shattering the upstairs windows, were fanning through the open frames and spreading to the eaves. Realizing their efforts could not save the house, the slaves stopped pumping water from the well. They dropped their buckets and stepped back to watch in horrified fascination.

The child in Zelma's arms began to wail. She struggled to free her arms from the binding blanket Clabe had wrapped her in. Clutching at Zelma's neck, she buried her face in the strange woman's bosom and began to scream.

"There, there," Zelma murmured. She crossed the yard with the child to put a greater distance between them and the excited yelling of the slaves.

The sheriff and his deputies came out with another load of articles, but they made no effort to return to the burning house again. Claudine Faviere joined them, stood her ground, but kept screaming at the slaves to continue to haul things from the house until they fled in terror of both their mistress and the fire.

Zelma kept watching the doorway for Clabe to emerge.

It seemed like an eternity before he appeared. Alone. He had failed in locating the child's mother. He had tied a cloth about his lower face, but he was still hacking from the smoke and heat. He looked about for his mother, spotted her, and came across the yard to join her. "She hid," he explained. "We couldn't find her."

Zelma clutched the child more tightly. "My God!" she cried. "Are you saying she didn't want to be saved?"

Clabe nodded toward where Claudine stood with the sheriff and his men. "Apparently she was right," he said. "Her stepmother was. . . ." He stopped in midsentence when the girl in his mother's arms lifted her head and stared at him.

Solomon and Jingo came running around the side of the house. They were excited, ran up to Claudine Faviere and the sheriff. Zelma saw their exaggerated hand motions and how they kept pointing toward the back of the burning house. Claudine Faviere began to scream at them, at the sheriff who intervened.

"See what's happening," Zelma told Clabe. "Get Jingo and Solomon away from that woman. If she suspects they're Granville people, she's as soon shoot them as listen to them."

When Clabe reached the group, he could make neither heads nor tails of their excited exchange. He grabbed Solomon by the shoulders and spun him around. "What the hell's going on?" he shouted.

" 'Round back," Solomon stammered. "A shed. Her people say there's slaves locked inside. The fire's spreadin' to the roof, and we can't get the lock off the door."

"The key, Miss Faviere!" the sheriff shouted, flushed with rage.

"The key's inside, you bastards!" Claudine screamed.

"Go in and get it if you want to save them worthless niggers!" She turned and ran away from them, laughing.

"She's mad," the sheriff said. "Madder than she's said her stepmother was."

Zelma saw Claudine rush for the stables, then the men disappear around the side of the house. She called to one of the Negro women and told her to take care of the child. As she was running around the side of the house after the men, she saw Claudine Faviere ride out of the stables. Her horse reared when the smoke struck its nostrils. She struck it repeatedly with her riding crop and dug her heels into its flanks. The horse made for the road and was lashed into a fast gallop by its rider.

Clabe and the deputies were trying to force the door of the shed with a timber when Zelma reached them. The roof was smoldering, ready to burst into flame at any moment. Solomon had managed to coax some of the slaves back to the well to form another bucket brigade. The roof shingles had just begun to flame as the first bucket of water reached the shed.

"Now!" Clabe shouted.

They slammed the battering ram against the locked door. It groaned, bowed, and then was knocked from its hinges.

Zelma saw Clabe disappear into the shed ahead of the other men. She heard him cry out, "Good God!" Unable to hold back, she hurried forward and into the shed behind the men.

She had to cover her mouth to force back the sickness rising from the pit of her stomach. The shed was filled with slaves, some bound to the walls, others tied together. They had been forced to live in their own excrement. The stench was horrendous. But it was not the stench that affected those who'd broken into the shed. Many of the slaves looked like cadavers. It was later learned they had been confined for a period exceeding five months with only a handful of meal per day. Most bore marks of sadistic torture, burns and lash marks, and one woman had knife slashes across both her cheeks. A young man had had his leg amputated apparently for no cause other than he had displeased his mistress with his slow, loping gait.

Zelma ran from the shed.

She found a spot in the yard behind some shrubs and gave in to her sickness.

Clabe found her. "Mother, are you all right?"

"I will be," she told him. "Just give me another moment." She steadied herself and stepped out from behind the shrubs. "I knew that woman was a monster," she cried, "but this . . . this staggers the imagination."

"The sheriff's looking for her now," Clabe told his mother. "She'll be arrested and tried."

"He'll never find her," Zelma prophesied. "She knew what would happen when they broke in the door of the shed. She's fled." She saw the Negroes from the shed being helped away from the nearness of the burning house to a place in the yard. "Good God. Those poor people."

Clabe took her arm to steady her when he said, "Mother, some of them are our people."

Zelma caught her breath. "Our. . . ? Those we thought were runaways?"

Clabe nodded.

Zelma stood silently watching the group of Negroes huddled in the yard for several moments. Then she told Clabe, "Have Jingo and Solomon hitch up one of the Faviere wagons. We're taking our people home."

Later when the injured slaves were being loaded into the wagon, the sheriff approached Zelma and Clabe. His wrinkled face was covered with soot. He pointed back to where the Negro woman stood holding the Faviere child. "What about that there girl, Mrs. Granville?" He averted his eyes and shuffled the toe of his boot through the dirt. "Course I could take her into New Orleans. I know the bad blood between your family and the Favieres, and I wouldn't expect. . . ."

"The bad blood doesn't extend to helpless children," Zelma interrupted coldly. "New Orleans families will have enough on their minds digging out from the flood. No one would take the child." She motioned the Negro woman to bring her charge forward. "Are you the girl's mammy?" she asked.

"Didn't have no mammy," the woman answered. "Her mother wouldn't let nobody touch her baby."

Zelma reached for the girl. "What's her name? Paulette, wasn't it?"

"Yes'm."

"I'll take Paulette home with us to Plantation Bend," Zelma told the sheriff. The child had been whimpering and immediately became hushed in Zelma's arms. Zelma cuddled the girl, speaking to her in reassuring whispers.

"You knew she'd take the child, didn't you, Sheriff?" Clabe asked with a smile.

"I was countin' on it," the sheriff admitted. He touched the brim of his hat with his fingertips in a gesture of appreciation and, turning, moved back to join his men, who were watching the flames consume the Faviere house.

"What about the Faviere people?" Zelma asked Clabe with concern. "What will be done with them?"

"That's up to the authorities to decide, Mother," Clabe answered. "Come on. We've done enough. Let's get home to Plantation Bend. Vienna will be worried." He left his mother and went to call Solomon and Jingo and to claim their horses.

A woman in the wagon behind Zelma said, "I'll take the baby, mistress."

Zelma turned. "Oh, thank you." It was the woman with the slash marks across her cheeks. Zelma had passed Paulette into the woman's arms before recognition struck her. "Good God!" she cried. "Matilda!"

After Clabe and Zelma had ridden away with the sheriff and his deputies, Vienna went upstairs, had hot water brought to her room, and bathed. The bath revived her, rid her of some of her tension. Tonight, she told herself, she would sleep as soundly as her husband. She dressed and went into her son's room.

Pearl was sitting cross-legged on the floor amusing Dester by building a pyramid of a stack of colored wooden blocks. The boy looked up, happy to see his mother, but then quickly turned his attention back to his play. Pearl left him on the floor to amuse himself and came to sit beside her mistress on her charge's bed.

"You look worried," the slaves observed. "No need t' be. Claudine Faviere ain't goin' to do nothin' with the sheriff present, 'cept maybe run them off her property."

"What? Oh, I wasn't thinking about that," Vienna told her.

"New Orleans, then?" Pearl murmured. "You goin' to tell me 'bout that?"

"Maybe later," Vienna said. "Right now I'd like to just blot it out of my mind."

"That bad?" Pearl persisted. She'd already heard spatterings of the tales the coachman had told at the slaves quarter. Still, she knew she didn't dare press for her mistress's account, not now. Sighing, she rose. "If you goin' to be with Dester," she said, "I'll go down and help Dolly with supper. Mistress Zelma invited the sheriff and his three deputies." Her voice expressed her disapproval. Since Africa's hanging, none of the Granville people trusted the authorities.

"Yes. Run along," Vienna told her. "I'll put Dester to bed before I come down." Rising from the bed, she went to join her son on the floor. "What are you building?" she asked, pretending interest in the lopsided pyramid. "Here. Let me help. . . ." She looked up, suddenly alert.

A strange rumbling sound came from the distance.

Pearl, standing in the open doorway, turned. "Can't be thunder," she said. "Sky's clear. I jest looked. We're goin' to have a pretty sunset."

The sound was growing steadily louder.

"No, not thunder!" Vienna cried. She sprang to her feet, upsetting Dester's blocks, and ran to the window. The scream that escaped her struck terror into both Pearl and Dester.

Pearl rushed to her mistress's side and peered out.

From around the bend of the creek came a high wall of water.

"Lordie!" Pearl shrieked and grabbed at her mistress in terror.

Vienna pushed her away. She ran back to Dester and snatched him from the floor. Memories of Madame Celine's wall collapsing flashed through her mind. She knew she had to get to the far side of the house away from the onrushing water. She yelled at Pearl to follow her and ran out into the hallway. She heard screams from below as others became aware of the source of the rumbling sound. Dester, at first too startled by suddenly being snatched away from his play to cry, burst into tears. He began to struggle in his mother's arms, but Vienna tightened her grasp to keep from dropping him.

She had reached Zelma's room when the water struck. The sound was more terrifying than the damages caused. The water had not been as high as it had appeared, not at their distance away from the funnel of the creek bed. It hit the lower halves of the windows, shattered the glass, and poured into the main floor. The impact overturned tables, chairs, and the study bookcases, and then the water subsided almost as quickly as it had struck.

Trembling and clinging to Dester, Vienna remained pressed against the wall of her mother-in-law's bedroom until she heard Pearl whimpering with fear in the hallway. The rumbling grew fainter as the wake of the water moved beyond the house.

Trying to quiet Dester, she came out into the hallway.

Pearl was huddled in a corner away from the banister. "The Lord's sendin' another flood," she wept when she saw her mistress.

Vienna felt herself calming. "The flood was most likely sent by Claudine Faviere," she said. "Take Dester back to his room and stay with him."

Vienna came down the stairs and into the mess of the lower floor. She moved through the rooms Zelma had been so proud of, inspecting the damages, and she found herself fighting to hold back her tears. In the kitchen, she was grateful none of the slaves had suffered more than fright. Dolly had already taken command and was shouting instructions to the still-terrified girls for putting things back into order.

Vienna came back through the house and out onto the

long porch. The water in the yard was quickly falling back, but she knew that the fields, much lower in elevation, would now be lakes. The crops had been ruined.

Vienna was still on the porch when she saw Clabe and Zelma ride up across the creek. There was a wagon behind them filled with people, Jingo and Solomon driving.

The bridge had not been washed away, but it had apparently been seriously damaged. Clabe motioned for his mother to wait while he tested the weakened structure. Edging his horse slowly over the planks, Vienna caught her breath and held it until he reached the safety of the opposite side. Then she left the porch and ran across the muddy yard to meet him. When she reached him, Clabe had dismounted and was shouting instructions to Jingo and Solomon to abandon the wagon because the bridge would not take its weight. "You'll have to help the others across on foot," he yelled. Turning to Vienna, he drew her into the curve of his body. "Anyone hurt here?" he asked.

Zelma, who had made the crossing, swung down off her horse beside them.

"No one hurt in the house," Vienna answered. She told herself she should prepare her mother-in-law for the destruction she'd find inside. "But the house itself," she said. "The water's ruined. . . ." She saw by Zelma's expression that she need not continue.

"Claudine Faviere's hate was so strong she stopped in her flight long enough to open the floodgates of the dam," Zelma said incredulously.

Vienna suppressed a cry when she saw the condition of the Negroes being helped across the bridge. She lifted her head and stared up at Clabe, but his expression told her he'd explain later.

Clabe took his mother's arm. "We'll rebuild," he told her. "We'll drain the fields and replant. We're not beaten."

Zelma, watching their people approach from around the side of the hill, turned back to her son. She straightened, tilted her head, and looked into his eyes. "Of course, we're not beaten," she said. "Not us. We've survived yellow fever and an attack by the British army, your father's death and your own personal difficulties. We're not going to be beaten by a flood. We inherited your father's dream, and nothing will take that from us."

Zelma turned as Matilda approached. She took Paulette Faviere protectively into her arms and walked away toward the house.

CHAPTER TWENTY-SIX

IT WAS A warm spring morning.

Glancing through the window and seeing new buds on her moonflower vine, Zelma came out onto the porch for closer inspection.

Dester, now eight, was sitting on the lower step, elbows on his knees, chin cupped in his hands as he stared solemnly out across the yard at a group of farmers passing on the road.

Zelma sat down beside him and put her arm about his shoulders. "Why so glum?" she asked. She knew he had been arguing with Paulette and his sister, Katrina. The three of them were very close, but being the only boy, Dester was frequently excluded from their games.

Her grandson at the age where embarrassed by overt displays of affection, wriggled free of her embrace and rose from the step. "That road go to New Orleans?" he asked.

"*Does* that road go to New Orleans?" Zelma corrected. "Yes, it does."

"I want to go there someday," the boy told her.

"Why?"

"Just to see it," he answered.

"Well, if New Orleans keeps growing, it'll come to you before then," Zelma murmured.

Paulette and Katrina, tired of their girls' games, came around the side of the house in search of Dester. The three of them ran off to resume their play, and Zelma remained on the step watching them as they ran laughing across the yard in a game of tag.

She sat for a long while before gathering the strength to

rise. She no longer had the energy for quick movements. That morning she had awakened with a tightness in her chest and a peculiar numbness in her limbs. She stretched to get the circulation moving in her body, then came down off the porch and wandered into the field beyond the yard to gather the wildflowers growing there. She carried them up the hill, but when she reached the cemetery she was too exhausted to distribute them on the graves. She sank onto the edge of her husband's great stone slab and sat there quietly listening to the birds and the laughter of the children carried up from below by the morning breeze.

A sense of contentment swept over her.

For the first time in her life, there was nothing she could ask for to make her happier. Under Clabe's devoted supervision, Plantation Bend was now the greatest cane-producer in Louisiana. She had two beautiful grandchildren and a third on the way. Paulette was like a daughter to her. She had seen that the ownership of the Faviere plantation had been awarded the girl when her stepsister had not returned.

Claudine Faviere, she'd heard, had returned to Paris. Her reputation, however, had preceded her, and it was said that even there she was shunned and driven from every public house or store into which she ventured. The abolition movement to put an end to Negro slavery was in progress in America, and Claudine Faviere was often used as an example of owners' cruelty to the blacks.

True to her promise to Africa, Zelma had welcomed Matilda back to Plantation Bend. Now married to Pearl, Aaron had been united with his mother and had taken her into his house. He had also taken charge of the mulatto Jojo after Naome had died of cholera and was raising the boy as his own.

Sighing, Zelma leaned her head back against her husband's stone marker and closed her eyes. She felt contented, fulfilled, but dreadfully exhausted. The bouquet of wildflowers slipped from her hand. She did not bother to retrieve them. A strange weightlessness overcame her. She felt light-headed as the aches and pains of her aged body left her. She did not need to open her eyes to know that she was no longer alone in the cemetery. She could sense them there—those she had loved. Dester and Vance. Bessie Lou. Zona and Madame Celine.

Smiling, she let them welcome her.